ROSARIO FERRÉ is Puerto Rico's leading woman of letters, with several books of poetry, short fiction, biography, and feminist criticism to her credit. A 1995 National Book Award finalist for *The House on the Lagoon*, she has publis[...] English: *Sweet Diamond Dust* (Plume), [...] and *The Youngest Doll*. A frequent lect[...] she lives in Puerto Rico, where she is c[...] tional memoir," *Eccentric Neighborhood*[...]

D1113326

THE HOUSE
ON
THE LAGOON

❧

ROSARIO
FERRÉ

Ⓟ

A PLUME BOOK

I wish to thank both Susan Bergholz and John Glusman for their generous help
during the writing of this book. Their literary expertise and spiritual support
were crucial to me, and made this novel possible. I also wish to thank
my husband, Agustín Costa, for sharing the novel's difficult moments
with me, as well as its joys.

PLUME
Published by the Penguin Group
Penguin Books USA Inc., 375 Hudson Street, New York, New York 10014, U.S.A.
Penguin Books Ltd, 27 Wrights Lane, London W8 5TZ, England
Penguin Books Australia Ltd, Ringwood, Victoria, Australia
Penguin Books Canada Ltd, 10 Alcorn Avenue, Toronto, Ontario, Canada M4V 3B2
Penguin Books (N.Z.) Ltd, 182–190 Wairau Road, Auckland 10, New Zealand

Penguin Books Ltd, Registered Offices: Harmondsworth, Middlesex, England

Published by Plume, an imprint of Dutton Signet,
a division of Penguin Books USA Inc.
This is an authorized reprint of a hardcover edition published by Farrar, Straus and Giroux, Inc.
For information address Farrar, Straus and Giroux, Inc.,
19 Union Square West, New York, NY 10003.

First Plume Printing, October, 1996
10 9 8 7 6

Copyright © Rosario Ferré, 1995
All rights reserved

 REGISTERED TRADEMARK—MARCA REGISTRADA

LIBRARY OF CONGRESS CATALOGING-IN-PUBLICATION DATA
Ferré, Rosario.
The house on the lagoon / Rosario Ferré
p.   cm.
ISBN 0-452-27707-8
1. Women novelists, Puerto Rican—Fiction.   2. Married women—
Puerto Rico—Fiction.   3. Family—Puerto Rico—Fiction.   4. Puerto
Rico—Fiction.   I. Title.
PS3556.E7256H68   1996
813'.54—dc20   96–18819
                                                                       CIP

Printed in the United States of America

PUBLISHER'S NOTE
This is a work of fiction. Names, characters, places, and incidents either are the product of the
author's imagination or are used fictitiously, and any resemblance to actual persons, living or
dead, events, or locales in entirely coincidental.

BOOKS ARE AVAILABLE AT QUANTITY DISCOUNTS WHEN USED TO PROMOTE PRODUCTS OR SERVICES.
FOR INFORMATION PLEASE WRITE TO PREMIUM MARKETING DIVISION, PENGUIN BOOKS USA INC.,
375 HUDSON STREET, NEW YORK, NY 10014.

Any shade to whom you give access to

the blood will hold rational speech

with you, while those whom you

reject will leave you and retire.

HOMER
The Odyssey, XI

⬖

Before I ever loved a woman

I wagered my heart on chance

and violence won it over.

JOSÉ EUSTASIO RIVERA
The Vortex

FAMILY TREE

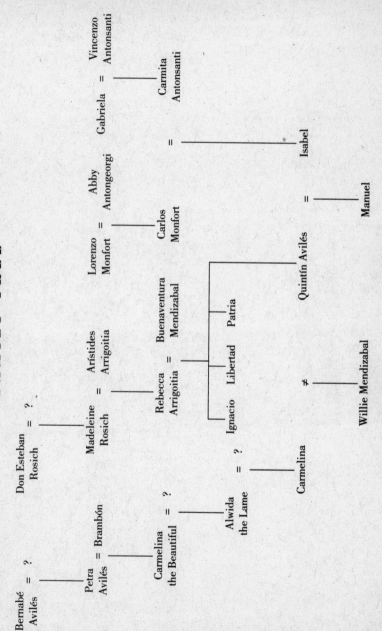

The House
on the Lagoon

QUINTÍN AND

ISABEL'S PLEDGE

My grandmother always insisted that when people fall in love they should look closely at what the family of the betrothed is like, because one never marries the bridegroom alone but also his parents, grandparents, great-grandparents, and the whole damned tangle of the ancestral line. I refused to believe her even after what happened when Quintín and I were still engaged.

One evening Quintín came to visit me at the house in Ponce. We had been lounging on the veranda's sofa, when a sixteen-year-old boy who was sitting on the sidewalk in front of the house began to sing me a love ballad.

The singer, the son of a well-known local family, had been secretly in love with me, although we had never met. He had seen me occasionally when our paths crossed in the streets of Ponce and at parties. Recently, my picture had been in the society columns, announcing my engagement to Quintín Mendizabal.

The young man became very depressed when he read the news, and in his deranged state the only thing that would ease his sadness was to sit under the flowering oak tree which grew in front of my house on Aurora Street and sing Love Me Always *in a haunting tenor voice.*

That night, as I sat next to Quintín on the veranda's sofa, I was mesmerized by the song. I had never heard anyone sing with such a voice; it sounded like a silver bell as it filtered through the terrace's white iron grillwork, and I thought that if there were angels in heaven, they would probably sing like that.

When the unexpected serenade began, Quintín had one of his fits of temper, which he inherited from his ancestors. He rose from the sofa, walked unhurriedly to the door, crossed the garden path under the purple bougainvillea vine massed over the veranda's roof, went through the hedge of hibiscus that grew in front of the house, his belt in his hand, and mercilessly lashed the unfortunate bard. I ran after him crying, but I couldn't make him stop. When she heard my cries for help, Grandmother ran out of the house, too, and tried to hang on to Quintín's arm, but he went on beating the boy. Abby and I stood there horrified. As the brass buckle whistled at the end of Quintín's belt, he coldly counted the blows aloud, one by one.

I had begged the boy to get up and defend himself, but he refused even so much as to look at his attacker. He went on sitting on the ground, singing: "Love me always, / sweet love of my life. / You know I'll always adore you. / Only the memory of your kisses / will ease my suffering," until he fell unconscious on the sidewalk.

Soon after this, the young man slashed his wrists with a razor blade, without even trying to contact me. I was tormented by guilt, and for a while deeply resented Quintín for his brutal behavior. Many years later I still couldn't listen to that song without tears welling up in my eyes. It always made me remember the young man who had wanted to serenade me, spreading the balm of his voice on a beautiful summer night.

It took my family a long time to recover. From then on, Grandmother was obstinately opposed to my marriage to Quintín Mendizabal. "Someday you'll be sorry, that's all I can tell you," she said to me repeatedly. "There are enough kind, educated men in this world so that you shouldn't have to end up in the arms of a common bully."

Abby had married a Frenchman's son, and this perhaps had

something to do with her dislike for everything Spanish. "Quintín's ancestors," she would insist, "are from the most backward country on earth. 'Spain never had a political or an industrial revolution,' my husband used to say, and it's been our tragedy that it was the Spaniards who colonized us. If I ever travel to Europe, the only reason I would visit that country would be to relieve myself, and then I'd leave."

For years the episode stayed vividly in my mind, though at the time I refused to see it as a bad omen. I never forgot the unhappy singer, however. Whenever I thought of him, I remembered what Grandmother had said. Unfortunately, I did not mind Abby's advice, and on June 4, 1955, I walked down the aisle on Quintín's arm.

Quintín was very much in love with me. After the young man's suicide, he began to have trouble sleeping, and he would wake up in the middle of the night bathed in sweat. One day he came to visit me in anguish and asked me to forgive him. "An ungovernable temper is a detestable thing," he said. "One ceases to be oneself and becomes another; it's as if the devil himself crept up under your skin." He didn't want to be like his father, his grandfather, or the rest of his ancestors, he added, who were descended from the Spanish Conquistadors. They all had wrathful dispositions and, worse yet, were proud of it, insisting that rashness was a necessary condition for bravery. But there would be no getting away from them if I didn't help him wrench himself from the morass of heredity.

It was after lunch, the hour of the siesta, and everyone else in the house was sleeping, stretched out lightly on their beds without bothering to take their clothes off. We were sitting as usual on the veranda's sofa, and the afternoon heat intensified our wooing. We kissed and embraced a dozen times under the flowering jasmine that hid us from intruding eyes. "Love is the only true antidote to violence," Quintín said to me. "In my family, terrible things have happened which I find difficult to forget."

It was then that we made our pledge. We promised we would examine carefully the origins of anger in each of our families as if *it were a disease, and in this way avoid, during the life we were to share together, the mistakes our forebears had made. The rest of that summer, we spent many afternoons together, holding hands on the veranda and telling each other our family histories as Grandmother came and went busily through the house, performing her household chores.*

Years later, when I was living in the house on the lagoon, I began to write down some of those stories. My original purpose was to interweave the woof of my memories with the warp of Quintín's recollections, but what I finally wrote was something very different.

PART 1

The Foundations

1

Buenaventura's
Freshwater Spring

❧

WHEN BUENAVENTURA MENDIZABAL, Quintín's father, arrived
on the island, he built himself a wooden cottage on the far side
of Alamares Lagoon, a forgotten stretch of land that had been only
partially cleared of wild vines and thickets. There was a spring
nearby which the residents of the area had once used. A stone
fountain built around it had been maintained by a caretaker, since
it was considered public property. In recent years, however, people
had forgotten all about it. The caretaker, an arthritic old man who
lived next to the spring, had stopped keeping it up, and soon the
mangrove swamp had enveloped it completely.

Half a kilometer down the beach stood the beautiful houses of
Alamares, one of the most exclusive suburbs of San Juan. Alamares
stood on a strip of land crossed by a palm-crested avenue—Ponce
de León Avenue—with water on either side: the Atlantic Ocean
to the north, and Alamares Lagoon to the south. The more public
side of the avenue looked out to the Atlantic, where the surf was
always swelling and battering the sand dunes; and the more private
one opened onto the quiet beach of the lagoon. This beach ended
in a huge mangrove swamp, and only the tip of it was visible from
Alamares. When he moved to the area, Buenaventura built a
modest cottage precisely at this site, where the mangrove swamp
met the private beach of the lagoon.

The swamp was a mysterious place, full of exotic wildlife and strange botanical specimens, with creatures both amphibious and terrestrial. The mangroves had bushy tops with all sorts of birds nesting in them. The white heron roosted there, and at sundown turned the branches of the trees a ghostly white, as if a snowstorm had just blown through. Albatross were often seen gliding over the swamp, looking for a safe place to spend the night, and from time to time one could even see a tiger-eyed *guaraguao*, the nearly extinct local eagle, perched on one of its branches. But the mangroves were also aquatic, and their roots spread an intricate maze over the water. Inside this labyrinth of knots and sinews a whole universe of mollusks, crustaceans, and fish proliferated freely, half immersed in the mud, half encrusted in the mossy cartilage of the wood.

It was a strange territory to navigate in, and although several wide channels crossed it from end to end, if one were to get lost in its tangle, there was only a slim chance of finding one's way out. Following the waterways, one came eventually to Morass Lagoon—thus named by the Spanish explorers and later renamed Molasses Lagoon by the slum's inhabitants—and after crossing it would finally end up in Lucumí Beach. A sugar mill, the Central Oromiel, had been established on the lagoon's shores and emptied the foul-smelling sludge from its rum distillery into its quiet waters, turning the lagoon into a quagmire. The sugar mill had closed down at the beginning of the twentieth century, but the waters were still contaminated. Many of the city's sewers emptied into it; it was cheaper to get rid of raw sewage that way than pollute the white sand beaches, which tourists had begun to visit. On the shores of Morass Lagoon was one of the city's worst slums, Las Minas. Most of the servants who worked in the houses of the elegant suburb of Alamares lived there, and frequently crossed the intricate waterways of the mangrove swamp in their rowboats.

Ponce de León Avenue, the capital's longest boulevard, began in the Old City, cut straight across Puerta de Tierra, and converged into Alamares, before losing itself in the distance as it penetrated the country's interior. When Buenaventura moved into the area there were still a good number of old-fashioned horse-drawn carriages driving by, as well as fashionable Stutz Bear Cats, Packards, and Silver Clouds belonging to the affluent residents. Everyone knew everyone else in Alamares and waved cheerfully from their motor seats, dressed in white cotton jackets to keep off the dust from the road and wearing rubber-rimmed goggles that made them look like owls.

In the afternoon, when nannies came out to take their charges for a walk, they always preferred to stroll down the sidewalk of Ponce de León Avenue, where the wind from the ocean playfully pulled at their starched aprons and coifs. There the Atlantic broke in long blue waves over the bathers, who had to swim energetically to keep their heads above the crests of the waves. The nannies felt secure and invigorated. But when they walked down the quiet beach path which bordered Alamares Lagoon, they insisted they could hear strange moans coming from the nearby swamp that reminded them, they said, of things dying or being born. Once the sun began to go down, mysterious lights sometimes glowed through the bushes; crabs and lizards crept through the undergrowth. For this reason no one walked in the direction of Buenaventura's half-hidden cottage at the end of the lagoon at dusk.

One day the caretaker of the spring was found dead, lying by the rim of the fountain, from a mysterious blow to the head. A small item appeared in the morning papers, but nobody paid much attention, and the event was soon forgotten. The residents of Alamares didn't need water from the spring any longer, since they were connected to the city's aqueduct. Soon after that, Buenaventura moved to the caretaker's house and nobody seemed to mind. He cleared the spring of undergrowth and put it back in use. Afterward, Buenaventura married Rebecca Arrigoitia and took her to live with him on the shores of Alamares Lagoon.

The caretaker's fate was a stroke of good luck for Buenaventura. Since the outbreak of the First World War, San Juan Bay had been filled with merchant marine ships, as well as navy destroyers that would sail past the looming stone walls of San Felipe del Morro, the Old City's largest medieval fort, crowned with Spanish cast-iron cannons, to anchor not far from Alamares Lagoon. There were so many ships that the municipal aqueduct could not supply fresh water for all of them, and before long the captains of the Spanish merchant ships, like the *Virgen de Purrúa* and the *Virgen de Altagracia*, came knocking at Buenaventura's door to ask if he could provide them with fresh water from his spring. Buenaventura felt it his duty to oblige and he did all he could to accommodate them. There was no other well for twenty miles around, and Spanish ships were always left for last, since government officials in the city were understandably partial to serving those merchant ships which sailed under the American flag. Yet, despite the increasing American influence, there was always a lively market for Spanish foods on the island: most well-to-do people favored the paella valenciana, Segovian *sobreasada, ensaimadas* from Mallorca, and other such tasty dishes over American-style food. Trade with Spain was impossible to eliminate completely.

Buenaventura was, above all, a good Spaniard, and he never pressed his countrymen to pay cash for his services. He preferred to exchange his water casks for a few cases of the Riojas and Logroños which the Spanish captains brought him. In turn, he would sell them to his customers in the city at a favorable price. Soon after he arrived on the island, he proved so successful at this friendly bartering that he built a small warehouse next to his spring. There he stored his wines; the ruby-red hams he began to import from Valdeverdeja, his hometown; the ivory-white asparagus from Aranjuez; the honeyed nougats and marzipans from Jijona; and the exquisite Moorish olives from Seville. He brought most of his goods into the island illegally in flat, covered barges that navigated through the mangrove swamp. The barges would load their merchandise off the deserted coves of Lucumí Beach, where the Spanish merchant ships arriving from Europe made discreet stops before going on to the port of San Juan.

2

Buenaventura

Arrives on the Island

✂

WHEN BUENAVENTURA ARRIVED on the island in the *Virgen de Covadonga*, he was twenty-three years old and without a cent to his name. An orphan since he had turned fifteen, he was raised in Spain by two maiden aunts, who set great store by his good looks. He was six feet tall, tan-skinned and dark-haired, and had eyes so blue they made you want to sail out to sea every time you looked at them. Quintín told me the story of his arrival when we were first engaged to be married, and many years later he repeated it from time to time for our two boys, Manuel and Willie, to remind them of who they were and where they came from.

All during his trip across the Atlantic, Buenaventura had wondered what the island of Puerto Rico would be like. He had read something about the history of the Caribbean before setting sail from Cádiz, but he had also learned much of it firsthand. The Spanish-American War, which had ended nineteen years before, was still fresh in the mind of many Spaniards. He knew his country had fought tooth and nail to keep Cuba, the last jewel in the crown of the Spanish empire. After the Seven Years' War, in 1763, Spain had traded Florida for Cuba to the British. Later, thousands of Buenaventura's countrymen had died at Punta Brava, Dos Ríos, Camagüey, shot down in bloody combat by Cuban rebels during the Revolution. But when Spain lost the Spanish-American War, it simply let Puerto Rico go. Was the island too poor and not worth fighting for, Buenaventura asked himself. Or was Spain just too exhausted to go on fighting?

Buenaventura landed in the port of San Juan on July 4, 1917, the same day President Woodrow Wilson signed the Jones Act, which granted us American citizenship. Luis Muñoz Rivera, the bill's chief proponent and our Resident Commissioner, had died the year before and President Wilson, in deference to his memory, had signed the new bill with the Resident Commissioner's gold pen. Muñoz Rivera was a poet as well as a statesman, and like many of the island's politicians at the time, he juggled American interests with nationalist conceits, fighting for Puerto Rico's independence on the sly.

As Buenaventura's ship dropped anchor in the harbor, the festivities celebrating our brand-new American citizenship were going full blast. Now each of us would have the right to an American passport, a talisman so powerful it opened doors all over the world. For nineteen years, since the Americans had landed on the coast of Guánica in 1898, we had lived in a political limbo. Spain had given us our autonomy six months before the Americans arrived, but we were never granted Puerto Rican citizenship. We still traveled with a Spanish passport, and lost it at the end of the Spanish-American War. A new document had not been issued, and for a while we were citizens of nowhere at all.

Not to be citizens of any country, however insignificant, was uncomfortable enough. Then we were told we couldn't travel anywhere. The greater part of our island's bourgeoisie consisted of seafaring immigrants, people from the Canary Islands, the Balearics, and Corsica, as well as from mainland Spain and France. Some had come to the island from Venezuela, and others from neighboring Caribbean islands, fleeing the wars of independence, which inevitably brought ruin—if not death—to the well-to-do settlers. They were used to traveling freely to and from the Continent, migrating with the seasons. Travel was imperative to establishing stable commercial relations with business partners. Not having a passport meant growing poorer every year.

For this reason, our brand-new American citizenship was hailed as a godsend, and a first-class celebration was in order. We would now have a definite identification with the most powerful country in the world, and the golden eagle would be stamped on the cover of our passport. Henceforth, we would cherish it as our magic shield: we could travel anywhere, no matter how far or exotic our destination; we had the inalienable right to political asylum at the local American Embassy; and the American ambassador would be our civil servant.

Buenaventura disembarked from the *Virgen de Covadonga* and found lodging near the wharf where the ship had docked. Don Miguel Santiesteban, a longtime friend of his family who had immigrated from Extremadura some years before, owned a warehouse at La Puntilla, the harbor area where most of the merchants' depots were. Buenaventura dropped off his satchel, put on his black *sombrero Cordobés*, and walked up the street to where the festivities were in full swing.

The heat was stifling, as suicidal pelicans nosedived into the molten steel of the bay. Buenaventura walked along the harbor, admiring the *Mississippi* and the *Virginia*, steamships anchored at the dock, decorated with streamers flapping gaily in the wind. He passed the new Federal Post Office and admired the impressive pink Federal Customs House. A handsome new building, it had guava-colored pinnacles on the roof and garlands of ceramic grapefruits and pineapples decorating the windowsills. Near the Customs House was the National City Bank, which reminded him of a Corinthian temple. Several gaily painted pushcarts were parked under the huge laurel tree in the plaza, selling "hot dogs," a snack which was evidently very popular because the line of people went around the Post Office building. Buenaventura asked what "hot dog" meant and burst out laughing when he was told. He bought one and it didn't taste like dog meat at all; it reminded him, instead, of a cross between salami and a German wiener. Another vendor sold beer from a barrel, but it was warm and he couldn't swallow it. He would have given anything for a glass of red wine from Valdeverdeja. He settled for a glass of fresh sugarcane juice, which he found delicious.

As he walked on, the Atlantic glimmered at the end of the street like a jewel. He felt as if he were still on deck; the road was paved with large polished blue bricks, and for a moment it seemed to be rocking gently under his feet. A huge crowd gathered on the sidewalk and he stood on a corner to watch the Fourth of July parade go by. A lady standing near him, wearing a starched white cap with a red cross sewn on it, gave him a small American flag. "You must wave it above your head when Governor Yager arrives," she said to him, "and call out 'God Bless America' as he rides by in his open convertible." He took the flag and thanked her, doffing his hat.

Nearby was the new capitol—still under construction—the dome of which was to be "an exact copy of the one Thomas Jefferson built at Monticello," as someone proudly told him on the street. He looked at the corner sign and noticed that the avenue was named after Juan Ponce de León, one of the Spanish Conquistadors, and his heart skipped a beat. Several floats went by, pulled by army mules and covered from top to bottom with American flags. From them waved a chorus of beautiful girls with red, white, and blue sashes draped across their chests—the names of the States of the Union written in glittering silver dust.

A mob of barefoot children stood cheering on the sidewalk; they were brought there from the public elementary school by the superintendent, who was dressed in black and carried a bowler hat in his hand. It was the first public school on the island, a passerby confided to Buenaventura, completely funded by the American government. Every time a float went by, the children cheered and waved their flags spiritedly, but they shouted the most when they saw Uncle Sam walk by on stilts, wearing long silk pants with red, white, and blue stripes on them, his top hat aglitter with silver stars. He threw handfuls of brand-new pennies at the crowd, and they gleamed on the ground like gold.

Buenaventura observed everything around him with a keen eye. He had come to the island to stay, and any knowledge about his new situation would help him get settled. He noticed that the people sitting on the dais, at the foot of the unfinished capitol, and the soldiers marching down the avenue were foreigners. Most of them were blond, tall, and well-built, whereas the natives were of sallow complexion, medium height, and a delicate frame. The well-to-do had parked their open carriages and motors on the side of the avenue and were watching the parade from the comfort of their leather seats, sitting under opened parasols. They were fashionably dressed, the men in dark cloth coats and the women in white cotton percale, with intricate lace frills at the neck and sleeves. The people standing on the sidewalk looked thin and pale, as if they rarely had three meals a day. But they were in good spirits. Most of them were barefoot and wore straw hats on their heads, with the fringe turned down to shade their faces from the blazing sun.

A tall man with a large mustache, wearing a tuxedo and top hat, was sitting next to a large-bosomed lady carrying a wide-brimmed hat with a silk cabbage rose pinned on the side. Buenaventura found out from his chatty neighbor on the sidewalk that they were the governor and his wife. A detachment of cadets marched behind the Marine band, wearing red caps with patent-leather visors and carrying their rifles on their right shoulders. They marched down Ponce de León Avenue to the beat of Sousa's *Semper Fidelis*. Buenaventura liked the music immensely; he found it so inspiring he almost went two-stepping along behind them. Any nation that marched to that kind of music was bound to be optimistic, he thought. He would like very much to belong to it. The scathing heat, the screaming children—none of it would matter as long as he could be part of the brave and the free.

His native land was very different. Spain was a decaying country; its buildings were crumbling with age and everything seemed outdated. In Valdeverdeja, water was still sold house to house from earthenware jars hauled by mules, and the villagers went around in two-wheeled carts pulled by donkeys. It seemed to him that his countrymen had been disenchanted with the world from the time of Segismundo, Calderón de la Barca's hero, and that skepticism had sapped their spirits. They didn't believe in anything anymore—not in the values of patriotism, not in the dogmas of faith. Religion was no more than a convention of respectability. But here the young men were full of spirit as they marched down the avenue; he could see it in their eyes, which shone with enthusiasm every time the cry "God bless America and America will bless you!" was heard from one of the bystanders.

Buenaventura was still standing there watching the parade when someone announced through a loudspeaker that all citizens over twenty-one were expected to sign up as volunteers in the U.S. Army. Tables would be set up at the end of Ponce de León Avenue once the festivities were over. Suddenly people began to run here and there, calling to one another excitedly. Buenaventura thought that, despite all the hoopla about the new citizenship, the natives wouldn't risk their skins for it, and would run home and hide under the bed. But the reverse happened. In no time at all, there was a line of several dozen young men eagerly waiting to sign up beside Uncle Sam's portrait, and in less than three hours the quotas were filled.

"They must have good reason to leave. I'm beginning to suspect famine on this island has been even worse than in Valdeverdeja," he wrote to a friend in a letter he sent home the next day. "I'm amazed at the eagerness with which the young men of San Juan lined up to board the *Buford*, the military transport ship anchored at the wharf. In Extremadura it's not surprising if people want to sign up in the Spanish Navy. Land there is dried-up leather, and everyone wants to leave. But this place is as green as the Garden of Eden, and no one can go hungry. One has only to squat by the roadside and shit a few guava seeds, and in no time a full-blown tree is growing there, laden with fruit and flowers. Puerto Rico must have been a miser's paradise in days gone by, and who knows but it may still be so today."

Buenaventura had acquired an accountant's certificate in Spain, but it didn't do him much good here, because it didn't conform to federal standards. It was proof of his experience, though, and he went searching for work in the city's commercial district with his certificate in his pocket. As he passed by the wharf, he saw a ship loaded with casks of rum which were being thrown overboard by the crew in view of a group of government officials. He asked what they were doing and they said the cargo's owner was abiding by the Dry Law, which had just been imposed on the island. Buenaventura marveled that the islanders should want so fervently to be good American citizens. They had been drinking rum practically from the cradle, and he didn't see how giving up liquor was going to make them better citizens.

Farther down the street, he came to an open circular building, a wooden arena with bleachers all around, where a cockfight was about to take place. People were placing bets and yelling, ready to pit two cocks against each other. Two men blew mouthfuls of rum into the birds' beaks to make them more aggressive, and everyone was drinking openly. Apparently, rum was not forbidden at cockfights. The men were affixing razor blades to the spurs of the struggling fowl and they glinted in the sun like tiny scythes.

Buenaventura had seen plenty of bullfights in Valdeverdeja. But when the men let the cocks loose and one of them in a minute trailed its innards in the sawdust, he suddenly felt like vomiting and had to leave. That evening, when he arrived at his lodgings, he wrote another long letter to his friend back in Extremadura. "Here islanders have kept many African rites alive. It's going to be difficult to teach the Congolese and Yorubas the good manners of the *Mayflower*."

To a cousin in Madrid he remarked: "Soon this place will be a fakir's paradise, where everybody will live on air. The present war in Europe has made the economy more precarious, but the main concern of the islanders is to prove to the United States that they can be good American citizens. Their most popular refrain at present is 'Food can be as effective as bullets.' They have tightened their belts dramatically, cutting down on their intake of flour, sugar, rice, and milk, and donated the proceeds to the troops fighting overseas, so that American soldiers will be better fed.

"The sale of Liberty Bonds has been extraordinarily successful, and even public-school children have bought some of them with their penny savings. Although hungry and often dressed in rags, these islanders have managed to purchase twelve thousand three hundred and eighty-three dollars in bonds, their contribution to the defense of the powerful nation that has adopted them. Sometimes they're so generous they remind me of Don Quixote."

3

The Queen of the Antilles

BUENAVENTURA DIDN'T HAVE a cent to his name when he arrived in the city's old port, but he wasn't exactly destitute. He had his good looks, and he brought with him an old parchment in which his family pedigree was inscribed. This moth-eaten document claimed he had the right to a title from his great-grandfather, a descendant of Francisco Pizarro, conqueror of Peru.

At the time of his arrival, our bourgeoisie all descended from one exuberant family tree, and everybody was kin to everybody else through this or that offshoot. If you wanted to know who someone's relatives were, you only had to visit your grandmother slumbering in her rocking chair, wake her up, and ask her to whisper you her secrets. Since colonial times, a clean lineage was worth a family's weight in gold. In every town, marriages were carefully inscribed in two books, which were jealously guarded in the parish church. They were called the Bloodline Books by Spanish priests. Originally, they had been instituted to keep the blood free of Jewish or Islamic ancestry, and separate records of all white and nonwhite marriages were kept in them.

Even though Quintín pretended not to share such absurd prejudices, I always suspected he felt the same way as the rest of his family. When he fell in love with me, this wasn't a problem, since my lineage was clean. But Quintín's hidden feelings would surface

later, and create tension between us. In any case, at the time of
our engagement, very few of our friends or relatives thought differently, which must be counted as a point in Quintín's favor.

When the Americans arrived on the island, the Bloodline Books
were abandoned. Priests became poor and many of their records
perished in random fires or during fierce island hurricanes, when
the wind blew away many a leaky parish roof. But the Books
disappeared also because the practice was considered unworthy
of American citizens. For this reason, it was useful to have a
grandmother you could ask about bygone days; she usually remembered how the Bloodline Books had read and knew exactly
who might have hidden stains in his or her pedigree.

Keeping track of these things was getting to be more and more
difficult, Rebecca, Quintín's mother, confessed to him. As the
new habits of democracy gradually took over, unsoiled lineages
were becoming almost impossible to find. With the exception of
exclusive gathering places like the Spanish Casino, anyone who
could pay for it could go to the Tapia Theater, the Palace Hotel,
or the Condado Vanderbilt Hotel, and there were absolutely no
racial restrictions on who could apply to the recently founded State
University in Río Piedras, which was paid for with American
dollars. The warm tropical breezes, the swaying palm trees, the
waves which sighed and gave way to festoons of foam on the
beach—everything on the island contributed to the loosening up
of old Spanish customs, and eventually people forgot about the
Bloodline Books.

A balmy climate can be a dangerous seductress, Rebecca used
to say to Quintín, and before long the sons of the well-to-do began
to eye the bare arms and shoulders of the beautiful mulatto girls,
who, following the American custom, went everywhere unaccompanied and worked where they pleased. The beauty of the quad-
roons, which until then was a hidden treasure, was suddenly
discovered by the young men of "good families," and there was a
veritable epidemic of racially mixed liaisons on the island.

A few well-to-do families, those who were really wealthy,

like the Mendizabals, stubbornly kept to the old Spanish ways and countered the loosening up of mores with an even stricter code of behavior for their children. They urged them to be extremely careful of their friends and advised them to ask for last names, so their parents could check on pedigrees.

These families were also influenced by our new American citizenship, but in a very different manner. Rebecca often told Quintín how in the past many of their friends' families had traveled by steamer to Europe for the holidays, and only a few had ever set foot in the United States. Most were born in the Old Country and still had relatives there; others owned property which had belonged to their ancestors; some even cherished the dream of returning one day, though in the end few did so.

Once they became American citizens, rich families traveled often to the United States and began to send their children to first-class universities on the East Coast. Reaching the mainland at that time involved a complicated voyage by ship and train; airplane travel wasn't commercialized until the end of the twenties. Pan American Clippers, which were amphibious at the time, would land in San Juan Bay, fly from there to Port-au-Prince, and then on to Santiago de Cuba and Miami. Before the Pan Am Clipper, one booked a steamship from San Juan to Jacksonville and there boarded a Pullman coach on the Florida railroad line to Washington, D.C., Philadelphia, or New York. As trains had coal engines and no showers, it didn't matter how light the color of your skin was. By the time you arrived at your destination, you were black as soot from head to toe.

It was during these trips to the United States that well-to-do families began to realize some surprising facts which reaffirmed their belief that the old ways were still the best, and that it was important their children abide by them. When they boarded the train at Jacksonville, for example, they learned that black passengers couldn't travel in the same Pullman coaches as whites. As long as the train traveled through the South, Negroes had to use a different bathroom and go to a different restaurant car. This was an alarming discovery and at first these families were so amazed they couldn't believe their eyes. It would never have happened in their country, they thought, where everyone could eat or make water in the same place. The concept of equality under law, which the new democratic regime supposedly had brought to the island and which they had so earnestly embraced because they wanted to be good American citizens, was interpreted very differently on the mainland.

The situation caused Puerto Rican visitors considerable distress. Even though they were Caucasians, their skin was never as white as that of the Americans milling around them; it had a light olive tint to it, which made them suspect in the eyes of the conductor when they were about to board the first-class coaches to New Orleans, for example, or in those of the concierge when they were about to check into the Plaza Hotel or the Sherry Netherland, once they had arrived in New York. At those moments they were very conscious of what they wore, and realized that wearing a genuine pearl necklace or carrying an authentic alligator bag on your arm made a difference when you stepped into an elegant hotel lobby, especially if one "came from down South." People looked at you with respect. For this reason, once they set foot in the continental United States, the well-to-do families from the island never spoke Spanish but always addressed each other in perfect English.

Back home, on the other hand, when a son or a daughter from one of our better families was being courted or about to become engaged, mothers would visit their confessors and ask them in secret if the old Bloodline Book from their particular parish by chance still existed, because they needed to see it. They would wipe the cobwebs off the covers, blow the dust from the parchment pages, and peruse them carefully until they verified the spotlessness of the suitor's stock. Until this was done, permission for the marriage was withheld. Since they were now part of the United States, they told themselves, this was the only way to ensure that their grandchildren would be accepted at the best universities on the mainland, or that they could travel first-class by train or boat all through that great country, just as they had been used to doing in Europe.

As a result of this close scrutiny, it was becoming more difficult for the daughters of the bourgeoisie to find appropriate husbands. American young men, although desirable from every point of view—they were fair-skinned, well educated, and often connected to the prosperous sugar refineries on the island—were a tricky business. More than once, engagements were dissolved literally at the church door, when, arriving from the mainland for the wedding, a suitor's family might find the bride's hair to be suspiciously curly or her skin to have a slight cinnamon hue. They would point out these details to the bridegroom and decry the reliability of the Bloodline Books, cautioning that they could be altered or false, that it was better to trust your own eyes. The engagement would be broken off and the family would return to the mainland en masse, taking along the repentant suitor. This kind of unfortunate occurrence was much rarer when the fiancé was from Spain. Spanish immigrants were usually more lenient than Anglo-Saxons about exotic physical traits. Colonized by the Moors for seven hundred years, they were less suspicious of olive skin or curly jet hair.

The Spanish Casino was an important institution, because it was where young people from the better families got to know each other. Quintín told me how, the same year Buenaventura arrived on the island, the Casino was planning its most splendid carnival in years. Rebecca, Quintín's mother, was to be crowned Queen of the Spanish Antilles. Rebecca was sixteen years old, the beautiful daughter of prosperous parents, and the committee unanimously chose her to be queen. When it came time to find a king to escort her, however, things did not go so well.

The committee was made up of a group of middle-aged ladies who were the organizers of many of the balls given in the city.

They were responsible for preparing the lists of eligible young men who could be partners at such events. In the case of the Spanish Casino's king, for example, they would visit the elegant mansions of Alamares, sit on the terrace drinking coffee, and from there look over the children of the family. As soon as they saw a teenager with down on his cheeks who might serve their purpose, they would ask his parents to let him meet the future queen, to see if she liked him and if they looked well together.

It usually took only one or two visits with a lanky young man in tow to get the job done, as at their tender age girls weren't that particular about their escorts. More often than not, they were more interested in the coronation gown, train and crown, and all the paraphernalia that being carnival queen entailed, than in their pimply sixteen-year-old escorts. For the parents of the young man, on the other hand, to have their son accepted as king was a privilege not easily refused. Once he was chosen, the young man's family became members of the exclusive Spanish Casino without the steep entrance fee.

Quintín chuckled every time he told me how the ladies of the committee had an especially hard time with Rebecca's escort, because his mother knew exactly what she wanted. An only child, Rebecca had been thoroughly spoiled. The ladies of the committee brought half a dozen candidates to her door who were unceremoniously "beheaded," as Rebecca kept shaking her golden curls. This one reminded her of a lily of the valley and might wilt at the first sign of heat; that one was sinewy and athletic but had a nervous tic; this one was a ninny who slobbered compliments in her ear whenever she danced with him; and that last one was as brawny as a bull but just as thickheaded. What she wanted was an intelligent king.

She wanted a true monarch, one who could subdue her with a single glance. A sovereign with shoulders spread like infantry battalions, strong cavalry thighs, and eyes so blue they made you want to sail out to sea. A real commander in chief, who would raise her slumbering regiments at a command. She wanted a prince who longed for the whole of her: her marzipan throat and her cream-puff shoulders, her coconut-custard breasts, her dainty rice-and-cinnamon feet, and her delicate ginger pussy; one who would eat her, lick her, nip her, and drink her, and then grind her into powdered sugar in his arms. Not a trace would be left of the porcelain doll her parents kept hidden in her silk-lined boudoir at the end of the bedroom corridor, where neither the dust nor the noise nor the heat of the street could harm her, and where every night her bed was a dark whirlpool of loneliness into which she plunged, weighed down by icy sheets.

Exhausted from her endeavors, Doña Ester Santiesteban came to Rebecca's house one last time with a photograph of a dark-haired young man in a red-velvet frame under her arm. He was broad-shouldered and stood very straight, and he wore a black *sombrero Cordobés* on his head, of the kind people wore at *corridas de toros* in Spain.

"The young man is perfect for the part," Doña Ester said. "He's twenty-three years old and recently arrived from Spain. His family is not too well off, but he has all sorts of papers which say he's from a good family, and I thought you might be interested in meeting him." She said nothing about his good looks on purpose, because she feared Rebecca might repeat her litany that good looks were not all that important, compared to what was inside.

Doña Ester was Don Miguel Santiesteban's wife, and the couple had emigrated to the island from Extremadura thirty years before. During his first night in San Juan, Buenaventura slept in Don Miguel's warehouse at La Puntilla. During the next couple of weeks the old gentleman did everything he could to help him find a job, but there were so many immigrants in the city that it was no simple task.

He invited Buenaventura to lunch at his house, and the young man made a good impression on Doña Ester. He had dark hair and blue eyes, but she felt sorry for him because he was so awkward and looked so lost. All during the meal he stared at his food, not knowing which silver fork to use. He overturned the wine goblet and dropped his knife several times, so that it clattered against the rim of the plate. Doña Ester asked herself how he would manage to get ahead in the finicky island society and on that very day began to teach him that gentlemen didn't eat chicken with their fingers, stood up to help a lady with her chair whenever she rose, didn't barge ahead through a door in front of her but opened it courteously, and other basic rules of etiquette. When dinner was over, she asked him to stop by the studio of the family photographer to have his picture taken.

Doña Ester planned to send the photo to Angelita and Conchita, Buenaventura's maiden aunts in Extremadura, so that they might see their nephew was doing fine, in spite of the mosquitoes and the bad drinking water. But when she came back from Rebecca's house after the girl had rejected the fourth would-be king, the first thing Doña Ester saw in her living room was Buenaventura's portrait on the marble-topped table, waiting to be mailed to Spain. She dropped her handbag on one of the Victorian rocking chairs, gave a deep sigh, and said to herself, "Here I am, searching all over town for a scrawny teenager for Rebecca, and the King of Hearts is sitting on my drawing-room console all the time."

Rebecca chose him as her official escort the next day, even before seeing him in the flesh. Buenaventura went to visit her and kissed her hand; he was a fast learner of the ways of kings. On the day of the coronation ball he escorted Rebecca to the throne with perfect decorum, and on their wedding day a month later he walked her down the aisle, her hand poised on his arm light as a heron's wing. In his black tuxedo and silk top hat he not only looked like a patrician, he behaved like one. His courtly demeanor, the elegant way he carried himself, seemed to say: "Here is someone who did not learn the rules of etiquette yesterday, but sucked them with his mother's milk."

4

When Shadows

Roamed the Island

✕

AT THE BEGINNING of this century, our island acquired an unexpected strategic significance for the admiralty of the Third Reich. Being a history fan, Quintín was very well informed about that period of our past, and would tell me about it when we were first married. They were exciting times, and I liked to hear him talk about Admiral Alfred von Tirpitz, for example, who insisted, during endless royal audiences at the court of Kaiser Wilhelm II, that Puerteriko be made a German naval base, which would secure the commercial routes to the Antilles and to the Gulf of Mexico. "If they had made El Yunque, the highest peak on the eastern coast, a nest of Krupp artillery cannons as they had planned," Quintín said, "it would have helped them considerably in their aim to acquire greater control over the Panama Canal, which was becoming more and more important for the American fleet. An open sea lane from the Atlantic to the Pacific would have permitted them to come and go as they pleased between California and the East Coast."

I found the whole matter fascinating. The result of von Tripitz's plans for the Caribbean was a German siege of the island, and in 1917, the year of Buenaventura and Rebecca's wedding, we suddenly found ourselves surrounded by hungry sharks. German sub-

marines were everywhere and, as they sailed in and out of the
crevices of the Puerto Rico Trench, were perfectly visible when
they surfaced. People made a hobby of watching them come up
from the deep from the rooftops of Old San Juan, using the same
binoculars they used at the horse races.

Our strategic importance became evident, and the United States
began to establish new military bases on the island, quartering
thousands of American soldiers among us. Despite their presence,
ships continued to sink in front of the city, taking with them to
the bottom of the sea drums of gasoline, rolls of paper, bags of
salt, rice, beans—all the things that began to disappear from our
shops. People survived thanks to the emergency programs of the
U.S. government, which sent us war rations along with the soldiers.

San Juan merchants started to count their assets in rubber tires,
gasoline drums, and pounds of salt pork, and Buenaventura Mendizabal was one of them. Every cellar in the city became a dry-
goods warehouse where things that were indispensable for survival
were hoarded. The people bore their adverse destiny patiently.
They were used to tightening their belts on empty stomachs and
they survived in spite of everything, killing hunger with *carajitos*,
shots of rum in their coffee, and sweet-potato skins boiled with
orange leaves for their midday meal. Children went barefoot, their
heads full of lice and their bellies swollen with parasites. When
they ran down the street, their souls barely clung to their bones,
like fragile kites made of tissue paper.

5

The Merchant Prince

ꗥ

BUENAVENTURA INHERITED a Spanish coat of arms from his
ancestor, Don Francisco Pizarro, depicting an armed warlord beheading a hog with his short sword. "The Pizarro Mendizabals had
always been successful merchants before they turned into soldiers," he said to Rebecca on the day of their wedding. "Before
they sailed off to Peru during the Spanish Conquest, their business
had been selling smoked hams, which they peddled with great
flair all across Castile." And as he spoke, he slid a heavy gold
ring, emblazoned with that uncouth heraldry, on her finger.

Things went well with Buenaventura after the marriage. He was
doing good business selling water, and Don Esteban Rosich, his
wife's grandfather, was proud of him. Don Esteban was in the
shipping business and decided to help his grandson-in-law by
making him a present of two small steamships of eight thousand
tons each, so that Buenaventura could transport his provisions
from Spain to the island. Rebecca christened them herself, the
S.S. *Patria* and the S.S. *Libertad,* breaking a bottle of champagne
on the side of each ship and toasting the future of Mendizabal &
Company, her husband's newly established enterprise.

My future father-in-law wasn't as intelligent as Rebecca believed
him to be, but he had an unfailing commercial instinct. "These

are difficult times, my dear," Buenaventura would say to Rebecca. "No business is foolproof except in food, because, no matter what happens, people always have to eat."

In 1918, when German submarines laid siege to our city and people were literally dying of hunger, Buenaventura decided it was the right moment to expand his business. So he bought a shipload of dried codfish in Newfoundland, which he somehow managed to get through the blockade. When he put the fish on the market, it sold out in less than a week. The fish fillets were thick and lush, their juices stored under a layer of hardened salt which protected them from the rain and the flies and preserved them from rot. They had, furthermore, a sky-high protein content which began to work wonders on the starving population. All through the mountains, one could see peasants boiling codfish slabs with green plantains, *yuca* and taro roots, in large tin cans poised over an open fire, under the shade of mango trees.

Buenaventura discovered that cod actually saved people's lives, and on top of this, it was excellent business. He bought it dirt cheap: for a ten-pound package of cod he paid one American cent to the Canadian company, Viking Co., and he sold it for ten cents a pound. Business was so good that soon after a second shipload managed to slip into port, he made Rebecca a splendid gift for their wedding anniversary. He bought her a white Packard, which she named Dulce Sueño in honor of the *paso fino* horse that won the trophy that year at the racetrack.

A windfall like that couldn't last forever. Soon other wholesalers were buying cod by the shipload in Halifax and squeezing it past the German submarines. Buenaventura saw danger coming, and he wrote to Viking Co. asking them to identify his product by stamping each crate with the seal of Francisco Pizarro. But they refused to comply. "No cod is better than the next cod, and to distinguish yours from the rest would go against our company policy," the president of Viking Co. replied dourly.

Competition was fierce, but Buenaventura's ships always managed to dodge the German U-boats, and he sold more cod than the others. At first, people thought it was just happenstance. If Buenaventura's lucky star made it possible for him to marry an heiress a month after his arrival on the island, his ships could very well wiggle out of the range of German guns and cross the blockade unscathed.

Bit by bit, however, people began to suspect foul play. Rumors flew that Buenaventura's Spanish friends, who traveled everywhere as tourists on his ships, were not ordinary passengers. The minute his ships landed, they would go wandering around the island, making detailed maps of the major roads and bridges and taking note of the radio-transmission towers. Once the ships unloaded their merchandise, they would board them immediately and sail home with the documents.

One day, something very odd happened after one of Buenaventura's ships docked. He always drove out to the wharf to wait for the ships to come in after they'd been sighted from El Morro's lighthouse. On that day, the minute the gangplank was lowered and before anyone got off, a huge Doberman pinscher trod gingerly down the incline, sniffed his way to where Buenaventura's black Packard had driven up, and jumped in as he opened the door. Buenaventura was curiously nonchalant about the whole thing. He never asked who had sent him the dog or where and when it had gotten on board. He named it Fausto, and from then on, it slept at the foot of his bed.

Quintín, of course, would deny these stories about his father if he ever read them. I admit they're no better than hearsay. But everyone who knew Buenaventura at the time suspected that he was a German sympathizer, although people later forgot all about this. The mysterious immunity of Buenaventura's ships lasted only a year, the war being over by 1918. But it brought him a great deal of prosperity. He relocated his merchandise from the small wooden depot he had built next to his bungalow on the lagoon to a large brick-and-mortar warehouse on La Puntilla, close to where the rest of the city's commercial entrepreneurs had their store-houses and business offices.

He liked to eat and drink in style, and five years after his marriage to Rebecca he had forfeited his slender silhouette for a considerable girth. His hair had thinned out on his head, so he let sideburns, black as tongs, grow on each side of his face. He was fiercely loyal to his products, and business for him was a point of honor. He would have challenged his detractors to a duel had he thought it necessary.

Quintín once told me the story—passed on by Rebecca, since he hadn't been born yet—of how one day his father invited four American businessmen to dinner at his house. They were investors in a large new hotel to be built on the strip of beach near the lagoon, and the residents of Alamares were thrilled at the prospect, because it would provide a casino, a swimming pool, and tennis courts they could use. Rebecca and Buenaventura were sitting with their guests at the table when the maid drew near and whispered something in Buenaventura's ear.

"The cook is up in arms," the maid was saying, "because the can is rusted and swollen, and he doesn't think it wise to add Mendizabal asparagus to the salad. They might poison the guests."

Buenaventura looked at her in disbelief. "Poison our guests just because of a little rust on a can?" he cried, his cheeks trembling. "How can anyone say such a thing? Tell the cook to be careful what he says, because slander can be much worse than rust, and if he criticizes Mendizabal products, he may end up without a job." And when the maid brought in the salad bowl, he put four large asparagus spears on his plate and proceeded to eat them boldly, making fun of the whole episode and pretending not to notice the green slime covering them.

"Asparagus are good to ward off impotence and other disorders of the infirm," he told his guests jovially as he ate. "They work wonders in bed, and a few hours later you piss them into your chamber pot." Fortunately, the American entrepreneurs declined to eat any salad, because that evening Rebecca had to drive Buena-ventura to the emergency room at Alamares Hospital to have his stomach pumped due to food poisoning.

PART 2

The First House on the Lagoon

6

The Wizard from Prague

❧

REBECCA AND BUENAVENTURA had been married for eight years and they still hadn't had any children. This was a disappointment for Buenaventura, who wanted a large family, but Rebecca didn't mind it at all. She didn't want children. She felt she was a free spirit; if she had children, she'd never be able to dance and be one with nature the way she wanted.

Rebecca had made many friends in the artists' community of San Juan and often invited them to the bungalow, where they would sit in the garden by the lagoon and talk about poetry and painting. Buenaventura knew about these gatherings, but he was busy and didn't give them much thought. He would leave the house at seven in the morning and wouldn't return until eight at night, so Rebecca had most of the day to herself. She wrote poetry in the morning, practiced an improvised style of dance along the lagoon's edge in the afternoon, and invited her friends to dinner almost every evening.

In 1925 Buenaventura decided they should move to a place more in keeping with their new prosperity. Their bungalow stood on choice property and could easily be torn down to make way for a new building. One day he was driving down Ponce de León Avenue on his way home and he saw a beautiful mansion being built on a palm-shaded hillock. It had a wide-terraced front, stained-glass windows, and walls decorated with golden mosaics that gleamed in the afternoon sun. He immediately decided he wanted a house just like it, only larger and more luxurious.

Buenaventura stopped the car and got out to inspect the house more closely. There were workmen coming and going with wheelbarrows loaded with sacks of cement, and he asked one of them who the architect was. The man pointed to a sallow, curly-haired man dressed in black, with a black silk cape thrown over his shoulders. Buenaventura approached, smiled, and introduced himself, complimenting the architect on his work. But the man stared back sullenly, muttered under his breath, and stalked off.

Quintín had done research on the architect and even contemplated writing a book about him once, before he let himself be swallowed up by his work at Mendizabal & Co. He was an admirer of Milan Pavel's work and was convinced he was an important figure in the artistic history of the island.

Milan Pavel lived in San Juan from 1905 to 1928. He had emigrated from Prague to Chicago when he was ten years old, the son of a carpenter. He never studied architecture formally, but was probably an apprentice to one of Chicago's well-known architects. When he saved enough money, he established his own construction company and began to build homes in Chicago's West End, where many immigrants lived. Chicago was at the center of an architectural revolution; those were the golden years of the Prairie School.

Pavel became Frank Lloyd Wright's protégé and assisted him first as a blueprint copy boy and later as a draftsman. He had a natural ability for design; his architectural drawings were delicate and executed with a precise drafting hand. He had a photographic memory as well, and in time was able to reproduce, line by line, Wright's unique plans for his buildings.

Pavel became more and more obsessed with his master's work. He hardly ate, and slept only fitfully. He drove by the master's studio at Oak Park and marveled at the beauty of the low, horizontal buildings which gathered all the beauty of the prairie light at dusk. He admired the avant-garde designs of the homes Wright had built in the elegant suburbs of Chicago. He would have given his right hand to be able to design one of them, but in the modest bungalows of the West Side he was commissioned to build he didn't dare take a chance like that. He was, after all, only an obscure contractor of immigrant origins.

A few years after he established himself in Chicago, something happened to Pavel which drastically changed his life. In 1898 he had married a young violinist of Bohemian descent, María Straub, but they became estranged and María took up with a lover. Pavel found them in bed one night when he returned home unexpectedly. He beat her and pushed her down the stairs. Fearing he had killed her, he left the house in a panic.

He fled Chicago and, taking with him a copy of Wright's Wasmuth Portfolio, went to Jacksonville, Florida. Jacksonville was experiencing a building boom, following the great fire of 1901, which had destroyed many of its downtown structures. Pavel was bound to find work there. He attended a Methodist Episcopal church, asking forgiveness for the crime he thought he had committed, and was befriended by the minister, who was about to build a new church in the parish. Pavel offered to draw the plans free of charge, and the minister was delighted. Pavel designed a beautiful building, an exact copy of one Wright had built in Chicago. But someone on the committee of parishioners was familiar with Wright's work and accused Pavel of plagiarism. Pavel was stunned; he couldn't understand how anyone could say such a thing. His church would have been a faithful re-creation, stone by stone, of Wright's masterpiece, not a mere copy.

Pavel used to like to take walks on the Jacksonville waterfront in the evenings, wrapped in his black silk cape, and he would see groups of fashionably dressed Spanish-speaking people getting off ocean liners and boarding limousines that drove them to the train station. He asked where they came from and was told many were from Puerto Rico, a territory of the United States. At Jacksonville they boarded the Florida train and headed north.

Puerto Rico was often in the news at the time; it was described by the press as an exotic, far-off possession, where there was a dire need for public works. The island had been a colony of Spain for four hundred years and, as William Randolph Hearst's newspapers often pointed out, was mired in poverty. This situation more than justified the United States taking over the island after the Spanish-American War. Ninety percent of the population was illiterate, and bilharzia and hookworm were rampant. A roster of projects was to be undertaken by the federal government to better the lot of the inhabitants.

Pavel was a keen observer. He took note of the well-heeled, elegantly dressed travelers who got off the boats from Puerto Rico, and he also read in the press about the plight of the Puerto Rican people. He surmised there must be two Puerto Ricos— one in serious need, and one which was booming. Both offered him ample opportunity for work as a contractor, and he began to consider emigrating to the island. There was another reason that moved him toward that decision: Puerto Rico was isolated enough so very few people there had heard of Frank Lloyd Wright.

Pavel sailed for his new destination, and for the next twenty-three years he lived out his dream: in Puerto Rico he managed to become his hero. He re-created much of Wright's work with absolute fidelity; he filled San Juan with beautiful copies of the master's houses, which the islanders hailed as gems of architecture.

Soon after he arrived in San Juan, he became a member of the Elks Club. It was a wise decision, because the Elks were very well connected. Only foreigners could become members, and he was immediately made to feel welcome. The Elks spoke English among themselves and were active both in private and in public institutions. They had government connections and owned many of the important businesses involved in the development of the island—the telephone company, electric power plants, foundries. Many of the Elks were Masons, like Pavel himself.

On the day of his initiation as an Elk, Pavel inscribed his profession in the members' book as "architect." Many of the club's members commissioned him to design their private homes, but these were usually modest buildings, because the Elks were puritanical and didn't believe in extravagance. Through the Elks, however, Pavel got to know the criollo landowners, who were all members of the Association of Sugar Producers. These were the people he had seen getting off the passenger ships at Jacksonville, with silver fox draped over their shoulders and expensive Stetson hats on their heads: the Calimanos, the Behn-Luchettis, the Georgettis, the Shucks—the sugar barons of the island. Soon many of them wanted him to design them ultramodern mansions. Pavel didn't have to worry about a budget at all; he could spend whatever he wanted.

Buenaventura called on Pavel several times and finally got him to have lunch with Rebecca and him at their house. Before the meal was served, Buenaventura took the architect around and showed him the site. It was truly paradisiacal. By that time most of the wild vegetation surrounding Alamares Lagoon had been cleared away, except for the mangrove swamp, and several beautiful homes had been built near Buenaventura's bungalow. The lagoon was clear and peaceful, and because of the buildings that had gone up around it, at night it shone like a perfect aquamarine set in a necklace of diamonds.

Buenaventura showed Pavel the gentle slope where he wanted to build his new house, with "a magnificent terrace from where he could watch his ships go in and out of the harbor." "This place we're living in now can't properly be called a home," he said to Pavel. "It's only a temporary residence. I want you to build a mansion more suited to our social standing. I'll pay whatever you ask." But Pavel refused.

"It has nothing to do with fees," Pavel said. "I simply have too much work and can barely keep up with the commitments I have already." He knew Buenaventura would have paid him a good sum, and the site was certainly beautiful. What bothered him was Buenaventura himself—his large peasant's hands and the unruly tufts of hair that grew out of his ears, which he never let the barber clip for him, though Rebecca begged him to. Above all, he resented Buenaventura's ignorance, his coarse, country ways. During his walk through the site, his host emphasized that he wanted the house to be impressive, but that it should be comfortable. "I want to live in a home, not a controversial work of art," he said. Pavel suspected the real reason Buenaventura wanted him to design the house was that he liked his golden-mosaic decorations—which gave off an affluent glitter under the noonday sun—and not because of his avant-garde architectural lines.

It was Rebecca who made him change his mind. When Buenaventura excused himself after lunch and went back to his office, Rebecca and Pavel were left by themselves, and she invited him to go for a walk along the lagoon's edge. Rebecca was twenty-four and her beauty was in full flower. Pavel saw that she had a keen sensibility and lived for art. She wrote poetry in secret, she said, and brought out a folder of poems from the house. It had an elaborate binding with a water lily carved on the front and silver clasps on the sides. Rebecca was reading one of her poems to Pavel when a breeze from the lagoon blew away several pages. Instead of running after them, she did an elegant little dance, managing to capture them in midair. Pavel laughed as he watched her admiringly.

"I've always wanted to be a dancer and a poet," she said to him. "When I was a child, my parents took me to Europe. We went to the great opera houses and saw the best dancers: Anna Pavlova in London, Nijinsky in Paris. But my favorite was Isadora Duncan. From the moment I saw Isadora dance, she became my ideal. In Puerto Rico, artistic currents arrive years later than in the rest of the world. That is why I believe your work is so important. You could teach us about modern art."

The young men and women from well-to-do families who came to Rebecca's salon were the *jeunesse dorée* of San Juan, and they had the same tastes she did. Far from belonging to San Juan's demimonde, where the struggling artists came from, they had traveled widely in Europe, knew the best wines and cheeses, could play a Shubert impromptu on the piano, spoke French fluently, and above all did not have to work for a living. They wanted to lead beautiful lives, both inside and out, wear beautiful clothes, visit beautiful places, and occupy their minds with beautiful thoughts.

This type of existence unfortunately was not conducive to the disciplines of learning, so their compositions—the light dramas, boudoir vignettes, and playful piano pieces they put together— were never very good. Some believed that to write a poem or a musical composition one had to slave for hours learning difficult techniques, but Rebecca's friends didn't agree. Like Rebecca herself, who thought one could learn to dance simply by "imitating nature," they subscribed to the Muses' inspiration. They loved to go to the beach, buy expensive jewelry and clothes, and were fervent admirers of Rubén Darío, the modernist poet then in vogue in Puerto Rico.

While in Argentina and Peru the rising stars were avant-garde writers such as Vicente Huidobro and César Vallejo, in the back-water of Alamares Lagoon the modernist poets Darío and Herrera y Reissig, who sang the beauties of the bejeweled Art Nouveau world, were still the darlings of the moment. In Europe as well as in Latin America, rhyme and meter were passé and poetry now strove to express the conflicts of modern civilization—the lone-liness of the city, the protests of the exploited masses, the loss of religious belief. The world was bursting at the seams, but in Rebecca's literary salon poets still sang of gardens full of roses, ponds skimmed by snow-white swans, and foam-crested waves spilling over the beach like lace-hemmed gowns.

Rebecca thought maybe Pavel could change all this. He was a cultivated man. In Chicago he had led an intense life, having made contact with the cultural elite there. He was well versed in the latest artistic movements from Europe: Expressionism, Constructivism, Cubism. He understood her when she talked about modern art.

Rebecca had been feeling more and more estranged from her husband. Buenaventura had begun to pay less attention to her, so preoccupied was he with business matters. After the First World War the price of sugar had soared, and the well-to-do were living in style. They often gave parties at home and wine and champagne flowed like water. Buenaventura was very busy at the warehouse, since he was in charge of sales.

As she walked with Pavel by the water's edge, Rebecca told him about her life. There were no ballet schools in San Juan, so when she returned to the island with her grandparents, she decided she would learn to dance on her own. "Isadora Duncan never had professional training, either," Rebecca said to Pavel. "She became a dancer by identifying with nature. That's why I like to spend as much time as I can in the garden. I'd like to reach, through nature, the divine expression of the human spirit.

"When I came back from my trip to Europe, I began to dress in flowing robes and I read everything I could get my hands on about her. My parents were worried, and started to invite young people to the house often. They took me to picnics, concerts, as many social events as they could think of. Finally they contacted the committee of the Spanish Casino and offered to foot the carnival's bill that year if I was elected queen. They hoped the social activities would take my mind off my supposedly bizarre interests. The ladies' committee complied and suggested a newly arrived stranger—a Spaniard from Extremadura—as my escort. I was so taken with Buenaventura's good looks I fell head over heels in love with him. We got married a month later, when I had just turned sixteen. Then I discovered that he didn't like poetry and hated ballet."

Milan was sympathetic. "Now that you've met me, everything

will be different!" he said. "I'll teach you all about modern art."
Rebecca was overjoyed. She was sure that, with Pavel near, her
talents would be rekindled. Pavel talked to her about the need for
the artist to make a total commitment. Rebecca shouldn't go on
spending time with dilettantes; if she wanted to become a true
poet and dancer, she had to do serious work. As she listened to
him, Rebecca felt transformed.

She's like me, Pavel thought. An inveterate dreamer, as well
as the most beautiful woman I've ever met. I want to build a special
house for her that will enable her to go on living for beautiful
things in spite of being married to a boor. He hadn't told her he
had turned down Buenaventura's commission. He pretended to
have accepted, as Rebecca described what she wanted.

"You mustn't just draw the plans for a beautiful house," she
said as they walked by the beach. "You must build me a masterpiece where everything will be carefully planned to preserve the
illusion of art. I want Tiffany-glass windows, alabaster skylights,
and floors made of *capá* wood from the cool forests of the island."
She laughed when she finished her fanciful description, but their
conversation had brought a flush of pleasure to her cheeks.

Pavel looked around the property, which ended at the lagoon's
shore. To the left there was a large thicket of mangroves. Near
Buenaventura's bungalow, there was an old wall with a weather-
beaten sign which read *Cristal de Alamares*. "That's Buenaventura's spring," Rebecca said. "He used to sell water to the Spanish
merchant ships just after we were married."

"I'd like to see the spring," Pavel said, his curiosity piqued.
They walked toward the enclosure. Rebecca searched for the key,
which was hidden under a stone, and opened the padlock. They
entered, taking care not to dirty their shoes in the mud. Inside,
there was a well about four feet deep, full of water. A pipe drained
the well in the direction of the lagoon. Pavel drew near and bent
down to scoop some water into his cupped hand. "It's delicious,"
he said, taking a long drink. "Cool and sweet. Taste it." And he

offered Rebecca some. But when he felt Rebecca's breath on the palm of his hand, he couldn't resist the temptation and kissed her on the lips. Rebecca didn't say anything. She just looked at him. "You should build your house right here," Pavel told her. "That way the Muses will always inspire you."

When he returned home that night, Pavel took out his copy of the Wasmuth Portfolio and picked out one of Wright's masterpieces as his model. He wanted to build Rebecca the most beautiful house in the world. As he worked on the plans he grew inspired and added many new elements which would make the house more in keeping with life in the tropics. At the front entrance, the one which opened onto Ponce de León Avenue, there was to be a magnificent mosaic rainbow. Through this rainbow Rebecca would dance out into the world, swathed in her silk chiffons and reciting her love poems.

The bedrooms would be in the front wing, facing the boulevard, and an elegant open pavilion would connect that wing to the dining and living rooms, which would face the lagoon. As the terrain sloped gradually toward the back of the house, one could drive under the open pavilion, which would serve as a carport and at the same time add a colorful accent because of its mosaic decorations. Under the house would be a large cellar. The kitchens would be there, as well as a large number of storage rooms, and a special chamber for the spring. The ceilings were to be twice as high as those of Wright's houses, and the edge of the gabled roofs would be decorated with a glittering mosaic of olive boughs—the token gesture Pavel made toward Buenaventura, since olives were one of Mendizabal's best-selling products. The house would be surrounded by a garden, and the glassware used at table would repeat the motifs of the flora: the water goblets would be lotus-shaped, the wine goblets would resemble hyacinths, and the champagne flutes water lilies.

Pavel designed a beautiful golden terrace at the back of the house, floating over the lagoon. He would be more than glad to meet with Rebecca's artist friends there, he said, and together they would stimulate the lazy artistic climate of the island. The next day Pavel accepted Buenaventura's commission. It was the first time in his life he designed something truly original. He created the house on the lagoon as one would create a poem or a statue, breathing life into its every stone.

7

Rebecca's Kingdom

❧❦

BUENAVENTURA AND REBECCA moved into their new house in 1926, and a few months later he was named Spanish consul for the island. This strengthened his economic situation even more. Now he didn't have to sneak his merchandise into the city in covered barges that crossed the swamp, but could bring it directly into port, still without having to pay taxes on it. He sold his black Packard, bought a silver Rolls-Royce, and put a Spanish flag on its radio antenna. "Spain's flag is the same color as the bullring's," he would say proudly to the diplomats he ushered around the city. "Gold for its sand and red for the blood that brave men spill on it."

As Buenaventura's wife, Rebecca was required to be at his side at all formal receptions for Spanish dignitaries and for goodwill ambassadors from other European countries. When Puerto Rico became a territory of the United States, diplomatic relations virtually ceased between the island and the rest of the world. Every business or legal transaction had to be processed through the Department of the Interior in Washington, D.C., and this office was so flooded with work that dealing with Puerto Rican affairs was like looking for a needle in a haystack.

Buenaventura acquired an unexpected political prominence as

one of the few businessmen who could still import merchandise directly from Europe. His house became a meeting place for envoys from all over the Continent. Dinners were always seven-course affairs, and the elaborate social receptions required constant supervision. Buenaventura expected Rebecca to make everything run smoothly.

Rebecca herself told me about this time in her life during the months when Quintín and I were engaged and she was still my friend. Once our family difficulties began, though, this kind of confidence ceased. But in the summer of our courtship I used to travel from Ponce to San Juan often, and as I waited at the house for Quintín to come home from work, Rebecca would talk to me about herself.

Rebecca, as I've said, began to be unhappy in her new house. Once he was made Spanish consul, Buenaventura refused to let her meet with her artist friends, because it wasn't seemly for a diplomat's wife to patronize such bohemian goings-on. As a result, a year after they moved to the house the poetry readings, concerts, and dance recitals ended and the sparkling mosaic terrace went unused. Rebecca had wanted a Temple of Art, and instead they lived in a Temple of Commerce and Diplomacy where her husband reigned supreme. She maintained that a man's kingdom is his business and a woman's is the home, but Buenaventura wouldn't take her seriously. "A man's home is like a rooster's coop: women may speak out when chickens get to pee," he said to Rebecca, giving her a pat on the behind. Rebecca anguished about it for several weeks and then accepted giving up her artistic soireés for the time being, because she didn't want to damage Buenaventura's career as a diplomat.

In Extremadura, Buenaventura's family wasn't rich but they lived in a nice house and kept a moderate number of servants, in accordance with their modest prominence. After a number of years in Puerto Rico, however, he observed that the local bourgeoisie were very tight-fisted. They never spent a penny more than they needed to on their homes, and their servants lived in miserable conditions in underground cellars.

When they moved into Pavel's house, it was as if Buenaventura enjoyed behaving in open contradiction to his opulent surroundings. He forced Rebecca to walk around the house with a sheaf of keys hanging from her waist with which she would lock up the wines, the coffee, the oil, and the sugar in the pantry. Mendizabal's smoked hams were considered a great delicacy, and in their new home Buenaventura hung them from bronze hooks in the pantry's cupboard. The hams were aged—sometimes five or six years old —and had a round tin cup at the bottom, into which the slow tears of lard dripped day and night. After a while, Buenaventura began to be afraid that someone would steal them, and he had Rebecca store them in her closet, next to her fashionable Paris outfits and lace lingerie. So, when Rebecca was invited to dinner at their friends' homes, there was always an odor of smoked ham about her that left no doubt as to the prosaic origin of the Mendizabal family fortune.

Occasionally, Rebecca would defy her husband's decrees, smiling sweetly under her Mary Pickford curls. Buenaventura had ordered that no broken porcelain plate or drinking glass should ever be thrown out before he inspected it, so he could keep track of how much waste there was at the house. Rebecca and the servants were so terrified of his outbursts that they would secretly glue the pieces together and put them back in the dining-room cabinet. On one occasion, when Buenaventura needed a loan for his cod-importing business, he invited the president of the Royal Bank of Canada to dinner at the house, and Rebecca poured him his coffee in one of the porcelain cups with a reconstructed handle. Unfortunately, the heat melted the glue and the cup fell into the man's lap, staining his white linen pants and scalding his groin. When Rebecca saw his grimace of pain, she smiled charmingly and said without losing her composure: "Please excuse my clumsiness, sir. My husband abhors waste and never throws anything away, even broken cups. That's why he fully deserves to be trusted by the Royal Bank."

Buenaventura and Rebecca traveled to Spain for the first time in 1927. They drove south from Madrid to Valdeverdeja, but he wouldn't stay with his aunts Angelita and Conchita at their quaint whitewashed home, with its geranium pots on the windowsills and its inner courtyard with the ancient well still in use. He insisted they set out immediately for the austere plains of Extremadura, where the Conquistadors were born. So they crossed the valley of the Tajo River in their rented Bentley without stopping until they reached the Monastery of the Virgin of Guadalupe, high up in the Sierra. He stayed there with Rebecca for a week, and visited the place every three or four years throughout most of his life.

Buenaventura had had the monastery restored as soon as he could afford it. It was from Guadalupe that several of the Conquistadors had set out for the New World, after being blessed by the prior at the chapel. Trujillo, the town of Buenaventura's ancestor Francisco Pizarro, was nearby, and Pizarro had also been blessed at the monastery before he set sail for Peru.

When Buenaventura stayed at the abbey, he liked to sleep in the same spartan cell that King Charles V of Spain had used on his religious retreats; he strolled in the Mudéjar cloister, bathed in the freezing waters of the monastery's pond, and shat comfortably in the white-porcelain toilet he had ordered built. It was the only building with modern plumbing in the province, and the monks had had the toilet raised on a velvet dais and draped with red damask curtains to keep the icy mountain drafts which seeped through the louvered windows from chilling their benefactor's bottom.

Rebecca hated the place. The monks had whitewashed the cells and fixed the leaky roof, but there was no heating system; they still relied on braziers to heat the rooms. The walls and floors were so cold Rebecca swore a white mist breathed out of them at night. The first time she stayed at the abbey, she was so chilly she slept fully clothed in the cell adjacent to Buenaventura's and refused to take a bath the whole week they spent there.

Ten years had gone by since Rebecca's wedding, and she was no longer as much in love with Buenaventura, but she liked being married to him because he was a powerful man. When they attended parties in San Juan together, the minute the orchestra began to play a paso doble—*The Kiss*, for example, which went: "A kiss, in Spain, is carried by a woman deep in her soul!"; or *My Tawny Beauty*: "Step on my cape, my tawny beauty, and the imprint of your foot I'll carry in a locket deep in my heart!"—Buenaventura would walk over to Rebecca in his silk tuxedo and puckered shirt, and ask her to dance. Rebecca's misgivings would all melt away as she sailed across the crowded dance floor in Buenaventura's arms, the envious looks of her friends falling by her side like dead birds.

By the time Rebecca was twenty-seven, she had begun to tire of Buenaventura's stubborn disregard for her artistic vocation. They had lived in their new house for two years and she had been a model wife, but Buenaventura hadn't let her hold a single artist's soirée. Pavel hardly dropped by anymore and Rebecca had no one to talk to. She didn't have any children and she was bored to death.

Pavel visited Rebecca often during the construction of the house on the lagoon, but once the family moved in, he stopped coming. In the past year he had been ill and withdrawn. A rumor was going around that people who lived in the houses Pavel built went gradually out of their minds. The Behn brothers, for example, the owners of the local telephone company—known in San Juan as "los hermanos Brothers"—were so happy with their beautiful house at the entrance to Alamares that they refused to go out and took care of their business by telephone instead. Eventually the brothers went bankrupt and the government expropriated their company; the house was torn down. The Calimanos, powerful hacienda owners from Guayama, began to spend their days planting water lilies in the Japanese pond at the back of their house and stopped ordering the modern crushing mills and flywheel gears necessary for their business. They produced less and less sugar and their house was also torn down. The collapse of sugar in the world market—in 1920 a ton of sugar was worth $235.87 and by 1926 it was worth $83.31—put pressure on other sugar barons, too, and they no longer commissioned lavish homes from Pavel.

To forget his woes, Pavel began to drink a purple liquor made from sugar beets which he distilled himself in the cellar of his house. His grandmother had made it in Czechoslovakia when he was a child, and now he drank it to feel closer to his Czech roots. He stopped working and became a recluse. He built a moat around his rural-style cottage on the outskirts of San Juan, so no one could approach it from the street.

One morning Pavel, half drunk, stepped into his car to go downtown, but the car wouldn't start. He opened the hood and tried to get the motor going, but nothing happened. He stood in front of the car, cranking it over and over, thinking it wouldn't budge. But the car suddenly shot forward and crushed him against a telephone pole. People were afraid of his bad luck and no one went to his funeral; he was carted off, unaccompanied, to the Municipal Cemetery. Rebecca was the only person who put flowers on his grave.

Soon after Pavel died, Rebecca decided she couldn't bear to live with Buenaventura any longer. She approached him, head hung low, her blond curls almost hiding her face, and told him she was leaving him. Governor Horace Towner, who was a friend of Don Esteban Rosich, had offered her father, Arístides Arrigoitia, an office job in Atlanta, and she had persuaded him to accept. Her mother, Madeleine Rosich, had always wanted to go back to the States. They would take Don Esteban with them, as he was well on in years. They would be living in a house with a pillared portico at the end of an avenue of ancient mahogany trees. Buenaventura couldn't believe it. It had never crossed his mind that Rebecca might desert him.

"And what will we do with our beautiful house?" was the only thing that occurred to him to say. "Frankly, I don't know," Rebecca replied sadly. "For all I care, you may use it as a warehouse for your precious hams and your cursed codfish." And she went on packing the flowing robes, the dancing slippers, and the books of poetry into her suitcase.

When Buenaventura found himself alone, he fell ill. For the first time since he arrived on the island, he didn't have the energy to get out of bed. He stayed there all day like a beached whale, not shaving, not even dressing for breakfast. He couldn't stand living in Pavel's house, where everything reminded him of Rebecca. A week later he got out of bed, took a bath, dressed, clipped the tufts of hair growing out of his ears, and traveled to Atlanta to ask her forgiveness.

On the day Buenaventura arrived, Rebecca found that she was pregnant. She didn't want the child to be born without the father's knowing about it, so she told Buenaventura the news. He was exultant. He apologized for everything and promised Rebecca she could have all the artistic soirées she wanted if only she would return to the island with him. Rebecca consented. Her mother and father were happy with the decision—they had hoped the rift would be temporary—and a few weeks later the whole family boarded the ship back to San Juan. Rebecca returned triumphant on Buenaventura's arm, and from that day on she reigned as undisputed mistress of the house on the lagoon.

8

Salomé's Dance

❧

BUENAVENTURA WAS SO HAPPY he wanted to please Rebecca in everything. She could invite as many artists as she wanted to her cultural gatherings, which would alternate with Buenaventura's diplomatic meetings. Dressed in elegant gowns and velvet suits, Rebecca's friends came at least one evening a week to the house, to lounge on the terrace and discuss poetry, art, and music until the early hours of the morning. They made fun of Buenaventura's acquaintances—the businessmen, lawyers, and politicians he invited to dinner, who dressed in dark suits, had generous paunches, and ate with napkins tucked under their chins. But Buenaventura didn't mind.

Rebecca wrote poetry every day. She visited the spring in the cellar and drank its waters, convinced that they nourished her inspiration. Her friends wrote poetry also, and they read their compositions aloud to each other on the terrace, commenting on them and making suggestions. They read books on modern art and became politically conscious. They admired Luis Palés Matos, the son of a white *hacendado*, who in 1929 had published a collection of revolutionary poems titled *Tún tún de pasa y grifería* in which black ethnic roots were regarded as fundamental to Puerto Rican culture. The bourgeoisie was scandalized, but Rebecca's friends fell in love with the poems, which echoed with the mysterious rhythms of Africa. Rebecca was so proud to have these meetings in her own home that she kept her racial prejudice in check and never complained when her friends recited Palés's poems.

Thanks to these *rendezvous*—the cultural and the diplomatic—Buenaventura and Rebecca got along better than they ever had in eleven years of marriage. Rebecca was content and didn't even notice when Buenaventura brought Petra Avilés to work for them at the house. Brambon, Petra's husband, moved in with them, too, and the couple installed themselves in the cellar. Petra worked as cook and Brambon became Buenaventura's chauffeur.

Petra's ancestors were Angolan, and when people told her she was strong as an ox she would smile and say that was to be expected, her ancestors drank ox blood. She was six feet tall and her skin wasn't a watered-down chocolate but a deep onyx black; when she smiled it was as if a white scar slashed the darkness of the night. She wore brightly colored seed necklaces around her neck and steel bracelets on her wrists, and she went barefoot, so the only thing you heard when she walked into a room was her bracelets tinkling like spearheads. Petra was born in 1889 in Guayama, a town famous for its sorcerers and medicine men, and her parents had been slaves. As slavery was abolished in 1873, she was born free.

Petra's grandfather, Bernabé Avilés, whose African name was Ndongo Kumbundu, was born in Angola. Petra herself told Manuel and Willie Bernabé's story when they were children, and it would make their hair stand on end. Bernabé was chieftain of a tribe living in Bié Plateau, an area six thousand feet above sea level and one of the richest in Angola, when one day Portuguese traders raided his tribe and made him a prisoner. He was taken to the port of Luanda and put aboard a ship that landed in nearby St. Thomas. That same year he was brought to Puerto Rico in a small frigate and sold to Monsieur Pellot, a sugarcane hacienda owner in Guayama, which had lush cane fields all around it.

The black insurrection of Saint-Domingue at the beginning of the nineteenth century had kept Puerto Rico in constant fear of slave revolt. Saint-Domingue had been burned to a cinder, and practically no sugar was being produced there. This had caused sugar production to increase on the other islands, and many new slaves had been brought to the plantations. By the middle of the nineteenth century, the black slave population in Puerto Rico totaled almost one-fourth of the inhabitants. The neighboring St. John and St. Croix had had horrendous slave insurrections and became floating torches, their white populations mercilessly slaughtered with sugarcane machetes.

Slaves from Angola, Kongo, and Ndongo shared fundamental beliefs and language, part of a rich culture. They had their own religion, and their chieftains were spiritual leaders whose duty was to look out for their people. They believed in Mbanza Kongo, a mythical city of ivory minarets surrounded by a forest of date palms, with an underground river flowing beneath the city. The river separated the world of the living from the world of the dead, and was both a passage and a barrier. In Mbanza, each tribe had its own street and the inhabitants lived in peaceful coexistence; the fields of corn, wheat, and cereal around it belonged to everyone. The duty of every Angolan chieftain was to turn his own village into a Mbanza Kongo.

Bernabé had been chieftain of his tribe, and when he first arrived in Guayama, he couldn't understand why all the land on the island belonged to a few white *hacendados* dressed in white linen suits, with panama hats on their heads, when the rest of the population lived in abject poverty. Nor could he understand why he was baptized into a religion where God was called Jesus, when he had always prayed to Yemayá, Ogún, and Elegguá, whose powerful spirits had guided him, helping him heal the people of his tribe. But what had really overwhelmed him was that he was forbidden to speak Bantu with the other Angolans and Kongos living in La Quemada.

Bernabé, like the rest of the adult *bozal* slaves recently arrived from Angola, spoke Bantu. But if anyone was caught speaking it, even if he was speaking only to himself, he would be punished with fifty lashes. Bernabé had a terrible time accepting this. One's tongue was so deeply ingrained, more so even than one's religion or tribal pride; it was like a root that went deep into one's body and no one knew exactly where it ended. It was attached to one's throat, to one's neck, to one's stomach, even to one's heart.

Bernabé was as black as midnight, and he was very intelligent. Five years after his arrival there was a false rumor that Spain had granted freedom to the slaves in its colonies but that the news was being kept from distant towns like Guayama, which were cut off from the rest of the world. Bernabé got wind of the rumor and began to organize a rebellion, swearing that if freedom wasn't granted to them the slaves of La Quemada would fight to the death. He spoke secretly in Bantu with the other *bozales* and was able to plan an uprising without any of the criollo slaves—many of whom were loyal to their master—finding out about it.

The uprising was to take place on New Year's Day, the only time slaves were allowed to leave the hacienda and celebrate in the town square, where they danced the *bomba* to the rhythm of African drums. Bernabé had organized his men into three groups. One group would go to the square to dance the *bomba* in front of the Casa del Rey, which served as an armory—where the Spanish militia kept its rifles and swords. This would create a diversion, so the militia wouldn't notice anything was amiss. The second would set fire to the cane fields nearest to La Quemada, on the outskirts of town. And the third would be lying in wait behind the shrubs of sea grape by the road, to intercept the people of the hacienda, who on that morning would all be in church. When they came out of Mass the fire would be going full blast and they would run back to La Quemada. The slaves would ambush them. Bernabé had given orders that they were to take Monsieur Pellot and his family prisoner, without harming them. The Pellots would serve as hostages until the slaves got the mayor to declare officially that they were free. By that time, the *bomba* dancers would have stormed the armory and taken the rifles of the Spanish detachment, to give the abductors of the Pellot family the necessary support.

Bernabé crouched silently behind the sea grape shrubs, trying to make himself invisible. He had seen the first wisps of smoke rising like black strands of hair against the blue of the sky, when Conchita, Monsieur Pellot's twenty-year-old daughter, came galloping up the road on her mahogany-colored mare. Evidently she had overslept and her family had left her behind. She woke and saw the fire and was on her way to warn the family. But she didn't get more than a mile from the town. The slaves sprang on her like cats and made her a prisoner; but her horse got away.

When the riderless horse arrived at the church, the people of the town summoned the militia, marched to La Quemada, and were able to put out the fire. The revolt was aborted. Nothing happened to Conchita Pellot. The *bomba* dancers never had the chance to attack the armory, and the slaves were herded back to the hacienda and locked up in their quarters. With the help of the *becerrillos*, the fierce hunting dogs trained to follow a slave's scent, the conspirators were rounded up. Five of them received a hundred lashes each; but Bernabé, the leader, was sentenced to a special punishment, as an example for the rest.

Petra hadn't been born yet, but her mother told her the story of what happened to her grandfather on that day, and Petra passed it on to us. The Sunday following the attempted revolt, all the slaves of La Quemada were brought to Guayama's town square. His Excellency the Governor-General traveled all the way from San Juan to be present. His golden throne was brought from the capital in a mule cart and set under a huge laurel tree in the plaza, right in front of the whitewashed colonial church. Bernabé was brought out to the square after the special Mass celebrated in honor of the governor. They had tied his arms behind his back with rope, and his legs were secured to a post that had been thrust deep into the ground, so that he couldn't move. Everybody waited. The governor was served coffee and sweet cakes on a silver tray passed around by a Spanish orderly as he conversed with the mayor, the parish priest, and the Pellot family. The other *hacendados* and their wives strolled around, elegantly dressed, wearing hats and gloves, delighted to have the island's most powerful magistrate in town. A local guitar trio played a *zarabanda* under the trees and everyone was in a festive mood. Nobody paid any attention to Bernabé, who watched the spectacle with flashing eyes. In his tribe a man's execution was a solemn affair; no one would have dared to play music, eat sweet cakes, or make small talk. He was tense, but he wanted to die with dignity. He had refused to eat or drink in the last twenty-four hours, so as not to soil the clean clothes his wife had brought to prison for him.

Strangely enough, no firing squad or drummer was in sight. The slaves murmured restlessly under the trees, kept in line by the militiamen, who were there to protect the governor. All of a sudden Bernabé saw Pietri, the town barber, carrying his black instrument case and flanked by two Spanish soldiers in uniform. An aide walked by his side, holding a red-hot iron rod. Bernabé realized what was going to happen and strained desperately at his bindings, moving his head up and down like a strapped bull. When the barber opened his bag and took out his scalpel, Bernabé let out such a howl that the governor dropped his coffee cup on his lap and the Spanish orderly overturned his silver tray. "Olorún, ka kó koi bé!" Bernabé cried, looking straight up into the sun as he prayed to his gods to be merciful. One of the soldiers hit him on the head with a club and he passed out. The barber then pried his mouth open with a wooden spoon and sliced his tongue off, cauterizing the wound with the red-hot iron. So said Petra's mother.

BUENAVENTURA LIKED to visit his clients, the owners of the small grocery stores that were supplied merchandise by Mendizabal

& Co., and during one of these trips he had a stupid accident. He had driven all the way to Guayama, on the southeastern tip of the island, and when he reached the outskirts he felt the need to relieve himself. It had been a long trip, almost three hours up the winding mountain roads, and he preferred to urinate behind some bushes rather than enter one of the establishments in town for that purpose. But as he stepped out of his car he twisted his right ankle.

At first he didn't pay any attention and strolled half a kilometer up the road to stretch his legs, but his foot began to swell, until it looked like an eggplant. He saw a stream cascading down the side of the hill to the left of the road, sat down on a large rock, and took off his shoe and sock. He was bathing his foot in the cool waters when Petra walked by. She knelt in front of him and, without a word, took some *yaraná* leaves from her pocket, wrapped his foot in them, and had him dip it in the stream again. Then she got up and went on down the road. A few minutes later Buenaventura could stand as if nothing had happened. He walked back to his Rolls-Royce, got in, and ordered the chauffeur to drive back to San Juan. The next day he sent the car to Guayama with orders to find the tall black medicine woman and bring her to him.

Petra became Buenaventura's personal servant. She took care of his clothes, polished his shoes, cooked him special dishes, and would have kissed the ground he walked on had he asked her to. She worshipped him like a god. Buenaventura came from a family of warriors like her grandfather, and if he had been born in Angola he would also have been a chieftain. Petra was very poor; the terrible punishment her grandfather had received had been a curse on his descendants. The Avilés family had the reputation of being a rebellious lot. Petra knew she wasn't worth anything, but she meant one day to have Buenaventura's heart.

Petra settled herself in the cellar, where she built an altar to Elegguá, her favorite saint, behind the door of her room. Elegguá was so powerful he was known among blacks on the island as "He who is more than God." He was a strange idol—I saw him many times when I went down to the cellar of the house on the lagoon. He looked like a peeled coconut; with a coconut's dark brown skin, two knobs in place of eyes, and a small stem at the top of the head, which Petra rubbed with her finger whenever she asked him to do something for her. An unsmoked cigar, a red ball, and a large conch shell were always on the floor next to him. The tobacco and the red ball were to please Elegguá—he was a man and he liked to smoke cigars, but he was also a little boy and liked to play with toys. The conch shell was to speak with the dead. Through it Petra spoke with her ancestors, and it was from them she gleaned her medicinal wisdom.

Rebecca assigned the bulk of the household chores to Petra—the cooking, cleaning, and laundering. When Quintín was born, Petra served as midwife. When the birth pains commenced, Rebecca panicked. She was twenty-seven and was sure she was going to die in labor. She lay in bed screaming, "I can't do it! I can't! The baby's head is too large, it will never come out!" Petra went to her room and rubbed Elegguá's head. Then she went back upstairs, knelt by Rebecca's bed, and gently massaged her belly with coconut oil for the next twenty-four hours, repeating the words "Olorún, ka kó koi bé!" until the baby found its way out of Rebecca's womb.

Quintín was born in November of 1928. He was born before Rebecca's pregnancy reached full-term—he was an eight-month baby—and as she managed to hide her swollen abdomen under layers of silk gauze, his birth went almost unnoticed. Petra brought her niece Eulodia—her first relative to come to the house on the lagoon from the slum across the mangrove swamp—to take care of the baby and be its wet nurse. Most of the time Quintín's crib stayed in the kitchen, which was in the cellar. Quintín got used to playing on the cool earthen floor of the servants' quarters.

Two weeks after his birth, Rebecca went back to her artist friends, without even spending half of the forty days devoted to

San Gerardo in bed. She was soon totally involved in her dancing and other creative pursuits and for the next seven years led an intense artistic life.

REBECCA LIKED to dance for her friends on Pavel's golden terrace. One day one of her friends brought a copy of *Salomé*, Oscar Wilde's drama, to the literary salon. They read it aloud and found it extraordinary, and one of them translated it into Spanish. Then they decided to act it out on the terrace one evening. It was a risky decision. Buenaventura would be having guests of his own that night, and they might stop by. But Rebecca was adamant. She was determined to be true to her artistic vocation, as she had promised Pavel, and announced that she would play Salomé herself, and do the Dance of the Seven Veils.

She visited a famous couturier, who designed a beautiful costume for her, and she went to see a local coppersmith, who took her measurements and made her a special bustier. Two golden goblets would cover her breasts, which she would remove at the end of the performance and use to pour water from the lagoon on St. John the Baptist's severed head—a wooden sculpture an art collector had agreed to lend them. It was supposed to be a literary joke as well as a statement, a kind of local baptism of San Juan's revered patron saint by the members of the salon.

The day of the performance, everything went according to plan. When the moment arrived, Rebecca appeared onstage and began her dance. She took off each of her seven veils and was almost stark naked, except for the golden goblets, when Buenaventura's Rolls-Royce arrived in front of the house and he walked up the stairs with several of his friends. When he saw Rebecca, he didn't say a word. He simply took off his cordovan belt, livid with rage, and flogged her until she fell unconscious to the floor.

Quintín was seven years old. He got out of bed when he heard music, and he wandered out into the living room, which opened onto the terrace. It was dark, but he saw everything. His mother's naked body remained etched in his mind all his life. When Quintín told me this story on the veranda of the house on Aurora Street many years later, his voice shook with emotion. Rebecca's dance had been a strange ceremony; her purple veils fell to the floor one by one, until a single streak of gauze covered her golden pubis. Quintín was both fascinated and terrified by what he saw.

It took Rebecca several weeks to recover. When she was finally able to get up from bed and join the family at dinner, she hardly dared look at her husband. She sat there like a broken doll, dressed in one of her flowing gauze gowns, and wouldn't say a word. Quintín didn't look at her; when he kissed her good night he had to close his eyes, because he was scared to see her bruises up close. Buenaventura was convinced Pavel was to blame for the whole situation. "It's all his fault she behaved so shockingly," he would grumble when he saw Rebecca so silent and withdrawn. "If she hadn't known him, she wouldn't have lost touch with reality. I had to give her a lesson to make her come down to earth."

When Buenaventura got together with his cronies at the Spanish Casino's bar, he would say to them over sherry and aperitifs: "Pavel may be dead and gone, but his house is still breeding fantasies around us like Anopheles mosquitoes. If Rebecca goes mad, it will be his fault; everyone knows his buildings are jinxed and the owners end up in an asylum. But I'm not going to let that happen to us. My aunts brought me up in Valdeverdeja to be a hardworking squire, even if that meant learning how to turn hogs into hams and knead bread out of stones."

Buenaventura was worried for other reasons, too. The Spanish Civil War had broken out in July of 1936. Sales were slow. Merchandise from Spain—the wines, olives, and white asparagus which made up a good part of Mendizabal's staples—began to grow scarce. Moreover, he had many friends among General Francisco Franco's Nationalist forces, who had invaded Spain from Morocco and were fighting to overthrow the Republic. He had heard that many of the artists in Spain were sympathetic to the

Republic: Picasso, Pablo Casals, the poet García Lorca, and he vilified them every time he had the chance. He was convinced that Rebecca's artist friends were socialists and perhaps even Communists. It didn't matter that Rebecca repeatedly pointed out that her friends were the sons and daughters of some of the richest families on the island. Buenaventura still saw them as dangerous, because now all art to him was dangerous.

One day he came home for lunch, and as he sat with Rebecca at the table in Pavel's beautiful dining room, he looked around reproachfully. "We need to get rid of all this useless bric-a-brac," he said loudly, taking in at a single gesture the stained-glass lamp hanging from the ceiling, the lotus water goblets on the table, and the silver wine cooler on the buffet. "Tear it all down and let fresh air and sunlight into these rooms. This house is too dark, and only vermin like to breed in twilight." When the servants brought him a tray of partridges stuffed with French plums, he refused to eat them. He ordered Petra to go back to his aunts' hearty recipes, like pig's feet stewed with chickpeas, or white-bean *fabadas* with stewed *chorizos*, which made one think straight and not lose one's bearings.

A few days later Buenaventura made his threats come true. He moved Rebecca and Quintín to a hotel, called in a demolition crew, and had Pavel's house razed to the ground. In twenty-four hours the Tiffany-glass windows and pearl-shell skylights were shattered to pieces, and Rebecca's mosaic rainbow was ground to bits. In place of the old house, Buenaventura built a Spanish Revival mansion with granite turrets, bare brick floors, and a forbidding granite stairway with a banister made of iron spears. From the ceiling in the entrance hall he hung his *pièce de résistance*, a spiked wooden wheel that had been used to torture the Moors during the Spanish Conquest, which he ordered made into a lamp. The construction went quickly, and the family was able to move into the new house in less than a year.

"I want us to have more children, and they must grow up strong and healthy," Buenaventura announced to Rebecca once they had moved in. "From now on, everyone in this house will get up at daybreak, take a cold shower before going to Mass, and work for his keep." Rebecca laughed to herself. It had taken her eleven years to get pregnant with Quintín, and she doubted very much that she would have any more children. But Petra began to give her brews to drink, and they were very effective. She soon found that she was pregnant again, and was surprisingly submissive.

Quintín loved going with his mother early in the morning to the chapel on the other side of Water Bridge, at the entrance to the lagoon. It was one of the few buildings Pavel had built that were still standing. Buenaventura never went with them: he liked to open the heavy, iron-studded doors of his warehouse at La Puntilla himself and was usually at his desk at seven, when his employees arrived. Quintín was only eight but he remembered this time of his life clearly. He was happy: the other children hadn't been born yet and he didn't have to share his mother with them. Mass was the one time of day when he was alone with Rebecca. He would walk with her down Ponce de León Avenue holding hands, and together they'd jump over the rain puddles from the night before.

At that early hour the lagoon was shrouded in mist and the vessels coming into San Juan seemed to float in the distance like ghost ships. As they entered San Juan Bay, their wailing horns reverberated through the windows and woke people up, just as they do today. The haze seemed to seep through everything, giving the lagoon a fantastic air. The royal palms that grew around the lagoon's edge were plumed mermaids standing on their tails; the black boulders the Spaniards had dropped at the entrance to the bay to keep pirate ships away were fierce dogs baring their fangs at the enemy. Everything seemed possible to Quintín at that hour: Buenaventura might go back to Spain to fight alongside his Fascist friends, and then Rebecca would belong only to him.

The only section of Pavel's house Buenaventura didn't order destroyed was the terrace. The contractor said it might weaken the foundations of the new house, so the terrace was left standing and was made part of the Spanish Revival mansion. Ignacio was born in 1938, a year after they had moved into the new house. Patria and Libertad followed soon after, in 1939 and 1940, respectively. Rebecca bore her frequent pregnancies patiently, seemingly reconciled to her fate. But she was exhausted. She put away her dancing shoes and her poetry books and slowly faded from view.

QUINTÍN

One Saturday afternoon Quintín made a disconcerting discovery. He was in the study reading Plutarch's Lives of the Noble Romans when he needed to look up a word in Latin. He went to the bookcase to take out the Latin dictionary, a two-volume affair bound in red leather, and he came upon a manuscript hidden behind it, in a tan folder tied with a purple ribbon. He read the first few pages quickly, then sat down in amazement on the study's green leather couch. He knew he didn't have time to examine all the manuscript before Isabel came back from the market, so he put it back carefully in its hiding place. Around two in the morning, when Isabel was sound asleep, Quintín got up quietly from bed, returned to the study, and took the folder from the back of the shelf. He sat in front of Rebecca's ornate desk and began to read with intense concentration. The manuscript had no title, but the first page read: "Part One: The Foundations." There was also "Part Two: The First House on the Lagoon"—eight chapters in all.

Quintín remembered saying to Isabel long ago that it would be an interesting project to write down the story of both the Mendizabal and the Monfort families. They had been so young, so idealistic! He didn't want Isabel to be just another bourgeois housewife; he wanted her to amount to something, so he could be proud of her.

Isabel wanted to be a writer, and being a historian himself—he had a master's degree in history from Columbia University, although life had forced him to travel a different road—he thought they could embark on the project together.

History is one of fiction's most important quarries, he had told her, imagination being the other important source. He was at her disposal with whatever historical information she needed to write her autobiographical novel. He could help her with the research, he said, and leave the literary part to her. But Isabel had let the matter drop; after writing a few chapters, she hadn't done any more.

Some of the pages were yellowed; others looked relatively fresh, as if they had been typed recently. Quintín had thought it curious that since they came back from Manuel's graduation at Boston University, Isabel had been asking him so many questions about the Mendizabal family history. He had answered as well as he could and had seen her take some notes, but he hadn't given the matter much thought.

As he read on, Quintín began to feel uncomfortable. The manuscript was an authentic effort at writing fiction; Isabel definitely intended it as a novel. But she had made up incredible things about his family and left out much of what had really happened.

"The Pizarro Mendizabals had always been successful merchants before they turned into soldiers," she said in the chapter "The Merchant Prince," and it was from Don Francisco Pizarro that they inherited their uncouth heraldry: a warlord beheading a hog with his short sword. What a way to turn things around, Quintín thought. The Mendizabal coat of arms had a chevalier hunting a wild boar, not beheading a hog. In the Middle Ages the Spanish nobility used to hunt to keep in good shape while they awaited the moment when they would wage war against the Moor, and this was what Quintín's great-great-grandfather had done. But Isabel had altered everything. She was manipulating history for fiction's sake, and what was worse, she was putting words into his mouth as if the false information had come from him.

Quintín was dumbstruck. How could Isabel write such things about his parents? At first he was angry, but then he began to see the humor of it. If she's been writing this all along, he told himself, Isabel must hold the record for wives who have shared the same bed with their husbands for years and still have managed to keep secrets from them!

Some of the allegations Isabel made were truly shocking. She accused Buenaventura of being a German sympathizer during the First World War, then implied that his mother had been secretly in love with Milan Pavel, the Czech architect. Her description of Rebecca taking a stroll with Pavel by Alamares Lagoon beneath her lace parasol as she talked him into building them the house, and the scene of the kiss in the spring's shed, would have been romantic if it weren't so preposterous, almost as preposterous as Rebecca dancing naked on the terrace for her artist friends—something he never witnessed. What Isabel had written was absurd; it was impossible to take seriously.

"Writing lies means writing lies," he had once heard a famous author say. And yet that wasn't always so. Many writers had a rich imagination; they could make everything up from scratch without having to resort to personal experience. Isabel simply hadn't learned to apply Turgenev's advice: an author must cut the umbilical cord that binds him to his story.

On the other hand, all writers interpreted reality in their own way—and that was why Quintín preferred history to literature; literature wasn't ethical enough for him. There were limits to interpretation, even if the borders of reality were diffuse and malleable. There was always a nucleus of truth, and it was wrong to alter it. That was why Quintín didn't consider writing a serious occupation, like science or history.

Isabel's lack of professionalism bothered him even more than her fantastic fabrications. She was a truant, a brain picker, an intellectual pickpocket! She had unscrupulously plagiarized the historic material he had given her—she could never have written the chapters

*without his help—and yet she never acknowledged it. Not only had
he confided to her with naïve sincerity the story of his family; he
had given her all the historical background she needed.*

*She owed him the picturesque story of how Rebecca had met his
father when she was sixteen, for example, and of how she chose
him to be King when she was Queen of the Antilles. She also owed
him Milan Pavel's story; Isabel could never have found out about
the Czech architect on her own. Quintín had been an admirer of
the man and had collected information about him for years. No
books about Pavel had been published, and Quintín had come by
his material through interviews with the owners of Pavel's few houses
that were still standing. The owners of these houses were all friends
of his family. Would they have talked to Isabel Monfort about Pavel?
Would they have bared their family secrets to her? He didn't think
so. She wasn't a Mendizabal by birth; she belonged to San Juan's
bourgeoisie by marriage, and people tended to be clannish.*

*Not content with her plundering, Isabel had blatantly altered
Pavel's story. Her description of the famous architect as a Bohemian
Count Dracula who went about the city with his black silk cape
fluttering in the wind was ludicrous. True, Pavel was a scoundrel,
but he was a refined scoundrel. Quintín had seen photographs of
him wearing starched white linen pants and white suede shoes.
Isabel had also suggested that Milan had returned Rebecca's favors,
and had become infatuated with her himself, building the house
on the lagoon to please her. The whole story was a sham and yet
perhaps there was a seed of truth to it. Perhaps Rebecca would have
been happier married to someone like Pavel.*

*Isabel had made some inexcusable mistakes. Some of them were
silly; for example, pretending there were hot-dog stands in 1917,
and that Buenaventura had eaten a hot dog on the day he arrived
in San Juan. Quintín laughed again. No one knew for sure when
hot dogs had arrived on the island, but he doubted it was before
the Second World War.*

A more serious error was saying that Puerto Rico's siege by

German submarines had taken place during the Great War, when actually it had happened during the Second World War. Von Tirpitz's plan for an invasion remained a dream, an insubstantial report in the archives of Kaiser Wilhelm II. It wasn't until 1942 that Nazi submarines roamed Caribbean waters. But Isabel needed to invent the siege of Puerto Rico in 1918; the German submarine blockade was important for her development of Buenaventura's supposedly Fascist sympathies. She had consciously altered the facts of history to serve her story.

Quintín didn't feel guilty about reading the manuscript; he felt he was doing the right thing. He was discovering something important about Isabel and was examining his family's history in a way he'd never done before. It was true, Rebecca had sometimes been unhappy in her marriage. But to suggest that she had been in love with Pavel was a big leap. His father had been a difficult man; he had a vile temper and Quintín had had a hard time getting along with him as a child. But he was a generous provider and a kind parent. With time Quintín had come to understand Buenaventura better, and now that he was middle-aged, he could fully appreciate his father's goodness. His mother and father had been happy and unhappy together, as is usually true of any marriage.

By Chapter 8, Quintín had ceased to be amused. His mother had been a beautiful, delicate creature, both spiritually and physically, and he resented Isabel for ridiculing her. Rebecca was an accomplished poet and her literary salon had been a success in the San Juan of the twenties. When Quintín was born, she had given up her artistic career and had devoted herself to him. She hadn't ignored Quintín, and he couldn't remember at all having been relegated to the cellar when he was a child. Petra must have spread that vile rumor; she couldn't stand Rebecca.

From the moment she arrived at the house Petra had wielded an inexplicable power over Buenaventura. Being a Spaniard, he found African voodoo rites exotic. He loved to hear Petra talk about her embrujos and Quintín himself joked about her hocus-pocus with his friends at the San Juan Sports Club. But somehow those *embrujos* had had an effect on Buenaventura. Rebecca sensed this, and she tried to get rid of Petra, but it was useless. Petra had entrenched herself in the cellar like a monstrous spider, and from there spun a web of malicious rumor which eventually enveloped the whole family.

By four in the morning, Quintín had finished reading Isabel's work-in-progress. He gathered up the pages, put them back in their tan folder, and tied the purple ribbon around it. Then he hid the folder behind the dictionary. He wasn't angry with Isabel, but he was uneasy. He didn't want to mention the manuscript to her. But he would watch her behavior closely, very closely, during the next few weeks.

PART 3

Family Roots

9

Carmita Monfort's Promise

❦

QUINTÍN OFTEN CAME to visit me in Ponce when we were engaged, and he used to stay at the Texas Motel. It was a square cement building with four furnished rooms where traveling salesmen stayed one or two days, and it stood right next to the gas station. Texaco was the first gas station to open in our town, and I remember the first time its red star stayed lit all night. It thrilled everyone in Ponce, and we were naïve enough to think it was a herald of progress.

Quintín had no money then, but we were very happy; we looked forward to the day when we would get married. But we were going to have to wait a long time to see our dreams come true. Buenaventura was adamantly opposed to our marriage until Quintín had saved enough money to be completely independent; we had no idea how long it would take.

That summer we were both on vacation, home from our respective schools up North. A warm, sweet-scented breeze blew from the cane fields near town, and as there was no air-conditioning, we often went to sleep without any clothes on. I was twenty-one and Quintín was twenty-four. I was going into my senior year at Vassar College, and Quintín had just finished his master's degree at Columbia University. He worked all week at Mendizabal & Co., lowering codfish crates with a forklift from the transport trucks at the warehouse, in order to save enough money to board the *público* which brought him to Ponce on weekends.

There was very little to do in the town. We would go for a stroll around the plaza in the evening or maybe to the movies, to an Ava Gardner or a Rock Hudson film. We said good night early by the iron gate. Around one o'clock, though, when everybody else was asleep, I would get up and walk barefoot to the garden. I would remove my nightgown and walk naked into the shrubbery. Quintín would be waiting for me, deep in the groves of myrtle and fern.

More than thirty years have gone by and I can still remember our lovemaking—how we rolled on the grass under the stars, with the dogs from the house wagging their tails as if it were all a game. At the end of that summer, after returning to college, we began to see each other every Sunday in New York.

We would meet at the Roosevelt Hotel, which had already begun to deteriorate, with its sprinklers running the length of the ceiling in dark corridors, and its stained faux-marble and electrified gas fixtures uglying its walls. The Roosevelt had an underground tunnel connecting it to Grand Central Station. It was convenient in two ways: in winter, one didn't have to go out into the cold weather —which I hated—and relatively few people used it, which cut down on the chances of meeting anyone from home. Getting her reputation compromised was just about the worst crime a girl from a good family could commit back then, and I remember trembling at the thought of meeting someone from home in the hotel lobby. The Roosevelt tunnel was a perfect escape route: one could go in and out of New York unseen.

As I boarded the train in Poughkeepsie I felt I was already in that tunnel. It was an exhilarating feeling. The moment I left my dormitory at school, I was already in Quintín's arms. At Grand Central I nearly ran down the Roosevelt's passageway, took the elevator, and entered the corridor at the end of which there would be a bed where Quintín was waiting for me. It was like walking into a maze where desire and distance melted into one. Mother, father, Rebecca, Buenaventura were all left behind, shut out equally by the intricate turns of the labyrinth. There, in that prenuptial chamber, on that nondescript mattress far from the prying eyes of family and friends, we both lost our virginity, purified by an innocent lust.

When I met Quintín, my heart was thrown into turmoil; I lived at the very center of desire. Everything around me was confusion; only meeting Quintín in the garden in Ponce or in our hideaway in New York would soothe me. Nor did the powerful attraction I felt for Quintín ebb after the sad episode of the tenor's suicide.

Quintín was very good-looking; he had inherited Buenaventura's swarthy Spanish looks. He had broad shoulders, a young bull's neck, hazel-green eyes, and hair black as a raven's wing, carefully combed back and dabbed with eau de cologne. The only thing that worried me was his fiery temper. The moment I saw him on the verge of anger, I'd shake my head and refuse to look into his eyes. This was to be our secret signal. Quintín had lived in terror of Buenaventura's ferocious temper, and our signal was a way of preventing his own anger from surfacing. It proved effective for a while; Quintín would laugh and forget what he was angry about. In fact, it brought us closer.

"Life is like a war," Abby would say to me when I was growing up. "The longer we live, the more scars we carry around with us. There's a maimed veteran hiding inside each of us; some have lost an arm, others a leg or an eye; we've all been buffeted by life's blows. We can't grow our missing limbs back, so we have to learn to live without them."

I believe my mother, Carmita Monfort, was responsible for my hidden wound, though she was not aware of it. When I was three years old, something dreadful happened which I've never been able to forget. At the time we were still living in Trastalleres— Father, Mother, Abby, and I. Trastalleres was a lower-middle-class suburb of San Juan, and it was there that Carmita became pregnant for the second time. I have a blurred recollection of the day. I was playing with my dolls under the terebinth tree which grew at the back of the house and I could feel the noonday sun on the nape of my neck. Mother's bathroom window was high over my head and it was open; I couldn't see her but I heard her cry out. I dropped my dolls and ran to the other side of the house, went up the stairs, and flung open the bathroom door. She was lying on the floor unconscious; a pool of blood lay on the white tiles like lacquer.

Mother's parents, Doña Gabriela and Don Vicenzo Antonsanti, were both from Corsica, where, according to my grandfather, there was only the sea, the soaring cliffs, and mountains covered by scrubby vegetation pared down by goats. When they were in their twenties, Gabriela and Vicenzo came to our island to visit relatives who lived near the town of Yauco. They fell in love with its velvet-green mountains, which harbored valuable coffee shrubs beneath a canopy of *guamá*, *yagrumo*, and mahogany trees. Gabriela and Vicenzo were first cousins, and to get married they had to get a Papal dispensation. Once that problem was taken care of, they were married and they worked hard as a team. Soon they owned a prosperous coffee farm on the outskirts of Yauco, where they lived.

Abuela Gabriela was a beautiful woman, but beauty was unfortunately her nemesis. There was very little to do in the mountains, and Abuela had a hard time keeping Abuelo's mind off his favorite pastime. He loved guava shells with goat cheese, and Abuela would prepare them for him almost every day. When she boiled the guavas, the aroma would fill the whole house and waft in and out through the windows. Abuelo could smell it before he got off his horse. The moment he climbed the stairs, he would start peeling off his clothes and chase Abuela through the house until they wound up in bed. Abuela Gabriela's skin was a delicate guava pink, and when they made love he nibbled playfully at her breasts and felt himself to be more and more potent. Abuela finally realized the guavas were an aphrodisiac and stopped cooking them, but it was too late. For six years in a row she had a baby every year. Abuelo was delighted with his wife's productiveness, which he saw as a gift from God. "My wife is so fertile," he would say to his friends, "that I just have to sneeze by her side once, and nine months later she's as big as a pumpkin. But I don't mind it at all, because being so close to nature is one of her many charms."

Abuela Gabriela did her duty and lived with a clear conscience. In their seventh year of marriage, Vicenzo was still moonstruck every time he came near her, but she couldn't stand it anymore. She chose to fall out of favor with God rather than lose her inner peace. That December she pushed Vicenzo out of her room before she turned into a pumpkin again.

It wasn't an easy victory; she had to fight for her bed as if it were a castle under siege. Vicenzo importuned her nightly with his poems and serenades, standing like a lovesick calf by her locked door, but Abuela was proud of her Corsican blood and withstood his assaults with an iron will. "If this goes on for one more day, the cradle will be my tomb," she cried to Vicenzo. She pleaded with him to accept chastity as a way of life, but it was no use. When he insisted she honor a husband's prerogatives, Abuela rose up in arms. Like a mountain-born Lucretia, she defended her celibacy with brooms, dust mops, and even kitchen knives. When in the dead of night she saw Abuelo's shadow creeping silently near her bed, she sat up, knife in hand, and cried out at the top of her lungs: "Get out of here, Vicenzo; this is my private bastion! From now on, whoever tries to climb these ramparts will end up in one of Río Negro's ravines."

It was a struggle for both of them. They still loved and needed each other. Abuela Gabriela didn't want to exile Abuelo from her side; she tried to convince him that true love didn't dwell in the bottom half of the body but in the mind, and that a chaste embrace could be as effective an antidote for incurable wounds as a lustful one. But Abuelo wouldn't give in. His eyes would fill with tears, he would look at her reproachfully, and then would try to kiss and embrace her. When he finally realized that she meant what she said, he tried to practice continence for two weeks, but on the fourteenth day he felt as if he were burning in hell. He stole out of the house and went off to the nearest town.

Abuelo began to visit two mistresses in Yauco once a week, and no one thought him the worse for it. "Only the exercise of nature's most elemental pleasure can reconcile a man to the suffering of this world," he said to the priest of the town, who was one of his best friends. When he went to confession, the priest didn't make anything of his new situation and gave him absolution anyway. Soon both of Abuelo's mistresses became pregnant. Abuela was so relieved that it was someone else's task to give birth, nourish, and bring up the new babies that she gave them both her blessing. She attended the christenings and had Abuelo recognize them as legitimate.

Not long after she chose a celibate life, Abuela stopped going to church. She would lie alone in bed at night and miss Vicenzo terribly. Instead of praying to the Virgin Mary, whose image stood in a corner of her bedroom on a little shelf surrounded by candles, she would reproach her for allying herself with St. Peter and St. Paul, and with the Fathers of the Holy Church, who were all unfair to women. St. Paul had told his male brethren it was better to marry than to burn; but he had no palliative for his female brethren, who would burn whether they were married or not.

Abuela was a sensual woman and had enjoyed sex with her husband; abstention was torture. She resented the fact that a woman's fertility should condemn her to loneliness. She consulted with the midwife, who told her menstruation would last only twenty years, and at the end of that time she would be able to live a normal life, free from the terror of becoming pregnant every time she made love.

Abuela simply had to be patient and wait it out. In time she pardoned not only Abuelo for his sexual dalliances, but also St.

Peter and St. Paul for being so unrelenting. But it wasn't until she was able to forgive herself that she was finally at peace. Sexual sins were not important, after all; what really counted was shared responsibility and companionship, and even though they slept in separate beds, she went on living with Vicenzo on excellent terms. When Abuela was finally blessed with menopause, she let Abuelo climb back into her bed, and they began making love with the same gusto as at the beginning; he still preferred her to either of his mistresses. Abuelo and Abuela got along very well after that. When he sold the farm in Río Negro and moved to Ponce to open his coffee warehouse, Abuela went on being his business partner and worked side by side with him for many years.

Abuela kept only one secret from Abuelo during all this time. When her six daughters were born in Río Negro, she swore to herself she wouldn't let them undergo her terrible trial. She made them promise they would have one child every five years, and they would surreptitiously do everything to prevent consecutive pregnancies. "An only child is portable," Abuela said to them. "The mother may carry it with her everywhere. But two babies are a powerful link in the iron chain with which men tie women down and make them their prisoners."

This was the promise Carmita was supposed to keep and recklessly broke three years after I was born. When Abuela learned her daughter had become pregnant a second time, she traveled from Ponce to San Juan with the midwife to remind Carmita of her pledge. Abby was away at the time; she had gone to visit her nephews in Adjuntas because Father's Uncle Orencio had just passed away. If Abby had been home, none of this would have happened. Abuela Gabriela, left to her own designs with my mother, forced her to drink some brew to terminate the pregnancy. But it was so strong it caused hemorrhaging.

When I ran into the house and saw Carmita unconscious on the floor, I was terrified. I couldn't understand what Abuela Gabriela was whispering about with the midwife, but I knew something

dreadful had happened. I saw Abuela and the maids carrying
Mother to bed, then scurrying about to change the bloodstained
sheets and take them to the laundry house in the garden. Then I
heard Abuela say to Mother that she mustn't worry, that something
at least four moons old had fallen into the toilet bowl, and how
relieved she should feel. A little later the doctor was smuggled
into the house through the back door, so the neighbors wouldn't
see him. When Father came back from his workshop that evening,
the crisis was over and Mother was lying neatly in bed, simply
getting over a bad headache.

I remember feeling both excited and afraid. I was part of an
adult plot, a secret female conspiracy which Abuela Gabriela said
would be of benefit to me when I grew up, so I did my best to say
nothing to Father. The whole thing would probably have blown
over if Mother hadn't developed a serious infection (the pregnancy
was too advanced and complications set in) and was unable to
have any more children. This was a hard blow for Father, who
never found out about the miscarriage but eventually discovered
that Carmita was sterile.

Year after year Father had hoped for a son. Carlos was an
orphan, and he felt that not having a father was the saddest thing
that could happen to a child. He planned to do many things with
his son and teach him to grow up to be a fine young man. Carmita
was silent when she heard him talk like that, but she became more
and more depressed.

Abby and I talked this over many years later and she told me
what had happened. When Abuela arrived from Ponce, she convinced Carmita that every woman had the right to determine what
took place in her own body, and that she would be able to take
good care of her second child only when the first one—meaning
me—was grown enough so that it wouldn't be a constant worry.
Carmita had gone along with the abortion. Then the unexpected
had happened.

Carmita suddenly felt guilty; something had been uprooted from her heart that she hadn't known was there. A mantle of affection had already wrapped itself around the faceless baby in her womb. A deep sadness came over her, and one day Abby discovered that all the knives had disappeared from the kitchen drawer, the scissors from her sewing box, the pruning shears from the gardener's tool box, and Father's razor blades from the medicine cabinet. She went looking for Carmita and found her in the sewing room, where she spent her mornings after Father went to work.

Carmita was sitting in front of her black Singer sewing machine, the one decorated with gold miniature roses that Father had given her for her last birthday. She had put the knives and scissors in a row on the table, next to her needles and spools of thread, and was staring at them intently. When Abby came into the room, she looked up at her in a daze. "I know there's something important I have to do with these knives and scissors, Abby," she said, "but I can't remember what." Abby was terrified; she made a thorough search of the house and put all sharp-edged objects under lock and key until Carmita came out of her depression a few months later.

All of a sudden it was as if Carmita weren't there anymore. Her eyes grew absent and her black clothes, wet with tears, were always cold when I hugged her. It was as if she lived in a perpetual mist. She wouldn't let me kiss or embrace her, because I reminded her of the dead baby.

10

Madeleine and

Arístides's Marriage

❧

QUINTÍN'S GREAT-GRANDFATHER Don Esteban Rosich was Italian by birth. He lived in Boston for many years and was naturalized in 1885. One day—it must have been around 1899—he walked with his seventeen-year-old daughter, Madeleine, into La Traviata, a store in Old San Juan. Spread over several polished mahogany counters were rolls of imported silk from France, lace from Portugal, Belgium, and Venice, colorful linens from Ireland. Arístides Arrigoitia, Quintín's grandfather, worked in La Traviata as a store clerk. He was twenty and had a difficult apprenticeship: the store's owner had a habit of kicking him in the shins every time he found mouse nests in the goose-down pillows at the back of the shop. But the real reason he hit him was that he hated foreigners. He saw them as leeches who took income away from Puerto Ricans, and he employed them only because they worked for half the pay. Arístides was an affable young man and made the most of his unpleasant job. Elegant ladies who led an active social life in San Juan came to shop in La Traviata almost every day, looking for the laces and silks that their fashionable couturiers would make into beautiful gowns. Arístides knew their tastes by heart.

Don Esteban was a widower. He had decided to retire to the island for reasons of health, after making a fortune selling Italian shoes in Boston. He also owned a steamship company—the Taurus Line—which did a lot of business between San Juan, Boston, and New York, and he could easily go on supervising it from the island. Don Esteban had arrived in San Juan only a month before and had purchased a country house in the blue hills of Guaynabo, because he liked the cool temperatures there. The house had a sloping tile roof, wooden rafters, and a brick chimney—built to please the fancy of the previous owner, a rich islander who dreamed of owning a home in the snow-covered hills of Maine.

Don Esteban took his daughter to La Traviata so they could buy linens for their house.

"How may I help you, sir? We have some beautiful new merchandise just arrived from Europe," Arístides said, smiling, as Don Esteban strolled in, silver cane in hand. He spoke perfect English, and Don Esteban was taken by surprise. At the time, almost no one in the city could speak English.

"What part of the States are you from, young man?" he asked pleasantly. Arístides's blond hair and easygoing manner misled Don Esteban into thinking he was an American. "I was born right here, sir," he said, politely pulling out a chair for Madeleine. "My parents immigrated from the Basque provinces just before my birth."

Quintín used to talk to me about Don Arístides often, because he was very fond of him. In fact, there has always been a photograph of him in a silver frame on our library table. He never met his grandfather on the Mendizabal side of the family; Buenaventura talked to him about his ancestors from Extremadura, but they were always heroes, not flesh-and-blood people. Don Esteban, on the other hand, was a lovable old man, with pink cheeks and snow-white whiskers on either side of his face.

Arístides was tall and robust; Quintín said he looked like a peasant from the Pyrenees. Don Esteban immediately took a liking to him. He identified with people who came from humble backgrounds and had learned to make a go of it in a difficult situation.

"*Il piacere e mio,*" Don Esteban said in Italian, and asked Arístides where he had learned to speak English so well. "The American nuns from the School of the Annunciation were my teachers, sir," he replied. "They taught us it would be our duty to speak English when we knocked on the doors of heaven, asking to be let in." Don Esteban and Madeleine burst out laughing. They knew he was poking fun at a comment the governor had made recently in the local press. The governor had decreed that English be mandatory in all the island's schools, and four thousand copies of Appleton's *First Reader in English* had been handed out to schoolchildren. Both Don Esteban and Madeleine thought it was preposterous to make children take all their classes in a language they couldn't speak. "Of course, this means we'll be an educated people when we get to heaven, even if we don't understand what God says," Arístides added with a wink at Madeleine.

Arístides knew he had made a good impression and decided to take advantage of it. He brought out a roll of ivory Alençon lace to tempt his customer into buying it; it would make a beautiful gown. "I need a roll of plain white percale to have a dozen sheets made for our new house," Madeleine said in a no-nonsense voice, vigorously shaking her head. "We never attend formal parties." Arístides brought out a roll of fine Belgian linen and showed it to her. "You should have sheets made of this," he said. "It's impossible to sleep on anything else on this island. At night it gets so hot that cotton sticks to you like sour gum. That is, unless one sleeps in the nude. Then it doesn't matter what kind of sheets one sleeps on."

Madeleine stared at him unabashed. She was a forthright young woman with few inhibitions, in spite of having been brought up by the nuns. "I wouldn't mind sleeping in the nude," she replied in a lilting voice, "but only on sheets that have my initials on them." And she asked Arístides if he knew someone on the island who could embroider them for her. "At the convent next to the Church of Our Lady of Miracles, of course," he answered cour-

teously. "I can take you there myself tomorrow if you like. The
nuns are friends of mine."

A year after her visit to La Traviata, Madeleine walked down
the aisle of the Church of Our Lady of Miracles carrying a beautiful
bouquet of white orchids, and returned on her husband's arm. Don
Esteban gave them his blessing. He was going to need a young
man like Arístides to help him manage the offices of the Taurus
Line, he said, and Arístides was very sociable and knew a lot of
people in San Juan.

Arístides's father was born in Bilbao, and worked as the head
chef at the Spanish Casino—where his granddaughter was to be
crowned Queen of the Spanish Antilles seventeen years later.
Arístides's mother died when he was a child, and his father sent
him to the orphanage in Puerta de Tierra, which was run by
American nuns. Before the Marines landed in Guánica in 1898,
there were practically no schools for children on the island; the
orphanage at Puerta de Tierra was an exception. By the time Don
Esteban had settled in Guaynabo, however, there were six hundred
public schools, all of them built by the American government.

The school Arístides attended as a child was run by an order
of missionary nuns who did valuable work in San Juan. It was
because of the nuns of the Annunciation that Arístides admired
the United States so much. They were very good teachers and were
careful to instill in their students a true civic spirit. The history
of the United States was taught thoroughly at their school, yet
Puerto Rican history was never mentioned. In the nuns' view, the
island *had* no history. In this they were not exceptional; it was
forbidden to teach Puerto Rican history at the time, either at private
or at public schools. Can history be so dangerous as to be revolutionary? I've often asked Quintín that question, but he never
answers me.

The nuns of the Annunciation taught Arístides that the island
had begun to exist politically when the American troops landed
at Guánica. President Wilson had said so himself in a speech in

1913. "The countries the United States have taken in trust, Puerto Rico and the Philippines, must first accept the discipline of law. They are children and we are men in these deep matters of government and justice." It was for this reason that Arrigoitia had so loyally embraced the ideals of Republicanism and American democracy.

As Arístides grew up, the world seemed to endorse the lessons he had learned from the nuns. His employer at La Traviata exploited him, something the American government would never have done. Arístides tried to get a job at the post office before he took the one at La Traviata. Postal officials were highly regarded; they got paid the federal minimum wage, which very few people earned on the island; obtained health insurance and were given a paid two-week vacation each year. But he had no luck. He never forgot the painful lessons he had learned at La Traviata. "The day we become an independent nation," he would tell Quintín years later, "the local bourgeoisie will throw the more recent immigrants off the island and take away our rights and properties. We owe everything we have to the American Constitution, and for this reason you should cherish and defend it."

After Madeleine and Arístides were married, they stayed on in the Guaynabo country house with Don Esteban. Arístides was a capable man. After his marriage he went to work in his father-in-law's steamship company, but he also joined the local police force as a part-time volunteer officer. He had a mystical approach to politics and saw Puerto Rico's becoming a part of the United States as almost a religious crusade. Arístides found his father-in-law very congenial. Don Esteban was getting on in years and somebody had to take care of him, so there was no sense in their moving away. Madeleine kept house like no other woman Arístides had ever met. She brought two *jibaritas* from the mountains of Cayey to help her keep the country house spick-and-span, and taught them to mop the floors with Clorox, disinfect the toilet bowl, and scrub the bathtub. In the kitchen, her pots and pans were so bright they shone like silver, hanging on the wall. Quintín says he never saw anything like it. The contrast between Madeleine's and Petra's kitchens always impressed him as a child. In Madeleine's kitchen there was an electric stove and one could eat off the floor with a spoon, the tiles were so clean. But food had no taste at all: it was always honey-glazed baked chicken, Idaho potatoes with a dab of Brookfield butter, and "squeezed cloud juice"—Madeleine's euphemism for plain tap water—in one's glass. In Petra's kitchen, on the other hand, there was a coal stove with burning cow dung, and cockroaches often dove merrily into the stew, but everything tasted like a *pio nono*, like a bishop's fancy blessed with a fresh sprig of basil.

At first Madeleine was afraid to have children. She dreamed of returning to Massachusetts someday, where she had had a happy childhood. A baby would be a powerful reason to remain on the island, and she wasn't sure she wanted to establish herself permanently where she felt a little bit like a stranger. Don Esteban still owned a beautiful turreted brownstone near Boston Harbor, in the Italian quarter of the city, and he decided not to sell it in case Madeleine might someday want to go back.

Madeleine enjoyed sports. She played tennis every afternoon on the military base nearest to Guaynabo. Island women never played any sports at all, so she played with the young recruits at the base, which gave tongues something to wag about. She was an admirer of Helen Wills Moody, the first American woman tennis player to become nationally famous. Madeleine was tall and willowy, wore her skirts much shorter than women on the island, and was always in a hurry to get where she was going. She loved taking long walks by herself or driving out to the mountains in her father's Reo, looking for wild orchids, which she would bring back with her to town.

Orchids were her hobby and she bred cattleyas, laelias, and phalaenopsis in a nursery Arístides had built for her behind their country house. Madeleine grafted them herself and created extraordinary specimens; some looked like pink-legged spiders, others like golden scorpions or blood-speckled butterflies. She liked the sense of privacy the nursery gave her; it was so quiet under the protective green canopy it felt almost like being in the mountains: one was at peace and in total control of one's self. Arístides enjoyed orchids, too, but for other reasons. He found them erotic and liked to collect them because they made him feel as if he were surrounded by beautiful women. A few years after they were married, he bought a farm high up in the hills of Barranquitas, where he bred orchids by the dozens.

Madeleine never learned to speak Spanish. She spoke English at home with her father and with her husband, and sign language with everyone else. Even thirty-seven years later, when she finally returned to Boston, she still couldn't speak a word of Spanish, though she understood most of it. When Arístides's friends invited them to their house, she suffered. For the first ten minutes, everybody in the room tried to be polite and spoke mincingly in English so as not to exclude Madeleine from the conversation. Slowly but surely, however, a bit of juicy gossip would slip out, or a risqué joke or expression which could only be rendered in Spanish: *"Estaba más jalao que un timbre e guagua"* (He was as drunk as a skunk); or *"Eramos demasiados y parió la abuela"* (There were already too many of us, and then Grandma got pregnant). Then everyone would jump in, speaking Spanish like mad. They would slap each other on the back, laugh and curse and jabber away like magpies, as if they wouldn't be able to talk again for the next fifty years. No one listened to what his neighbor was saying; people spoke for the pleasure of hearing themselves speak.

Madeleine cringed and began to inch toward the wall. She felt like a soldier caught in the cross fire, bullets whistling this way and that over her head, while she was unable to fire a single salvo. It was as if Spanish were the only way to assert one's presence in the room: if you didn't speak it, you simply didn't exist, you were completely invisible. One's tongue was almost a magic peduncle with which one reached out to touch one's neighbor. One groped around with it to examine a face, tweak a nose, or poke into someone's eyes and ears. Madeleine, accustomed to her peaceful life surrounded by orchids, shuddered when people were milling around her or anyone tried to touch her. Soon she was next to Arístides, pulling him by the elbow and then nudging him toward the door. Only when they were outside did she feel safe again, in control of her own mind and body.

The result of these unhappy episodes was that Arístides's friends slowly withdrew. They didn't want to seem impolite to Madeleine, but they couldn't help it. The uncomfortable situation only repeated itself again and again. So they stopped inviting them to their homes, and loneliness closed in around the young couple like an iron hoop.

Quintín's mother, Rebecca, was born two years after Arístides and Madeleine's wedding, and this helped the marriage considerably. Arístides had wanted to have children right away, but Madeleine forced him to observe the rhythm with steely determination. The rhythm, in the opinion of the nuns of the Convent of the Immaculate Conception in Boston, was God's law. One wasn't supposed to use anything that thwarted Him—like prophylactics, creams, or vinegar sponges—which were all *contra natura*, preventing life from engendering. If one wanted not to have children, one made love only on those days when the egg had already been discharged from the uterus, flowing down the tide of life. The trouble was, one never knew for sure when this happened, and making love became as dangerous as ducking bullets. The only safe time was during the six days following menstruation, but this wasn't always easy to observe. Once Madeleine and Arístides were spending a long vacation on the Barranquitas farm, where there was very little to do. On the seventh day they made love, and Madeleine became pregnant.

When the nuns at Auxilio Mutuo Hospital asked Arístides to come to the nursery so he could meet his daughter, he was amazed at what he saw. Thanks to her long walks, Madeleine had an easy delivery and the baby's face was neither red nor swollen. She had Madeleine's peach complexion and upturned nose, with a delicate golden fuzz on her head. Wrapped in her pink embroidered blanket, she looked like a little rosebud with petals still curled tight. "You never would have guessed she's the granddaughter of a Basque highlander," he said to the nun who held her in her arms. And kissing her on the forehead, he added, "Now I can sleep soundly, because I know I'll have someone to take care of me in my old age."

Arístides was overprotective of his daughter. After Quintín and I got married, Rebecca herself used to tell me about the trouble he gave her when she was growing up. When a boyfriend came to visit her in their Guaynabo home, he always sat with them in the living room and made small talk. The visitor would feel so self-conscious he wouldn't say a word, eventually leaving the house in dejection. When Rebecca was invited to parties, Madeleine stayed home and Arístides was the one who chaperoned the young woman. Her father enjoyed following a tune and loved to dance with Rebecca, so her friends rarely had a chance to dance with her. When they did, Rebecca was so accustomed to her father that she invariably stepped all over their toes.

Arístides wasn't aware that anything was wrong; he thought his daughter was enjoying herself as much as he was. One evening he asked Rebecca to dance with him for the third time and she burst out crying. "Don't you see what you're doing, Father? If I dance with you all the time, I can't keep step with anyone else."

Arístides shamelessly spoiled Rebecca; he bought her everything she wanted, but in return he expected her to obey him in all things. She became a virtual prisoner; he never let her do anything on her own. When she wanted to do volunteer work at Presbyterian Hospital, he refused permission. When she was offered a job proofreading at *The Clarion*, San Juan's largest newspaper, he called the owner on the telephone and pressured him not to hire her. When she wanted to visit her cousins in Boston, he wouldn't allow it. After she graduated from high school, she wasn't permitted to go to the university; she had to stay home and help Madeleine with the housework. Soon she was so bored she began to retreat into a fantasy world. When she turned sixteen, the ladies of the committee from the Spanish Casino fortunately paid her a visit. Who knows what would have happened to Rebecca if they hadn't arrived with Buenaventura's portrait in its red-velvet frame.

I suspect Rebecca's difficult relations with her father were at the root of her advocacy of political independence for the island. I remember her telling me that when she was a child she had a stamp collection, and her favorite stamps were from France. Many of these commemorated the French Revolution and had the initials RF printed on them. As her full name was Rebecca Francisca, they were also her monogram. Blazing cannons, flying banners with cries such as "Long live the Republic!" or "Liberty, Equality, Fraternity!" in blue, white, and red completed the picture. Rebecca swore that one day she would gain her freedom and fly to all parts of the world, like the letters her stamps gave wings to. "Every woman should be a republic unto herself!" she often whispered into her pillow before she went to sleep at night.

Years later, after she began to hold her literary soirées in the house on the lagoon, Rebecca's artist friends were all Independentistas—albeit of the salon type. When they argued that the island should be a sovereign nation and cease being a territory of the United States, she agreed wholeheartedly. If she couldn't be independent herself, she would say, at least her country should have control over its own destiny.

11

The Courage of

Valentina Monfort

❧❧

ABBY WAS MY FAVORITE GRANDMOTHER. She was petite, no more than five feet tall in her bare stockings, and she liked to remind you that Letizia Bonaparte, Napoleon's mother, had been the same height. She had delicate features and her skin was as smooth as ivory. After Abuelo Lorenzo died, she always dressed in black and wore her gray hair pulled back in a knot, which made her coal-black eyes look even darker and livelier.

What I admired most was her presence of mind. She was convinced that greedy people always ended up badly. "Ambition," she used to say to me, "is like a plague of termites. It makes inroads from father to son, from brother to brother, and before you know it, the beams of your own house are eaten through and through. Termites never sleep, they bore tunnels underground day and night until they finally reach the heart."

Abby's maiden name was Valentina Antongeorgi, and she was also of Corsican descent. She was born in San Juan in 1885; her father was a schoolteacher and her mother a social worker. Abby was preparing to be a nurse, but her mother died, and she had to take care of her younger brothers. She was forced to abandon her studies when she was sixteen and a sophomore in high school. The federal government had instituted health programs all over the island, teaching people the value of vaccines and modern sanitary methods, and she had planned to work in hygiene after her graduation. But she also enjoyed literature and music and took courses in both at school.

When Abby's father remarried, her stepmother took over their house in Old San Juan, and Abby was practically relegated to the status of a servant. She had to cook, clean, and sweep the *zaguán* every day, because her stepmother was pregnant. The house was on San Justo Street, near the wharf. One day Abby was sitting on the balcony when Lorenzo Monfort rode by in his tilbury.

Lorenzo was a coffee planter from Adjuntas and he had come to San Juan to see about the arrival from France of a new crushing mill. One morning he rode by the house and saw Abby sitting there with a live chicken in her lap. She looked almost like a little girl, her features as delicate as porcelain. Her hands, though, were very strong, and as Lorenzo looked on, Abby took the chicken by the head, gave its neck a lightning twist, and in an instant the chicken was dead.

The next afternoon Lorenzo passed by the house again and heard someone playing the piano. He looked in through the window and saw the same girl, but this time her hands were flying up and down the keyboard as daintily as butterflies. He needed someone like that by his side, he thought, who could kill a chicken at devilish speed and play music like an angel. A few days later he went to see her father and asked for her hand. The year was 1903, and Abby considered herself very fortunate.

Abby and Lorenzo went to live at San Antonio, the coffee farm near Adjuntas which the young man co-owned with his brother. The town was high up in the mountains; the steep terrain made its houses look like eggs at the bottom of an eagle's nest. Lorenzo was a gentleman farmer. He had studied agronomy in Barcelona and knew about all the modern inventions related to the coffee industry. He imported the latest hydraulic crushing mills from France and had the two-ton boulder of the *tahona* pulled up the steep hills of the farm on palm husks tied to six mules that almost burst their guts with the effort. He had several turbines made to order in the United States and used them to move the machinery which husked and polished Arabian coffee beans. The farm had ten springs which provided it with water power. Lorenzo had them channeled into an aqueduct which he set up with dozens of sluices so he controlled the force of the water as it ran down the mountain. But as he also had an artistic sensibility, he built a fountain with marble dolphins which sent water down the other side of the hill. Coffee shrubs surrounded benches which allowed one to sit under the trees and read books or just talk to a friend. One of the most valuable assets of the San Antonio were the hundred-year-old *capá*, *yagrumo*, and mahogany trees which spread their protective mantle over this arbor.

Abuelo Lorenzo had a twin brother, Uncle Orencio, who also lived on the farm. Orencio was a merchant and took care of the commercial side of the business, while Lorenzo supervised the planting and harvesting. It was Uncle Orencio's responsibility to get the coffee beans to Adjuntas in large hemp sacks. Thanks to Orencio's entrepreneurship, the brothers had their own mule train to carry the sacks down the steep mountain road to Ponce, which entailed considerable savings. They also had their own warehouse in Ponce's harbor, where their merchandise could be stored for months. Orencio would wait for coffee to go up in Europe and the United States, and would sell it only when the price was sky-high.

They were identical twins and it was difficult to tell them apart. Uncle Orencio was born a few seconds before Lorenzo and considered himself the older, so he expected everyone to obey his orders. He was very different from his brother; he had absolutely no aesthetic sensibilities and didn't give a damn whether the Arabian coffee beans "shone like drops of black gold on the palm of your hand," as Lorenzo used to say. He made everybody work from dawn to dusk and paid his workers the same salary year in, year out.

Lorenzo was a kind man, and he didn't agree with his brother's policy of squeezing the last drop out of the local peasants. But he was afraid of Orencio and seldom stood up to him. He worshipped trees. He saw them as minor deities which purified the atmosphere and kept the island's sparse soil from running out to sea. "Trees are our best executors," he used to say to Abby when they took long walks around the farm or sat on the benches near the dolphin fountain. "They hold on to the soil. Let us plant coffee and make a living from it, and when we die they'll make a good resting place when we're buried under their shade."

When Abuelo Lorenzo brought Abby to live at the farm, he thought Uncle Orencio would move away, but Orencio acted as if nothing had changed. He didn't move out his bed or his dresser. The only concession to privacy he made for the newlyweds was to have his meals in the kitchen instead of in the dining room, and to bathe in the cement cistern at the back of the house instead of in the enameled iron tub with griffin feet that Lorenzo had installed on the second floor after he got married. Lorenzo didn't dare ask him to leave, though Abby would have liked him to. There were no decent lodgings around, and Orencio would have had to move into one of the peasants' shacks or travel every day by mule to and from Adjuntas, a two-hour trip each way.

Abby was very happy with her husband. They understood each other and shared the same tastes. The house they lived in was extremely pleasant. It was two stories: the first floor served as a warehouse where the coffee ready to be sold was stored; the living quarters were on the second floor. Lorenzo lived in considerable luxury. He had his food served on delicate china, used silverware, and slept on linen sheets. He also had a Pleyel vertical piano and a small but well-provisioned library with the novels of Balzac and George Sand standing side by side—which Abby took over.

A balustered balcony was wrapped around the house like a harmonica, and Abby loved to spend time there. It was never hot and there was a magnificent view of the mountains. The *yagrumo* trees always seemed to be waving their shimmering leaves at her, and the African tulips sprouted tiny flames from their dark treetops.

She practically lived in this gallery, and on breezy days she swore it hummed her favorite tunes.

At first, Abby thought she would find time to read novels and play the piano as much as she wanted to, but she found out she was wrong. There was a shantytown called Los Caracoles close by, where many of the farm workers lived. The huts had thatched palm roofs and walls made of wooden crates, and there were no sanitary facilities. People bathed in the river and relieved themselves in the plantain patch behind the workers' barracks. The plantains that grew there were the largest and thickest Abby had ever seen, but when she learned the reason why, she wouldn't eat them. She asked Lorenzo to build latrines for the workers, but Orencio refused.

Children ran around naked, their bellies swollen with tapeworm. Abby began to go there every day to help. She taught the children basic hygiene: they should wash their faces and hands before supper, and take a bath every day. There was a Methodist school in the vicinity, and Abby met the young American missionary who taught the children to read and write. One day she asked Lorenzo to buy three cows in town and had them brought up to the farm. From then on, she sent fresh milk to the schoolchildren daily.

One Sunday morning, Abuela was sitting out with Abuelo on the balcony when the overseer came by. The young couple had been married a year and Abby was pregnant with Father. "It's been raining for a week and a lot of rubbish has collected upriver," the overseer said. "If we don't clear it up soon, there could be a flood and the mud will drown the newly planted seedlings in the lower part of the farm. If you want me to, I can dynamite the dam today, rather than wait until tomorrow when the workmen will shovel it out. But you'll have to pay me extra, because today is Sunday and it's a dangerous job." Lorenzo agreed. He knew it was a difficult task. The man would have to climb on the pile of debris to leave the dynamite, and could easily be swept away.

The foreman went ahead with the job and soon there was an explosion; the dam had given way. The rain lasted all day; the farm seemed about to be buried under an avalanche of dark clouds. The deluge shook the coffee trees and the red beans fell to the ground as if raked by a steel comb. Lorenzo and Abby ate lunch and went to their room to take a nap; there was nothing else do in that kind of weather. By three it was as dark as if it were six in the evening. They were still resting in bed and Orencio was sitting on the balcony poring over his account books when the foreman came up the stairs and mistook Orencio for Lorenzo. "The job's done; pay me now," he said. But Orencio didn't know what the foreman was talking about. "You were only doing your duty," he said. "We could have waited until tomorrow and wouldn't have had to pay you extra."

The foreman left in a rage. He stayed up all night drinking rum and went back to the house the next morning with his sharpened machete in his hand. He stepped out on the balcony; it had stopped raining, and Abby and Lorenzo were having breakfast. Lorenzo smiled at the overseer when he saw him come near and went to take out his wallet from his jacket to pay him. But the machete flew by and hit Lorenzo on the side of the head. Abby was sitting next to him, pouring a cup of coffee, and the crimson jet left a wide arch on her skirt and spattered the soft mound of her belly. For a few seconds that seemed like an eternity, she saw what she saw and heard what she heard without understanding any of it. Then a long, woeful cry rent the silence of the magnificent woods around them.

Abuela had Abuelo buried under the copse of trees where they used to take walks holding hands. She locked herself up in her room and was so torn with grief she didn't even try to find out the reason for her husband's murder. She was told by Uncle Orencio the foreman had killed him because he was drunk. Her daze lasted for weeks; she couldn't concentrate on the legal matters that needed her attention. Uncle Orencio saw his chance; his brother hadn't drawn up a new will after the wedding, so Orencio claimed ownership of the entire property. A month after his brother's death, Orencio gave Abuela her three cows and title to the five wooded acres with the dolphin fountain and the copse of trees where Lorenzo was buried, and told her to leave the farm.

Abby moved to San Juan, but she didn't go back to live with her father. She rented a small house in Trastalleres and there her son, Carlos—my father—was born in 1904. I was born there, too, twenty-eight years later, and I remember clearly what the house was like. It had a corrugated tin roof which glinted in the sun, a small balcony in front, and walls painted fern-green. The roof made the house hot as a frying pan in the summer, but when it rained, it was wonderful; you felt you were sleeping under a waterfall. Abby had wanted it this way, because it reminded her of life in the mountains.

The house was behind the city's foundries, a place that hadn't been developed yet, and there was enough land so she could fence in her cows. She set up a small business making curd cheeses wrapped in plantain leaves which she sold from house to house, and later began making delicious desserts which she sold to the local fancy restaurants on a weekly basis. Her specialties were "ladyfingers," "coconut kisses," and "guava meringue on custard," a dessert she proudly renamed "floating island" in homage to Puerto Rico. She hired several women to help her and soon had a successful business. She brought Father up by herself, and sent him to an artisan's school, where he learned cabinetmaking. Later, Father set up his own furniture business, using wood from the trees on the five acres of land next to my uncle's farm.

Uncle Orencio died peacefully in bed when I was three years old. I remember it clearly because it was the same day Abuela Gabriela came from Ponce to force Mother to abort the baby, and it all happened because Abby went to my uncle's funeral. I never met Uncle Orencio, but I felt as if I had known him all my life. I used to picture him in my mind every time a truck full of wood arrived from the mountains. The logs looked like sawed-off limbs and I always imagined they were his butchered remains; that was the fate he deserved for having robbed us of our inheritance.

QUINTÍN

In the days following his discovery of Isabel's manuscript, Quintín was able to confirm his suspicion that she was writing a novel. Whenever he telephoned the house from the office, the maids would answer that Isabel was busy in the study and had given orders not to be disturbed. She spent the day writing and seldom went out of the house; she had stopped seeing her friends and no longer did errands such as picking up his suits at the dry cleaner's or going to the market. She sent the maids, instead.

Quintín was worried. He wanted to know what else Isabel had written, but though he checked several times behind the Latin dictionary, he didn't find any more pages hidden there. The tan folder lay undisturbed, as if Isabel hadn't realized someone had tampered with it.

Quintín wanted to know why Isabel was writing a novel. To escape from reality? Was the novel a panacea for a secret discontent he hadn't detected? He had felt secure in his marriage until then; it never occurred to him that Isabel might be unhappy. For twenty-seven years they had had a good marriage, in spite of the tragedies that had sporadically visited them. He admitted he was a bit strait-laced; he had to be, it was the only way he had been able to make a success of Gourmet Imports. He had started from scratch, with the odds stacked against him; his brother and sisters had bitterly opposed him from the beginning. But he had been loyal to his principles. There was a true and a false, a right and a wrong in his mind. Isabel was different, though. "Nothing is true, nothing is false, everything is the color of the glass you're looking through" was one of her favorite sayings—which she had picked up from a famous Spanish baroque poet. This was what distinguished the historian's point of view from that of the writer.

Isabel had become more and more inaccessible. When he came back from the office in the afternoon, she hardly spoke to him. They usually had dinner early, and afterwards would sit out on the terrace and read awhile, enjoying each other's company. Once a week they would take in a movie or go visit friends. Lately, however, she would say she was tired and didn't want to go anywhere; she'd usually go to bed early or sit by herself reading in the study. If Quintín asked her if something was wrong, she'd shake her head and not answer.

A week after his first find, Quintín got lucky again. It was six o'clock in the morning and Isabel was still asleep. None of the servants had come up yet. Quintín went into the kitchen to browse through the Fannie Merritt Farmer's Boston Cooking School Cook Book, *which Rebecca had inherited from Madeleine Arrigoitia; he was looking for a recipe for rum punch. It was the Fourth of July, and he was giving a party for his employees at Gourmet Imports. When he took the book down from the shelf in the pantry, another tan folder fell out. Quintín put it back in its hiding place and took down the recipe for the punch. He could hear Eulodia coming up the pantry's back stairs and he didn't want to arouse her suspicions. He had breakfast by himself on the terrace and went off to the office. That night, however, he got up at two in the morning and went silently to the pantry to look for the manuscript. Sitting on one of the kitchen stools, he began to read. This time the manuscript was headed: "Part Three: Family Roots," and it included just three chapters.*

Quintín read with amazement what Isabel had written in Chapter 9, where she described their love affair in Ponce, after they were engaged. She revealed secrets he wouldn't have whispered to anyone. How could she be so callous? They were both so young, so much in love! He was pained at her shameless depiction of how they would meet in the garden of the house on Aurora Street in Ponce, and later in the Roosevelt Hotel in New York; he felt embarrassed as well as betrayed. Quintín's face went red with shame. Just thinking what people in San Juan would say if the manuscript was ever published made his head reel. It didn't matter that twenty-eight years had gone by; Isabel had no right to bare these secrets to the world.

Quintín was less and less amused by Isabel's novel. It would be better to do away with it now than when she finished writing it. He got up from the stool and went to the kitchen sink to burn the pages he held in his hand. But as he was about to touch the match to the bottom of the first page, curiosity got the better of him.

He sat down again with the manuscript in his lap and took a deep breath. He had to cool down, to keep his Mendizabal temper under control. He decided the best thing was to create a distance between what he was reading and his own personal feelings, and he would do that by adopting a critical attitude. He would read the manuscript as if he were a conscientious literary critic; after all, literature, like history, had to be well written. Style was enormously important. He had never been a passionate reader of novels, but he had to admit this one was riveting; he hated and at the same time loved reading about his family and about himself. It gave his life more substance, made it more interesting. But he also found it humiliating to see its events tarnished by embellishment or downright falsehoods.

The manuscript had its good points. Isabel's chapter about Buenaventura's arrival in San Juan, for instance, had a nice flow to it, even if it was too historical, borrowing from the factual material he had provided her. In these last three chapters she struck out more on her own. But melodramatic phrases like "When I met Quintín, my heart was thrown into turmoil; I lived at the very center of desire" made him laugh aloud, they were in such bad taste.

Worse still was the way the manuscript was tainted with feminist prejudices. Obviously, Isabel wanted to be in tune with the times, but really, it was deplorable. Feminism was the curse of the twentieth century! He could see it at Gourmet Imports, where there were more women employed than ever before. Though, it was true, never at jobs where important decisions were made. His accountants at Gourmet Imports were women, even his comptroller, a good-looking mulatto who was full of energy and often worked late. But his sales managers, his sales representatives, his vice president, were all men.

What was happening at Gourmet Imports wasn't unique. The same thing was occurring in private businesses all over the island; his friends at the Sports Club said so. At the investment firm Barney and Shearson; at Green Vale Real Estate. Even the government was besieged by skirts! The Secretary of Education was a woman, the Secretary of Acueductos y Alcantarillados—the Water and Sewer Authority—as well. Quintín was a fair man; he thought women should have equal legal rights. But he believed men had an ingrained fortitude that was indispensable for leadership.

Was Isabel writing this novel because she wanted to have control over their lives? She was imposing her opinions and making the decisions; creating or destroying characters (and reputations!) at will. But she was neither discreet nor diplomatic enough. She liked to play with a loaded deck, often pointing a finger at the male characters. The Spanish Conquistadors, for example, were scavengers; Buenaventura, a spy and a brute; Milan Pavel had ended up a drunkard; Don Vicenzo Antonsanti, Isabel's grandfather, was a stud who lived for the thing between his legs; Orencio Monfort, her great-uncle, had been responsible for her grandfather's violent death. Well, there were good men and bad men in the world, and the same was true of women.

The women in the novel, on the other hand, were all portrayed as victims. Isabel's account of how Doña Gabriela Antonsanti—her maternal grandmother—had forced Carmita to abort her baby was a dreadful story. Quintín had never heard it before and was unpleasantly surprised. He was a religious man and abortion was a mortal sin; he was amazed Isabel should have kept this from him. Finding her mother in such a sorry state must have been a traumatic experience for Isabel as a child. He felt sorry for her, but that didn't excuse her airing family skeletons which had been hanging peacefully in the closet until now.

Her story of Doña Valentina Monfort was simply wrong, as maudlin and juvenile as a Corín Tellado romance. If Isabel were to say what her grandmother was really like when she lived in the mountains of Adjuntas, she'd have a much better chapter. Here Doña Valentina was a do-gooder, and he knew better. But it's always more interesting to write about evil than about goodness, as Dante well knew when he wrote his Inferno, an instant bestseller, while Paradiso was never read by more than a handful of people. Merchants in Florence must have been well educated, very different from those in San Juan today, Quintín surmised in a mental footnote. If I had written this novel, I would have followed Dante's example and explored some of the more controversial aspects of Isabel's grandmother.

In fact, just for the hell of it, he would. He would prove to Isabel that he could tell his own story, which she might take to be a delusion, a voluntary misinterpretation of facts, but which he knew to be the historical truth. Give her a taste of her own medicine, and see how she felt, reading about her own family. Quintín considered this for a moment. Then he opened a drawer in the pantry cabinet, took out a pad and pencil, and began to write with almost manic intensity.

"Isabel has inherited many of Doña Valentina Monfort's traits; she shares her grandmother's fantasies of social justice and independence for the island, as well as her Corsican bad temper. Corsicans have the typical personality of the colonized, envious of other people's successes and prone to inferiority complexes. Many of those who support political independence for the island today are of Corsican descent. There was a large Corsican immigration during the nineteenth century. Thousands came and settled in the steep hills of the interior where few had dared venture before. They developed a burgeoning coffee industry, cruelly exploiting their workmen.

"Doña Valentina Monfort was a classic example of the Nationalist Independentista syndrome. As soon as she married Lorenzo Monfort, one of the Monfort twins from Adjuntas, she saw herself as a Jacobin, red bonnet on her head and razor-sharp scythe in her hand, singing the Carmagnole down the mountains of Adjuntas. During the year and a half that Valentina spent in the mountains she didn't just help out in the elementary school at Caracoles; she actually founded the Independentista Party in the shantytown next to the farm. She was an active campaigner, collecting funds and making incendiary speeches whenever she had the chance. I got to know her well during my visits to Isabel at the house on Aurora Street, and I never saw eye to eye with her.

"The Monfort twins were notorious in Adjuntas because of their violent family history. I remember hearing people talk about them years ago. One of my salesmen at Gourmet Imports heard their story during one of his business trips there. He still visits Don Alvarado's grocery store monthly to replenish his stock of goods— usually rice, beans, and codfish, because it's a very humble establishment—and he heard Don Alvarado tell the story himself.

"Don Alvarado is a trustworthy man. He has been our customer for over twenty years and has unfailingly paid his bills. I've gone by his place a couple of times. There must be a thousand little stores like Don Alvarado's colmado on the island. They're practically an institution with us. They are always perched on a bend of the road leading in or out of the nearest hill town, a mango tree with a wooden bench next to them, a greasy window covered with flies and the remains of a roasted pig. Usually the head is the only thing left, a pole sticking out of its mouth. And next to the colmado sits *the eternal* cafetín, *with pints of rum on the shelves, two or three tables covered with oilcloth, and a sign that says 'No women or dogs allowed,' or 'Forbidden to talk about politics or religion,' nailed to the wall.*

"What really happened to the Monfort twins was this: Lorenzo and Orencio were equally ambitious and tight-fisted. The San Antonio coffee farm, which ceased to exist around the turn of the century, wasn't the affluent establishment Isabel has romantically made it out to be but a run-down mountain ranch. The brothers didn't live in a balconied two-storied mansion, but in a low wooden shed they built themselves. The place was no more than a hovel. It had earthen floors and walls made of rough boards they had hewn out of nearby trees with their own saws. There was practically no furniture and there were no sanitary facilities. A latrine stood outside the house, and if it rained, one had to get wet to use it. The brothers bathed in the nearby river and slept in identical iron cots in a large barnlike room divided by a sheet hanging from the ceiling.

"They guarded their privacy jealously. The farm was perfect for illegal deals: bootlegging, rustling, and in times of political unrest—the Independentista uprisings which periodically shake the island—smuggling and storing arms. They were each other's worst enemy but had established a precarious truce between them in order to survive. Unfortunately, they had inherited the property equally, and each owned exactly the same amount of land. Neither had enough money to buy the other half, and no stranger would have been interested in buying the godforsaken place.

"The brothers had also inherited the same fiery temper. They were both redheads—-Isabel is a redhead, too, by the way, although until I discovered this manuscript I never suspected she had a violent nature—and at night their heads would flame on their pillows like twin bushes of anger. When Lorenzo arrived at the house with Valentina, Isabel's grandmother, riding on the rump of his horse, the truce between them ceased to exist. The marriage took Orencio by surprise. He never expected it. His younger brother was a weakling

in his eyes; he couldn't have convinced a beautiful girl like that to come out to the boondocks with him unless she had her own reasons. And Orencio soon believed he had found out what they were.

"Orencio moved his iron cot to the other end of the barn, as far away as possible from the flimsy sheet that served as a divider and kept the passionate newlyweds to themselves. Nights were a torture to him. The heaving and sighing went on for hours; and he couldn't sleep out in the open because of the frequent rains. One day Lorenzo went on a trip and Orencio stayed behind on the farm. It was a warm day, and Valentina had removed her clothes to take a nap. There wasn't a breath of air, and the mosquito net hung over the bed like a cloud of heat. Orencio crept under its folds. The rough feel of the hands on her body, the arms covered with red down were so familiar Valentina mistook them for Lorenzo's. She later claimed she had been half asleep and hadn't noticed the difference, but Orencio insisted she had known all along.

"When Lorenzo came back from his trip, Orencio demanded they share Valentina, because she had given herself to him. Lorenzo was afraid to say no. If he refused, he would have to leave and it would cost him the farm. An uneasy truce was reached which lasted a few months, but Valentina couldn't hide her preference for Lorenzo. She loved him and saw him as her legitimate husband, despite the fact that he had betrayed her when he had accepted this unholy arrangement. At night when she went to bed with Orencio, instead of responding to his caresses, Valentina would simply lie there under the mosquito net, a log floating on the tide of sleep. That was why Orencio Monfort ordered the foreman to chop off Lorenzo Monfort's head, and not for the puerile reason that Isabel gives in her novel."

Quintín was almost finished with his story when he saw a light under the kitchen door. He stuffed the pages into his pocket and put Isabel's manuscript back into its tan folder and hid it behind the Boston Cooking School Cook Book. *He had changed his mind about letting Isabel read his version of things.*

PART 4

The Country House
in Guaynabo

12

Thanksgiving Day, 1936

❧

HE WAS SEVEN YEARS OLD. Quintín remembered it clearly. Don Esteban Rosich was still alive, and he enjoyed having the family over for turkey. Don Esteban must have been almost ninety, but he was very sociable, and Quintín was his favorite grandson. He insisted that Quintín was a big boy now, and when dinner was over, he told him he could sit with them out on the terrace. Madeleine served him his apple pie à la mode, and Quintín sat down in his grandfather's white Thonet rocking chair to eat contentedly.

Quintín loved his grandmother's pies; nobody made them like that; the crust was so light it melted on your tongue before you closed your mouth. It was one of the reasons he liked to visit the country house in Guaynabo, another being the grass-covered slope behind the house, where he could slide as fast as lightning on his red sled all the way to the fern-shadowed creek at the bottom of the hill. His grandparents' house was the only one he knew where people celebrated Thanksgiving. None of his friends had heard of it or understood what the word meant. They pronounced it "San Gibin," as if in honor of an obscure Catholic saint. They knew nothing about the Puritans, Plymouth Rock, or the four wild turkeys of President Washington. In fact, as there were very few turkeys on the island and no one ate them on that day, Madeleine's fowl was a large hen, fattened especially for the feast.

Quintín finished his apple pie and began slowly swaying to and fro, leaning as far back as he could in the rocking chair that reminded him of a bicycle with huge wheels on its sides. He liked to listen to grownup talk, and the family forgot all about him.

Don Esteban, Quintín's great-grandfather, never saw eye to eye with Buenaventura, and there were always fireworks when they got together for cigars and after-dinner drinks. Usually they ended up talking about the island's disquieting political events. "Autonomists are all Independentistas in disguise," Don Esteban said to Buenaventura. "They'll argue about the moral virtues of being an independent nation, while they profit shamelessly from the wealth of the United States. Let's see what they do after Senator Millard Tydings presents his bill calling for immediate sovereignty for the island."

"A barking dog never bites!" said Arístides, with a reassuring smile at Madeleine. "I don't believe anything serious will come of it. The Nationalists are trying to intimidate the United States into giving up the island, and Senator Tydings has fallen into their trap. But it's just a lot of propaganda, and the other senators know better!"

They were talking about Millard Tydings, a senator from Maryland who was a personal friend of Governor Blanton Winship. Tydings had introduced a bill in Congress which proposed independence for Puerto Rico in a matter of months, freeing the United States from the official guardianship of a possibly mutinous island.

Governor Winship was incensed by the latest shootout of the Nationalist Liberation forces of Pedro Albizu Campos, during which several police agents had been murdered. Pedro Albizu Campos was the son of an *hacendado* from Ponce and of a mulatto woman; he had studied law at Harvard, where he became friendly with Irish nationalists. He believed the Irish had won their independence through the "blood sacrifice" of the martyred Catholic rebels executed after the Easter Rebellion of 1916, and he thought Puerto Ricans could do the same. He came back to the island, founded the Nationalist Party in 1932, and began a frontal assault on what he termed "American Imperialism." Albizu maintained that Puerto Rico had been illegally ceded to the United States by Spain at the end of the Spanish-American War, since in 1897 we had been granted autonomy by the Spanish courts. He named himself President of the Republic of Puerto Rico and began publicly to harangue the masses, encouraging them to fight the "invader" by every violent means possible. Four years later, in 1936, he was arrested and tried for sedition.

"Nombrare il Diabolo e vederli venire sono due cose molti diversie: Calling the Devil and watching him come are two very different things," said Don Esteban, shaking his head. "People on this island were given a great gift when they were made American citizens nineteen years ago. They should be going to Washington on their knees, to persuade the Senate that Puerto Rico should be made a state as soon as possible, instead of bickering about when or even if they should ask for statehood. Now we'll see what happens with the Tydings Bill!"

"I'm not as afraid of Pedro Albizu Campos as of Luis Muñoz Marín," said Arístides. "That young politician is a smart one; he wants us to achieve the maximum degree of independence through negotiation, using autonomy as a stepping-stone to a Nationalist Republic. It was all done in Ireland fourteen years ago; there's nothing new under the sun."

Buenaventura blamed President Franklin Delano Roosevelt's supposedly socialist measures for the divided opinions on the status of the island. "That man is a turncoat," Buenaventura said. "He betrayed his own class when he made us pay income tax, and no one who's anybody in Puerto Rico is going to want the island to be part of the Union as long as he's President. We might as well stay as we are now, don't you think?"

Don Esteban didn't reply. His father had been an anarchist

laborer in one of the marble quarries of Bergamo, in northern Italy, and he felt a great admiration for President Roosevelt, precisely because he had passed a law that made everybody pay taxes on their income. He didn't want to discuss President Roosevelt with Buenaventura.

"Taxation is a mistake. In Valdeverdeja no one ever paid taxes and the town always had enough money for public works," Buenaventura went on morosely. Whenever he mentioned his hometown, he became nostalgic and pulled more deeply on his cigar. Don Esteban looked at him disapprovingly. He knew that, in spite of his complaints, Buenaventura hardly paid taxes at all, because he charged cash for most of his merchandise and never declared his real income. "I don't see why we should give those lazy representatives in our local legislature a third of our hard-earned money," Buenaventura added, extending his arm to flick a sliver of red ash into a flowerpot.

"Well, there's no need to worry about independence for now," said Arístides. "I'm a friend of several Statehood Republican Party leaders, and they assure me the Tydings Bill isn't going anywhere. Taking our citizenship away from us would raise an outcry and make the United States look like a bully. They are in a difficult position—they're not sure they want us, but they can't let us go."

Rebecca sat demurely in the chair next to Buenaventura, drinking iced lemonade and listening absentmindedly to all that was said. Madeleine, however, was all pins and needles when she heard this kind of talk. She took out a handkerchief from her sleeve and began to dab at her forehead with eau de cologne. "God have pity on the people of this island if they ever take away their American citizenship!" she said to Buenaventura in English. "Chaos will reign and no one will know what to do. I was born in Boston; I could never live in a foreign country."

Don Esteban looked despondently at his daughter. He had to admit she was right. If the island were ever made a republic, they would have to sell the Taurus Line and go back to Boston. Still, there was very little they could do to prevent it. Politics on the island were a complicated affair; it was better to keep a low profile and not get mixed up in any of it. In any case, they didn't really have to get involved. Don Esteban's son-in-law, Arístides, was an officer in the police force, even though only part-time, and he took care of them very effectively. He saw to it that their businesses were never unduly investigated for back taxes by the Departmento de Hacienda and that their homes were under adequate police protection.

Don Esteban had been very upset when he found out Buenaventura had beaten Rebecca because she had danced for her friends in a risqué evening gown. He went to visit her and he was shocked: Rebecca had a blue ring around her right eye and several cuts on her brow. He insisted Rebecca leave Buenaventura and come to live with her own family again. But this time Rebecca didn't go back to her parents as she had when they went to live in Atlanta. Instead, she became pregnant with Ignacio.

It was almost as if, taking her penance to heart, Rebecca was determined to prove she had more willpower than anyone else. One can be a rebel by being obedient; in fact, absolute obedience can be the most perfect kind of rebellion, as saints who embraced the hairshirt under silk garments discovered long ago. Rebecca's metamorphosis was something of the kind. Before, she admired Oscar Wilde and Isadora Duncan. Now she went to Mass and to Communion daily. She was one of those people who, if told by the Pope they should be poor to save their souls, the next day give everything away and go barefoot to attain their goal. But it was also as if she were acting out a role onstage. In the thirty-seven years she had lived, she had given several very intense performances. Now she was set on being the perfect wife.

The house on the lagoon was always spotlessly clean. Industriousness became the Mendizabal family's supreme virtue, and no one was ever supposed to be sad. Order and discipline were very important. One day Rebecca went down to the cellar, where the servants lived, and made inquiries as to who was married and who was not. She found out Petra and Brambon had been living in sin for years, and she was horrified. Rebecca made them dress up as bride and groom, got them a marriage license, and took them to see the judge. Petra and Brambon did everything she told them, as if it were all a game. They thanked her for the wedding gifts, drank champagne, and ate a slice of wedding cake, but the next morning they secretly went back to the civil court and asked the judge to divorce them. They had been married a long time ago, in a voodoo ceremony in Guayama, and were afraid the legal marriage might put a hex on them.

When Ignacio was born, Rebecca took care of him herself. She was almost fanatical about it: she bathed him, fed him, and wouldn't let anyone else near him. On the other hand, she began to neglect Quintín again. He was born in the old house, and his mere presence reminded her of a different time. In Pavel's time she often went down to the cellar to drink water at the spring or to take long baths. She wrote poetry and her house had been full of her friends. But since Buenaventura's beating, she hadn't gone down there once. Precisely because she didn't want to remember, she hardly ever asked to see poor Quintín. Petra and Eulodia kept Quintín with them in the kitchen. They would sit him down on a red stool and give him a bowl of green beans to snap, or in front of the revolving ice-cream maker and let him pour the rock salt on the crushed ice.

That Thanksgiving Day in 1936, as Quintín remembered it, did not have a peaceful ending. After Don Esteban's speech on the blessings of American citizenship, Buenaventura kept a hostile silence. Just before he left the house, however, he decided to get even. "I heard that the Taurus Line had a very good year, Don Esteban," he said as he was going out the door. "I want to congratulate you. Profits are much higher here than in Boston, thanks to our new coastal trade laws, which force the island to ship everything through the mainland. Before, we could ship directly to Spain, and Mendizabal & Company was doing good business. Now things have changed and it's *your* turn. American, Spanish, who knows! At this rate, we're never going to make up our minds what we'd like to be!"

Arístides was furious. He was sure Buenaventura had meant to insult Don Esteban and the United States. He took hold of him by the lapels of his jacket and pushed him unceremoniously out the door.

13

Chief Arrigoitia's Ordeal

❧❧

ARÍSTIDES ARRIGOITIA LIKED to take part in the military maneuvers the police held in San Juan, and, being an officer, he
always marched at the head. When he became bored with his
office job at Taurus, he joined the police force full-time. He didn't
get paid much, but he didn't need the money. His wife was rich
enough for both of them, and he wanted instead to serve the
community. The only thing that saddened him was that he was
fifty-eight and had little chance of becoming police chief because
of his age. It was during one of those marches, in January of 1937,
that Governor Blanton Winship first saw him.

Winship was impressed by Arrigoitia's physical appearance. He
was tall and muscular; his back was broad as an oarsman's, and
when he wore his white gala uniform, silver saber at his side, he
looked like an admiral who has just stepped off his ship. Governor
Winship also liked to dress in white. He wore a white linen suit,
carried a gold pocket watch in the vest under his jacket, and
sported a panama hat on his head. He was always smiling; he
looked like a benign Southern grandfather.

Most American governors before him had led carefree lives at
the Governor's Palace—better known as La Fortaleza of Santa
Catalina. It was true, language isolated them; very few people

spoke English on the island, in spite of the ordinance that everything should be taught in English at school. Besides, governors
usually had a difficult time understanding the Byzantine convo-
lutions of the local political scene. In 1936 there were four parties
in *Porto Rico*, as the American governors had officially rebaptized
the island: the Union Party, which stood for autonomy; the Statehood Republican Party; the Socialist Party, temporarily affiliated
with the Republican Party because the labor movement was fiercely
pro-statehood; and the Nationalist Party, which fought for independence. The first three parties had representatives in the local
Chamber, but as they were usually embroiled in bloody combat
for federal funds, the governor and his executive cabinet tended
to look on them as a troublesome lot.

The governor was appointed by the President and had absolute
powers. He, in turn, appointed the executive cabinet and the
senators. The members of the House of Representatives were
elected locally, but they could only advise the governor and had
no clout. A civil servant, the governor was usually named to the
post to repay a political favor at the level of national politics,
making his involvement with events on the island frequently
halfhearted. It was the executive cabinet that really ruled. The
governor rarely went out of the mansion and preferred to exercise
his authority from there, keeping his distance from the local
population.

The last appointee before Governor Winship who had tried to
be a de facto governor and got involved in risky island affairs was
Emmet Montgomery Riley. Riley was born in Kansas City. He
came from a humble background—his father had been a farmer
and he was a real-estate agent before going into politics. He was
a Mennonite and an authentic reformist, in favor of the Temperance
Law, banning cockfights, and jailing all prostitutes. He found out
most marriages on the island were common-law marriages, because
the Catholic Church charged an absurdly high sum to perform the
ceremony, so he ordered an army of Mennonite ministers to visit

the hills. Everyone wanted to get married for free by the plainly dressed men from Kansas with black homburgs on their head, and didn't mind if they were also baptized, because they got free Bibles. They could attend services in the modest white-steepled churches that were cropping up all over the hills. This unnerved the members of the local bourgeoisie, who were all Catholic. They began to undermine Riley's reputation, spreading rumors that he was a bigot and a religious fanatic. They renamed him the "Marriage Monkey" and the "Mule from Kansas City."

Riley was equally disgusted with the local bourgeoisie. He thought it was a disgrace to live in opulent mansions, be served by an army of servants, and travel to Europe every year, when ninety percent of the island was illiterate and lived at a level of poverty that would have horrified people in Kansas. In the Sunflower State, where cattle, wheat, and sorghum were the main sources of income, land was distributed a lot more fairly. There were no throngs of peasants in rags who worked in the fields for a few cents a day.

Every time he drove out of the city to the countryside, Riley was shocked by what he saw. The peasants lived in thatched-roof huts and languished without work during the "dead time," the months between harvests when the sugarcane fields lay fallow. So Riley tried to make the local sugar planters pay their workers better salaries. He also set out to force the huge American sugar mills like the South Puerto Rico Sugar Company to do the same. But the businessmen banned together and defeated his efforts in Washington. Riley became despondent; he stopped driving out to the hills to see how he could help the starving peasants and rarely left the Governor's Palace, just as his predecessors had done. Francisco Oller, the famous Puerto Rican painter, did a portrait of him around that time—now unfortunately lost—in which Riley is standing on the ramparts of La Fortaleza in a plain black suit, his fair hair blowing in the wind, and a sad look in his eyes. A few months later President Harding ordered Riley to leave the island.

Governor Winship was very different from Governor Riley. He had been a planter himself in Virginia and got along splendidly with the local *hacendados*. He enjoyed cockfights, *paso fino* horses, roast pork, and green bananas pickled in onion and garlic. In spite of being a Protestant, he was frequently asked to be godfather to the children of the local gentry and often suggested picturesque names for them, half English half Spanish, such as Benjamin Franklin Pérez Cometa or George Washington Cerezo Nieves. He had faith in tourism and, to promote it, commissioned a photographer to do an album of the island's natural wonders, paying for it with his own money. When the album finally came out, it was an instant success—especially on the mainland. The photographer obeyed Winship's orders and captured the island in all its splendor: there were angel-hair waterfalls, cotton-candy clouds, sugar-white beaches, cows pasturing up and down velvet-green hills—and not a single starving peasant to mar the beauty of the landscape. Everyone who saw it thought the United States had done well in acquiring a Caribbean island that looked like Switzerland but where everybody spoke Spanish and ate rice and beans.

The year 1937 was a fateful one for the island. When the Nationalist terrorists intensified their attacks, trying to intimidate the United States into making Puerto Rico independent, Winship was approached by the local sugar-mill owners and other well-to-do citizens, and was asked to put a stop to the bloodbath. Arrigoitia was among the citizens who visited Winship at the Governor's Palace, and he later told Quintín about it. Bombs were going off all over the city, and at night one could hear machine-gun bursts, fired from black Oldsmobiles with "Nationalist hoodlums" at the wheel, as the official news report put it. Statehooders, Autonomists, and those who believed in independence had been playing at make-believe politics for years when Pedro Albizu Campos appeared in their midst, dressed in black and spewing fire and brimstone, like the Devil himself.

Governor Winship never did things by halves, and when he realized what was happening, he put Nationalists and independence sympathizers all in the same boat. The Nationalist Party was outlawed. People who wanted the island to acquire independence by peaceful, democratic means were also placed on the subversive list and hunted down mercilessly.

The governor invited his longtime friend, Elisha Francis Riggs, to visit him at the Governor's Palace. "Up to now," he told him, "patrol officers here only know how to direct traffic; they're not prepared to fight a gang war. The local police force has to undergo a total reorganization. I want it to become part of our armed forces—and I need someone who has my utmost confidence to put this into effect. I believe you're the right person for the job."

Riggs was a war hero; he'd been decorated during the First World War and was chief of operations for the Russian field mission in Petrograd. He accepted the post and was most effective: he armed the police force with the latest artillery weapons and trained them at Fort Buchanan, a new military camp. He was so successful at turning them into professional soldiers that a year after his arrival he was gunned down by the Nationalists on Sunday as he was coming out of church.

Winship was incensed, but he kept his anger under control. A few months later he summoned Arístides Arrigoitia to the Palace. They were sitting out on the terrace at La Fortaleza, accompanied only by an aide and two of Winship's bodyguards. "The Nationalists who murdered Colonel Riggs are still on the loose," Winship said icily. "I'll make you chief of police if you promise to catch them." Arrigoitia looked at him in surprise. There had never been a Puerto Rican chief of police before. But he took the offer to be a proof of confidence and he was flattered; the governor evidently considered him a friend.

"Puerto Ricans are loyal American citizens, and we're just as upset about Riggs's assassination as you are," he said to Winship energetically, getting up from his chair to give his words more emphasis. "What happened was your fault; we wouldn't have any of these problems if we were a state. Congress is taking too long to decide our status." Winship's bodyguards, alarmed by Arrigoitia's excitable stance, slid their hands under their jackets, but Winship signaled them to ease up. Arrigoitia excused himself and sat back down sheepishly. A servant offered him a mint julep; he took it from the tray with a trembling hand.

The sun was just setting on the bay and a white passenger ship sailed silently before them, about to pass through El Morro's channel. Winship looked out toward the blue hills of Cataño, surrounded by lush cane fields. "I'm a lover of the land, Arrigoitia; and your island is very fertile. I admired it from afar, when I lived on my tobacco plantation in Georgia, and I still do. I feel I did the right thing in accepting President Roosevelt's appointment as governor. We can teach your people to take care of the land: how to make it more productive with modern methods. But you're a different country from us. It'll be much better for you if you stay as you are, enjoying the protection of the American flag but keeping your own personality. To do that, we must fight terrorism together. That's why I'm offering you the appointment of chief of police."

Arrigoitia felt discouraged, but he didn't want Winship to see that. He said he'd think about the offer and politely took his leave.

When Arrigoitia left, Governor Winship commented to his aide: "These people understand each other better than we understand them. I have a feeling that appointing an honest Puerto Rican to be chief of police is going to be the solution to our problems with the Nationalists."

Don Esteban Rosich heard about Governor Winship's offer, and he told Arístides: "Don't accept. You'll be pitting brother against brother. You'll never be able to live it down." But the governor's offer was too big a temptation for the ex-salesman from La Traviata. He thought it the perfect chance to prove to Winship that he could trust Puerto Ricans, that they were loyal American citizens, so he took the job.

During the next few months Arrigoitia had to hunt down a specific number of Nationalists a day, put them in prison, and let

Governor Winship have a count. These expeditions made him unpopular, but Quintín's family refused to believe the ugly rumors that were circulating. On Easter Sunday, the Nationalist Liberation Army announced that it was going to hold a march in Ponce and that they would be unarmed. Pedro Albizu Campos was in jail, and the march was supposed to be a peaceful protest against his sentencing. The Nationalist Party was officially banned, but Ponce's mayor was a liberal, and he told the Nationalists they could hold their march if they were respectful of the law. He issued them a permit. Governor Winship was immediately suspicious and ordered an investigation. His spies furnished him with contrary facts: the long-awaited Nationalist revolution to bring down the colonial government was to begin that day.

When Easter Sunday arrived, Chief of Police Arrigoitia was ordered to stop the demonstration, and he traveled from San Juan to Ponce to carry out the command. The Nationalists purposely sent their youngest cadets to march, as well as nurses and old men. Arrigoitia telephoned Governor Winship, who was dug in with a group of officers near the hill town of Villalba to wait for the coup, and told him the evidence furnished by his agents was all wrong. There were no bazookas, rifles, or machine guns in sight in Ponce, he said. But the governor didn't believe him. He insisted the Nationalist terrorists had sent their women and children to the fake parade as a cover. Armed men were probably hiding on the rooftops or in the branches of Ponce's many trees. There might even be terrorists hiding under the manholes in the streets of the town.

Early that morning the cadets started to arrive from all parts of the island. They stood four abreast, in military formation, down the middle of Marina Street. The men wore black cotton shirts and white pants and the nurses wore white uniforms with a red cross on their caps. Some of the cadets carried wooden rifles on their shoulders—they trained with them in their makeshift military camp—and others carried fake swords hanging from their waists.

Chief Arrigoitia deployed his police troops, and the two armies faced each other across twenty feet of pavement for over an hour. Ponce's mayor realized a bloodbath was imminent and announced on the loudspeaker that he was canceling the permit to hold the march, but the cadets pretended not to hear.

Arrigoitia then went behind his troops to tell the governor over the field telephone that everything was under control but that he thought it was a mistake to prevent the march. The governor told Arrigoitia he was a jackass and that it wasn't his job to think: his orders were to get the job done. Arrigoitia went back to the front lines and ordered the captain of the Nationalist troops to move out, but he refused to budge.

Many of the cadets couldn't have been more than fifteen or sixteen years old, and they looked straight at Arrigoitia, as if daring him to fire. The fake arms made them look even more like unruly children playing at war. Arrigoitia began to perspire and swore several times under his breath. "This absurd mission had to be in Ponce, the hottest town on the island," he grumbled. "You could fry an egg on the pavement right now, and my uniform is soaked."

Arístides couldn't bear it any longer. His heart racing, he went over to one of his aides and told him to take his place at the head of the troops. He walked down Marina Street and entered the Chapel of the Servants of Mary. He was a friend of the nuns at the convent; it would be a good place to rest. It was quiet inside; a single votive candle glimmered in a red vase that hung from a silver chain, and several nuns were kneeling in prayer before the Holy Sacrament. Arístides sat down on a bench and closed his eyes. When he opened them again, he wasn't sure how much time had gone by. It was so peaceful that for a moment he thought what was going on outside was a nightmare. The white sphere of the Sacrament, exposed in a monstrance surrounded by golden rays, gazed at him serenely and seemed to be saying, "What will all this matter thirty, fifty, a hundred years from now, Arístides? Why are you in such anguish? Kneel in front of me and entrust me with your suffering."

Arístides took off his white cap with the golden eagle on it, knelt, and began to pray. Gradually he calmed down; the governor's insult didn't sting so much anymore. He still had hopes that at the last moment someone would give way—either the cadets or Winship, and that nothing would happen. Shooting children wasn't going to solve anything, especially on Easter Sunday, a day of peace.

As the pressure eased, his mind began to wander, and he looked around the beautifully decorated chapel. He admired the white orchids the nuns had gathered in vases around the Tabernacle. They were his favorite flowers because they made him think of Madeleine. The delicate froth on the lip of the blossoms reminded him of the golden down on her mound of Venus. Governor Winship was single, maybe that was why he was so stern and cold-blooded. He was a lot like Pedro Albizu Campos. Both were fanatics in the service of a cause, and it was so much more pleasant to serve a beautiful lady.

When Arístides Arrigoitia walked out of the chapel, his aide was waiting for him at the door, holding a yellow telegram in his hand: Governor Winship's order to attack the Nationalist cadets. Arístides walked to the front of the line of his men and gave the command to fire.

14

Tosca the Soothsayer

❦

SEVENTEEN PEOPLE DIED IN PONCE, mostly teenagers, and dozens of demonstrators were wounded. The island's press was ordered to protect the governor's public image and Chief of Police Arrigoitia was blamed for the decision to open fire on the unarmed cadets.

Don Esteban Rosich was ninety, and he never recovered from having his son-in-law publicly accused of murder. A few months later he had a heart attack and died. Madeleine took his body back to Boston on one of the Taurus Line steamships. She was fifty-three, and for a long time she had debated whether to go back home or not. Now that her father was dead, she finally made up her mind. She would never come back to the island—and I never got to know her, except through Quintín. She spent the rest of her life in her family's brownstone on the North End.

Arístides Arrigoitia lived by himself in the country house in Guaynabo. He could not stand the white orchids in the nursery at the back of the garden, and one day he dowsed the plants with gasoline. Then he went back into the house, took his white gala uniform out of the closet, and his white jacket with the gold epaulets and his cap with the eagle on it, and put them alongside the orchids. Then he set fire to the whole thing. As he walked away from the blaze, he thought he heard Madeleine cry out, lamenting as she always had that God had condemned her to be as frail as an orchid when she had a soul as sturdy as a man's.

His loneliness was a torment to him. He had broken with his longtime friends because Madeleine didn't speak English, and once she was gone, her friends—the couples with whom they played bridge every Friday evening—never called back. After the Ponce incident, people looked at him as if he were a monster. Even Governor Winship refused to see him at the Governor's Palace. He was officially accused of ordering the attack, and was tried and found guilty. Soon after that, he was dismissed as Chief of Police. Fortunately, he wasn't sent to prison. He was from too good a family for the law to be applied literally, so he was put under house arrest. After the first year of the sentence, he was able to slip out of the house often, in spite of his detention officers' surveillance.

Arístides put the Guaynabo country house up for sale and asked the parole authorities to let him move to a smaller house in Puerta de Tierra, the barrio where he was born. He sold the Taurus Line and put all the money in Rebecca's name; he could live well enough on social security. Rebecca had two children and the money would permit her to be independent of Buenaventura if she ever needed to be.

Puerta de Tierra was where the main gate to the citadel of Old San Juan had once stood, and part of the city walls. They had been torn down a hundred years earlier to make way for Ponce de León Avenue, and a lower-middle-class barrio sprang up in the area. Arrigoitia liked living there; it reminded him of Quevedo's famous sonnet *"Miré los muros de la patria mía, si un tiempo fuertes, ya desmoronados"* (I looked upon my county's bastions, once proud and strong and now fallen into ruin), and he would meditate on the fate of empires. If the Spanish empire had fallen despite its might, something similar might happen to the United States one day. He would be terribly sorry to see it; he still admired the U.S. enormously. But then what had happened to him wouldn't seem so shameful.

Arístides began to take long walks around Old San Juan. He had always loved the city, and now it was all he had left. His hair had turned almost completely white; he let it grow long and stopped shaving, so people wouldn't recognize him. Every day he walked up Fortaleza Street and bought the newspaper from the vendor at the corner of González Padín, where the sea breeze was as stiff as on the deck of a sailboat. The sidewalk was steep, and walking up its slant gave one the feeling of rolling through waves. The wind blew his hair about and invigorated him as if he were setting out on a trip. He cut across Plaza de Armas, where there were always beggars sitting on the edge of the Fountain of the Four Seasons, and doled out a few quarters from his pocket. Then he walked up Cristo Street and entered El Morro fort. There he truly felt at ease—he loved to sit on the ground and watch the children fly their kites like colorful pieces of glass set against the sky; he petted the dogs which came up to smell his baggy pants and unkempt shoes.

He went down to the Paseo de la Princesa to watch the sun set over the boats of the old fishermen who still ventured out into the bay every day at five in the morning and came in at eight with their catch. Usually there wasn't much to sell—a couple of red snappers; a spiny *chapín,* good for only one *empanadilla;* a black moray eel, still staring ferociously with its beady eyes. The endless traffic of huge ocean liners coming into the bay had done away with most of the fish, and the beach was dotted with plastic bottles, disposable diapers, and all sorts of trash. But Arrigoitia didn't look down at the polluted beach at his feet; he gazed toward the horizon, where the sea melted into the sky and you could set out in any direction you pleased. At the water's edge there was nothing to hold you back; nothing to remind you that you had lost everything and that people laughed at you wherever you went.

There was something special about living in a seaport. It was as if the sea were constantly licking your wounds, telling you not to worry, not to feel disappointed. The world was out there; life and love were promises glinting on the tips of the waves. You just had to find a way to reach them. You didn't need money for a boat ticket or anything like that; you could travel with your imagination, the sailboat of the soul.

During one of his strolls down Luna Street, Arrigoitia saw a pink house with a curious sign over its door. The house was at the less reputable end of the street, near San Cristóbal fort. It was a dilapidated neighborhood occupied by lottery vendors, prostitutes, the owners of the small *cafetines* and *bares* of Old San Juan. Arrigoita stopped to read the sign: "Visit Tosca the Soothsayer and find solace." Below, there was a hand with the palm divided into five sections: "emotion," "self-respect," "energy," "inner strength," and "the spirit." Over each finger was a picture of an African saint: Elegguá, Changó, Obatalá, Ogún, and Yemayá. The Anima Sola stood at the center of the palm, a naked soul surrounded by a circle of flames.

Arístides identified himself with the Anima Sola. He pushed aside the curtain of colored beads and entered a dark hallway. "Please take off your shoes before you come in," said a voice from the end of the hall. It was a young voice, and there was a light-hearted sound of water coming from the cool interior. "Now take off your tie and jacket," said the voice. Arístides looked around him, wondering how she could tell what he was wearing in the dark. There was a small altar at the end of the hallway decorated with papier-mâché flowers, with a picture of the spiritualist Allen Kardec, and over him a full moon surrounded by seven stars. He walked toward it and put his shoes, tie, and jacket on a bench in front of the altar. A door opened and a beautiful mulatto girl in a flowered robe entered the hallway.

"The full moon is the godmother of all *mayomberas*," she said, taking him by the hand. "She gives power and light to those who worship her, and helps them to find the road." And she made him kneel in front of the image. Then she led him into a small room at the back of the house. There was no furniture; they sat on the floor, on worn velvet cushions. An incense burner released a single spiral of smoke into the room and the water in a fish tank bubbled in the corner.

Tosca lowered her head and placed her hands before her in prayer. She had flowing dark hair which hid her face when she looked down, so that Arístides felt that he was staring into the shadows. "You don't have to say anything," she said. "Simply turn your thoughts loose, let them fly toward me." Arístides was sitting in front of her. He gave a deep sigh. "Everybody has abandoned you: your wife, the governor, your friends," Tosca whispered, still holding her hands in front of her forehead like a chapel of slender fingers. "But you mustn't worry about it, you've come to the right place. I've had many terminally ill visitors who were worse off than you are."

Tosca took Arístides's hand gently and followed the lines of his palm with the tip of her finger. She began to talk in a funny voice, as if reading from a book. "You had a good marriage for many years," she said, still holding his hand. "But your father-in-law died, and he left orders in his will that he should be buried far away. Your wife didn't want to be parted from him, so she took his coffin back home with her. Your daughter, the apple of your eye, is married to someone you dislike and you hardly ever see her. Loneliness can be harsh punishment, and you haven't done anything to deserve it." When Tosca finished, she lowered her hands slowly and gazed at him intently. Arístides just sat there, his head slumped on his chest.

"I came to see you because I want to kill myself and I don't have the courage," he said. "I've been accused of a crime I'm not guilty of." Tosca looked sadly into his eyes. At fifty-nine, Arístides was still handsome, with long silver hair and an imposing physique. "You've always wanted to be a good man," she said. "But one man's good is another man's evil, and you never made up your mind about what's good for *you*. You shouldn't kill yourself until you find out." And she put her hand on his thigh and bent over to kiss him on the mouth.

Arístides closed his eyes. He felt as if he were dissolving into thin air, like the incense burning on the small lamp next to Tosca. All of a sudden he sensed Madeleine was near; he could almost smell her favorite orchid perfume, her peach-like cheeks. He let Tosca press him down gently on the cushions strewn over the floor. He didn't offer any resistance as she took off her clothes and lay naked alongside him, silent and still. Her dark skin was like quail's flesh; it was tender and at the same time tasted of wilderness, of tangled bushes and acid earth. Arístides closed his eyes and penetrated her to the farthest corner of her being. When he lay back on the bed, exhausted, he had forgotten all about Madeleine and her peach-like cheeks. He was amazed at how relaxed he felt. "Thank you, Tosca," he said to her. "You know how to soothe a man's soul."

Before he left, Tosca said to him: "Madeleine's road was very different from yours. Come and see me once a week and I'll show you." She was right. After making love to his wife for thirty-seven years within the holy bonds of matrimony, loving Tosca was a liberation. Sex with her was a mystical experience, inseparable from finding one's spiritual way in the world. Arístides began to spend more and more time with her and was truly happy for the first time in his life.

The detention officer followed Arístides to Tosca's house. He didn't report the visits to his superiors, but he told Rebecca all about them. Rebecca was furious when she found out about her father's love affair with the soothsayer; she couldn't forgive him for taking a colored mistress. When Arrigoitia came to visit the house on the lagoon, he would sit for hours on the terrace waiting to see Rebecca, but she never appeared. Even Buenaventura, in spite of his antipathy toward Arrigoitia, was more humane. He thought the affair with the soothsayer was picturesque, and healthy besides.

"Tosca sounds like just the right medicine for him," Buenaventura said to Rebecca. "If she's made him forget about his ridiculous gala uniform and about being chief of police, good for her! If a man is still alive in bed, it means he'll be around for a while!" When Buenaventura came home from work and found Arrigoitia at the house, he would sit on the terrace and chat with him for a few minutes. He would ask Arrigoitia how he was doing and if he could help him in any way, before going up to his room to take a bath and dress for dinner. But if Rebecca walked by, she would turn her head and pretend there was no one there.

Arrigoitia couldn't bear to have his daughter ignore him. He was a Basque, and Basque families are close-knit. He began to act strangely. He would stop at a corner in Old San Juan and suddenly launch into a speech. He would praise statehood and independence in the same breath. "Puerto Rico will one day be the forty-ninth state in the Union," he would say to anyone passing by, "and will thus bring greater glory to our fallen Nationalist cadets. Praised be our American Constitution, as well as our American congressmen, who one day will grant us statehood so that we can become an independent nation."

When Rebecca found out about her father's eccentric behavior, she was convinced he had lost his mind. She began to badger Buenaventura, insisting that Arístides be put in a sanatorium. Buenaventura resisted for a while, but when rumors began to fly around Alamares that his father-in-law was wandering the streets of Old San Juan looking like a beggar, his clothes all ragged, and raving about the island's political status to whoever stopped to listen, he had no choice but to acquiesce. A few days later, the sanatorium's van with two male nurses aboard went to Arrigoitia's house in Puerta de Tierra to pick him up, but he had disappeared. They looked high and low, but he was nowhere to be found and no one knew what had happened to him. During one of his trips to San Cristóbal fort a few days later to deliver merchandise to the U.S. Army stationed there, Buenaventura noticed that Tosca's sign had been taken down. The neighbors told him she had moved away a few days earlier, with the help of a white-haired man who "was very tall."

Buenaventura never mentioned any of this to Rebecca, but whenever he heard talk about Arrigoitia's tragic fate, he would wink and look down at his feet. He was the one who told Quintín the story of Arrigoitia's disappearance many years later, and Quintín later relayed it to me.

15

Carmita and
Carlos's Elopement

FATHER, CARLOS MONFORT, was more than just a cabinet-maker; he was a true artist. That's why it was such a tragedy that he stopped working at his craft and became a run-of-the-mill businessman. He was never any good at investing large sums of money, and when Abuelo Vicenzo died and Carlos started managing Mother's fortune, everything began to go wrong. Carlos lived for the art of carving wood. Among my earliest memories as a child are the silver swish of the handsaw, the smell of wood glue and varnish, and the coolness of turpentine when it touched my skin. The hammer, the plane, and the chisel were always near my crib, and Father used to make beautiful furniture with them.

Carlos was thin and sallow, like many people who come from the mountains. He had spindly arms and legs, and when he was bent over a piece of wood, he looked like a water spider. Although he was born in San Juan, there was something countrified about him. He liked to dress in jeans, wore water-buffalo sandals, and talked in funny, antiquated proverbs, such as *"Calma, piojo, que el peine llega"* ("Be patient, lice, your comb will come"), *"Entorchó la puerca el rabo"* ("When the sow sticks out its tail, keep out of her way"), or *"Lo fiao es pariente de lo dao"* ("Credit is giveaway's first cousin").

I remember watching him as he worked. He had his own style of decorating furniture with all manner of tropical blossoms: hibiscus, orchids, bougainvillea, gardenias. People admired his work: his rocking chairs, easy chairs, and side chairs were to be found in all the elegant living rooms of San Juan. His tall marble consoles were popular with the casinos and ballrooms of the period—with their baskets of pineapples and elegant palmetto leaves carved on their crest. At the society balls, girls danced gaily before his beveled mirrors, admiring their own reflections.

Carlos married Carmita against Abby's will, and against the wishes of Abuelo and Abuela Antonsanti, too. They were very different. Mother was taller and heavier than Father, and she had absolutely no artistic sensibility. She had large, cow-like eyes and skin like tightly packed vanilla ice cream. From the moment Abby laid eyes on her, she didn't like her. Carmita had a smug way of sitting, with a smile on her face, as if she knew a secret that made Carlos happy.

She was never in a hurry; she never lost her temper. When she met Carlos, she was twenty-eight (two years older than Father, and in those days almost a spinster), and she had never had a serious beau. Carmita was the youngest of six sisters, and when she met Father, the other girls were all married. They had met their husbands before Abuelo became rich. Abuelo Vicenzo did all he could to have Carmita marry someone of her own status, rather than a fortune hunter. She was a coffee heiress, he would say to her, and if she married beneath her station, she had everything to lose.

Father and Mother met at Ponce's *fiestas patronales* for the Virgen de Guadalupe. Carmita slipped out of the house for a stroll around the plaza and was standing next to the tin-horse roulette, about to bet on one of the horses, when Carlos approached. "Put a dollar on number 13," he said. "Today is Tuesday the 13th and it should bring you good luck." Carmita looked up in surprise. Carlos was dressed in a faded blue suit and was carrying an old suitcase in his hand. He had come to the fair to sell his furniture and had a stand nearby full of chairs and rockers. She liked his thin mustache, which spread a little wing of brown hair over his smiling lips. She bet two dollars on the yellow horse with the number 13 painted on its red saddle, and won twenty dollars.

"It's the first time I've won at anything," Carmita said. "Tell me which horse to bet on next." Carlos said to bet on the red horse, number 2. "Two is my favorite number, because people should never be alone," he said. She won another twenty dollars. "How splendid!" she exclaimed, clapping her hands like a little girl. Carlos left a friend in charge of his stand, took Carmita by the arm, and they began to tour the booths together. "You and I are going to have to stay together," she said, laughing, as she counted the money she had won. "You're definitely bringing me luck."

A little later, a man walked up to them selling papier-mâché masks for *Vegigante* costumes from a tall pole he carried on his shoulder. He twirled it this way and that, advertising them over the heads of the crowd. Most were of devils, and the young people from the barrios wore them at carnival time. Carlos thought they were beautiful and put one on. It was fire-engine red, with a green horn on its chin, two yellow horns sticking out of the temples, and a blue horn perched on the nose. He started to jump up and down like a grasshopper, waving his arms and crying, *"Vegigante a la bolla; Contigo, pan y cebolla!"* ("Marry me tomorrow, and we'll live on radishes with bread and onion!"). Carmita laughed till tears came to her eyes.

"Buy me the Sad Princess," she asked him, pointing to the mask of a girl with a sequined crown on her head and a rhinestone tear on her cheek. "Next time my parents tell me not to fall in love with a scoundrel who is after my money, I'll put it on and cry: *'Contigo, pan y cebolla!'* ('Hurrah for radishes with bread and onion!')."

The next day Carlos went to see about a truck to take the

furniture he hadn't sold at the fair back to San Juan. He then went to the Línea Cofresí station, at Plaza Degetau; the *público* would be leaving at one o'clock. Carmita was waiting for him, still wearing her princess mask, her blond hair braided in neat tresses. In her right hand she carried a small suitcase, and in her left a large bunch of honeyberries. "One has to eat what's available," she said, winking at him and smiling. "Coffee has to be ground and paid for before we can drink it, but honeyberries grow free by the road all the way from Ponce to San Juan." Carlos took the suitcase and they boarded the *público* together.

Abby couldn't understand what Carlos saw in Carmita. She reminded her of a Raggedy Ann doll, with her long braids and her sad way of laughing at everything as if she were five years old. "She's a nitwit. If she lives with us, she'll have to earn her keep, and she can't cook, clean, or sew. All she does is comb her hair and sleep until eleven in the morning. We can't afford to take in a woman like that."

So the next day Carlos moved his bed to the workshop and took Carmita to live with him. He didn't ask her to do anything at all. He just liked to look at her. "Her skin reflects the light in a special way," he said to Abby. "She helps me to see things differently. I can carve much better when I have her around." Carmita sat naked on one of his chairs all day long, watching him work, her hair flowing like honey over the back seat as she brushed it. They were very happy together. Abby, and Abuelo and Abuela Antonsanti, had to accept Carmita and Carlos's affair post facto, long before they finally decided to marry.

I was born in 1932, when we were still living in the workshop of Trastalleres, which my parents turned into a home. We lived there for almost ten years, and when we moved to Ponce, we were still a close-knit family. I'll never forget the day we walked into the beautiful house on Aurora Street. None of us except Carmita had seen anything like it before. Abby had lived very simply after she left the farm in Adjuntas, and when she entered the living room at Aurora Street and saw the Beauvais tapestries, the chairs and settees upholstered in blue damask, the chandelier that hung like a huge chrysalis from the ceiling, her black eyes narrowed to granite points. *"Porvou que ça dure!"* she said, shaking her head reproachfully as she quoted the words of Napoleon's mother, Letizia, when she learned that her son had crowned himself Emperor in Paris. Carlos managed to calm her down. "Never look God's gift in the mouth, even if you don't agree with His methods," he said. "Just enjoy it while it lasts."

We went into the kitchen and Abby asked the cook to make us some rice and beans, as well as *empanadas* and *piononos*, my favorite ripe-plantain pies. We took the silver, china, and crystal from the pantry's cupboard and had a banquet that very day. But the real feast came when we walked into the library, where Abuelo Vicenzo kept his collection of books. Abby and Father loved to read, and I took after them. At the dining-room table, we would talk about music and literature for hours. Abby always said that a family that reads together stays together, and it probably would have been true if it hadn't been for Carmita's confounded hobby.

I loved Father deeply, but he was a weak man. Maybe that's why I can't remember what he looked like. When I try to picture him, I see a faded photograph; sadness has washed away the sharp contours of his face. He could never say no to Mother—no matter how harebrained her requests. If Carmita wanted to spend a fortune on beauty creams, Danish chocolates, or French perfumes, it was fine with him. He was always eager to please her, as if she were a child, and at first he thought it amusing when she started to sneak out of the house to gamble in San Juan's elegant casinos.

After Abuela Gabriela made Carmita got rid of the baby, Carmita began to gamble more and more. At four o'clock every afternoon she would begin to feel restless, as if Poe's "Imp of the Perverse" had taken hold of her. She would hurry to the corner, hail a taxi, and have it take her to the Continental Club, the only casino in San Juan that was open during the day. She enjoyed the Lady

Luck Afternoons, when until eight in the evening a lady got six chips for every dollar, instead of three. She met all kinds of women there, housewives running away from unhappy marriages, widows bored with their lives and afraid to travel by themselves, prostitutes looking for an early customer. Carmita was running away, too, though none of us could ever figure out what she was running away from. She lived in a fantasy world; reality was the roulette table. Between the *"faitez vos jeux"* and the *"rien ne va plus,"* everything was possible: trips to Europe, Dior's latest fashions, Tiffany jewels—all the privileges she had had to give up when she married Carlos and moved to his workshop.

Father carved his furniture in the morning, Carmita played roulette in the afternoon, and there was often little to eat on our table when dinnertime came around. Abby had to prepare stews like the ones she had learned to cook at the farm, with the yams, roots, and tubers they sent us from Abuelo Lorenzo's land. Carmita's hobby soon became an addiction, and she didn't just gamble at the casino; the minute she went out on the street, she was looking for the lottery vendor, or she would go to the racing agency to bet on next day's favorite horse. If she didn't have any money, she would simply take whatever jewelry she was wearing to the pawnshop. She was hardly ever home, but spent the greater part of the day wandering the streets, asking people for money. Father worried about her all the time. At dinner he hardly spoke to me; it was almost as if I wasn't there. That was when Abby insisted we move in with her. She could take much better care of me at her house than at the workshop, she said, and after that she bathed, dressed, and fed me, and took me to school every day on the bus.

Abuela Gabriela died one day unexpectedly of pneumonia, and Abuelo didn't want to live without her, so he went a week later. Carmita inherited a considerable sum of money, in spite of the fact that she had five sisters. Abby and Carlos were both amazed; they thought Abuela and Abuelo had disinherited their youngest child when she had married below her station. "May God bless them and keep them both in heaven!" cried Abby when she heard the news. "Now Carmita can stop complaining about how sick she is of '*pan y cebolla*,' as she's been doing since she met Carlos!"

Carmita's sisters were all married and had their own houses, so they let us move into the house on Aurora Street. Abuelo Vicenzo had long ago sold his coffee farm in Río Negro and invested the money in real estate. Mother's part of the inheritance—several houses and some commercial properties in Ponce—needed tending, so Father closed his workshop in Trastalleres and the family moved south. From then on, he spent all his time administering Carmita's money and ceased to be his own man.

QUINTÍN

Several times Quintín had been tempted to leave his own version of Doña Valentina Monfort's story inside the manuscript of Isabel's novel, to let her know he'd been reading it. But then he thought better of it and destroyed it. He was afraid Isabel would be angry and hide her novel somewhere outside the house—she could rent a safe-deposit box at the bank, for example, or leave it at a friend's house—and then he'd never be able to finish reading it. That was a chance he wasn't willing to take.

As much as he didn't want Isabel to know he was on to her project, he had unwittingly added a few commentaries here and there in pencil, in a tiny script which was almost invisible; perhaps Isabel had noticed them. He had thrown Doña Valentina Monfort's story into the wastepaper basket. Perhaps she had found and read it as well.

Every night, when Isabel was sound asleep, Quintín would creep out of bed and search the house high and low, but he didn't find any more pages. Either she had hidden them so well he would never find them (like most men, he could barely find the socks in his own dresser drawer without her help), or she had destroyed the manuscript entirely. But what if someone else had it? He immediately rejected this last possibility. Isabel wouldn't risk someone else's reading it and telling him about it.

One night, after looking in all the closets and cupboards, Quintín went back to the study at three in the morning and sat down despondently at Rebecca's desk. It was an elaborate affair, with gilded tendrils decorating its sides and four Egyptian caryatids serving as legs. There was a secret compartment, where long ago Rebecca had hidden her own portfolio of poems. He was curious to see if they were still there, so, gingerly, he removed the center drawer and slowly put his hand in the hollow behind it. He groped around for the tiny key that was usually in the lock, but it wasn't there.

Quintín was suspicious, but he went back to the bedroom and lay down quietly on the bed. Isabel, as usual, went on sleeping undisturbed. The next morning, when Isabel was in the shower, he searched in her jewel chest, which was open on her dressing table, and found the tiny bronze key. Quintín left it there and finished dressing, but the following night he returned on tiptoe to the study, key in hand. Breathless with excitement, he opened the desk's secret chamber and, sure enough, instead of Rebecca's elaborate portfolio of poems, with its silver clasps on the side and water lily embossed on the front, he found Isabel's tan folder with her manuscript inside.

Quintín's anger and disappointment vanished. She was so crafty, he thought, and in a way he admired her for it. They had always argued a lot, but people who fought a lot often loved each other very much, and he loved Isabel more than anyone else in the world. But would she really be able to write a good novel? He didn't know. At any rate, to substitute her own manuscript for Rebecca's poems in the secret compartment was a clever touch.

Quintín sighed deeply and sat down on the study's green leather couch with the manuscript in his lap. A shiver—of pleasure? anguish? he didn't know for sure—went down his spine. The room was absolutely quiet, and dark. There was no wind in the mangroves that night; all one could hear was the gentle lapping of the waves of the lagoon against the walls of the house. He turned on the bronze lamp next to the sofa, and a bright spot of light fell on the manuscript's first page. It was the fourth part of the novel and was entitled "The Country House in Guaynabo." Quintín stared; it was sure to be full of appalling stories and yet it would be impossible to resist. Two of the new chapters were about the Rosich history, Rebecca's side of the family; a third chapter was about Carmita and Carlos—Isabel's star-crossed parents.

As he began to read, Quintín saw himself as a child at his grandparents' house in Guaynabo. What was Isabel going to do with him now? What metamorphoses would she make him undergo? He was sitting on his grandparents' terrace, listening to his father argue heatedly with his grandfather, without being able to do anything about it. It was an eerie experience, reading himself as if he were someone else.

He smiled wistfully as he turned the pages. Obviously, Isabel sympathized with his mother's relatives more than with his father's. Don Esteban, his great-grandfather, as well as Madeleine, his grandmother, were given a good press, whereas Buenaventura was described once more as a brute and a provincial Spanish rustic. He had beaten his wife black and blue after her enactment of Oscar Wilde's Salomé, and then had had the gall to attend Thanksgiving dinner at his in-laws', where he complained to Don Esteban that he was unhappy because he had to pay taxes, something he supposedly never had to do in Valdeverdeja. The absurdity of the scene was hilarious. Would Madeleine and Arístides have invited Buenaventura to Thanksgiving dinner after he had beaten up their daughter? Didn't they know? Could Rebecca have kept something like that from them? It was all a fantastic fabrication.

Quintín was overwhelmed with curiosity. Why would Isabel portray his family that way? There was an irony underlying the whole scene which must have a definite purpose. Maybe Isabel meant his mother had been psychologically battered by his father, and wanted to show how some women reacted under the circumstances.

But there was a grain of truth in what she said. Rebecca often put up a quiet resistance to Buenaventura's authority, and she had been able to get away with a lot, thanks to her "dead fly" technique. It was the traditional way for a married woman to behave in those *days; very different from today. Rebecca's apparent meekness and "obedient" stance were often highly effective. Quintín was amused, remembering that whenever she acted that way, Buenaventura turned to putty in her hands. If Isabel's purpose was to describe the tactics of married women in the past, she had been entirely successful.*

In the next chapter, "Chief Arrigoitia's Ordeal," Puerto Rican history was again at the center of the novel. Isabel's Independentista sympathies clearly got the better of her, and her style grew stilted and didactic as she depended on historical data more than was necessary. What was worse, she made another historic slip: when Isabel talked about San Juan Bay, she was describing the way it looks now, polluted by the huge tourist ocean liners that visit the city daily, not the way it appeared in 1937. In 1937 there was very little tourism on the island and very few ocean liners. The waters of San Juan Bay were crystal-clear, and fishermen brought in a good catch almost every day.

Quintín and Isabel would never see eye to eye politically. Quintín was for statehood and liked to think of the United States as his real country. He considered himself not a citizen of Puerto Rico but an American citizen—a citizen of the world. "If Puerto Rico ever becomes an independent nation, like the Nationalists and Independentistas would like," Quintín would tell Isabel, "we'll be on the first plane to Boston, where my family still owns some real estate."

Quintín considered Nationalists and Independentistas a dangerous lot. Nationalism was more a faith than a political conviction, and Nationalists were fanatical. They were touchy and capricious; one day they might wake up feeling worthless and decide to shoot the President. It had happened more than once, and it might happen again. In 1950 there had been a shootout at Blair House—an attempt on President Truman's life. A few years later, in 1954, a seamstress named Lolita Lebrón, the son of a furniture-maker named Rafael Cancel Miranda, and Andrés Figueroa Cordero—who looked more like a jockey than like a fire-spewing terrorist—had showered bullets on the House of Representatives in Washington.

Quintín was pleased that a plebiscite was to be held on the island in five months. Puerto Ricans would finally choose whether they wanted to become a state of the Union or an independent nation. He felt sure statehood would win. Commonwealth status, which had come into existence in 1952, didn't really count. Voting for commonwealth wasn't going to solve anything; it would be perpetuating the status quo. Becoming a state would be the only way to put the lid on Nationalist and Independentista terrorism.

But statehood wouldn't resolve the language problem. Isabel had attributed his grandmother's failed marriage to the fact that she had never learned to speak Spanish. The American governors never learned to speak it, either, and in Isabel's opinion the Nationalist riots during the thirties and forties were in part a consequence of that situation. Commissioner Easton's ordinance making English the official language at school seventy-nine years ago was a historical fact, and everyone agreed today that it had been a mistake. But the truth was that learning English had given the island a great advantage over its Latin American neighbors. English had made it possible for Puerto Ricans to be a part of the modern world, whereas Cuba, the Dominican Republic, and Haiti were still in the Middle Ages. Today English and Spanish were official languages in Puerto Rico, and this was so by public consent. The official use of both languages was inevitable because of the intricate way the island's industrial and economic development was linked to the mainland. Declaring Spanish the island's only official language —as Isabel would no doubt prefer—would cause a huge outcry. People would be up in arms, in the legal and in the business world. Quintín believed the island was well on its way to becoming bilingual, especially with the three million Puerto Ricans commuting to and from the U.S. "Today the Bronx is practically a suburb of San Juan," he used to say, "and American Airlines is Puerto Rico's most popular bus line."

By now, everyone knew what Thanksgiving was, everyone ate

turkey and was thoroughly acquainted with the Pilgrims and George Washington. Would Isabel herself give up English if the island became independent? Would she have written her manuscript in English if she didn't think English was important? If she had written her novel in Spanish and published it in Puerto Rico, why, only a handful of people would read it! But if she published in the United States, thousands would read it.

What troubled Quintín the most was Isabel's blatant disregard of history. For example, she described the Nationalist cadets almost as if they were martyrs. "Many of the cadets couldn't have been more than fifteen or sixteen years old," she had written, "and they looked straight at Arrigoitia, as if daring him to fire." This, of course, was inaccurate. People of all ages were part of the Nationalist cadets, and they were from all walks of life. They had only one thing in common: if they could let themselves be murdered in cold blood, it was because they could kill in cold blood. Governor Winship was right to insist that the Nationalists be wiped out. They were bloody fanatics as well as experienced guerrillas—just like Uruguay's Tupamaros or Peru's Sendero Luminoso.

The shooting of the Nationalist cadets had taken place on Easter Sunday, 1937—nobody could deny that. But the lens through which the event was seen had been subtly altered, and the blame laid on the wrong party. That was what Governor Winship had done when he held Arístides, Quintín's grandfather, responsible for the Nationalists' massacre. And Isabel perpetuated the error in her manuscript.

Arístides was a tough police chief, absolutely loyal to Governor Winship. His ferreting out of the Nationalist terrorists was hardly the reluctant crusade Isabel made it out to be; it was a heroic endeavor. He had put his life on the line, trying to establish law and order. On the morning of the parade, he went to the Mayor of Ponce's house, got him out of bed at gunpoint, and forced him to sign a document canceling the Nationalists' permit to hold the march. Then he went to Marina Street, where the cadets were already *assembling, and showed them the document. But they refused to budge.*

Arrigoitia had been a hero in the island's struggle for statehood, and here was Isabel, who didn't know a chit about politics, daring to sling mud at him and stain his reputation. His grandfather would have his niche in island history when it finally became a state; he was sure of that. And how dare she describe him fantasizing about his grandmother erotically just before the shooting of the cadets! There was no way Isabel could have known what Arrigoitia was thinking at that moment, and her description certainly wasn't like him.

What was Isabel trying to prove? That Quintín was wrong? That she knew more about the Ponce shootout than he did, in spite of his being a historian? And why would she try to prove that, anyway? It would be impossible to respond to all the false statements Isabel had put in her novel. Such an effort would turn into a historical treatise, and he certainly didn't have time for that.

PART 5

The House
on Aurora Street

16

The Kerenski Ballet School

⚹

ONE OF MY FAVORITE STORIES concerning my side of the family
began on the day we arrived in Ponce, after my grandparents died.
It was Sunday, and Father, Mother, Abby, and I had traveled in
the *público* and got out at Plaza Degetau in the center of town. I
was ten years old.

I had never been to Ponce before, and the first thing I noticed
when I stepped out of the *público* was the heat. The Indian laurel
trees planted around the square had been trimmed to look like
giant mushrooms, but they did little to diminish the sultriness that
rose in waves from the pavement. A band played gaily by the
firehouse; people were streaming in and out of church and strolling
along the square very elegantly dressed. They milled around the
marble fountain of Plaza Degetau, listening to the music and ex-
changing greetings.

The Firemen's Band was playing Puerto Rican danzas, and once
in a while they worked in "I'm Dreaming of a White Christmas."
The bandstand was decorated with frosted accordion paper bells
and tinsel Christmas trees that shimmered in the breeze. This was
no puny small-town band. There were forty musicians in all—
dressed in navy-blue uniforms, and wearing bright red caps with
shiny patent-leather visors—and they were playing brand-new in-

struments, or at least it seemed so to me. Six trumpets, four tubas, four trombones, and at least a dozen clarinets and saxophones gleamed in the sun as if they were made of gold. The first thing I thought when I saw them was that in Ponce firemen must be very rich. Men strolled on the right and women on the left side of the plaza, listening to the music, and when I looked at their reflections in the tubas' brass bells, they seemed to be gaily chasing each other in circles.

I asked Abby if the firemen were trying to cool down the crowd with their music, and she laughed. She said she doubted it; they were playing in honor of Secretary of the Interior Harold Ickes, who was on an official visit to Ponce and was sitting right there next to the mayor, on the dais in front of the bandstand. I liked everything I saw at Plaza Degetau: the fountain with its six bronze lions spewing water from their gaping muzzles, the stone benches with verses from local poets carved on them, the huge laurel trees whispering secrets over us.

In Old San Juan—which was near Trastalleres—plazas were narrow and treeless. They had been used by the Spaniards for military maneuvers, and there was an austere, martial air about them. Houses were crowded together like dominoes on each side of the narrow streets. They had cramped balconies and balusters that looked like rows of matchsticks, and there were no trees to provide shade. Ponce, on the other hand, had wide streets and plazas, as if it had been built with elegant parties in mind. Houses were set comfortably back from the street; they had wide terraces in front and enclosed gardens at the back where mangoes and honeyberries leaned over the walls like dark green anemones. They were usually one story high and were painted light colors—pastel blue or peach, or ivory. It was a beautiful city. From afar, it looked like a wedding cake put out to set in the sun.

After we tired of strolling around Plaza Degetau, we walked to Aurora Street, where I had been told our house was. As we approached it, I saw a tall building with a Greek portico in front.

"That's La Perla Theater, where the Kerenski Ballet School performs every year," Abby said. "Our house is just a little farther down the street."

I had heard wonders about the Kerenski Ballet School in San Juan, and a few weeks after we got to Ponce, Abby enrolled me in it. I began to attend the studio on Acacias Avenue every day. André Kerenski and Norma Castillo exerted a strong influence on the artistic life of Ponce in the forties and fifties, and their ballet school was one of the best in Puerto Rico at the time.

André was twenty-nine and Norma twenty-five when they arrived in Ponce in 1940, two years before we did. Kerenski was born in Russia and had been a student at the Imperial Ballet School in St. Petersburg. His mother, a red-haired White Russian aristocrat whom André had been very attached to, had emigrated with him to the United States when he was twelve. When he was twenty-two, she managed to enroll him in the chorus at the Metropolitan Opera Ballet. She died a year later, leaving him the last of her Fabergé cigarette cases, which he sold and lived from for the next four years.

The penury André Kerenski was forced to endure, and his mother's untimely death, made him turn his back on his aristocratic roots. He became friends with socialist sympathizers at New York University, where he earned a degree in liberal arts. He believed in a better world, one he had lost when his mother took him out of his own country before he could decide what he wanted. He was convinced that the Revolution his mother had run away from had been justified. Private property should be abolished and everything should belong to the state; that was the only way to prevent the abuses of the rich. He sympathized with Lenin from afar, and was in complete agreement with the transformation of Imperial Russia into the Union of Soviet Socialist Republics. Later he refused to believe that Stalin was the monster the press made him out to be. André met Norma Castillo at the Metropolitan Opera Ballet and he fell in love with her, forgetting all about politics.

Norma was the daughter of a sugarcane hacienda owner from Ponce who had sold all his land at the end of the First World War. A staunch believer in statehood for the island, her father had invested all his money in U.S. municipal bonds and had retired to live on the interest. Norma was his only child, and he had wanted only the best for her. She showed a special ability for ballet and in 1935 he sent her to study in Paris; later she joined the School of American Ballet, affiliated with the prestigious New York City Ballet. When she graduated, she was offered a job at the Metropolitan Opera Ballet, where she met André, fell in love, and married. Soon after that, André renamed his wife Tamara, because of her jet-black hair, which she wore in a sleek chignon at the back of the head, in the style of Tamara Toumanova, the famous dancer from the Ballet Russe de Monte Carlo.

Tamara's skin was satin-white and she had a robust constitution. She reminded Professor Kerenski of the beautiful young peasant women he had seen as a child outside St. Petersburg. His mother used to take him to spend the summer in a countryside dacha which had a silver-plated balcony, an onion-domed roof, and a long avenue of firs leading up to its entrance. André and Tamara had come to Puerto Rico for their honeymoon, and André had fallen in love with the island. He was enchanted by the Castillos' old house on Acacias Avenue, which also had silver-plated balconies and a carriage house with a wrought-iron gate with the initial C at the top. It must have been more than a hundred years old.

The Kerenskis had come to Ponce during carnival week. One afternoon they were sitting on the balcony which opened onto Acacias Avenue when the carnival parade went by. André was amazed by what he saw. The revelers were a fountain of energy: they danced up and down the street as far as the eye could see, their costumes a sea of colors. There were snake charmers, flamenco dancers, battling angels, and dozens of *Vegigantes* of all sizes and hues. They had absolutely no inhibitions, shimmying, quivering, and rippling, as if they wanted to get rid of the flesh on their bones and fly away like spirits. They spun on their toes and swiveled their hips, as if possessed by demons. Professor Kerenski couldn't believe his eyes. "This town is full of natural-born ballet dancers," he said to Tamara. "A ballet school would be a great thing here. With a little training, one day they'll have their own Anna Pavlova and Vaslav Nijinsky to boast of. I think we should move to Ponce."

At first, Tamara didn't even want to consider it. She had been a disciple of Mordkin, the great dancer in Sergei Diaghilev's company in Paris, and her career was on an upturn. She was about to be named to one of the principal ballet roles in the Metropolitan Opera Ballet's performance of Adam's *Giselle*, and she was looking forward to it with great excitement. André didn't have as much to lose as she did, but he had always wanted to be a ballet teacher more than a dancer and moving to Ponce was his opportunity to do something for the common people. Tamara thought it over for a few weeks; she was in love with her husband and finally consented.

Tamara informed her family of their decision, and they moved to the island soon afterwards. Her parents were not as well off as they used to be; the value of municipal bonds had plunged after the Second World War, and the Castillos had begun to feel the pinch, so the house on Acacias Avenue was not kept in good repair. When André and Tamara seemed so enamored of it, however, Tamara's father presented it to them as a wedding gift, and her parents moved to a small modern apartment. Tamara's mother gave her her diamond earrings to wear at the social events she would now be attending in Ponce, and Tamara pawned them and used the money to fix the leaky roof, paint the walls, and scrape and polish the floors of the old house.

The romantic, turn-of-the-century atmosphere of the place was perfect for a ballet studio. It had arches over the doors, carved to look like filigree fans, and a fine burlwood floor. Professor Kerenski had the interior walls torn down and the whole house became a sixty-foot-long ballet studio. A wooden barre was screwed to the wall on the right and a mirror to the wall on the left, and there students "could learn to interpret the soul through the outline of the body," as André used to say.

Soon the first full-page ad for the school came out in the local newspaper: "Ballet training for beginners and amateurs, with special attention to children." André wanted to have some pupils from the slums, to teach them free of charge, and Tamara agreed to it. But when Tamara's friends saw the advertisement, they flocked to the Castillos' old mansion with their daughters, leaving no room for the poor children.

The first two years of the school were prosperous. André and Tamara had as many students as they could handle—there were at least fifty at the school at one time, girls between eight and sixteen—and they were making more money than they had ever dreamed of. But André wasn't completely happy with the way things were going. He didn't like the fact that the school had only girls. His yearly production at La Perla Theater, for example, had to be put on stage without boys. In *Peter and the Wolf* the role of Peter had to be danced by a girl, and that was not satisfactory. Kerenski himself had to dance the part of the Wolf, because no girl could ever dance *that* part convincingly.

One day he called a meeting at the school and asked all the students' mothers to attend. He told them about the ballet schools in St. Petersburg and in Monte Carlo, where male dancers often became prodigies. Ballet could open the doors to the world of art and fame. Why didn't they bring their sons to his school, too? The mothers listened to him politely, fanning themselves and winking at each other as if what he was saying was terribly funny. Kerenski asked them why they were laughing. Hortensia Hernández, a buxom lady wearing a gold charm bracelet, who had two daughters at the school, finally put up her hand. "Ballet is a risky career for boys," she said, giggling. "It encourages effeminate behavior and they can end up being fairies." André was horrified, but there was little he could do to change their minds. No boys were ever brought to the Kerenski Ballet School on Acacias Avenue.

After I joined the school, I had to go through four years of rigorous training before I could dance in Kerenski's production at La Perla Theater. In Ponce, girls my age were treated like hothouse flowers. They ate quantities of cream puffs, cakes, and all kinds of desserts and had no idea what discipline of the body meant. The first thing Professor Kerenski did was put us on a diet. Fritters, *tostones*, and rice and beans were strictly forbidden. For two years he spoke to us only in French and made us learn by heart all the names of the steps we had to perform in class. During the day we walked down the street doing developpés, arabesques, and coupés, and at night we went to sleep murmuring the names of the steps under our breath like a prayer.

At the studio we practiced for hours on end, our slippers whirling over the floorboards like silk drills. We struggled to learn to balance our bodies and govern our minds, "to do a pirouette on your toes, and end it poised on a dime," as Professor Kerenski would say. The heat in Ponce was stifling all year round; as we practiced, we perspired like legionnaires, but we bore our sufferings with a smile.

The Kerenskis' school was divided into two sections. There were the run-of-the-mill students, who were in Tamara's charge, and whose mothers had enrolled them to lose weight and learn to behave gracefully in public. They were not expected to amount to anything, but they made up the greater part of the academy, and their monthly dues kept the studio afloat. Then there were the serious students, who were under Professor Kerenski's personal care.

Professor Kerenski lived for ballet; he saw it as the expression of the soul's most profound emotions. He was as romantic as he was Russian. He did not believe in Balanchine's theory that the dancer should be as unemotional and impassive as a metronome and must simply follow the rhythm dictated by the music. "If you let the music flood you when you dance," André used to say to us, "one day you'll attain enlightenment." He was the perfect maître de ballet. He established three levels in his classes—A, B, and C—and when a student reached the last level, it meant she was ready to be a star. That year she would dance a solo in the school's production at La Perla Theater.

I was one of those fledgling swans, trained and groomed by Professor Kerenski himself, and my life began to revolve completely around ballet. The Ponce Lyceum, where I went to school, was two blocks from the studio, so it took me five minutes to walk there after class. When I arrived, I was already wearing my black leotard, which I had pulled on in the bathroom at school. I worked out until six, when Abby sent Abuela Gabriela's chauffeur to pick me up in our blue Pontiac. When I arrived home, I took a bath, had dinner, and did my homework. By nine I was so tired I went right to bed. I hardly spoke to anyone at home except Abby, but no one seemed to mind.

Professor Kerenski was very conscious of what he wore. I think he wanted to impress on us the fact that he was Russian, so we would appreciate his skills all the more. He always wore a red silk jacket and black pants. The jacket had a mandarin collar and had a sash tied at the waist. His hair was dark blond, and he wore it carefully combed about his ears like the dome of a small basilica. His Russian good looks dazzled the students—especially the new ones—but he never took advantage of it. He was very serious about his art and kept his distance. When he gave a class, he stood before the mirror, baton in hand, keeping the rhythm as he tapped on the floor, and he never ventured too close to the girls. Whenever he performed one of the sequences from *Le Corsair* or from *L'Après-midi d'un faune*, for example, we would all sit in awe on the floor watching him, hardly daring to breathe.

Tamara was still a beautiful woman, but lately she had gained weight. She always wore a black leotard, with a long gauze skirt covering her generous hips. Sometimes she danced by herself in the early afternoon, before any of her students arrived at the studio. I got there earlier than most, and I used to love watching her; the minute she started to move, you forgot she was overweight because she was so graceful. Professor Kerenski never danced with any of the students. He always danced solo in front of the class when he wanted to show us how to do a new step.

Tamara didn't have anything to do with the advanced classes; she taught only beginner and intermediate classes. She had to teach the nine- and ten-year-olds to stand correctly, shoulders down and fanny tucked in, and train the twelve- and thirteen-year-olds to walk elegantly down the aisle, preparing them for the debutante pageant which took place at the Ponce Country Club every summer.

One day I was resting in the Kerenskis' living room and I saw Tamara come out of the bathroom after a bath (the Kerenskis had restored the carriage house next to the studio as their private apartment; it had a living room, a bedroom, a bath, and a modern kitchenette). She was naked and I was surprised to see how beautiful she was. She reminded me of Ingres's *Odalisque*—a reproduction of it hung in the living room of our home on Aurora Street. She had her back to me, so she didn't see me, but when she stood before the mirror I thought she looked sad. She often had that same expression in class, as if she wanted to get away from everything. I thought maybe she was bored with her job, and I couldn't blame her.

Professor Kerenski was more enthusiastic than ever. Sometimes he would take off his red silk jacket and show us how to dance a particularly difficult sequence, in his black pants and T-shirt. It was then that we noticed his chest was covered with a red nap, very different in color from the blond page boy he groomed with such care. What was even more curious was a faint odor of crushed geraniums that came from his armpits whenever he lifted his arms to show us a new step.

I had a good friend at the ballet school, Estefanía Volmer, the daughter of the owner of El Cometa, Ponce's largest hardware store. Don Arturo Volmer was from a family of modest means, but he had married Margot Rinser, whose father was the founder of the largest rum distillery in Ponce. Her father had given them El Cometa as a wedding present, and Arturo had done everything he could to make it an ongoing concern, but he had had little luck. He wasn't a good businessman; he made little money selling "tinker toys," as he used to say—just enough to break even—and Margot still had to ask her father for the niceties she was used to.

Margot had been a great beauty, but she had developed bone cancer in her right leg a few years after her marriage, and the leg had to be amputated. Don Arturo never got over his wife's tragedy. He lived only to care for Margot; he took her everywhere, pushing the wheelchair himself, and wouldn't let a nurse near. He was so obsessed with his wife's tragedy he hardly remembered Estefanía existed.

Margot herself never gave Estefanía a second thought: when she got pregnant, she was already in a wheelchair. Margot had been an only daughter and was used to being the center of attention at home, even more so when she became seriously ill. Whenever she saw Estefanía walk into her room, she was always a little surprised, as if she had forgotten she had a daughter.

Estefanía had been brought up by nursemaids, with very little supervision. She was much more of a rebel than I. She had Coca-Cola and devil's food cake for breakfast—she wouldn't be caught dead eating the soggy porridge with bananas Abby made for me every morning. When she turned fourteen, she refused to put on any underwear and went around with her breasts swimming under her blouse like jellyfish. At fifteen she began to go to parties by herself. She never had a chaperone, and she was the only girl I knew in Ponce who went to the movies alone on a date. I admired her for it; the whole town talked about Estefanía, but she went on doing what she damn well wanted to. She was a beautiful girl, with milk-white skin, a long swan's neck, and red curly hair that reminded you of a burning bush when she stood under the noonday sun.

Estefanía was two years older than I. I had met her at the Lyceum, where we were both on the volleyball team. She was not a good student; she liked people better than books. But she enjoyed taking care of the younger children at recess time. She would organize games for them and play as if she were a child herself. She had a gay disposition and was always laughing and kidding, as if life were an ongoing party. She liked to dress to shock people, and sometimes we both did, as jarringly as possible—polka-dot pedal pushers with Hawaiian-style see-through blouses, for example—just to see people stare at us. Yet the reason I liked her was that I knew she was unhappy.

I remember that when Estefanía turned sixteen, her father gave her a red Ford convertible as a birthday present, a senseless gift. But her parents had no sense at all, so it didn't surprise me when I saw Estefanía drive up to school in it. Since her family lived near the rum distillery on the outskirts of town, she said, they gave her the car so they could get rid of the chauffeur, who was always drunk. Now she could go everywhere on her own at night, to the drive-in theater, even out to The Place, Ponce's cabaret by the sea, where she danced with the American sailors she met at the bar. But I know she never did anything she shouldn't have with them.

I was enchanted when Estefanía decided to enroll in the ballet school. She soon became an admirer of Professor Kerenski, and after that we shared all our secrets. We weren't in love with him; we didn't care at all about his good looks. We worshipped him for his excellence as a dancer, for the extraordinary ease with which he soared into the air and did eight entrechats in the *Don Quixote* suite, for example, or for the forty fouettés he completed during the Prince's solo in *Swan Lake*.

André was like a god to us; he ruled our lives in every way. He told us how many calories we could eat a day, what kind of shoes to wear to prevent bunions, and how to comb our hair so it wouldn't fly into our eyes when we danced. Most important, he forbade both of us to have steady boyfriends, because, he said, we had become his "spiritual" partners.

Our personalities changed as well. We turned meek and obedient, lost weight and looked more fragile every day. It was as if we had lost the desire to live our own lives. At home, our parents couldn't believe their eyes. Abby was particularly worried. She was used to sparring with me, and she couldn't figure out what was happening. She would come into my room to say good night and see me lying on the bed with a whimsical expression on my face, dreaming I was Giselle and had swooned on my tomb. Abby couldn't get over it. I never complained about anything; I did everything I was told, without answering back. When I did something wrong, I hung my head and humbly accepted her rebuke; it was almost as if I were a different person. She didn't guess I wasn't really there. I was simply waiting for my chance to escape from the house and run back to Professor Kerenski. "The minute you start getting bad grades at school, I'll punch that carrot-headed Petrouchka on the nose and take you out of the ballet school myself!" she told me one day. "You'd be much better off playing the piano for the poor children of the slums of Ponce at the charity bazaar next month." "Don't worry, Abby," I said. "I'll burn the midnight oil studying, just to please you."

It was 1946, and it was our turn to dance at La Perla Theater. When Professor Kerenski picked Estefanía for one of the solos in *Swan Lake*, I was genuinely surprised, but I didn't complain. It had taken me four years to reach C level and I had worked like a slave to get there. Estefanía, on the other hand, had been in our school only six months, and she had been selected for the part. When we found out that Professor Kerenski had chosen us to dance Odette and Odile from among a dozen advanced students, we squealed with delight and hugged each other. But things were never quite the same after that. Estefanía was a good dancer, but she was never better than me.

I simply couldn't understand it. For months I had been the star dancer at school; no one could hold an arabesque at almost a ninety-degree angle as I did; no one could whirl ten chaînés at an almost disappearing speed. The minute Professor Kerenski saw Estefanía, however, he had been partial to her. He was always using her as an example: when the students dragged their feet and couldn't get their grands jetés off the ground, he would make her walk to the front of the class and have her show everybody how to "soar into the air like a swan." I think it had to do with the fact that her hair was geranium-red and that she reminded him of his mother, the Russian princess.

17

The Firebird

※

ONE DAY I WAS EARLY TO CLASS and I heard Tamara and André arguing loudly behind the studio's closed door. André insisted that he wanted to dance the pas de deux of the Prince in *Swan Lake* with one of his advanced students. He was tired of teaching the girls to dance by themselves, he said: the crown of every ballet was always the adagio—the lovers' duet—and Tamara couldn't dance it with him because she was too fat. No ballet master of any reputation would ever put a performance onstage with female students only; it was even more shameful for a disciple of Balanchine. Tamara sighed and said it couldn't be; if he danced onstage with any one of the well-brought-up girls from Ponce, it would create such a scandal that all the fathers would come to the studio the next day and take their daughters away.

Professor Kerenski was furious, but he soon found a solution to the problem. If he couldn't dance the adagio with one of his advanced students, he would find someone who could. He visited the slum of Machuelo Abajo and interviewed several teenage boys from poor families. A few of them were on the neighborhood basketball team. He had them run two miles and jump the high bar to test their stamina and physical condition. He finally chose Tony Torres, a fifteen-year-old mulatto with finely chiseled features.

"Please drop by the Kerenski Ballet School in the morning," he said to him. "We're going to put on our new production at La Perla Theater, and I need a helping hand onstage."

Tony was a handsome young man. He had curly hair, and skin as smooth as bronze. He reminded me of one of those statues of Greek youths that turn up once in a while at the bottom of the Aegean Sea. Professor Kerenski didn't choose him for his good looks, however. He was the only young man among the athletic boys he interviewed that day who admitted to being gay. "He's the perfect partner for girls from good families," he said to Tamara, unable to keep an ironic tinge from his voice. "He can dance the Prince in *Swan Lake* and won't pose a threat to any of them. The fathers of our well-to-do students will be able to sleep in peace."

Professor Kerenski trained Tony Torres for several weeks before teaching him the role of the Prince. What Tony had to do was relatively simple. Professor Kerenski had pared down the part so Tony could learn it quickly, but I suspect he resented having to do it. He imagined what his artist friends who came to visit him periodically from New York would say: "André couldn't dance the part himself because, in that two-bit town where he lives, even Balanchine would be considered a pansy. He had to train one of the locals to substitute for him." It was all so silly he couldn't help being bitter about it.

"In classical ballet, the ballerina's partner is really nothing more than a mannequin," Kerenski said to Tony on his first day of coaching. "Your main role will be to put your hands around Odile's waist and lift her up as if she were a feather. Please don't grab her by the hips, or turn her around as if she were a roasting chicken." One day he told Tony not to shave the scant beard that grew on his chin: he had decided to add Stravinsky's *Firebird* to the program, and Tony would dance the main role as well. For that, he had to appear as virile as possible.

Tony was very sensitive, and at first he was hurt by Professor Kerenski's comments. He decided not to give them any importance, however, because dancing at La Perla Theater was a great opportunity for him. He hoped to be able to continue as a regular student at the Kerenski Ballet School once the recital was over. He was even willing to help out as a janitor if necessary, as long as he could continue taking classes. He meant to go to New York one day; he dreamed of dancing in a Broadway chorus or at a first-rate cabaret. When his family found out he would be dancing the two main roles in the ballet school's recital that year, they were ecstatic and gave him their full support. The young people in Machuelo Abajo saw him as a hero; it was the first time anyone from the slums had ever danced at La Perla or taken part in any of its elegant cultural events. When posters advertising the performance, with Tony's picture, appeared all over town—affixed to the telephone poles and to the walls of buildings and to fences— the people of Machuelo Abajo took them down, framed them, and hung them in their living rooms.

One afternoon Abby came to the ballet school to see me in class. Professor Kerenski went up to her and said I had possibilities; there was a chance I could become a serious dancer. He suggested that, once I finished high school, my parents not send me to the university right away but let me study ballet with him for a year or two. I should take my time before I made up my mind about what to do with my life. He was even willing to recommend me to the School of American Ballet in New York, where he had many friends. When I heard what he said, my heart skipped a beat. I was ready to do anything to become a first-class ballerina.

When we returned home, Abby began to rail against Professor Kerenski. "If you postpone your entrance to the university, it'll be over my dead body," she said. "I didn't sacrifice my whole life baking custards and cakes just so you'd end up dancing cancan soufflés in Radio City," she went on. I wasn't surprised at her outburst. But I was in my fourth year at the Lyceum and I could be as headstrong as Abby. I knew she couldn't force me to enter the university once I graduated from high school—not if I didn't want to.

Classes were over for the summer and now we could practice every day at the studio; the rehearsals were going well. Professor Kerenski was obsessed with the choreography, which he was doing himself. We wouldn't be dancing a complete ballet. This was impossible, not only because they were too long, but because we didn't have enough dancers to take the principal roles. We would interpret segments of works in an original Kerenski version. André spent hours listening to the music and thinking about the dances. "Choreography is the toughest trial a dancer must face," he would say. "The steps must come from the soul if they are to achieve the stature of art."

Soon we all went to the dressmaker who would make our costumes—a fat lady who lived on Victoria Street—and she took our measurements. Professor Kerenski supervised every detail; he was afraid the rhinestone crowns, the wired sequined wings, and the muslin petticoats which were so popular with Ponceños, who loved to wear elaborate costumes at every opportunity, might inhibit the dancers and make their movements stiff or awkward. He made it clear that the tutus of the girls in the corps de ballet in *Swan Lake* were to be exactly the same; otherwise, the mothers of the girls would start to compete, insisting that their little girl should have "the most ethereal wings" or "the most bouffant skirt," and this would spoil the uniformity of the line.

Professor Kerenski had assigned the role of Odile, the white swan, to Estefanía, and I was to dance Odette, the black swan; we'd wear tutus made from real feathers. This decision created a conflict: feathers were expensive, and our parents didn't want to spend a lot on our costumes. It took a lot of convincing to make them come around. Estefanía and I would both wear silk masks, delicate ovals with slits for the eyes. The most spectacular costume of all, however, would be worn by Tony in *Firebird*. Professor Kerenski had designed it himself. It was to be in the style of Marc Chagall, who had sketched the costumes for Stravinsky's ballet at the Metropolitan Opera House. It had a gilded bodice with a flame-colored feathered cape and a mask with a golden beak which completely covered the face. Tony's friends from Machuelo Abajo had all chipped in to pay for it.

The first half of the evening would consist of five scenes from *Swan Lake*. Estefanía and I would each dance a solo in the first scene; the second one was to be a duet; in the third and fourth scene each one of us would dance with Tony; and the last would be a trio. The corps de ballet would be made up of beginners and was entirely Tamara's responsibility. Every single student in the school would take part, to keep the mothers happy. The second half of the evening would be taken up by *Firebird*, in which Estefanía, Tony, and I would dance again. Professor Kerenski gave me the role of Prince Ivan, and Tony the role of the Firebird. Estefanía was to be the captive princess who is saved at the last moment by the Firebird in the adagio.

Tony was no mere prop; he proved to be a natural dancer. He was as agile as a deer and had the stamina of a basketball player. In his entrechats he soared almost four feet off the ground, higher than Kerenski ever did; and every time he made a grand jeté he seemed about to take off over our heads like a bird. He had an ingrained elegance and would hold us delicately by the waist, so that Estefanía and I had no trouble performing our arabesques and pirouettes. Professor Kerenski was pleasantly surprised, so he choreographed a more complicated interpretation of the *Firebird* than he had initially planned. Two weeks before the performance, when we began to rehearse at La Perla Theater, Tony's friends from Machuelo Abajo would come to see him dance every afternoon. Each time he did a difficult step, they cheered and applauded as if it were a basketball match and he had put the ball through the hoop. In spite of Tony's success, Estefanía and I would have preferred to dance with Professor Kerenski, and we couldn't help feeling let down about it.

When a new advanced student enrolled at the school, Kerenski studied her personality to see which side to bring out when he assigned her the part she would dance at the recital. Estefanía was, in his opinion, a jarreté dancer: she had a lyrical, sensuous way of moving. With her red hair and milk-white skin, she was perfect for the romantic role in the adagio, when the ballerina is supposed to melt like a snowflake in the arms of her partner. I was an arqué dancer, brilliant and rhythmic, more suited to energetic solos and Mediterranean allegros con fuoco. Raven-haired and olive-skinned, I danced with so much energy Professor Kerenski was impressed. "I like your fiery spirit, your sense of independence on the stage," he once told me. "I hope you never lose your style, because it's what makes you so special." He didn't know that when I danced I wasn't expressing any particular style. I was just trying to forget my troubles at home.

The last month before the performance, Professor Kerenski spent hours rehearsing *Firebird* with us. He had created something very special, and we were euphoric that he should have invested so much time in us. After the recital, the new choreography would always be associated with our names. We thought it was his way of making us the keepers of his legacy. Stravinsky's music was like a typhoon. It pulled us in its wake as it rushed us toward the unknown. The mystery of nature seemed to throb in its sway.

Estefanía was often late for rehearsals, so Professor Kerenski, Tony, and I usually began without her. When she finally got to the studio, Tony and I had already practiced the main scenes, so we left early. Abby was after me not to be late for dinner, and Tony had to take care of his mother, who was in a wheelchair, until his father came home from work. Estefanía would stay on with Professor Kerenski, and they always practiced late. He would rehearse Tony's part in *Firebird* with her, teaching her all the secrets of the adagio.

The night of the recital, the entire school came out of the studio at seven o'clock and walked down Aurora Street. No one in Ponce was surprised to see us in our black leotards and pink practice slippers walking single-file down the street, carrying our tutus in hangers before us so they wouldn't get wrinkled. Ponce is a city that loves spectacles, and people wouldn't miss them for anything. That's why houses there are like small theaters, with wide balconies opening onto the street. In the early evening, people sit chatting and gossiping, and as we went by that evening they waved and said they'd see us at the performance, which would begin at eight o'clock.

Professor Kerenski couldn't pay for a live orchestra, so the recital was performed to recorded music. Tamara operated the record player herself from the empty orchestra pit, and the music came out of two large speakers directed toward the audience. That week, tickets were sold by the hundreds. All the well-known families in town had at least one student at the ballet school, so everybody who was anybody was coming to the recital. Professor Kerenski, in keeping with his ideals of social justice, had also distributed a good many free tickets among the people of Machuelo Abajo, so Tony's friends and relatives could come and see him dance.

By a quarter to eight, La Perla Theater was packed; and everyone was dressed in formal evening wear. The relatives of the well-to-do students, in shimmering gowns and tuxedos, sat on the right side of the theater, where windows were left open and a cool evening breeze came in. Tony's relatives and friends sat on the left, where seats were cheaper because there were no windows, which made it hot. But they didn't seem to mind. Tony's friends were smiling, pointing this way and that to the lighted Murano chandelier—a gift from the Italian government when Adelina Patti came to sing in Ponce, accompanied by Louis Gottschalk, almost a hundred years before—or to the fresco of the Seven Muses, all dressed in pastel togas and wearing green laurel wreaths on their heads. Conspicuous among them was Terpsichore, the nymph of dance.

The first half of the show was as smooth as silk, without any problems. Estefanía and I danced Odette and Odile as if dancing on air, aided by our black-and-white feathered tutus. Tony was matchless as Prince Siegfried, outfitted in a magnificent blue silk jacket with gold buttons that his family had also paid for with contributions from his neighbors. The corps of beginners, aware that Tamara was close by in the orchestra pit and was keeping an eye on them, behaved very well and danced with perfect synchronicity. The audience was delighted, and at the end of the first act there was an explosion of applause.

The second act began with a mishap. The sets for *Firebird* were more complicated than those for *Swan Lake*. Professor Kerenski had wanted to use Chagall motifs for the backdrop and had superimposed two images one on top of the other: a quiet forest would be set on fire—the trees would erupt in a blaze of light—to create a feeling of vertigo. On the stage's outer edge, an inferno of red chiffon was illuminated by footlights. It fluttered in the wind, blowing this way and that, thanks to two large fans hidden behind the stage. The music started and Estefanía began her solo. She was supposed to jump over a barrier of flames, but her right shoe got caught in a red chiffon strip and she lost her balance and fell headlong to the floor. Tamara had to stop the record player, the curtain came down, and it wasn't until fifteen minutes later that the show resumed. Fortunately, Estefanía didn't injure herself seriously—just suffered a bruised elbow.

Professor Kerenski couldn't be found anywhere. When Estefanía stumbled, everyone seemed to be calling for him, but it was as if he had vanished into thin air. Tamara had to come from the orchestra pit to handle the emergency. The music started up, and once more we responded to Stravinsky's merciless onslaught. It was like dancing at the very tip of a flame. Estefanía performed her solo without further mishaps, and I confidently danced my own part. Then we both waited, holding our magic feathers in our hands, for the arrival of the Firebird.

I closed my eyes and remembered Professor Kerenski's words: "If you let the music flood you when you dance, one day you'll attain enlightenment." Slowly I let myself be drawn by the throbbing sounds; the music flowed around me like honey, like milk, like a swarm of bees. Stravinsky's hurricane enveloped me, as it did in the studio during rehearsal. When I opened my eyes, the Firebird was emerging from a forest of flames, dancing toward us. With every step he took, he defied the force of gravity, so high in the air did he soar. His costume was magnificent: his legs were sheathed in gold and looked like columns of fire; his arms were wings dipped in blood; his golden mask was the mask of life and of death. But what impressed me the most was the enormous spiral shell which lay curled between his legs.

First came the piece "Burning with Thirst," which the Firebird danced with me; then Tamara played "Unending Hunger" on the gramophone, and the Firebird turned to Estefanía. During the next fifteen minutes I performed a series of glissés alongside the Firebird. Then I did a set of pirouettes, ending in an elegant pasé, as we had rehearsed at the studio. It all went very well; it was clean and controlled dancing, the kind of performance Professor Kerenski expected of Tony and me. It wasn't until the last pasé, when the Firebird had to clasp me tightly around the waist to lift me up on his right shoulder, that I noticed the scent of crushed geraniums that came from his armpits. It was impossible to turn to look at his face; the mask hid it completely behind its shield of gold.

When I finished my part, there was a short burst of applause. I did a grand jeté and exited toward the side. I didn't go backstage, however. My throat was tight with anxiety as I watched the stage from the wings. Estefanía, totally ignorant of the Firebird's true identity, began the adagio with passionate brio. She was in top form, dancing with masterful ease; she looked happy and relaxed in the Firebird's arms. We were all supposed to know the choreography of the other dancers by heart, so that in case of emergency we could serve as understudies, and it didn't take me long to realize that the sequence Estefanía was dancing was something totally new. I had never seen it before. It was much more complicated choreography than anything we had rehearsed at the studio. More than classical ballet, it looked like a mating dance, a splendid rendition of the attraction the female wields over the male.

Estefanía and the Firebird were one with the music; it filled them completely. Estefanía wove her snow-white arms around the Firebird's neck, and his flame-red cape spilled over her shoulders and enveloped her in its blaze. When they finished dancing, I was on the verge of fainting, and the theater seemed about to collapse from the thunderous applause. I lost track of how many times the red velvet curtain rose and fell as Estefanía and the Firebird took their encores. They had completely forgotten about me. No one asked me to share in the standing ovation, so spectacular was the last duo.

Yet I had earned my place in the limelight, so I walked boldly out onstage. I took a quick bow standing next to Estefanía and the Firebird, but I could see it wasn't me the audience was applauding. I blushed, took another bow, and exited immediately. Estefanía and the Firebird took three more curtain calls, and finally the curtain came down for the last time and the stage went dark. But some people went on clapping. Suddenly a long whistle rose from the left side of the orchestra, where Tony's friends and relatives were seated, and the theater went silent.

"God bless our great Tony Torres," someone cried out. "Today he's brought great honor to Machuelo Abajo!"

At that moment an invisible hand pulled a lever backstage and the floodlights came up again; the curtain rose. Estefanía and the Firebird were still standing in the middle of the stage. Only the Firebird had taken off his mask and Professor Kerenski was kissing Estefanía on the mouth; he was kissing her and she was letting him kiss her, as if there was nothing she could do to prevent it. The audience, which had begun to file out of the theater, stopped in its tracks and stared at the couple onstage. At least ten seconds must have gone by while Estefanía and Professor Kerenski stood there kissing, deaf to the booing, whistling, and stomping which soon reached a crescendo as people began to turn back—especially Tony Torres's friends, who were furious, crying out that *The Fire-bird* had been a sham, that Kerenski had deceived them, that the ballet had been a cruel impersonation: Tony had never been given a chance to dance the second act.

His friends crowded together at the foot of the stage and began to throw shoes at Professor Kerenski, handbags, umbrellas, cigarette cases, whatever they could find in their handbags, yelling that he was a cheat and a liar, that he had led everyone to believe he was giving Tony Torres the star role when he had planned to take his place from the start. But it was as though Kerenski and Estefanía couldn't hear them; they went on kissing in front of everyone, the floodlights pinning them down like insects, wrapped in the blazing feathers of the Firebird's cape.

After the recital Abby walked me home without saying a word. Neither Mother nor Father had come to the theater to see me dance, and it was just as well. When we got home, I locked myself up in my room, but Abby came and knocked at my door. She brought me a glass of milk and a piece of pound cake she had just baked and put it on my night table. "Now you can eat everything you want," she said. "You won't starve yourself to death because of that preying vulture. Thank God you weren't the one to fall into his arms tonight, because right now I'd be in jail for smashing my umbrella over Kerenski's head. That's what I felt like doing when I saw poor Estefanía Volmer in her white-feather dress, helpless as a dove in his clutches." I couldn't say a word. I simply put my head on her shoulder and cried.

I never went back to the Kerenski Ballet School or saw André again. He was accused of child molestation by several students at the school and had to leave the island soon after. Estefanía's parents sent her to live with an aunt in Worcester, Massachusetts, until the whole thing blew over. When she returned to Ponce some years later, she was married to a yoga grand master, and they opened the first Sri Pritam Academy in town. She was as reckless and happy-go-lucky as ever. She used to bathe naked at the public beach with her husband and meditate in the lotus position as the sun went down. Once the police put them both in jail for indecent exposure, but being a Rinser Volmer, Estefanía didn't stay there very long. Tamara kept the ballet school going by herself, and in time she managed to establish a solid tradition of classical ballet in Ponce. Several of her pupils have gone on to be internationally known stars, and today she is worshipped as their beloved ballet teacher. Tony Torres, on the other hand, vanished from sight. He never went back to Machuelo Abajo, and no one ever heard of him again.

18

Vassar College

❧

AFTER THE KERENSKI EPISODE Abby and I became very close.
At least twice a week I went with her to the Silver Spoon, one of
the slums of Ponce, where she taught children to read and write,
and taught them skills like sewing and cooking as well. One day
she wrote to the president of a new Kodak plant that had just
opened in Ponce, asking him to donate twenty Polaroid cameras
for the children of the poorer neighborhoods. He replied that he
was sorry he couldn't accommodate her: he couldn't donate his
competitors' cameras. But he was sending her twenty Brownie
cameras as a gift, with fifty cartridges of Kodak film.

Abby thought teaching slum children to take pictures of their
surroundings might be useful. She had them take photos of trash
cans with hungry cats perched on top. The garbage, of course,
was ugly, but the cats were beautiful, because they were so alive.
The children might also photograph stray dogs. The Silver Spoon
was full of them; all one had to do was go to the butcher and get
a few large beef bones, and soon a dozen dogs would be milling
around. Abby thought all mongrels were special. She had three
of them at our house in Ponce, named Fly, Flea, and Tick. They
were brown, yellow, and white, respectively, with muzzles black
as tar and scruffy coats. Abby insisted they were more intelligent

than purebreds and also more grateful, because they knew you
had saved them from the dogcatcher and they owed you their lives.

Life could be transcendent even in the most squalid surroundings, and the contrast of the children's smiling faces with the
abject poverty around them was excellent artistic material. Abby
sent the children to take pictures of Ponce's huge municipal sewers, which emptied near the Silver Spoon, and had them pose
inside the cement cylinders, as if they were playing at an amusement park. When they finished their photographic excursions,
Abby picked out the best shots and showed the kids how to crop
the pictures at a photography lab. Then she sent the pictures to
a photo contest in the States which she had seen advertised in *The
New York Times*, and the Silver Spoon children won first prize.
Several of those children went on to become professional photog-
raphers, founding the first school of photography in Ponce.

FOUR YEARS AFTER the Kerenski episode, in 1950, I graduated
from the Ponce Lyceum. I had been accepted at Vassar College,
and Abby had promised to send me there so I wouldn't brood about
my failed dreams of becoming a dancer.

One evening, a few weeks before I was to go away to college,
Abby and I sat in our living room poring over the Sears catalogue.
I had picked out a handsome green trunk studded with brass nails,
six pairs of shoes, three sweater sets, two wool skirts, a camel's-
hair coat, a pair of black rubber galoshes, and an oilcloth rain-
coat—and had written it all down on the pink order form at the
back of the book. Stores at home didn't carry any of these items,
but thanks to the Sears catalogue we now had access to them, and
a lot more besides. During the forties and fifties, Sears had no
stores on our island. Sears wasn't a place, it was a state of mind;
ordering from the Sears catalogue was like ordering from heaven.

There was a Sears catalogue in every middle-class home in
Ponce at that time. Like most families on the island, ours was
divided politically. Carmita and Carlos were for statehood, whereas

Abby was defiantly Independentista. But we all liked to browse through the Sears catalogue. Having it at hand was reassuring—proof that Puerto Rico was an inseparable part of the United States. We weren't like Haiti or the Dominican Republic, where people still hadn't heard of the telephone and kept food fresh in wooden crates with blocks of ice instead of in General Electric refrigerators. Thanks to the Sears catalogue we had the same access as the people of Kansas and Louisiana to the latest inventions and home appliances, and we could import them from the States without paying taxes. The cardboard boxes and crates came by ship from "*el Norte*" and took months to get to the island, but when you opened them up, you felt the invigorating cool of the United States trapped inside like a breath of fresh air against your face.

Our family's Sears catalogue was always on the living-room table, and we used to thumb through it and dream of the wonderful things we'd never seen. When I was a child, I once ordered a beautiful Madame Alexander doll for Christmas. There were no Madame Alexander dolls in Ponce; dolls were made of ordinary plastic or stuffed with cotton, with clumsy paste hands and feet. My Madame Alexander doll had a delicately veneered face, real teeth, and soft brown hair. She came in a brown cardboard trunk with a complete travel wardrobe, exactly like the trunk Abby ordered for me when I was about to leave for college many years later.

Carmita purchased the latest Philips electric oven, Kelvinator clothes washer, and Electrolux vacuum cleaner from the Sears catalogue. Carlos enjoyed looking at the General Electric steel drills and automatic handsaws, and also at a special toolbox which came with all kinds of complicated contrivances for carving furniture. Even Abby liked to sit for hours with the catalogue on her lap. The section she liked best was gardening. She would read about the new revolving lawn sprinklers from Delaware, the pine-bark bird feeders from Maine, the redwood furniture from California, the golden zinnias, flame-red dahlias, and blue morning-glories from Arizona, which would never grow in the tropics but which Abby planted anyway, because she believed in the brightly colored flowers on the outside of the paper envelopes full of seeds. Looking through the Sears catalogue, Abby was tempted more than once to renounce her Independentista ideals, and vote for statehood, just like Carmita and Carlos. But she didn't.

I felt a great deal of sympathy for independence in my youth, perhaps because I was so close to Abby. When I saw how contradictory Abby's point of view was, however, I didn't know what to believe. She wanted the island to become independent for moral reasons, and in this I agreed with her wholeheartedly. She felt Puerto Rico was a different country from the United States, and that asking to be admitted to the Union as a state wouldn't be fair to the U.S., or in the long run to us. In a way, it would be like deceiving the American people, who had treated us well. But Abby also put great store in progress, and cherished her American passport as if it were a jewel.

In Puerto Rico we're all passionate about politics. We have three parties and three colors we identify with: Statehood and the New Progressive Party are blue, Commonwealth and the Popular Party are red, and Independence is green. Politics is like religion; you are either for Statehood or for Independence, you can't be for both. Someone has to be saved, someone must burn in hell, and if you're for Commonwealth you're floating in limbo. People become so fanatical at election time that they are capable of doing away with their opponents for the silliest of reasons. During the last election campaign, for example, an Independentista in a Barrio Canas basketball game was found with a flagpole buried in his back, an American flag still attached to it, because he didn't take his cap off when they played *La Borinqueña*, the Puerto Rican national anthem. I hate violence—I'm not a violent person at all, and this kind of thing horrifies me. That's why I like to think of myself as apolitical, and when election time comes around, I don't like to take a stand. Maybe my indecision is rooted in the Sears catalogue; it goes back to the times I sat as a child in the living room of our house in Ponce with the catalogue on my lap, wishing for independence and at the same time dreaming about our island being part of the modern world.

Many people believe that commonwealth is transitory. It's probably the most convenient status for us, but it can't last forever. People want to have a clear idea of who they are; they like to see things in black-and-white, signed and sealed at the bottom. The purpose of a commonwealth is precisely to preserve the possibility of change. It's the most flexible and intelligent political solution for us, but it makes others feel insecure, in danger of losing themselves. That's why one day we'll have to choose between statehood and independence.

The way I see it, our island is like a betrothed, always on the verge of marriage. If one day Puerto Rico becomes a state, it will have to accept English—the language of her future husband—as its official language, not just because it's the language of modernity and of progress but also because it's the language of authority. If the island decides to remain single, on the other hand, it will probably mean backwardness and poverty. It won't mean greater freedom, because we'll probably fall prey to one of the local political *caciques* who are always waiting in the wings for a chance to become dictator. There's no question in anyone's mind that independence would set our island back at least a century, that it would mean sacrifice. But we can't help being what we are, can we?

The day finally arrived when I was supposed to travel to the States to go to Vassar College. I folded my new Sears clothes neatly and put them in my new Sears trunk. Abby accompanied me to San Juan in Abuela Gabriela's old blue Pontiac and then to Isla Grande Airport. I cried as I boarded the Pan American Constellation flight which took me to Idlewild, but the minute I arrived at school, I was a different person. The four years I spent at Vassar were the happiest of my life. Fortunately, English was taught at every level of the Ponce Lyceum, so I was thoroughly bilingual and I never had any difficulty with my studies. I loved the college, with its winding pebble paths under the weeping willows, its fine departments of Greek and Latin and English literature, its brilliant professors and its liberated students. It was there I learned that Ponce, which seemed as large as the universe itself when I lived on Aurora Street, was really a very small town.

QUINTÍN

Two weeks had gone by since Quintín had found Isabel's novel-in-progress in the secret compartment of Rebecca's desk. He hadn't said a word to her, but he had been unable to stop thinking about it. In the early hours of the morning, he would steal back to the study, the small bronze key in hand, to see if there were any new installments, but he was disappointed each time. The folder was still there, but no new pages had been added. On the fourteenth night, when he took it out of the hidden drawer it seemed heavier, and, sure enough, there were three new chapters.

Quintín suspected Isabel knew he was reading the manuscript. It had all been too easy; he always found the little key in the same place, at the bottom of her jewelry box, and she never woke up or complained when he got in and out of bed in the middle of the night. It was almost as if they had a secret understanding: if they both kept quiet, Isabel wouldn't stop writing and Quintín wouldn't stop reading.

Quintín sighed with relief when he realized that the new chapters were all about the Monfort family. Because he wasn't in them, he wouldn't have to suffer at seeing himself through Isabel's eyes. He was amazed by his wife's perseverance. She had written the new material entirely without his help; indeed, she rarely asked him questions anymore. Her style had become more unencumbered; it flowed with a naturalness which surprised him. She was becoming a better writer as the novel progressed; she was blossoming before his very eyes. The Kerenski chapters were especially well written and could probably be published alone as a short story. He had read them eagerly, conscious of the aesthetic pleasure he was experiencing.

But his pleasure was tinged with resentment. He could have been an artist, too. After all, a good historian is as creative as a good novelist. But he simply never developed that part of himself. There were too many people to feed, too many obligations to attend to. First Mendizabal & Company and the Mendizabal tribe when Rebecca was alive, then Gourmet Imports and his own family. Like all men who were responsible heads of households, he had had to bite the bullet. He never had the opportunity to sit around doing nothing, fanning himself on the terrace as Isabel did, watching the pelicans dive into the lagoon and waiting for ideas to come to him so he could capture them in beautiful words. He felt he had been shortchanged. Creating a work of art must be one of the most satisfying experiences in life. If only he had time.

He wasn't bitter about his life, however; he'd always felt proud of his work. You had to be a daring spirit to be an entrepreneur, creative in a different sort of way. You had to be orderly and tenacious to keep a company going. Many of his employees had worked for Gourmet Imports for more than twenty years, and he had made it possible for them to live with dignity, earning an honest salary with the sweat of their brows so they could raise their families and educate their children. He paid taxes religiously and contributed to making the island a better place. But, in the end, nobody would remember what he'd done. The dust of anonymity would settle on his name; he would become just another cipher in the long list of citizens who had lived responsible lives. When he died, his family would rush to snatch their inheritance, and the government would take the rest.

Isabel, on the contrary, would be remembered as the author of The House on the Lagoon, a "work of art"—if she ever managed to publish it. Art was a much more effective way to perpetuate oneself, to achieve a kind of immortality.

He told himself he was being selfish, that he shouldn't begrudge his wife her possible success. But he wished she would share his anonymity with him. Maybe he could convince her not to publish the novel, to keep it a secret between them. She had accomplished something meaningful in life and he would be the first to compliment her on it. He would praise the way she had managed to hone her phrases and give body to the wraiths of her imagination. Was it so important that her novel be published? What mattered was that it existed, that it had been born and could compete with the rest of creation. That way, his family's reputation would be safeguarded and he wouldn't be forced to destroy the manuscript. If Isabel still loved him, she could make that sacrifice. It would be the utmost proof of her devotion, and he would be forever in her debt.

Quintín told himself he had to be patient and rise above the situation. His instinct told him it wasn't wise to pressure Isabel to talk about the novel right now. She had had a tragic family history. Her mother had been an addicted gambler. Her father had committed suicide, and Carmita had gone into a severe depression before losing her mind. He would just have to wait and hope that things would straighten themselves out.

Quintín turned once more to the manuscript at hand. He took out his pencil, sharpened the point, and concentrated as much as he could on the text. Maybe he could help Isabel write the perfect novel.

He read Isabel's description of her arrival in Ponce at the beginning of Chapter 16, and made a small note on the margin of the first page. "Eulogizing your own world too much?" She talked about Ponce as if it were Texas, the Lone Star State. Ponce was a beautiful town, but it could never compare with San Juan, which was a metropolis of a million and a half inhabitants. She had to keep things in perspective: Ponce had a population of a hundred and fifty thousand. "It's true, Ponce's houses look like wedding cakes. But that doesn't mean Ponce is architecturally more significant than the citadel of Old San Juan—even if San Juan's houses do have matchstick balconies," he noted farther down.

Another fault he found was Isabel's tendency to use her female characters as shadow players for her own personality. She had to be careful here; it was a pitfall for mediocre writers.

"You like rebellious characters," he wrote at the bottom of the next page, "but that doesn't mean you should identify with them. Be more careful—when you talk about them, the rebel in you suddenly rears its head. Perhaps that's why you could describe Rebecca with such gusto in the sixth and seventh chapters. In her young days, Mother was ungovernable; she was spoiled and was used to having her own way. But she changed later on. Father helped her to grow up and she accepted her responsibilities as a wife and mother."

When Quintín reached the end of the margin on the third page, he turned the page over and began to write freely on the back of Isabel's manuscript. He knew he was throwing caution to the winds, but he let his enthusiasm run away with him.

"What rings true in your manuscript is your passion for ballet dancing," he continued. "The reader can tell you love it by the way you warm to the subject. Your Isabel knows the names of all the steps and positions by heart, and must also have read a book or two on ballet theory. Rebecca, or the character you named after my mother, shares this passion with you. When Rebecca says, 'I'd like to reach, through nature, the divine expression of the human spirit,' she sounds a lot like Kerenski many pages later, when he tells his students, 'If you let the music flood you when you dance, one day you'll attain enlightenment.' But it's not Rebecca or Kerenski I'm hearing, it's Isabel.

"I remember the affair between Kerenski and Estefanía Volmer well; it was one of the biggest scandals in Ponce in the forties. You know what our island is like. Gossip is like Spanish moss; it knots itself around every telephone pole and hangs from the eaves of houses in no time at all.

"If you permit me, I'll add my version of the story here. It's different from yours, because it's based on facts. But, at this point, who can tell fact from fiction in this manuscript? For someone who never lived in Ponce, both versions could be true. It's the artistic rendition of the story, the telling of it, that's important. And I want to prove to you that history can be just as valid from the point of view of art if it is properly told."

So, as the early-morning light began to spill through the study's window, Quintín gave his historical version of Isabel's story—because all stories have a history:

"Kerenski had leftist leanings, and when he married Norma Castillo, they moved to Ponce. He was nicknamed by the townspeople Kerenski the Red Jew. No one would have sent his daughter to the ballet school if Kerenski had been its director. But everyone in Ponce knew who the Castillos were; all good families on the island know each other. Norma was very effective at teaching poise and etiquette to the girls, and the school was a success from the start. But after a while Kerenski began to resent the fact that only well-to-do students were enrolled. He wanted to work with all kinds of people, he said, so he could brag to his socialist friends about running a democratic institution where poor students were also admitted. He was embittered that the school was really under Norma's guidance. It was then that he started to look for ways to get back at her, and began stalking Estefanía Volmer.

"I knew Estefanía long before I met you, because the young people from Ponce's well-to-do families would often come to dances and parties in San Juan. That's how I got to know so much about the Kerenski Ballet School. You never saw Estefanía with me because you never went to parties at fashionable night spots at the time. Your father wouldn't let you go to them, he was such a Puritan.

Estefanía, on the other hand, was wild. I took her to dances a couple of times, and I can vouch for the fact that she wore no underwear. I remember on one occasion Estefanía was supposed to crown the Carnival Queen at the Alamares Casino. She asked me to be her escort. She was wearing one of those lavish wire-hoop gowns, with the skirt resembling a balloon full of air. When the moment arrived, Estefanía climbed the stairs at the end of the dance floor, carrying the Queen's crown on a red velvet pillow, and when she reached the top, she took a deep bow facing the throne. Her skirt rose perpendicularly behind her and revealed the prettiest pair of pink buns you can imagine. There must have been at least a thousand people there. All the men whistled and burst into applause. But Estefanía didn't even blush. She just laughed, fastened the rhinestone crown on the Queen's head with hairpins, and came bouncing back down the stairs to stand next to me on the dance floor. I never told you the story because I knew she was your friend and I didn't want to embarrass you.

"Estefanía's mother, Margot Rinser, was the first natural platinum-blonde I ever met. Her hair was the color of the rum her parents sold. But she liked to drink it, too. That was her problem.

"One day Arturo and Margot saw a traveling circus that had just arrived in Ponce. It must have been around six in the morning and they were returning from a party at the Ponce Country Club, when they went by the ball park and saw the big tent. Two lions were sleeping in a cage parked in a nearby gully. Margot told Arturo she wanted to see the lions up close. At first Arturo said no, but then he decided to humor her. They'd been married only a month. They came to the gully, parked their blue DeSoto, and got out.

"Arturo was in his white dinner jacket and Margot was wearing a long evening gown with a beaded train which shimmered in the morning half-light. As they approached the cages, they saw a man taking pieces of meat and bone out of a hemp sack. It was the

animals' caretaker, feeding the lions their breakfast. Margot came near and watched in fascination as the lions gorged themselves. She had never seen real lions before in her life, and she found them beautiful. They had large, golden eyes, and when they ate, their pupils dilated like tranquil pools.

"Margot asked the caretaker if she could feed one of the animals. The caretaker didn't think twice. The lions were old and were used to being hand-fed, so he gave her a small piece of meat. Margot approached the cage and called out playfully to the nearest female, a thin, squalid animal with tufts of hair on its head. Margot felt sorry for her. The circus was so cruel to animals—who knew how much this one had been through? Slowly she put her right hand inside the iron bars—Arturo was standing right behind her, holding on to her left arm, amused by her sentimentality. But just as Margot let the piece of meat drop to the floor of the cage, the lioness sprang at her. She thrust a paw between the bars and grabbed Margot's train—the shimmering beads had caught her eye—pulling Margot toward her with terrific force. For a few desperate seconds there was a tug-of-war. Arturo held on to Margot on one side of the cage, and the lioness on the other. Margot screamed, but the lioness had a tight hold. The train of the dress was made of strong material and wouldn't tear, so the lioness ended up mauling Margot's thigh through the bars.

"It was as a result of that accident—and not because of bone cancer, as you naïvely wrote—that Margot Rinser had to have her right leg amputated. A few weeks later she discovered that she was pregnant with Estefanía. It was a pathetic sight—pregnant and not even married six months—as Arturo Volmer pushed her wheelchair through the streets of Ponce. Arturo never recovered from the blow. He felt guilty for not being able to prevent the accident. In his dreams he kept seeing Margot's right hand offering the lioness a piece of meat, as he held on to her left and laughed as if it were all a joke. That was why he devoted himself to taking care of her, and why Estefanía was brought up like a wild child.

"*Estefanía was a rebel, everybody on the island said so. She used to drive her red Ford convertible from Ponce to San Juan, and she had a reputation for doing everything. She drove Arturo and Margot half mad with her carefree life, but there was nothing they could do about it.*

"*It was a well-known fact that Estefanía met Kerenski at the ballet school. It didn't take them long to realize they were made for each other. You seem to have been half in love with that scoundrel yourself. You know very well that you were the one who pulled the lever at the end of the recital at La Perla that night, Isabel! That you were the one who made the curtain rise so that the love affair of André Kerenski and Estefanía Volmer was revealed to the world! And a few months later—to help out Norma Castillo, who had sued for divorce—you accused Kerenski of child molestation during a court hearing. And as a result of your testimony, Kerenski was eventually deported from the United States.*"

Quintín was bent over the pages of the manuscript, completely absorbed in his writing, when he heard a noise outside the study where the mangroves grew near to the house. He hid the pages in the desk drawer and moved silently to the window. But it was just an owl, hooting morosely on a branch overhead, and its shadow flitted away as soon as Quintín showed his face. He went back and sat down on the chair in front of the desk, deep in thought.

He had discovered yet another facet of Isabel. Evidently she had been wildly in love with Kerenski. She had sworn she had never loved anyone before him and she had been lying all along. But that she should fall in love with a jerk like the immigrant ballet master only added insult to injury. Isabel was almost a child at the time, and yet she had been merciless. If what she wrote was true, she had viciously destroyed Kerenski with her slander, simply because she felt spurned. She was all innocence, all guileless spontaneity on the surface, and underneath, this terrible hate, churning. The intensity of her emotions, the violence she had been capable of, seeped through her words like a deadly poison. At fourteen she *was a little Medea, and like Medea, she had used words to wreak her vengeance on a pathetic Russian immigrant.*

Quintín felt a shiver of apprehension run down his back. If Isabel had been capable of doing such a thing simply because she had seen Kerenski kiss another student, what might she do to him if she ever got it into her mind that he didn't love her?

PART 6

The Second House

on the Lagoon

ISABEL

Quintín has found and read my manuscript. He's not only read it, he's put in commentaries in longhand, scribbling angrily in the margins, and even adding his version to mine on the back of some of the pages. What nerve, to accuse me of distorting the truth, of changing the events of our family histories around! He knows I know he knows. And yet he's left the manuscript undisturbed in Rebecca's desk.

Fine. His curiosity is piqued; he wants to find out how the novel will end. That's the reason he hasn't destroyed the manuscript or said anything to make me stop writing, confident that, at the very last, he'll be able to do away with it or prevent me from publishing. But he'll want to get even one way or another, I'm sure of it.

Quintín quoted the Bible at dinner tonight, just before we began to eat: "Whoever troubleth his own house shall inherit the wind," he said solemnly. Then he gave thanks for all the "blessings" we have received. That's fine, too. But at least I'll have had the satisfaction of having put down on paper the story of our marriage.

19

Abby's Wedding Shroud

✄

QUINTÍN AND I MET in the summer before my junior year in
college. It was June and we were both home from school. Abby
had taken me to San Juan for the weekend on a shopping trip and
we stayed at the house of Aunt Hortensia, one of Carmita's sisters,
who had moved to the capital. It was a sunny day and I had gone
out with my cousin to stroll on the Escambrón boardwalk. I liked
the boardwalk because of its magnificent view; on the left, one
can see the ocean, and on the right there is a small bay with a
crescent of white sand. We were wearing our bathing suits and
would dive in at the end. The waves are so transparent there that
they seem to be made of quartz, pounding the rocks as if trying
to reduce them to dust.

The Escambrón's Beach Club hadn't been torn down yet; from
the boardwalk, it looked like a white whale run aground on the
other side of the bay. The heavy black iron chain the U.S. Navy
had placed underwater during the Second World War to fend off
German submarines still hung at the entrance to the bay, rusted
and covered with barnacles. A group of street urchins in rags were
playing boisterously nearby, climbing up on the handrail and div-
ing from the edge of the platform like wild pelicans.

Suddenly someone pushed me from behind and I stumbled.

When I looked up, I couldn't breathe; something was strangling me. I clutched at my throat and the gold chain around my neck suddenly snapped; one of the urchins ran in front of me, then disappeared as he dived with the chain over the rail. Everything happened so quickly I didn't have time to think. When I put my hand to my neck, I realized I was bleeding.

A second shadow rushed past me and dove into the water. I peered anxiously at the ocean below; two shadows struggled under the dark blue surface, until the second one overpowered the first. A few moments later a dark-haired young man swam back to the boardwalk, holding my chain and medal in his hand.

"The Virgin of Guadalupe is the protector of my warrior ancestors," he said with a polite smile. "I let the boy get away because he was too young. But next time, don't come to the beach wearing jewelry. Urchins, like pelicans, attack anything that shines near the water."

He had broad shoulders and walked with a little bit of a swagger. "Thanks for the chivalrous gesture," I said, laughing.

Quintín took me by the arm. "You're hurt," he said with concern. "You'd better come with me." He escorted my cousin and me to his car and we went to the Emergency Room at the nearby Presbyterian Hospital, where a doctor took care of me. Then he drove us back to my aunt's house. Before he left, I thanked him again, and gave him my address and telephone number in Ponce.

I went back home with Abby and two or three days later Quintín called from San Juan. He wanted to know how I was and if I had gotten over the fright. I told him I was fine and that I was coming to San Juan the following week. We met again a few days later. After we saw each other several times, Quintín began traveling to Ponce every weekend. One day he asked me to be his steady girlfriend, and gave me Buenaventura's signet ring, which his father had once given to Rebecca. When Quintín was twenty-one, Rebecca had passed it on to him, because he was her oldest son. I remember the first time I wore it; we were sitting out on the

veranda on Aurora Street. I looked at the kneeling warrior beheading a hog, and thought how different it looked from anything
that was part of my world.

FATHER DIED at the end of the next summer, just before I returned
to the States for my last year in college. Carmita's gambling finally
did him in. When we moved to Ponce eleven years earlier, Carmita
had been almost cured of her habit; there were no casinos in Ponce,
and she had nowhere to gamble. But then the Ponce Intercontinental Hotel opened its doors atop a rocky hill behind the town.
The Intercontinental was the first truly modern hotel to go up in
Ponce, and it stood in contrast to the town's elegant turn-of-the-
century architecture. All the rooms had panel-glass windows; there
were balconies that jutted out over the dry, spiny vegetation, and
an absurd cylindrical stairway to the pool area made of round,
decorative bricks which faintly resembled the neck of a giraffe.

The hotel had a luxurious casino; the mayor had hoped it would
bring American tourists to Ponce. But he was wrong. The three-
hour drive from San Juan, the narrow, winding road, the hairpin
curves with dark green gullies which lured careless travelers to
the bottom proved to be too much of an obstacle. Ponce has no
beaches; it has never been a resort town, and Ponceños have always
wanted to keep it that way. Soon the Intercontinental was losing
thousands of dollars. Faced with a serious situation, the manager
began to advertise the casino among the local families, inviting
the ladies to its Lady Luck Afternoons, when each dollar would
be worth six chips instead of three, until eight in the evening.

Carmita was delighted. She began to go to the casino with her
friends, and soon she had a competition going as to who would
win the slot machine's pot. When she lost, she asked her friends
to lend her some money. If they refused, she just walked out into
the street and asked anyone she met for a loan. Pedestrians couldn't
understand why a well-dressed woman like Carmita Monfort was
begging for money, and some began to take advantage of her. They
would lend her ten dollars, then knock on our door and tell Carlos

they had lent her a hundred. It might very well have been true, but Carmita would never admit it, and Carlos didn't dare refuse. Months went by and the situation got worse. Every time Carlos went out of the house, there would be someone waiting on the sidewalk, asking him to pay a couple of hundred which Carmita owed.

After a while, Father was so embarrassed he stopped going to the office and stayed home all the time. He left the managing of Mother's properties to her accountant and didn't want to have anything more to do with her money. The only thing he liked was to sit under the white-oak tree he had planted behind the house on Aurora Street and to feed his two Florida parrots, Coto and Rita. He liked to see how much his oak tree had grown and would measure the expanse of its trunk every two or three months. White oak was one of his favorite woods for carving furniture, and when the tree was big enough, he planned to saw it down and make at least six rockers and a love seat. One day a tropical storm hit Ponce and felled many of its beautiful trees. The streets were littered with them, their roots exposed like huge molars extracted from the earth. It also uprooted our white oak and knocked down the parrot cage. Coto and Rita escaped. That was the evening Abby went looking for Father all over the house at dinnertime and found him hanging from the rafters in the attic, her shiny new garden hose from Sears tied around his neck.

Father's death was a nightmare. We only managed to weather the storm because of Abby. " 'It's when Corsicans lose everything that they know what they're really worth,' Napoleon's mother wrote to the Duke of Wellington after Waterloo," Abby said stoically as we stood by Father's coffin at the wake. "So stand up straight; keep your chin up, and don't cry. Just thank everyone politely for coming." I had no choice but to dry my tears and do as she said.

At the funeral Abby made a great effort to appear reconciled to her fate. But her mouth was like a bird that didn't want to fly; her lips drooped every time she tried to smile. Carlos was her only child. After he died, Abby shrank three inches and began to lose her sight. She knew Carlos would never amount to much, but she went on loving him as on the day he was born. When she found him hanging from the rafters in the attic, she put both hands to her mouth and fell unconscious on the floor. The maid and I heard the thud and ran upstairs. Mariana knelt by Abby's side to try to revive her, and didn't see Father's corpse. I saw him first. I ran down the stairs and out into the street, terrified. I wouldn't go back into the house for hours, but sat on the sidewalk, dry-eyed. Mariana had to call the ambulance that took Abby to the hospital, as well as the firemen who brought down Father's body. I didn't cry until the next day, when Abby came back and took me in her arms.

That summer brought a lot of changes. Carmita got worse, and we had to get a nurse for her; she couldn't be left alone, because she'd wander out into the street and start asking people for money. Abby wasn't feeling well, but she wouldn't admit it. She sold the piece of land she still owned in Adjuntas—which had appreciated considerably because Squibb, the pharmaceutical plant, had bought Uncle Orencio's farm to plant eucalyptus trees instead of coffee—and deposited the profits in the bank.

The following spring, I graduated with honors from Vassar. I had taken every course I could in Spanish literature, because I had made up my mind to be a writer. Abby was very supportive. She liked the idea from the start. She wrote me a long letter about the importance of being able to turn even our most painful experiences into art. Quintín was the only one who came to my graduation in May. From Poughkeepsie we flew together to Puerto Rico and I then traveled to Ponce by myself. When I got home, I ran up the stairs to the front balcony with my diploma in hand. The nurse opened the door. Abby was in bed, she said; she had been failing for the past month. I was upset; I had no idea she was so ill.

I went to her room and tiptoed to her bed. I wasn't prepared for the change that had come over her. Her eyes were closed and she looked even smaller than I remembered; she reminded me of one of Abuela Gabriela's miniature dolls in the vitrine in the living room. I kissed her on the forehead and put the diploma next to her on the bed. "Congratulations," she said when she opened her eyes. "I've lived fifty years after Lorenzo's death just to see you finish what I had to give up when I was nineteen. Now you can write the story of our family, with the dead and the living to help you, and I can rest in peace." I hugged and kissed her and said she was being silly; soon she would be well again and we would go to the Silver Spoon together.

The next day she woke up very early and got out of bed. She had breakfast with me in the dining room. Just as she was finishing her coffee, she said: "This afternoon I'm going to die, and I'd like everything to be ready. I need you to find me the wedding sheets I brought from Adjuntas, after I buried your grandfather. They're in a trunk in the attic." I told her not to joke like that, but my heart balled into a fist. The nurse chided her for talking about depressing things. Abby went on drinking her coffee, without saying another word. When she finished breakfast, she got up from the table and did something very strange. She walked to the terrace where Carmita was sitting in her rocking chair, and kissed her on the forehead. It was the first time she had kissed her since Carlos passed away. Then she went to her room and locked herself in.

A few minutes later I knocked on her door. I had found her wedding sheets; they were in an old chest in the attic, just as she had said. They were embroidered with miniature roses and had a scalloped edging of fine Brussels lace, and they were freshly laundered, as if someone had expected to use them soon. I was surprised at how fine they were. I had always heard Abby talk about how splendid her life at Abuelo Lorenzo's house had been, but I had only half believed her. I thought she was exaggerating, because one always remembers one's youth in a favorable light. But her wedding sheets were proof that she hadn't been making it up; life with Lorenzo must have been very fine indeed.

I gave Abby the bed linen and closed the door. After a while I heard the soft purring of Carmita's sewing machine. Abby had brought it to her room when Carmita became ill, and she had sewn all the new curtains and bedspreads for the house herself. I thought she must be feeling better and didn't want to disturb her, so I didn't knock on her door.

I went out to run some errands in town, and when I came back, I took dinner to Abby's room on a tray. But nobody answered my knock. Slowly I opened the door and found Abby lying in bed, her wedding linen perfectly ironed around her. She had made a shroud with the delicately embroidered top sheet, and she lay in it like a baby mummy, hands folded over her chest and face edged with Brussels lace. Around the bed lay a dozen envelopes, all duly addressed, with what was left of the money from the sale of the land in Adjuntas. There was a generous sum for the children of the Silver Spoon, and then the payment for her last bills at the house: electricity, water, and telephone. The final envelope held the money for her coffin and her burial expenses.

After Abby's death, the house on Aurora Street seemed larger and emptier than ever. I knew I had to put Carmita in an asylum, but I wanted to postpone that as long as possible. During the day the nurse and I had to feed and dress her, carry her to the bathroom and get her on and off the toilet; but at night she did everything on the bed. Every morning we had to give her a bath and change the sheets, because she woke up covered in excrement. After Carlos's suicide, Carmita refused to talk. She just sat in her rocking chair, combing her long, gray hair all day. I liked to sit and tell her about my things, even if she didn't hear what I said. She seldom smiled, but when she did, I felt as if she were pouring oil on my wounds.

20

The Wedding Vow

🜚

AFTER ABBY'S DEATH Quintín came to Ponce to see me every weekend, but it was impossible even to think of getting married, because he didn't have any money. At the end of the summer we had a stroke of luck. Madeleine Rosich died in Boston, and she left Quintín, her favorite, a considerable amount. Quintín proposed that same day, and we set the date for the wedding a year later. I decided to sell the house on Aurora Street but wanted to stay there with Mother until the last possible moment. A week before the wedding, I finally put her in an asylum.

Quintín gave his mother all the money he had saved from working at Mendizabal & Company, and he asked her to buy me an engagement ring. Rebecca went to see Doña Salomé Beguin, the Arab woman who sold jewelry in Old San Juan, and she picked a beautiful almond-shaped solitaire for her oldest son. It was an uncomfortable piece of jewelry; the diamond was razor-sharp, and it snagged my nylons every time I put them on. One day I was playing tennis with Quintín when the racket hit the back of my hand and the diamond split in two. I was terribly upset, thinking it might be a bad omen, but Quintín reassured me that his love would last forever, even if diamonds did not.

Quintín and I were married in June 1955, after two years of

courtship. The ceremony was in the Church of San José in Old San Juan, the oldest church on the island—and still one of my favorites. I've always liked the way it sits unassumingly in a corner of the square, its simple colonial façade rising like a whitewashed wave against the blue of the sky. There are no Conquistadors buried there; Ponce de León, whose house is just down the street from the church, is buried in the Cathedral of San Juan, several blocks away.

We had wanted a small wedding, but it didn't turn out that way. Quintín and I had invited very few people: my Antonsanti aunts and cousins from Ponce, whom I hardly saw any longer; Aunt Hortensia, Carmita's sister, in whose house I used to stay when I came to San Juan on visits; Norma Castillo, my ballet teacher; and several of my friends from the Kerenski Ballet School, among them Estefanía Volmer, who came to the wedding in a semitransparent shocking-pink gown, her breasts trembling under the delicate gauze. Esmeralda Márquez, who was still one of my best friends, hadn't been invited, but she sent us a beautiful present, a Madeira lace tablecloth I still use for formal dinners. Quintín, for his part, had invited several of his friends from Columbia University, as well as his Rosich cousins from Boston, but, unfortunately, very few of them could make the trip to the island.

Rebecca insisted that the reception be held at the house on the lagoon, on Pavel's golden terrace, and she asked us to let her take care of the festivities. She drew up a list of guests, and before we knew it, we had a full-blown affair on our hands. Rebecca invited all her San Juan socialite friends, Buenaventura's cronies from the Spanish Casino, and his diplomatic and business relations. Ignacio added a good number of his artist friends. Patria and Libertad wanted to have a good time also, so they asked several of their teenage friends. In all, almost three hundred guests were invited, and we had no choice but to accept graciously.

Rebecca seemed always to be in a bad mood and hardly ever spoke to me; it was as if she was jealous of our happiness. I didn't have much time to worry about it, however, because I was in a whirlwind. I had finally shut down the house in Ponce, and had moved to San Juan for the wedding. My dress was taken care of; I was to wear Abuela Gabriela's Chantilly lace gown and her point d'esprit veil, which Aunt Hortensia had graciously lent me and Doña Ermelinda had secretly altered in Ponce to fit me. My bouquet had been decided on also: a wreath of coffee blossoms from Río Negro—Abuelo Vicenzo's farm in the mountains—where Mother's family still owned a plot of land. But I had to see about my trousseau, and make a list of the presents that began to arrive by the dozen, so I could later write thank-you notes.

With the money he had inherited from Madeleine Rosich, Quintín bought a small apartment with a view of the ocean, in one of the new buildings of Alamares, and we went shopping together for all the things we would need: sheets, towels, dishes, kitchenware. We furnished it in part with the pieces I brought from the house in Ponce. My books were the first thing I unpacked; I lined one of the back rooms of the apartment with them, making it my study. Then I put Father's rocking chairs and settees in the living room, their crests gaily decorated with hibiscus, lilies, and bougainvillea. One of his wonderful marble consoles found a place in our dining room. When Quintín and I looked at ourselves in its beveled mirror, we felt truly happy. We embraced and kissed in front of it, as if sealing a pact. Having our apartment ready meant we would finally live our own lives and be able to get away from the house on the lagoon.

The day of the wedding, we rode to church in Buenaventura's silver Rolls-Royce, with Brambon at the wheel, wearing his black twill uniform. Abuela Gabriela's dress fit me like a glove and Quintín looked like a storybook prince, dressed in tails and wearing his father's silk top hat. Rebecca had kept it all those years in her closet, wrapped in tissue paper, so her sons could wear it on their wedding day. As we walked down the aisle together, I couldn't help thinking of Father, of how much he would have enjoyed being there with me. Abby would have liked to be at my wedding, too, but only if I had been marrying someone else. She wouldn't have wanted to see me marry Quintín.

After the ceremony, we drove back to the house on the lagoon for the reception. The house looked beautiful. The terrace's handrail had been decorated with a garland of white orchids, and tables for the guests had been set near the water. Petra herself had baked the wedding cake, a three-tiered fountain covered in icing, with two sugar doves drinking at the top. The morning of the wedding, she called us into the kitchen and showed us the cake before anyone else saw it. "Love is the only Fountain of Youth," she said to Quintín and me, her smile a half-moon shining on her face. "That's the secret Rebecca will never learn."

Buenaventura had decided that only Codorniu champagne would be served at the reception—the brand he imported from Spain—and the waiters hovered over the tables, pouring glass after glass for the guests. He had made his toast to the bride and groom and the orchestra had begun to play *Tú y yo,* the elegant nineteenth-century danza Quintín and I were supposed to dance together, when from under the golden terrace a whole string of rowboats floated out, lit with paper lanterns and full of people singing, accompanied by guitars. It was a serenade Petra and the servants had organized in our honor.

As the celebration continued, Quintín and I were absorbed in our own little world. We sat quietly next to each other, drinking champagne from the same glass, holding hands and feeling a little like strangers at our own wedding. We were counting the minutes until everything would be over and we would go to the airport, board a plane to New York, and from there fly to Paris. The terrace gleamed before us like a golden stage, and all of a sudden it made me think of Rebecca and her unhappy performance as Salomé. Rebecca had wanted to be a writer and a dancer, but she became neither, because of her unhappy marriage. I swore I wouldn't let that happen to me.

21

Rebecca's Book of Poems

❦

COMPARED TO THE MENDIZABALS, my family was little more than middle-class. The Antonsantis' inheritance was negligible next to the kind of money the Mendizabals had, and they probably would have preferred that Quintín marry a girl from one of San Juan's old, established families. Abby's side of the family, of course, didn't count. Buenaventura and Rebecca never mentioned the Monforts; even though they were landowners, they were too controversial for comfort.

In the eyes of Rebecca and Buenaventura, I was overeducated and far too Americanized. Sending me to study in the States had been my parents' great mistake; I had evidently enjoyed too much freedom during my years at Vassar. Patria and Libertad would both go to a finishing school in Switzerland after graduating from high school. Rebecca herself had studied only as far as her freshman year, marrying Buenaventura when she was sixteen. A university diploma was a sign of prestige, but it was also a subtle threat. A woman's education was supposed to be an asset; she could bring up her children better and it would give her the opportunity to help her husband at social gatherings. A degree from La Rosée in Switzerland would have been much more appropriate. Not only would I have learned to be a polished hostess;

I would have made friends among the children of European royalty. Being an orphan, on the other hand, and not having anyone but Quintín in the world was a point in my favor because it cast me in a vulnerable light. His parents could adopt me without reservation; I was to be part of the Mendizabal clan and participate in all their activities.

During the first months of our marriage, I got to know the Mendizabals better. Dinner was a very important occasion for Buenaventura, and the dining room was the most prominent room in the house. Up to forty guests could sit at the mahogany table, which had griffin feet and gargoyles carved at each end. The chairs had leather seats and backrests embossed with helmets of Spanish Conquistadors. At one end of the table, under the rug, there was a butler's bell that rang in the kitchen, so Rebecca could silently summon the servants.

Meals took forever, but Sunday dinners were the worst of all. Sometimes the family would sit down at two o'clock, and at five we'd still be there, like birds glued to a branch. I was very much in love with Quintín and wanted his parents to like me. But, still, it took all my willpower not to get up in the middle of the meal and run out to the garden to do a couple of jumping jacks, or simply to take a breath of fresh air. After a few months of this, however, I found a way to make dinners more bearable. I would simply sit there and closely observe everyone, finding out as much as I could about the Mendizabals by listening to the stories they all told me.

My own family's foibles were well known to me. Abuela Gabriela had been a feminist to the point of fanaticism; Abuelo Vicenzo had been a womanizer; Abby was a bit of a political radical; Carmita had been a compulsive gambler; Father, a born loser. Now I would get to know the Mendizabals' shortcomings.

Buenaventura's bad temper was legendary. Everybody in the house on the lagoon was afraid of him. One Sunday morning the whole family went to Mass and afterwards out to lunch. When we got back to the house, we heard an infernal noise coming from the

second floor. Buenaventura and Quintín ran upstairs and found
the plumber, his face red with indignation and dripping with sweat.
He had been unclogging one of the toilets when the family left for
church. Everyone had forgotten about him. When he finished his
job, he discovered that the gate at the top of the stairs was locked
and he couldn't get out. All the windows had grilles on them, so
he couldn't jump out, either. He called for help, but none of the
servants in the cellar heard him. After two hours, he became
desperate and began to bang the gate with a pair of pliers. When
he finally saw Buenaventura and Quintín coming, he began to
swear: a veritable stream of foul language spewed from his lips.
Rebecca, Patria, and Libertad covered their ears and began to
scream. Buenaventura was furious. He opened the gate with his
key—which hung at the end of a gold chain attached to his belt
—and escorted the man down the stairs and out of the house. He
paid him his fee, asked him for a receipt, and when the plumber
was about to leave, Buenaventura punched him and knocked him
out cold. He couldn't just let his wife and daughters be insulted
like that in front of everybody, he said.

Buenaventura was always trying to win me over in his rough,
unsophisticated way. "I'm over sixty and I feel as if I were made
of iron," he said to me one day, as Petra brought in dish after
dish of ham shank, rice with sausage, and pigs' feet stewed with
chickpeas. "Never pay attention to what doctors say; greasy food
is really very good for one's health." He couldn't understand why
I was so particular about what I ate. "You'll have to train that
queasy stomach of yours," he'd say to me. "People from Extremadura are primitive and hardy. They like to eat hearty foods
because when grease burns it gives off energy, in business as well
as in bed." He was proud of his teeth, and he liked to boast he'd
been to the dentist only once in his life and didn't need a single
filling. "When one is born with delicate teacup teeth like you, it's
a bad sign," he'd say to me in jest. "It means the genes have
degenerated and their owners have become too civilized."

Buenaventura was semiretired, and as Quintín gradually took

over the business, he began to go to the office only in the mornings. He had a small dock built under the terrace, and he kept a fifteen-foot motorboat there. Sometimes in the afternoon he would invite me to go for a ride through the mangrove swamp. We would cross Alamares Lagoon, and once we entered the bayous, he would cut the motor. We'd slide silently beneath the green maze. The mangrove swamp went on for miles, spreading lazily across the horizon, seemingly without end. Buenaventura would pilot the boat from the stern, and I would lean over the prow, taking in all the beauty and mystery of that strange place. From time to time I warned him that the water was too shallow, that there was danger of running aground. "These channels are frequently used for smuggling by the people from Las Minas," Buenaventura told me on one of our trips, pointing to a nest of huts on our right. "That's why I always carry a .42 caliber gun hidden in the first-aid kit under my seat." He never mentioned the fact that once he had used the swamp's intricate waterways to bring his own merchandise illegally into the island.

After cutting across Morass Lagoon, we would usually head for Lucumí Beach. For twenty minutes we could hardly breathe, floating over the stinking brown quagmire. Then suddenly the muddy water would clear and at the end of the mangroves we could see the white surf of the Atlantic roiling in the distance. The beach was spectacular, all golden sand dunes with miles of elegant palm trees weaving in the wind.

There were usually several black women waiting for us on shore. Tall and strong, with onyx-black skin, they bore a striking resemblance to Petra, and I wondered if they were related to her. But I never dared to ask. They always seemed to know in advance we were coming and they seldom spoke. The minute we arrived, they started cooking for us on their coal furnaces, silently dropping the batter for the fritters into black kettles full of boiling oil. Later they offered us fresh coconut water, which Buenaventura spiked with a shot of illegal *pitorro* rum.

"When I die, I want to be buried near this place," Buenaventura confessed to me one day as we sat on the beach, eating the golden, crispy morsels. "I want to fly up to heaven on the wings of a codfish fritter and lay my head on an *alcapurría* when they lower me down to my grave."

Once we walked inland for half a mile and visited the palm-thatched village of Lucumí, where the black women on the beach lived. At one end of a single mud street with huts on either side was a solid cement building with a sign reading "Mendizabal Elementary School." Buenaventura had donated the school to the village, and he took a special interest in having the children who graduated from it go on to study at a high school in town. One day I noticed that some of the black children coming out of school had gray-blue eyes like Buenaventura. When I asked Quintín about it, he bowed his head and didn't say anything at first. But I persisted, and Quintín confessed his father sometimes liked taking the black women of Lucumí to the beach, where he made love to them on the sand for a few dollars. Once he had even invited Quintín to join him, but Quintín had refused. I was incensed by the revelation. Buenaventura disgusted me, and I swore I'd never go back to Lucumí Beach with him.

When Arístides Arrigoitia died, Rebecca inherited her own money, so she didn't have to suffer from Buenaventura's miserliness anymore. She was always giving tea parties and luncheons for her friends at the house, and I was supposed to attend all of them. Patria and Libertad were sixteen and fifteen, respectively. They were interested in boys and had activities of their own, so I usually had to help Rebecca pour the coffee and pass the hors d'oeuvres among her guests. Each tea party meant a trip to the beauty salon and another one to the dressmaker. After six months of this, I was bored to death.

Rebecca had been friendly toward me, but after Quintín and I were married, she ceased being affectionate. It was as if she wanted me to prove that I loved her son as much as I should. I wondered why she was jealous of me, when she herself didn't care for Quintín. She was always caustic toward him; in her opinion, he could never do anything right. Quintín, on the other hand, never held his mother's peevishness against her. Rebecca was on a pedestal, and if I made the slightest disparaging remark, he would immediately draw the line. "Remember Rebecca is my mother," he'd say to me, "and she's suffered a great deal."

For years Rebecca had obeyed Buenaventura and lived the spartan life he had imposed on her, but when I met her she was tired of playing the martyr. She was getting old; her skin was wrinkled like yellowed ivory. Discipline and order were no longer so important to her. She wanted to enjoy life, and for this reason she preferred the company of Ignacio, her second son, and that of Patria and Libertad, to Quintín's.

Ignacio was always joking and made Rebecca laugh. Quintín, by contrast, seemed morose. He had such an intense look on his face that he made Rebecca uneasy. Blond, and with sapphire-blue eyes, Ignacio had inherited the Rosiches' northern Italian good looks. He had a cheerful personality; Rebecca had pampered him since birth. He had never lived in the cellar, as Quintín had for the first years of his life because he reminded Rebecca of happier times. And she did not let Buenaventura bully Ignacio into studying business as he had bullied Quintín, or force him to work long hours at Medizabal & Company, lowering codfish crates into the warehouse with a forklift. When Quintín and I were married, Ignacio had just turned seventeen and was a freshman at Florida State University. He didn't want anything to do with business, he said; he wanted to study something that had to do with art, but he didn't know exactly what.

Rebecca, meanwhile, had begun to live for the body, trying to postpone its deterioration for as long as possible. She needed more servants to pamper her, she said, so Petra brought several of her nieces who lived in Las Minas to the house. Every day, it seemed, a boat would arrive from Morass Lagoon bearing one of her rela-

tives. The boat would anchor at the small dock under the terrace
and the new servants would soon be installed in the cellar. Petra
then taught them their new jobs: one was to be Rebecca's masseuse;
another would do her hair and nails; a third would see to her
clothes.

One day Petra was on her knees, vigorously scrubbing the
dining-room floor. "Rebecca should have gone on dancing and
writing poems," she said to her niece Eulodia, who was polishing
the silver. "Maybe then she wouldn't be so tiresome, asking silly
questions like what's the secret of youth." Petra, in spite of being
older than Rebecca, didn't have a single frizzy white hair on her
head, and Rebecca wanted to know why. "Ask your husband,"
Petra said, her steel bracelets jangling as she walked by, carrying
a basket full of freshly ironed sheets on her head. "It was Ponce
de León, a Spanish Conquistador like Buenaventura, who went to
Florida looking for the Fountain of Youth. We Africans never grow
old." And when she got together with Eulodia and the rest of her
relatives from Las Minas that afternoon, I heard her laughing at
Rebecca behind half-closed doors.

I began to feel sorry for Rebecca, despite our being so different.
There wasn't a single book of poetry in the house on the lagoon;
Rebecca's library had disappeared when Buenaventura demolished
Pavel's house. One afternoon we were sitting out on the terrace
when I made up my mind to ask her about her writing. "Is it true
you once wrote a book of poems?" I ventured. "I'd like very much
to read it." Rebecca sat for a minute, head bowed, without saying
a word. When she finally looked up, she had tears in her eyes.
"How kind of you to ask," she said. "I'd be happy to show it to
you." And she went to her room to get it.

It wasn't so much a book as a folder of poems, and it was just
as Quintín had described it to me, with a beautiful Art Nouveau
binding, a water lily carved on the cover and silver clasps on the
sides. The pages were yellow and wrinkled; Rebecca hadn't written
a single line for years. I read the whole book in one night and the

next day I waited until after breakfast, when everybody had left the house, to let her know my opinion. I told her how much I'd liked it. Then I delicately suggested she change an adjective here, a metaphor there. I swear I said it candidly. I was still young and inexperienced; I didn't mean to hurt her. After all, Rebecca had never studied literature; she wrote poetry from inspiration and was ignorant of the intricacies of form. Naïvely, I thought suggesting how she might improve her verses would help us become friends.

"You think you know so much, just because you graduated from Vassar College!" Rebecca said angrily, snatching the folder from me. "You go around with a chip on your shoulder and you don't know a chit about life. One day you'll come asking for *my* help and you'll have to pay your dues!"

22

A Dirge for

Esmeralda Márquez

※

IT WASN'T UNTIL THE Esmeralda Márquez affair that I realized
how deeply I had wounded Rebecca. The incident was important
because in a way it was one of the strands in the skein of resentment
that later enveloped the whole Mendizabal family. Ignacio and
Quintín never felt the same toward each other afterwards, and
Rebecca never trusted me.

Esmeralda was from Ponce, and a childhood friend of mine. In
fact, she's still one of my best friends. We lived near each other
when we were teenagers—her house was on Callejón Amor, two
blocks away from Aurora Street—and even though Esmeralda is
four years younger than I, we went to the same teenage parties
and picnics. She had also been in the Kerenski Ballet School and
had danced in the corps in *Swan Lake* at our recital at La Perla
Theater.

Esmeralda was the daughter of Doña Ermelinda Quiñones, a
famous dressmaker from Ponce and the official mistress of Don
Bolívar Márquez, a well-known lawyer who often mediated in
sugarcane-labor disputes. Don Bolívar was married to Doña Carmela Márquez, a fat, pious woman who spent most of her day
praying in church. Doña Ermelinda had been Don Bolívar's mistress for years. He took her with him everywhere: to the Continental

Club, to the Ponce Country Club, even to private parties where
he knew his friends wouldn't turn Doña Ermelinda out. This
wouldn't have been at all surprising, since in Ponce gentlemen
with a certain social position often had official paramours. Doña
Ermelinda was a light-skinned mulatto—and a very beautiful one,
at that.

Ermelinda was born on a small farm on the outskirts of Mayagüez, a town on the west coast of the island, famous for its needlework. Her mother was a widow with seven daughters, and by the
time the youngest was eight years old, every one of them knew
how to sew. They would stay up all night huddled around a gas
lamp in their palm-thatched hut, plaiting, looping, and twisting
thread. By morning they would have finished the most beautiful
lace nightgowns, slips, and bodices that could be found in town.
When the First World War was raging in Europe, German submarines had made it impossible for the United States to import
lace lingerie from France. The owners of several large factories in
New York and Boston then turned their eyes to Puerto Rico, which
was already famous for its Mundillo pillow lace. They traveled to
the island and established dozens of workshops in the interior.
"Puerto Rican lacemakers," said the garment-industry ads that
appeared in the States, "had fingers as slender as flower stems,
and were as fragile and sensuous as the maidens of Ghent."

Ermelinda was the oldest of seven sisters, and once a week she
went with her mother to sell their wares at the garment factory in
Mayagüez, where they were paid twelve cents for each exquisitely
finished piece of underwear. Ermelinda's mother was a responsible
factory worker, and Mr. Turnbull, the factory manager, trusted
her. He let her have several rolls of silk and lace to take back to
the farm with her and only charged her a slight commission to
work at home.

One day Ermelinda was sitting on the sidewalk, waiting for her
mother to come out of Mr. Turnbull's office, when she spotted an
old copy of *Harper's Bazaar* lying near the gutter. Ermelinda attended public school in Mayagüez and had been taught to read

English, thanks to Commissioner Easton's decree. She picked up the magazine and began to look through the ads at the back. One of them struck her fancy: it showed a beautiful girl with blond curly hair, getting ready for bed. She was wearing the very same silk negligee she and her little sisters had finished only three weeks before, for which Mr. Turnbull had paid her mother exactly fifty cents. It was selling for fifty dollars at a store called Saks Fifth Avenue in New York. Ermelinda couldn't believe her eyes. She was so angry she told her mother she would never sew for Mr. Turnbull again.

She was sixteen and very good-looking—tall and willowy, with fine features. Her eyes were the color of molasses and her skin was a light cinnamon. Her only drawback was the mat of corkscrew curls that grew on top of her head, so wild and thick and spirited there was no way to comb them into a civilized hairdo. For this reason, ever since she turned fifteen, Ermelinda wore a red turban tied around her head.

In the nineteen-twenties, women on the island were becoming ever more conscious of the need to get out of the home. The local suffragettes, taking their cue from women on the mainland, marched in all the towns, fighting for the right to vote as well as the right to work. Needleworkers constituted more than half the labor force, but they were paid way below the minimum wage for men: six dollars a week for those over eighteen, four dollars a week for those under eighteen.

Ermelinda heard there was going to be a needleworkers' strike, and she decided to join it. She had read about strikes in a booklet published by the American Federation of Labor that had come her way. She went all over the island on muleback, wearing a pair of old U.S. Army pants she had acquired at the Salvation Army, and keeping dry under a huge arum leaf she held high over her head every time it rained. She began to make speeches at meetings, urging women to organize and join the strike; otherwise, they would never amount to anything.

One Sunday, at Plaza Degetau in Ponce, Ermelinda got up on

the Firemen's Band platform during intermission and began to make a speech. At that moment Don Bolívar Márquez rode by in his yellow Mercury convertible. His wife, Carmela, was at ten o'clock Mass in the Cathedral, and as Don Bolívar never set foot in church, he drove around in his car while waiting for her. Ermelinda was haranguing the women in the plaza to support the needleworkers' march the following week. She accused the needle industry of paying its workers a salary of hunger and of promoting a false image of Puerto Rico in their advertising campaigns. "If the lacemakers of Puerto Rico have fingers as slender as flower stems," she said, "it's not because they're born frail and sensuous like the maidens of Ghent, or any thick-witted nonsense like that, but because they have t.b. And if the children of Puerto Rico," she would add, "can sew as daintily as elves, it's not because they're born delicate by nature, or any shit like that, but because they have tapeworms and are starving."

The striking women, said Ermelinda over the megaphone, were to travel to San Juan the following Monday, and they would march to the capitol together to press their demands, wielding their scissors in their right hands and wearing red handkerchiefs tied to their wrists. The poor working conditions of the needlework industry were to be reassessed by the local legislature, since, as part of the United States, the island would soon be subjected to the new code of conduct of the NLRA, the National Labor Relations Act, which had recently been passed in Washington.

With her red turban glinting in the sun—she always stuck her needles in it before she made a speech—and her ample bosom resting on the rail of the platform, Ermelinda looked like an Amazon about to set the world on fire. Don Bolívar was impressed. He got out of the car and walked up to the wooden platform and waited for Ermelinda at the bottom of the steps. "Congratulations on your excellent speech," he said with a polite smile. "As a lawyer, I've always been opposed to the unfair way the needle industry operates on this island. If you get to San Juan and should meet with trouble, feel free to get in touch with me." And he gave her his card.

Ermelinda kept the card, but didn't pay Don Bolívar much mind. She had met his kind before; the sensuous lips and the lustful gleam in the eye gave him away. He wasn't so much interested in justice as in saving damsels in distress, and Ermelinda could very well save herself. She marched to the capitol the following week, but the strikers were not able to get their petition to the legislature. The local police were waiting for them, clubs in hand, as they walked down Ponce de León Avenue, and in the battle that ensued on the capitol's steps several women were wounded, and also a little girl. Puerto Rican legislators, bribed by the tycoons of the garment industry, had worked around the National Labor Relations Act, and the workers were not allowed to enter the building. The strike was declared illegal, and the poor conditions and low salaries in the needle industry stayed just as they were. Ermelinda landed in jail, and after two weeks of suffering indignities at the hands of her captors—she was raped twice, Esmeralda told me—she wrote a letter to Don Bolívar, asking for his help. Ermelinda was set free on bail the following day. When she walked out of La Princesa jail, he was waiting for her at the door in his yellow Mercury convertible. He drove her to Ponce himself, bought her a house in Callejón Amor, and moved in with her a month later.

The house was small but very beautiful. It had a raised balcony with columns; acanthus leaves decorated the capitals, and a small leaded-glass oval window graced the entrance. On the glass was a gay detail: a blindfolded cupid taking aim with his bow and arrow at whoever walked up to the front door. Don Bolívar would spend three days a week with Doña Ermelinda, and two with Doña Carmela in his official residence nearby. Everybody was happy. Next to her house, Ermelinda set up a small workshop with several Singer sewing machines, opened a boutique in front named Frivolité, and plunged into her work. She was so discouraged by the needleworkers' defeat she swore she would never bother to march for labor rights again. But she hadn't given up the fight. Fair or foul, one day she was going to win the struggle against powerful men.

Doña Ermelinda's lavish bridal gowns and evening dresses soon became famous in Ponce. All the young ladies and debutantes of the town visited her home. In fact, having a gown cut and sewn by Doña Ermelinda was the same as joining an exclusive fashion academy. But it was more than that. It meant becoming part of one of the oldest professions of all: that of woman of the world. Rumor had it, moreover, that Doña Ermelinda's ability with needle and thread went further than just good taste and a gifted sense of style. Tongues in Ponce wagged about the way her gowns made women mysteriously seductive, so that their escorts would inevitably become infatuated or fall head over heels in love with them.

After a customer of Doña Ermelinda ordered a new gown and paid for it (in advance), she would visit the boutique several times. First she would choose the material and the design of the dress; then she would go for three mandatory fittings; and finally she would pick out the accessories: what kind of doeskin glove to wear, whether up over the elbow or daintily trimmed at the wrist, what shade to dye her dancing slippers, what type of minaudière to carry in her hand. Everything had to be harmoniously assembled; to be a fashionable woman of the world entailed a wisdom acquired through the centuries, a knowledge just as important for one's survival as knowing when and where to invest one's savings. In Doña Ermelinda's opinion, a needle was as powerful an instrument of war as the lance had been for the Conquistador or the Mauser rifle for the American foot soldier during the Spanish-American War.

Doña Ermelinda's young clients knew each other well and would sit in rocking chairs in her living room, sipping passion-fruit juice with a nip of rum, and listening to her talk. She taught them a very important lesson, which she had learned during her tragic stay in La Princesa, San Juan's jail. Desire, she told them softly so the servants wouldn't hear, is the iron spike on which the world turns, the cause of its every happiness and of its every misfortune. And the way to oil desire's spike, she whispered to them, is to tantalize men. Everything a woman did should have temptation as its final objective. If she took a bath, put French perfume behind her ears, and dabbed herself with powder mixed with cinnamon, it should be to entice a man who was worth her while. If she cinched her waistline, making her bodice so tight that her breasts seemed about to spring playfully out of her dress, or spent hours making her hairdo into a work of art, it should be to seduce a convenient suitor, one who could support her in style. A woman of the world never wasted her ammunition on penniless candidates and only let herself be approached by millionaires.

Doña Ermelinda had three daughters with Don Bolívar, and she named the three of them after jewels: Opal, Amethyst, and Esmeralda, who was the oldest of the three. Don Bolívar had no children with Doña Carmela, so he gave his daughters everything they asked for: the best education, travel in Europe, exquisite clothes, membership in the best clubs in town. But as he was never married to Doña Ermelinda, the three Márquez girls were officially illegitimate and couldn't use their father's last name in their signature. Doña Ermelinda had hopes that one day this would change and Don Bolívar would do right by them.

The girls were equally beautiful: they had inherited their mother's willowy figure and light cinnamon skin, but only Esmeralda inherited the Márquezes' green eyes and fair hair, which fell in waves of honey over her dark shoulders. They were so beautiful that in town they called them the three sorrows, rather than the three graces, because every young man of good family in Ponce who set eyes on them fell madly in love.

Esmeralda Márquez met Ignacio Mendizabal in 1955, the summer Quintín and I got married, at the Bougainvillea Ball. She had come to the ball—which took place at the Escambrón Beach Club at the end of each summer—accompanied by Ernesto Ustariz, the son of a rich cattle rancher from the south of the island. Doña Ermelinda had married her other daughters to two prosperous merchants from Ponce, and wanted her oldest to marry into one of the prominent families of San Juan. Ernesto was a fine young man, and even though Doña Ermelinda had consented to have Esmeralda go out with him this once, she thought he was too much of a cowboy for her daughter. Esmeralda had told her Ernesto was studying at the university in Río Piedras and planned to go on to study law. But in the summers he worked on his father's dairy farm from dawn to dusk, milking cows and helping the farmhands lead the animals through vats full of chemicals to kill the ticks and gnats on them. This gave him a rustic aura that Doña Ermelinda didn't approve of.

Doña Ermelinda chaperoned her daughters everywhere, and she planned to bring Esmeralda to as many parties in San Juan as she could that summer, so she would have the opportunity of meeting young men from the capital. Thanks to Don Bolívar's political connections—he was a devoted Popular—they had already been invited to the Mayor of San Juan's *lechonada* at Christmas, and there Esmeralda had met several of the sons of local politicians, as well as the son of the owner of *La Prensa*, the most important newspaper on the island. But Doña Ermelinda didn't want Esmeralda to have anything to do with them. She wanted her daughter to meet the boys from the *really* good families of San Juan, the sons of the bankers, industrialists, and powerful merchants whose businesses were well established.

The night of the Bougainvillea Ball, Doña Ermelinda sat on a chair at the back of the Escambrón's ballroom, keeping an eye on her daughter, who was dancing a merengue with Ernesto Ustariz. Most of the men wore white dinner jackets with red carnations in their buttonholes, and from her vantage point, Doña Ermelinda recognized several of her young Ponce customers wearing her latest creations, which she had copied that season from *Vogue*. Esmeralda's evening gown was the most stunning of all. It was emerald-green silk, with an off-the-shoulder cowl neck which contrasted beautifully with the young woman's honey-colored hair, combed in an elegant beehive.

Doña Ermelinda herself always dressed in black. Ponce's tongues used to wag that her skirts were made of tar, better to catch the young men who fluttered around her daughters like flies. But she compensated for the severe look of her dresses with the elaborate turbans she wore on her head. That evening she was wearing a yellow silk one that looked exactly like a pineapple. A crowd of young people were shaking and shimmying to the beat of Rafael Hernández's ballroom orchestra, when suddenly she noticed an aristocratic-looking young man in a black tuxedo who approached Esmeralda and cut in as she was dancing with her partner. Ernesto Ustariz was so surprised he didn't know what to do when the young man in the tuxedo took Esmeralda by the hand and whirled her away. They sailed off together to the farthermost corner of the dance floor and soon were nowhere to be seen.

Ernesto stalked off to the bar to get a drink, and Doña Ermelinda sat up higher on her chair, her eyes skimming the dance floor like radar beams, until she finally spotted Esmeralda's glimmering green dress at one end of the ballroom. They made a handsome couple—both were blond and they were about the same height. The orchestra now played a tango and they looked like two skaters as they glided over the polished wood floor. Doña Ermelinda asked her neighbor at the table who the good-looking young man in the tuxedo was. His name, she learned, was Ignacio and he was Buenaventura Mendizabal's youngest son. Doña Ermelinda's heart gave a leap. If Esmeralda should marry Ignacio Mendizabal, who cared if Don Bolívar didn't officially recognize his daughter and if she couldn't use his last name as part of her signature? Esmeralda would never have to worry about such insignificant things again.

DURING THE REST OF THE SUMMER Doña Ermelinda designed Esmeralda's dresses with the utmost care, each more exquisite than the one before, so Esmeralda would hypnotize Ignacio as a candle will a moth. At first, Ignacio asked Esmeralda to dance with him only once in a while at parties. He was never very athletic and didn't like to dance—he tended to be a bit pudgy because he liked rich foods. He was also nearsighted and wore a pair of round-rimmed glasses that were constantly slipping down his nose because he perspired easily. But he was very sociable and liked to tell funny stories that made the ladies laugh. At every gathering there were usually three or four lovely girls flirting with him at the same time. This flattered him, because he didn't think of himself as handsome, but he couldn't make up his mind about any of them. After seeing how beautiful Esmeralda looked at parties, however, he began to ask her to dance more often.

Quintín was the first person in the family to perceive the effect Doña Ermelinda's strategy was having on Ignacio. He didn't know anything about Esmeralda or her family, except that she was a good friend of mine, and I decided not to tell him more than was necessary. He had met Esmeralda at one of the parties we attended that summer and was impressed by her looks, as was everyone else.

I didn't see anything wrong with Ignacio's falling in love with Esmeralda. I would have welcomed her as my sister-in-law. That way she would move from Ponce to San Juan, and we could live near each other. But I couldn't be sure how the Mendizabals would feel.

One day Rebecca told us Ignacio was acting strange. She was sure he was seeing someone, she said. He never got back home before three-thirty in the morning, and when he did, he'd lie down on the bed without taking off his clothes, smelling the white gardenia a girl called Esmeralda had given him before she said good-bye. Rebecca spied on Ignacio every night through the keyhole, and suspected he didn't sleep at all.

Ignacio had always been very particular about the way his food was prepared, but lately he had become impossible. Every morning at breakfast, when Petra asked him if he wanted his eggs scrambled soft or hard, or if he wanted goat or Gruyère cheese melted over his toast, he told her he didn't care. He didn't want any breakfast at all, because he didn't want to spoil the taste of mocha cream puffs he still had on his lips after kissing Esmeralda the night before. When at lunchtime Eulodia asked if he wanted his beef-steak rare or well done, his rice with red beans or white beans, he said he didn't care; he didn't want to forget the odor of truffled pheasant that came from Esmeralda's armpits when they had danced the mambo at the Copa Marina the night before.

Rebecca was near hysterics. When Ignacio went for a week without eating or sleeping, she asked Quintín to talk to him and find out who Esmeralda was.

Quintín went to Ignacio's room and had to wait up for him until dawn. "If you keep on like this, you'll get sick, and you'll never get back to Florida State University when summer vacation is over," Quintín told Ignacio when he came home at six in the morning. Ignacio looked up to Quintín and usually heeded his advice.

"I'm in love with Esmeralda Márquez and I need your help," Ignacio confessed, a pleading look in his eyes. "I want Father and Mother to meet her and I don't know how to go about it. First impressions are very important, and Esmeralda is so beautiful I'm sure, once they see her, Buenaventura and Rebecca won't mind who her mother is."

"And who is Esmeralda's mother?" Quintín asked cautiously.

"Doña Ermelinda, a well-known fashion designer from Ponce. She's been the official lover of Don Bolívar Márquez—a labor-relations lawyer—for twenty years. But Don Bolívar refuses to marry her, even though his wife, Doña Carmela, died, and he's been a widower for five years. I'm afraid this might put Esmeralda in a disreputable light," Ignacio added.

Quintín was open-minded then; he didn't think people living together without being married was anything extraordinary. It wasn't until later that he disapproved of that type of arrangement. He cautioned Ignacio, however: it wasn't wise to shock people, and their parents would undoubtedly be scandalized when they found out—especially Rebecca. Buenaventura and Rebecca had probably never heard of Doña Ermelinda or Don Bolívar. They knew very few people from Ponce—their friends were all from San Juan, and that would be to Ignacio's advantage. Quintín told his brother to go to bed, and that he'd think about helping him.

Quintín was more concerned about his parents' reaction than he had let on, however. That night, when he came back to our apartment, he complained that his brother was taking an unnecessary chance with Esmeralda Márquez. There were many beautiful girls among the young people Ignacio had grown up with in Alamares, and differences in how one was brought up were often more important than differences of culture and even of language. I tried to make him look at the whole thing from a different angle. Esmeralda was a friend of mine, I told him, and I knew her very well. She was not only beautiful, she was also very intelligent. She had managed to get a student grant and would soon be attending the New York Fashion Institute. She had inherited Doña Ermelinda's excellent eye for line and color and would probably be able to get a good job in a fashion house in the States after she graduated. If Ignacio liked Esmeralda, it was his business; there was no reason why he shouldn't ask her out. Doña Ermelinda, on the other hand, was a very elegant lady, who would do her utmost to make a good impression on Buenaventura and Rebecca, as on San Juan society. As to Don Bolívar, it was improbable that they would ever meet him. He was an old man and never went anywhere with Doña Ermelinda.

A few days later Quintín told his brother he was willing to help him out. Esmeralda was a sweet girl; with her blond hair and green eyes, she might convince Buenaventura and Rebecca to overlook her illicit home, of which she was the innocent victim. I was glad when Quintín decided to help Ignacio. He was still my old Quintín, the one I had fallen in love with when he came to visit me in Ponce.

Quintín and I went to parties regularly that summer and Rebecca often let us invite friends over to the house on the lagoon. Buenaventura liked to entertain, too. He particularly enjoyed trying out new wines and imported delicacies on his friends. It was no trouble for Quintín to organize a get-together for the following Saturday. Quintín invited a good number of his friends from San Juan, and some of my old friends from Ponce, and Esmeralda Márquez was among them. •

Esmeralda and her mother arrived at the house in a black Fleetwood Cadillac Doña Ermelinda rented for the occasion, with a uniformed chauffeur at the wheel. When Esmeralda stepped out of the car, she was wearing the most beautiful evening gown I have ever seen: the top was of Swiss embroidery and clung to her breasts like snow; the skirt was of silk organza and swirled around her like a waterfall. Right behind her came Doña Ermelinda dressed in tar-black taffeta, with a golden ziggurat sitting on top of her head. She was putting all her cosmetic wisdom to the test, and her skin looked almost pearl-white next to the opulent black of her dress.

Ignacio introduced Doña Ermelinda and Esmeralda to both his parents. Buenaventura was enchanted. He liked exotic people and felt immediately at home with Doña Ermelinda. He shook her hand warmly, took her around the living room to have her meet his friends, then offered her a glass of champagne. Ignacio took Esmeralda by the arm, so she would get acquainted with the young people, and after a few minutes of conversation drifted off with her to the golden terrace, to show her the moon trembling over the lagoon. When Rebecca saw them holding hands, a shiver of apprehension ran down her spine. Esmeralda Márquez looked like a nice girl; she was certainly beautiful in her white dress, which made her suntan very becoming. But Rebecca had absolutely no idea who she was and had never heard the name Márquez before.

Rebecca sat down next to a friend and began to observe Doña Ermelinda from afar. Buenaventura was showing her around the house and had taken her into the dining room, where Doña Ermelinda was busy admiring the Conquistador chairs. The dining room opened out onto the terrace, where the dance was soon to begin, and Doña Ermelinda decided to sit in one of the chairs because it offered a good vantage point. She pushed the chair to the edge of the terrace and made herself comfortable. From out of her bag she took a black lace fan Don Bolívar had bought her in Spain, and began to fan herself. She had finished her champagne and beckoned a waiter for another glass. Several ladies, the mothers of some of the other young ladies who had been invited to the party, came and sat next to her. They all began to talk and laugh among themselves.

Rebecca was amazed at Doña Ermelinda's uninhibited behavior. A total stranger, she was acting as if she had known the Mendizabals all her life. Rebecca scrutinized her more closely. She was elegantly dressed, but there was something about her that didn't ring true; she couldn't figure out what. She was still thinking about it when the music started playing the first paso doble of the night.

Ignacio had hired a popular band to liven up the evening and ordered them to play only Spanish music, to please his father. Buenaventura came over to ask Rebecca for a dance.

"You'll have to accept that girl as your daughter-in-law one day, Rebecca," he said to her. "If I know Ignacio, he's going to want to marry her as soon as he graduates from college; you know he's as headstrong as you are. I think you'd better get used to the idea." And when Rebecca didn't answer, but kept opening and closing her fan and staring over Buenaventura's shoulder to see what Doña Ermelinda was doing, he tightened his arm around her to bring her closer.

"Remember when *we* were almost the same age and fell desperately in love the night of your coronation ball? I was penniless but I was the happiest man on earth," he said. "Today we can afford to be lenient and spare our children some of the difficulties we had to face." Rebecca fanned herself slowly as Buenaventura went on whispering in her ear. He always got romantic when he danced a paso doble, and right now they were dancing *Pisa Morena*, one of his favorites.

All of a sudden Rebecca put her hand, sparkling with diamond rings, discreetly on his chest to make him keep his distance. "Stop behaving like a teenager and steer me as close as you can to Doña Ermelinda; I think I've discovered what was bothering me about her." They spun around the dance floor, picking up speed, Buenaventura's patent-leather shoes and Rebecca's rhinestone sandals sliding in perfect unison over the mosaic floor. Rebecca looked attentively at Doña Ermelinda. When they were close enough, she made Buenaventura spin around again, flung her right hand in an arc, and struck Doña Ermelinda's golden turban with her fan. The music stopped and everyone gasped.

When Buenaventura saw the turban fly off Doña Ermelinda's head, he stopped in his tracks. Rebecca bent down to pick it up and, looking surprised and dismayed, gave it back to Doña Ermelinda with a smile. She excused herself and insisted she had been looking the other way when Buenaventura unexpectedly whirled her around. Doña Ermelinda's face had turned gray. Several people began to laugh, pointing to the thick mat of hair that rose from her head, and some began to make unkind comments. But Doña Ermelinda didn't bat an eyelash. She stared right back at them, stood up proudly from the Spanish Conquistador chair, and shook her head vigorously, to make her wild curls stand out even more. Then she walked over to Esmeralda, took her by the hand, and they walked out of the house together, heads held high.

That sad event, which gave the San Juan social set something to gossip about for months, had serious repercussions in the Mendizabal family. Ignacio was furious at his mother for having shamed him. He began to court Esmeralda openly, in defiance of his parents' prohibition. If he persisted in seeing her, they told him, they would cut off his monthly allowance and refuse to pay for his airplane tickets to fly home from school on vacations. But Ignacio wouldn't listen.

Doña Ermelinda came every so often to the capital, to purchase the tulles and silks she needed to create her debutante gowns, and when Esmeralda was home from school in the States, she would accompany her on those trips. Usually they stayed overnight at a small but very nice house overlooking the bay in Old San Juan. During the rest of that summer vacation, they stayed there several times. Ignacio would come to the Márquezes' pink house in the evenings, stand under Esmeralda's balcony, and sing her romantic songs with a guitar trio accompanying him. He spent a fortune on these serenades, and on the bouquets of gardenias he sent up to her door every night. But Esmeralda never opened the balcony's louvered windows to see who was singing. The insult to Doña Ermelinda's pride had been so great she would feel vindicated only if Esmeralda roundly rejected Buenaventura Mendizabal's heir.

A few days before he left for school in September, Ignacio came to our new apartment to talk to Quintín in private. "You have to help me make Mother apologize to Doña Ermelinda," he said. "It's the only way she's going to let me see Esmeralda again." Quintín was sitting at his desk reading Suetonius' *The Scandalous Lives of the Caesars*. He looked up from his book and said, with sadness, "I'm sorry, but I can't help you, Ignacio." But Ignacio insisted, and he wouldn't leave.

Finally Quintín got tired of Ignacio's pleading and decided to stop beating around the bush. "You can't go out with Esmeralda Márquez, because she's part black. Father and Mother will never stand for it," he told him point-blank. They were sitting in the living room, and Ignacio was incensed. (And so was I, but I was too afraid to say anything.) Ignacio gave Quintín a violent shove, so he stumbled and fell. Quintín got up from the floor and slapped Ignacio, and his gold-rimmed glasses went flying across the room. It took all my levelheadedness to make them stop the fight.

Some weeks later Esmeralda was engaged to Ernesto Ustariz. Ernesto was head over heels in love with Esmeralda, and he had convinced his father to pay for Esmeralda's education at the Fashion Institute. As soon as they were married, they would move to New York, where Ernesto planned to enter New York University Law School. They set the wedding date for November in San Juan, because Doña Ermelinda wanted all of San Juan society to attend. Ignacio, Quintín, and I were invited to the reception at Alamares's poshest hotel. After the wedding, the newlyweds would spend the night in Doña Ermelinda's pink house on the bay before boarding a plane for New York, where they would honeymoon.

Ignacio left for Florida State University at the end of September and was back on the island two weeks later. He wasn't feeling well, he said, and wanted to take the semester off. The day of Esmeralda's wedding, Ignacio woke up sick. He suffered from asthma, and the emotional stress of the past week had induced a serious attack. He could scarcely breathe and went around the house on tiptoe, with an inhaler in his hand, as if walking underwater. He was by turn furious at Esmeralda and terribly unhappy. After lunch he went to a bar in San Juan to try to forget his woes. Rebecca insisted we all ignore him. He was only seventeen, and would eventually get over his silly obsession.

That evening we went to the wedding together. Ignacio had had more than a few drinks and was strangely silent. He said a courteous hello to Esmeralda and her mother on the receiving line, as if nothing had happened between them. At three in the morning, however, when Quintín and I were ready to go home, we couldn't find Ignacio anywhere. Finally we had to leave the hotel without him.

Quintín was worried about his brother, but there was nothing he could do. When we got to our apartment, we went directly to bed and fell asleep.

It must have been four in the morning when the phone woke us up. Quintín answered. It was Rebecca. "Ignacio is being held at the police station," she said, almost spitting out the words. "After the wedding he drove over to Doña Ermelinda's house and began to fire at everything in sight. I'd like to know why you left him behind at the reception and came back by yourselves. After all, he's your younger brother, Quintín, and you're responsible for him!" Quintín could hear Buenaventura in the background, his voice cracking with worry as he tried desperately to get a lawyer at that hour.

Quintín got out of bed and hurried to the police station. I called Rebecca and told her I was sorry; we had looked all over the hotel for Ignacio, but he had simply disappeared. She was terribly angry. "You may know a lot about books, young lady," she almost hissed, "but you know very little about responsibility and respect!"

It wasn't until later that I found out what had happened. Ignacio had gone to the wedding armed with Buenaventura's gun, waited until the bride and groom left the hotel for Doña Ermelinda's house in Old San Juan, and emptied it point-blank at the door. The newlyweds fled into the bathroom at the back of the building, but not before a bullet came through the front door and seriously injured Esmeralda's little finger. When he heard her scream, Ignacio stopped firing and collapsed on the sidewalk. The noise woke up the whole neighborhood; lights went on in the houses nearby, and not five minutes had elapsed before a police siren was heard.

Quintín got his brother out on bail that morning, and Ignacio never mentioned Esmeralda's name again. He went back to college the following semester and finished his four years at Florida State University. But he never fell in love again. When he came home for vacation, he enjoyed taking his fifteen-foot sailboat out on Alamares Lagoon all by himself. He named the boat *La Esmeralda* and insisted that sailing was the only love of his life.

23

Petra's Kingdom

❧

THE CELLAR OF THE HOUSE on the lagoon mesmerized me from the beginning. It dated from the days of Pavel, when Rebecca was a very different person from what she had become when I met her. The cellar gave the house much of its mystery, the feeling that events weren't always what they seemed but could have unexpected echoes and repercussions. My own house on Aurora Street had no cellar. Ponce's soil is dry and hard, very different from the swamps of the north, and its basalt foundations make digging into it almost impossible. At the house on Aurora Street, events were easy to classify: there was a right and a left, a front and a back to everything—there was little room for ambiguity or doubt. But at the house on the lagoon, things were often misleading.

The first thing that caught my eye when I entered that strange world were the huge steel beams that supported Pavel's golden terrace. They jutted out majestically from the walls of the house, all rusted and half eaten by the salt air. Even though they weren't supposed to be seen, they had an Art Nouveau elegance which seemed almost organic, as if Pavel had designed them to blend in with the nearby mangroves. The area under the terrace was used as a common room by the servants, and it was here that they ate, smoked, and sat talking and relaxing after work. The dirt floor was hardly noticeable; the servants sprinkled it with water and swept it carefully every day. Petra had furnished it with an old set of wicker furniture which had originally been used at the house and which Rebecca had discarded. Her wicker peacock throne was an important feature of the sitting room. Every night she would sit on it, wearing her brightly colored bead necklaces and bracelets. She would listen to the servants' complaints, and give them advice.

One by one, the servants would come and sit next to her on a low stool, pouring out their grievances in a whisper. If Rebecca had had a tantrum, for example, and given Eulodia hell for dropping a wineglass on the floor, Eulodia was to be patient with her and say nothing; Rebecca wasn't completely in control of her nerves. If Rebecca had ordered Brunilda to iron her new evening gown and had not bothered to take off the designer tag, and Brunilda was shocked to see the dress had cost five hundred dollars when her own salary was eighty dollars a month, Brunilda was to keep quiet about it. Rebecca was Buenaventura's wife, and she had the right to spend whatever she wanted on clothes, which were an important symbol of her husband's position in the world.

At the center of the common room, a door had been cut into the dirt wall. It dated back to Pavel's time; you could tell because of its Gaudiesque design. It was decorated with tendrils and leaves of a fantastic vegetation. It led to a dark tunnel into which twenty cells opened. The cells had earthen floors and no windows; they were ventilated by grilles imbedded into the top of each end wall. Originally, the rooms had been intended for storage: for wine, codfish, or Buenaventura's precious imported hams. When Buenaventura moved his merchandise to his warehouse on La Puntilla, however, the storage rooms had been turned into servants' quarters.

There must have been two dozen servants living in these cells when I visited the cellar the first time, and they were all related to Petra Avilés: Eulodia, Brígida, and Brunilda, her three nieces; Confesor, Buenaventura's tailor, who was Petra's nephew; Eustasio, the gardener, who was her cousin; Eusebia, Rebecca's seamstress, who was Petra's sister; Carmelo, the farmhand, who was her brother; and Brambon, her common-law husband, who was the chauffeur—among others. They got along very well together, and there were rarely arguments among them.

Buenaventura liked to bathe in the fresh spring water because he was convinced it kept him young. Every time he stepped in, he felt as if he shed years. Pavel had designed a marvelous underground chamber for the spring, decorated with a mosaic of indigo waves, and golden dolphins playfully chasing each other around. A bronze door, beautifully decorated with seashells and stars, opened onto it from the right side of the common room. Buenaventura had always liked this grotto and left it standing when he tore down the rest of Pavel's house. The servants bathed in a cement trough that had been built adjacent to it, which was also fed by the underground spring.

The cellar had a third door on the left, which opened onto the kitchen. From it one could step out into the yard, hidden from the avenue by a tall hibiscus hedge. This was where the family laundry was hung to dry after Brígida and Brunilda had scrubbed it on a rough stone slab. On the right side of the cellar, another door opened onto an enclosed patio where the animals were kept. Buenaventura's Doberman pinschers were there in a large cage. Fausto, the original black male who had mysteriously arrived from Germany on one of Buenaventura's ships, had long since passed away. But Buenaventura had paired him off with a handsome bitch before he died, and now he owned two black Dobermans: Fausto and Mefistófeles, who were the apple of his eye. Buenaventura also owned a cow, which was milked for him every morning; a dozen chickens, which laid fresh eggs for his breakfast; and a pigpen, from which Petra chose Buenaventura's beloved pigs' knuckles and ham shanks every week.

There was only one cage which didn't belong to Buenaventura

and his family—where the land crabs were kept and fattened up. The crab cage was made of wood and it was on stilts. A large stone sat on the lid to keep the crabs from pushing it open. Brambon, Petra's husband, had made the cage himself. Land crabs proliferated in the mangroves and had to be hunted down periodically by the servants, especially when it rained and the water in the mangrove swamp rose a few inches closer to the house. Otherwise, they would soon be seen scuttling down the cellar corridors and even climb up the terrace's iron beams. Fortunately, Fausto and Mefistófeles would sniff the crabs out and rip off their claws, so the crab population was kept under control.

Land crabs were considered black people's food at the house on the lagoon; no one in the Mendizabal family would have been caught dead eating them. But the servants loved crab. Petra said the crabs reminded her of warriors in full armor, and she swore they made people brave. Every Saturday night the servants would sit around a table in the cellar in front of what looked like a heap of blue cobblestones. Except that the cobblestones had spiny legs, huge claws, and eyes that stood out like red seeds on top of their heads. Then they would take a mallet, crack open the cobblestones one by one, and pry out the sweet white flesh with a fork.

Petra's room was the first one on the right at the end of the cellar's underground tunnel. The walls of her room were lined with bottles and jars filled with strange potions and herbal unguents. She always knew what remedy to prescribe for each ailment: orange leaf tea for nervous disorders, rue for menstrual pains, aloe for insect bites, witch hazel for ear inflammations or sties.

Petra ran Buenaventura's bath with perfumed bay leaves every day, and once every two or three months she boiled all kinds of roots which she said had magical powers and poured the liquid into the grotto's blue basin before Buenaventura stepped in. Buenaventura was convinced Petra's baths helped him do good business, especially when a price war was taking place at Mendizabal & Company. If he was trying to defeat his competitors from California, for example, who had slashed the price of Green Valley asparagus, he would take one of Petra's baths and his white asparagus from Aranjuez would miraculously begin to sell. Suddenly there would be a fad for them in the capital, and people would start eating rolled white asparagus sandwiches, white asparagus casseroles with cheese, lobster and white asparagus bisque. Buenaventura would make several thousand dollars overnight.

The servants respected Petra, and it was through her that order was established and maintained at the house. Petra was Buenaventura's marshal; everything he commanded was done by her. The servants considered Rebecca second in authority; before they did what she asked, they always checked with Petra. They were grateful because it was thanks to Petra that they had managed to leave the stinking quagmire of Las Minas in their rowboats and could live in relative comfort under Buenaventura's roof.

Petra always gave special attention to Quintín, although she made it clear that his privileged status depended on his carrying out Buenaventura's wishes. Buenaventura, as the years went by, felt a growing sympathy for the Independentista cause, and once had secretly donated money for it. He had lived on the island for many years, he'd say, longer than he had lived in Spain, and it was difficult for him to accept the fact that his adopted country was only partly self-governed. Not to be able to trade with other countries, for example; not to have a say in the election of the President; not to go to war with another country if the need arose—these were difficult things for him to accept as a proud descendant of the Conquistadors.

Quintín had been partial to statehood since he was a child—because of his closeness to his grandfather Arrigoitia. Arístides had taught him to admire the United States as one of the few true democracies in the world, and he believed the island had the right to become part of it. "We were invaded by the United States in 1898; and twenty years later we were given American citizenship without anyone asking our opinion about it. The United States made a commitment to us at that time, and now they must honor it."

When Quintín made his First Communion, his grandfather put Lincoln's Gettysburg Address in a little gold frame and gave it to him as a present to keep in his room. When Quintín graduated from high school, Arístides's gift was Toqueville's *Democracy in America*, and a volume of Thomas Jefferson's memoirs. Quintín read the books attentively, and his admiration for the United States grew ever more.

As a young man, Quintín loved to talk about these things at dinnertime, when the whole family gathered together. He maintained that the closeness of our island to the United States in the last fifty years had Americanized us even more than we realized. We should be able to vote for the President and pay federal taxes like the other American citizens—neither of which had been permitted us—and go on fighting for freedom as brave American soldiers had done in World War II. To do these things, he insisted, we had to become a state in the Union.

The minute Quintín brought up these subjects at the table, tempers would flare and Petra would have to intervene, chiding Quintín for being disrespectful to his father. "Are you a brave warrior like your father, or are you a ninny?" she would ask him, holding her head up high. "Don't tell me you're afraid of independence and would like your country always to remain a ward of the United States." And as long as Quintín kept quiet, Petra would forgive him.

The servants never used the front door of the house on the lagoon. Only the Mendizabals' relatives and friends came in through the Gothic granite archway Buenaventura had had brought from Valdeverdeja. Periodically, the servants went to visit their families in the slum, and they left the house by the back way, journeying to Morass Lagoon in rowboats. The food they ate was brought directly from Las Minas; it was never bought at the market. There was a constant flow of boats laden with fresh fish—blue sea bass, red snapper, yellowtail—as well as native fruits and tubers—mangoes, oranges, mameys, taro root, manioc, *yuca*, all still covered with fresh earth and smelling of the mountains—part of the servants' daily diet.

It was in one of those rowboats from Las Minas, laden with fruits and vegetables, that Carmelina Avilés arrived one day at the house, when she was a year old. She was brought there by Alwilda, Petra's granddaughter, who was lame in her right leg. Alwilda's mother, whose name had also been Carmelina Avilés, never came to work at the house on the lagoon. Carmelina was Petra's youngest child, and she had died in a bar in Las Minas when she was nineteen, knifed by her lover after Alwilda was born. Alwilda hardly remembered her. She had been brought up by her paternal grandmother, and when she was a baby she had had infantile paralysis. Their house, like most of the houses in Las Minas, was a wooden shack built on stilts, the stinking waters of Morass Lagoon flowing slowly beneath it.

Alwilda's grandmother raised carrier pigeons on her tin roof and chickens in a nearby coop. There were no telephones in Las Minas—people used the pigeons to send messages from house to house over the canals, and paid the old woman for the service. Alwilda sold the eggs in the city. This income, together with her grandmother's social security, was enough for them to survive. One day when Alwilda went to town to pick up her grandmother's social-security check at the general post office in Old San Juan, a sailor followed her and invited her for a drink at a bar near the waterfront. Alwilda was only fourteen, and she said no. The sailor followed her as she limped back to the slum, and after she hailed a boat at the dock he knocked the boatman down and pushed off into the swamp. He raped Alwilda under the mangrove bushes, rowed back to the dock, and disappeared. Alwilda never knew his name or where he was from; all she knew was that he was a brute and that he was black as night. His skin had been even darker than hers.

Alwilda discovered she was pregnant and decided to have the baby. She took care of Carmelina until she began to walk and then realized she wouldn't be able to keep her. Alwilda moved with difficulty and Carmelina never stayed still; there was no way she could follow the baby around the house. One day she had fished Carmelina out of the mud just in time, after she had fallen off the balcony. It was then that Alwilda thought of her grandmother, Petra Avilés. She decided to take Carmelina to her. Petra had given food and shelter to so many of her relatives in Buenaventura's house nobody would notice if she took a tiny baby under her wing.

As Alwilda's boat reached the pier, the boatman cried for her to bend over, because the iron beams of the terrace were lower at the entrance to the cellar and one of them might hit her head. Alwilda did as she was told, and when she looked up and saw the servants' common room, she let out a gasp of wonder. It was decorated with potted ferns and gay crepe-paper flowers in vases, several old wicker rockers and a dining table with chairs. At the end of the pier she saw a large black woman she supposed was her grandmother waiting for her on a dilapidated high-backed chair. Several green Cobras burned around her to keep the mosquitoes away. Petra was an impressive figure. She was fifty-eight years old, but her arms looked as strong as mahogany beams and her hair was charcoal-black. As Alwilda limped toward her with Carmelina in her arms, she wondered what she was supposed to do, whether she should kiss her on the cheek or get down on her knees to kiss her hand.

Alwilda had dressed Carmelina in her best clothes: a pink organdy dress with ruffles at the neck and hem. But she hadn't had time to bathe her; she had been afraid of missing the boat that came every afternoon to the Mendizabals' house from the slum. She drew near and was about to put Carmelina on the ground so she could embrace her grandmother, when Petra made her stop right there.

"Don't sit her on the floor. She's an Avilés and should be conscious of her rank," Petra said in a deep voice.

Alwilda murmured an excuse and put the child in Petra's lap. "She's the first of your great-grandchildren," Alwilda said. "Her name is Carmelina, just like your daughter's, but I'm afraid her skin is darker than Mother's." Petra looked at the child in wonder. Carmelina was a beautiful baby—as black as ebony, with large, amber-colored eyes and a dainty little nose which looked as if it had been chiseled in onyx.

"She looks just like I did when I was a child," said Petra, "when my color was still African black, and not watered down by age." And as she held the child in her lap she began to sing in a strange language that Alwilda had never heard before, and the little girl closed her eyes.

Alwilda explained her plight to Petra and asked if she would keep Carmelina and raise her at the house. The little girl had already fallen off the half-rotten balcony of her house once, she said; it was lucky she had been there to save her. The next time she might drown in the lagoon's mud.

Petra listened without saying a word. When Alwilda finished, she looked pensively at the child, asleep on her lap. "Carmelina was the most beautiful of my four daughters," Petra said to Alwilda, "and also the most high-strung. She was born during a terrific thunderstorm. Next to our house in Guayama there was a royal palm tree, and right after Carmelina was born a bolt of lightning struck it. The fire ran down the tree trunk and jumped into our house through the window; it missed Carmelina's crib by inches. But the spirit of the god of fire entered her body, anyway. Except, instead of in her heart, it lodged in the wrong place: her pussy. When she grew up, every time Carmelina crossed her legs, men were struck by lightning and fell in love with her. Many of them had been friends before they met her, but once they saw her they burned with desire and jealousy, and finally one of them killed her to eliminate the problem." Petra paused, as if trying to make up her mind.

"I'll do my best and see if I can smuggle the baby into the Mendizabals' house, but I hope she didn't inherit Carmelina's curse." Having said that, she went into her room with Carmelina still asleep in her arms, and closed the door. She put the baby on her bed and knelt on the mud-packed floor in front of Elegguá's effigy. And as she rubbed the stem on its head with her hand, she prayed, "Olorún, ka kó koi bé re," asking him to take pity on the little girl.

Alwilda returned to Las Minas, and Petra took Carmelina to the servants' bath at the spring. She undressed her and put her in the cement trough; she scrubbed her with a corn husk until she shone like a polished little coffee bean. Then she combed Carmelina's hair in two tight pigtails which stood out like tamarind pods on the sides of her head, sprinkled her with lavender water, put her pink dress on again, and took her upstairs. She had little hope that Buenaventura and Rebecca would let the baby live at the house, but maybe she could persuade them to let her stay for a few days.

It was five in the afternoon and Rebecca was playing bridge with three of her friends on the golden terrace when Petra appeared with Carmelina in her arms. "Isn't she beautiful? She looks just like a black Kewpie doll!" the ladies exclaimed. Petra put the baby in Rebecca's arms, and she was passed from one woman's lap to the next. They cooed and sang and made her laugh. "The backs of her hands are black as licorice," they noted with wonder, "but her palms are soft and pink!" Rebecca called out to Patria and Libertad, who were playing Chinese checkers on the other side of the terrace.

"Look what Petra brought you!" she said to them, smiling. "It's a new doll, only she eats real food and goes peepee in her diaper, not like the rubber dolls you're used to playing with!" The girls squealed with delight, and begged their mother to let them hold the child. Rebecca asked Petra to bring a blanket and a pillow, and soon Carmelina was lying on the floor, with the girls busily changing her diaper.

Several days passed, and the girls were still enchanted with their new toy. The first thing they asked for when they woke up was Carmelina, who was already giggling when Petra brought her upstairs, all spick-and-span and smelling of lavender. Carmelina was a placid baby; she liked to sit on the floor and let the girls do whatever they wanted: she ate porridge when they fed it to her, let them wash her ears, and was still as they changed the outfits Eusebia, Rebecca's seamstress, made for her.

After a week, however, Patria and Libertad began to tire of Carmelina. One afternoon Eulodia, who usually stayed with them and the baby, went down to the cellar and lost track of time, talking to a relative who had come for a visit. Patria and Libertad found a can of paint the housepainters had left behind, and as Patria picked up a brush from the floor, she said to Libertad: "I'm tired of playing with a black doll. Let's paint Carmelina white, to see how she looks." They took off her little gingham dress, Patria held her up, and Libertad spread the white oil paint all over her body.

At first Carmelina liked the new game, but then she began to feel uncomfortable and kicked Libertad, as if to make her drop the paintbrush. But Libertad was tall and gangly and she had long arms, so she stepped back and went on painting Carmelina. Once the job was done, the girls took Carmelina to the bathroom, so she could see how she looked. When Carmelina saw the little white ghost staring back at her in the mirror, she let out a terrified wail and Petra came running from the kitchen.

A few minutes later Rebecca, Petra, and Carmelina were in Buenaventura's silver Rolls-Royce with Brambon at the wheel, driving to Presbyterian Hospital, which was the nearest one to Alamares. Carmelina had lost consciousness; the lead in the oil paint was poisoning her. When they got to the hospital, she was taken to the emergency room, and the paint was removed with a special combination of mineral oils and soap and water. Another half an hour of being white, and Carmelina would have died.

The episode had unexpected consequences. Rebecca felt so bad about the baby's near-fatal accident that she let Petra keep her; and that was why Carmelina Avilés was brought up at the house on the lagoon.

QUINTÍN

The next time Quintín went into the study, he found five new chapters in Isabel's tan folder. He had begun to dread reading the manuscript, but after the first few sentences his forebodings began to dissipate. If in the previous chapters Isabel had tried to pull him into her web of lies and he had struggled to bring her back to reality, now they were in complete accord. She was his loving wife again; she remembered some of the happy moments they had shared—how they had met at the Escambrón boardwalk, and how he had retrieved the stolen medal of the Virgin of Guadalupe for her. Quintín remembered the incident clearly, and it was just as Isabel had described it. That was the day he had seen her for the first time. She looked like a goddess, with her jet-black eyes and beautiful figure. She was laughing with her cousin, holding on to the railing on the boardwalk, her red hair blowing in the wind.

Quintín remembered Isabel's graduation from Vassar, that rainy spring morning when he took her in his arms right after the ceremony. He recalled, too, how he had comforted her when Abby died and when she had to put Carmita in an asylum. How close they had been!

Quintín felt reassured that Isabel still loved him. For a while he had been afraid the novel was a kind of leave-taking, her way of saying goodbye.

Rebecca and Buenaventura had always feared that Isabel's back-ground was too different from Quintín's. Some of Buenaventura's salesmen who visited the interior of the island went so far as to call the Monforts little more than white trash. The Antonsantis were a well-known family in Ponce, but once Don Vicenzo died and Carlos, Carmita's husband, took charge of her inheritance, they quickly lost their capital. Abby had had to struggle tooth and nail to educate Isabel. She was probably the only Vassar College student who paid for her education in custards and cakes. Then Carmita went mad and Carlos killed himself. Quintín's parents cautioned him, pointing out these things and insisting that he should think carefully before making a decision. Psychological problems were often inherited, and Carmita's madness was not to be taken lightly. His children might develop it; Isabel, too. But Quintín was in love with Isabel. He would walk barefoot across the mountains from San Juan to Ponce for her, he told them. He would swim around the island just to be with her.

Steeped in his own thoughts, Quintín stopped reading. Something—birds, or maybe bats—rustling in the mangrove swamp brought him back to reality and he got up from the study's couch to pour himself a brandy. He drank it in one swallow and sat down again. The next chapter was "Rebecca's Book of Poems," and the minute he began reading, apprehension welled up in him. He laughed when she described Buenaventura as a glutton, gorging himself on pigs' feet and garbanzos. But he was shocked by her revelation that his father periodically took his black mistresses to Lucumí Beach and made love to them on the sand for a few dollars. He wondered how Isabel had found out; he'd certainly never mentioned it to her. But, unfortunately, he had to admit it was true.

What he didn't understand was why she insisted on baring his family's secrets to the world. He thought they had patched up their quarrel, and here she was again, going after his family with an ax. Instead of pointing out Buenaventura's good qualities—his loyalty to his family, his gentleness, his industriousness—she had made up yet another lie about him and now called him a wife beater. She could have been discreet about his foibles—his weakness for black women, for example—but she accused him of immoral behavior. Isabel was heartless. At least she could have been diplomatic about Buenaventura's shortcomings. What was the imagination for, anyway? Good writers should try to protect the people they love, not make bloody sacrifices of their reputations. Besides, what right had she to criticize Buenaventura when her grandfather, Vicenzo Antonsanti, had done the same thing? She didn't criticize him for it. Most men had mistresses at the time. Isabel didn't know anything about these things. She was a woman, how could she?

Granted, it was wrong of Buenaventura to have other women. It hurt Rebecca and broke the sacred vow of matrimony. But independence was part of a man's nature, the essence of his masculinity. A woman would say, "I love you and I'm yours forever." A man would say, "I'll love you forever," but he'll never say, "I'm yours." It wouldn't be in character. A man must always belong to himself if he wants to be a man. If the man she loves tells a woman, "I'm yours," what does she hear? That she'll have to take care of him. That he'll hide under her skirts when danger threatens. Women want their men to be strong, they don't want a wimp around the house. Rebecca knew about Buenaventura's trysts at Lucumí Beach and never reproached him for them. She was wise, like the women of her generation; she looked the other way. If she didn't acknowledge it, it wouldn't hurt. "Ojos que no ven, corazón que no siente"—Eyes that do not see, heart that does not feel—goes the old Spanish saying. For Rebecca, it was so. But Isabel was different. She was a modern woman and thought that one should be completely candid about one's mistakes. But no one was perfect, and so divorce was on the rampage.

The more Quintín read, the angrier he became at Isabel. Rebecca had now fallen out of favor and was ridiculed for not wanting to grow old, for being a self-centered egotist, for abandoning him to the servants while she doted on Ignacio. A pack of lies! The fact was that Isabel had been jealous of Quintín's special affection for his mother, to whom he had been closer than either Ignacio or his sisters. Isabel had seen Rebecca as a rival from the start. Something, someone, was pressing Isabel to write these awful things about his family. A mysterious force seemed to be driving her. Could Petra be behind all this? Could Isabel have fallen under her spell, as Buenaventura had so long ago? Petra had the ability to creep into people's hearts, and after she was entrenched in them, there was no way to get her out. She was a relentless gossip, endlessly spreading false rumors about his family in the house and even in the neighborhood of Alamares. Quintín began to suspect Petra was responsible for the web of lies Isabel was weaving around him. She wanted to show him that his family was a disaster, so he would lose his self-respect.

Why was Isabel so angry, so resentful? Hadn't he loved her enough? Had he mistreated her in any way? He'd always tried to be as kind and considerate as he could, not out of politeness, but because he truly loved her. Outwardly, they were a model couple; everyone in San Juan envied them their happiness. They were almost the only ones in their group who weren't divorced. It was inconceivable that after twenty-six years of marriage they should break up over a silly novel!

Isabel's description of the cellar of the house on the lagoon in Rebecca's time, when its dark labyrinth of tunnels had seethed with servants living off his father's magnanimity, and where all sorts of unholy activities took place, confirmed his suspicions. Petra, entrenched in the cellar's common room like a spider, made his hair stand on end.

Quintín made up his mind to destroy the manuscript. He would get up from the couch, go to the kitchen, and burn it. He had the matches in his pocket. He carried them with him all the time. But he didn't move. He knew, if he destroyed the novel, Isabel would leave him. Quintín felt like a fly, caught in Petra's web.

24

The Viscounts from Madrid

IN APRIL 1956 REBECCA AND BUENAVENTURA took Patria and Libertad on a six-month trip to Spain. The girls were about to enter La Rosée, in Lausanne, and they would travel with their parents until September before beginning school. Quintín and I were happy during that time. We both loved our apartment. It was very modern, one of the first condominiums to be built in San Juan. We were on the tenth floor, and the Atlantic Ocean was visible from all the windows, so it felt as if we lived aboard a ship.

I had begun to write short stories, none of which I liked enough to try to have published. Quintín was totally immersed in his job at Mendizabal & Company. By then he had the business well in hand, and since Buenaventura was away, he had been making all the decisions. He ordered new stock, kept track of sales, supervised the office personnel and the workers at the warehouse. He worked ten hours a day and was paid a very low salary, but he didn't mind; he considered it a necessary apprenticeship.

In the month of June, three months after the family left for Europe, we received a cable from Buenaventura and Rebecca, informing us that Libertad and Patria, who were sixteen and seventeen, respectively, had married two brothers from a distinguished family in Madrid, Juan and Calixto Osorio de Borbón. A letter to Quintín followed, with full details. The girls had met Juan and Calixto at a horse show sponsored by the Domecq family in Jérez de la Frontera—in the south of Spain—and they had fallen madly in love. The two couples were married in the Church of the Holy Spirit, and the Bishop of Madrid himself officiated at the ceremony. A Papal blessing from Pope Pius XII was read at the Nuptial Mass, and an exclusive reception was held in the gardens of the Ritz Hotel. Several of the Infantas had been present at the wedding, because the Osorio de Borbóns were directly related to the Spanish royal family. In fact, Juan and Carlos were both viscounts, which meant they were grandees of Spain and could keep their heads covered in the presence of the Spanish king.

Buenaventura invited Juan and Calixto to live in Puerto Rico, because he couldn't stand the thought of being separated from his two little girls. "Where there's food enough for six, there's food enough for eight!" he said to them genially, assuring them they would have a job at Mendizabal & Company. Juan and Calixto accepted his offer. The Spanish nobility had seen their living standards considerably lowered after the Civil War, when Generalísimo Francisco Franco had come into power. Franco had promised that one day he would reinstate the Spanish monarchy and young Juan Carlos de Borbón would become king, but no one knew how many years would pass before this might happen.

The family arrived in August, two months after the double wedding, having crossed the Atlantic in style on the *Queen Elizabeth*, which they had boarded at Southampton. At first, Patria and Libertad had wanted their father to buy them each an apartment in Alamares, so they could be on their own, but Rebecca had insisted the house on the lagoon was big enough for all of them. It was better for the Spanish viscounts to get used to their new environment gradually. In Spain, Juan and Calixto were accustomed to servants, four-course meals, and to having their shirts and their bed linen ironed by hand. Patria and Libertad had never ironed a handkerchief in all their lives.

Rebecca assigned each couple a private suite and furnished it with Spanish antiques. Petra was ordered to attend to the viscounts' every whim: they were to be served breakfast in bed, just as they were used to in Spain; their shoes were to be shined every morning and a clean shirt laid out on the bed. Brambon was to take them wherever they wanted to go in the family's Rolls-Royce.

A month after they arrived at the house, Patria and Libertad both announced they were pregnant. For the next two and a half years, each had a child every nine months, so at the end of the third year there were six babies in the house on the lagoon. Rebecca was delighted. She enjoyed waking up in the morning to the wailing of the babies, and ordered Petra to bring more servants to the house to take care of them. Petra complied; the next morning, seven of her nieces arrived from Las Minas by boat. The cellar became a beehive of activity. Each grandchild had to have a nanny, four dozen diapers had to be washed daily, double the amount of food had to be cooked in the kitchen, and three more cows were brought to the house, because Buenaventura's was soon milked dry. More and more boats came and went between Las Minas and the house on the lagoon.

Patria and Libertad were now both viscountesses, and enjoyed acting the part. Since their return to San Juan from Spain, nothing was good enough for them. Everything was boring. In San Juan there were no elegant cafés or five-star restaurants. There was only one musty theater, the Tapia, where old-fashioned dramas and second-rate *zarzuelas* were put on, whereas in Madrid there were dozens of gilded stages where the latest comedies could be seen. The only thing one could do was go shopping, and so they spent most of their time in San Juan's most exclusive boutiques, and charged everything to their father's account.

Rebecca got along wonderfully with her sons-in-law. She wanted all her friends to meet them, and began giving flamboyant parties at the house. San Juan society was in a turmoil; everyone hoped for an invitation to the Mendizabals' house, to get to know two authentic members of Spanish royalty. Buenaventura enjoyed the company of his sons-in-law well enough, but occasionally he made fun of them behind their backs. He liked to imitate Juan, who was very proud of his protruding chin—he boasted he had inherited it from Philip V of Spain. Whenever anyone mentioned Juan, Buenaventura would stick out his own chin and strut around the room in an arrogant pose, calling for Diego Velázquez, the Spanish court painter, to come and paint his portrait. When he pronounced the name Borbón, Buenaventura puckered his lips, which were thick and round, as if he were going to blow a whistle, and then he would immediately pinch his nose. He did this little routine every time he uttered his in-laws' last name, swearing they were of such high rank they stank. This behavior made me wonder if Buenaventura's legendary parchment with his family tree on it, which he had supposedly brought with him from Valdeverdeja— as well as his coat of arms—had all been a hoax. I always suspected Buenaventura, like many of the Spanish Conquistadors, was really of humble origin, though that was one of the secrets he took with him to his grave.

25

Buenaventura's Wake

꙳

MENDIZABAL & COMPANY paid very good dividends, but after
the viscounts' arrival, the family's expenses skyrocketed and soon
Buenaventura was spending more than he would have liked. Quintín began to be concerned; often, at two o'clock Thursday morning,
he'd still be awake, wondering whether he'd be able to pay his
employees on Friday. Buenaventura was worried also, but he always seemed to have money at hand. Quintín didn't know how he
managed it—Rebecca's private income certainly wasn't enough to
cover the new expenditures at the house. Where Buenaventura's
money came from was a mystery, but Quintín didn't dare ask him
about it. Be that as it may, the revenues from Mendizabal's sales
were never enough to pay for everything.

Quintín worked from six in the morning until five in the afternoon, and then he would drive to the house on the lagoon to talk
to Buenaventura about the day's business and reassure him that
things would eventually iron themselves out. Rebecca didn't seem
to notice anything amiss. She wanted to make a good impression
on her new in-laws, and help them meet the right people. Formal
dinners were held at the house every Saturday night, and Rebecca
would seat Juan and Calixto at each end of the dining-room table,
with their blue silk sashes across their chests and several medals

pinned on their lapels. On Sunday morning we were all supposed to go to Mass together and later perhaps attend a birthday party or a christening. During the week I was expected to accompany Patria and Libertad to the hospital whenever one of the babies got sick or a new baby was about to be born. I had to spend more and more time at the house on the lagoon, and I complained to Quintín about it. He begged me to be patient; it was important to keep Rebecca from becoming resentful, so she would be on our side. Trying to get away from the house on the lagoon was like trying to get out of a brier patch; when you pulled away, you took part of it with you, and it pulled you right back.

Having his in-laws working at the office was no help to Quintín. Every evening when he returned home, he complained to me about them. Juan and Calixto never got used to the heat in the warehouse; it was like working in a sauna, and at night they couldn't get a good night's rest. They woke up at nine after tossing and turning in bed, took a bath, splashed themselves with Eau Imperial, and half an hour later were drenched in perspiration again, so they had to go back under the shower. By the time they arrived at Mendizabal & Company, it was eleven in the morning. They worked for a couple of hours, and by one o'clock they were sitting at La Mallorquina, waiting for their daily crock of eels fried in garlic oil, followed by *arroz con pollo* and lobster *asopao*. At three o'clock they went home for their afternoon nap—as they had always done in Spain—and at five they rode back to the office in Buenaventura's Rolls-Royce. There they usually ran into Quintín, who was about to slide the crossbar of the warehouse's old doors into place. They joked with him for a few minutes—assuring him that La Puntilla was a well-chosen name for a place where people had to work from dawn to dusk, and warning him that one day one of them would drop dead like an overworked bull at the ring. Quintín stared, smiled politely, and the next day ordered the accountant to take half a day off their paycheck.

Quintín had entrusted Juan with keeping track of Mendizabal's stock of imported foods, but his inventories never tallied. He couldn't see a beggar in the street scavenging from a trash can without giving him half a smoked ham concealed in a paper bag. When the Spanish nuns from the asylum, which was close to La Puntilla, came asking for their weekly dole of ten dollars, Juan always added a case of the best asparagus from Aranjuez, as well as a string of Segovian sausages. Calixto, for his part, was much too lenient with the salesmen he supervised. He was an affable man who never rebuked the salesmen when they came back empty-handed if they failed to collect the monies owed by their customers, the small-grocery-store owners in the poor inland towns.

This upset Quintín, and whenever he saw Calixto at the house on the lagoon, he scolded him roundly. Mendizabal's salesmen, he told him, should see themselves as eagles returning to their nest at the end of the day, proud bearers of the fruits of their efforts.

On their first Christmas at the house, Rebecca gave Juan and Calixto splendid presents: Juan got a red Porsche and Calixto a *paso fino* horse, to compensate for the measly salary Quintín paid them. Rebecca didn't want to hear about Mendizabal's difficulties and was terribly upset if Buenaventura asked her to economize.

Buenaventura went down to the cellar more often now for his baths, and stayed longer in the spring's blue grotto. It was the only place he could find peace from the tumult of children and servants at the house, and from Mendizabal's increasing difficulties. As he drifted on his back in the water's cool darkness, sprinkled with Petra's magic herbs, he would forget his financial woes.

One day in the summer of 1958, a trespasser from Ponce de León Avenue jumped over the tall hibiscus hedge which grew at the back of the property, crossed the garden unseen, and wandered into the cellar. It was empty and quiet. Rebecca was celebrating one of her granddaughters' birthdays on the terrace, and the servants were all upstairs. The trespasser tiptoed across the common room and heard the murmur of water. He was thirsty, so he headed through the door that led to the grotto.

It was a hot day in July, and Buenaventura was floating peacefully in the gently flowing water of the basin, his eyes closed. The trespasser saw his clothes neatly laid out on a chair and began to go through his pants. Buenaventura opened his eyes and started to get out of the water, picking up a stone from the bottom of the spring. But the trespasser was much younger than Buenaventura, who was sixty-four, and he put up a fight. Buenaventura finally overpowered him, hitting him over the head with the stone and knocking him out cold. Buenaventura himself slipped on the wet floor and fell heavily to the ground. When he tried to get up, he realized he couldn't move. A few minutes later one of the servants found them and called for help. The trespasser lay unconscious on the floor; Buenaventura had suffered a fractured hip.

Buenaventura was taken to the hospital in an ambulance, and the trespasser was put in jail. The next day Rebecca made reservations on Pan American for the family to fly with Buenaventura to New York. Ignacio was contacted at Florida State University, where he was in summer school, and he also flew north. Buenaventura was operated on at Mount Sinai Hospital, and for three weeks the whole family kept watch over him. Quintín and I stayed at the Elysée, a modest hotel on 54th Street and Madison; but the rest of the family stayed at the Plaza on Fifth Avenue, running up a huge bill. The operation was a success, and when Buenaventura was released, we all flew back to the island together.

Once home, Buenaventura was able to walk perfectly well, but he had trouble urinating. He didn't sleep well; he had a burning sensation in his thighs and felt like urinating all the time. When he tried to relieve himself, however, there would only be a few drops. Rebecca wanted to call a doctor and suggested he go back to the hospital, but Buenaventura refused. He was fine, he said; it was nothing. Petra had always treated him for minor ailments and he didn't see the need to have more tests. Rebecca was afraid he would have one of his temper tantrums, so she didn't insist. She suggested they at least get a nurse, but Buenaventura wouldn't hear of that, either. Petra was giving him medicinal teas, which were bound to make him better. A few days later, he asked Rebecca to move out of their room. He wanted to be alone at night with Petra, who would sleep on a cot next to him.

Rebecca moved her things to one of the empty guest rooms, apparently relieved that she could now rest through the night. She went back to her tea parties and shopping expeditions, and decided she wasn't going to worry about Buenaventura anymore.

"He's a descendant of the Conquistadors; he's made of iron," she said to her friends at the bridge club, without a trace of bitterness in her voice. "Nothing can happen to him."

For the next few weeks Petra spent the nights rubbing Buenaventura with the cow-udder unguent and magic snake oil she had prepared. She put Elegguá's effigy near his bed and lighted a perfumed Cobra next to it. But it was no use. Buenaventura developed a high fever and worsened. One morning he began to hallucinate. He thought he was lying on Lucumí Beach and the waves were washing over him; he couldn't breathe. Something was troubling him, but when Petra knelt by the bed and put her ear to his mouth, no words came out. Petra picked Buenaventura up —she was still as strong as an ox, and her arms were as thick as tree trunks—and carried him down to the cellar grotto. Neither Rebecca nor anyone else in the family dared to keep her from doing this, since it was Buenaventura's wish. Quintín and I were the only ones in the family who followed them down. Petra got into the pool with Buenaventura and bathed him slowly, letting the cool waters flow over his trembling body.

As she rocked him gently, singing to him in her strange language, Buenaventura opened his eyes. "You must ask God to forgive me, Petra," he whispered—though Quintín and I were able to hear. "I had no right to build my house over a public fountain. My whole life was built on water, and water should be free because it comes from God." When Petra brought Buenaventura out of the bath, he was dead.

The servants carried Buenaventura's body upstairs to Rebecca, who was waiting in the bedroom. She had been told the news, but even so she couldn't make herself go down to the cellar. When she saw Petra helping to carry Buenaventura's body and holding on to his hand, Rebecca pushed her away and ordered her out of her sight.

Rebecca's hair was disheveled and her tearstained face was swollen red. Buenaventura's body was stretched out on their bed, and she sat down beside him, tears streaming down her face. "You were my king since the day I met you, and you betrayed me," she cried out bitterly. "One dies as one lives. That's why, instead of drawing your last breath in the arms of your loving wife, you drowned in the arms of a witch."

The wake was held the following day. Buenaventura's remains were laid out in a bronze casket set in the middle of the living room so all of San Juan society could pay its respects. Rebecca had the family's silver Rolls-Royce specially prepared to take him to the cemetery: the gray leather seats were removed and an opening was made through the trunk to accommodate the casket. Two days later Buenaventura rode in the car for the last time, and we followed behind, in a caravan laden with flowers. We drove to the family mausoleum, which Buenaventura had had built out of granite from Valdeverdeja. The Bishop of San Juan officiated at a Requiem Mass and blessed the remains, at Rebecca's request. Most of the servants went to the cemetery and left flowers on Buenaventura's grave, but Petra didn't go. Rebecca had forbidden it. She sat praying in the cellar in her high-backed wicker chair, making sure that Buenaventura's soul arrived safely in the Underworld, following the route of the spring to its source.

PART 7

The Third House

on the Lagoon

26

Rebecca's Revenge

＞Ｋ

AFTER BUENAVENTURA'S FUNERAL, the family came back to the house and we all went into the living room to wait for Mr. Domenech, the family executor, who was to read Buenaventura's testament. Eulodia and Brunilda went into the kitchen to prepare coffee and something light to eat. Everybody was in black: Rebecca, Patria, and Libertad wore black linen dresses with black lace mantillas on their heads; Ignacio, Juan, and Calixto wore dark suits with gray silk ties. As the family sat in a circle in Rebecca's stiff Louis XVI gilt chairs, I couldn't help smiling to myself. There was something amusing and at the same time sinister about the family; they reminded me of a flock of ravens sitting on a fence, just as in Hitchcock's *The Birds*.

Rebecca and her daughters carried rosaries in their hands and solemnly recited prayers for Buenaventura's soul. Rebecca leaned her head against the back of her chair and sighed, closing her eyes. Ignacio sat next to his mother, tenderly holding her hand. Quintín sat next to me without saying a word, mopping his brow with a handkerchief from time to time. He was sad to lose his father, but at the same time I knew part of him was glad. Now Rebecca would finally be free of his boorish ways, and Quintín would be able to take care of her as he had wanted to since childhood.

Everyone wondered about Buenaventura's will, which lay unopened in a burgundy leather case on the coffee table. I knew what they were thinking. Whoever got the largest number of shares of Mendizabal & Company would be its next president. Buenaventura's lawyer finally arrived, kissed Rebecca's hand, and sat at one end of the room. He had a cup of coffee and chatted for a few moments with the family. When the cups were cleared, he got up from his chair and ceremoniously opened the case. The will was half a page long, and he cleared his throat before reading it aloud: Buenaventura had left everything—the house and all of Mendizabal & Company—to Rebecca.

Quintín wasn't surprised. Buenaventura was bound to do just that. The problem was how to deal with his mother in the future, so business could go on as usual at the firm. The expenses at the house had gone on spiraling, and Quintín was very concerned. He had never dared ask Buenaventura about his mysterious source of income, and after Mr. Domenech finished reading the will, he realized there had been no mention of it.

Quintín had a poor sense of timing, and he chose that moment, with Buenaventura's body still warm in its grave, to inform Rebecca of the company's precarious situation. "Do you know where Father's personal income came from, Mother?" he asked Rebecca, as tactfully as he could. "I see he doesn't mention any bonds or securities in his will, but he must have had them. Incredible as it may seem, the dividends from Mendizabal & Company aren't going to be enough to cover the family's expenses this year; Father's personal revenues were essential to us."

Rebecca was astounded at the question. "Buenaventura had a secret account in a Swiss bank, where he had a large deposit in cash," she said. "But he never told me the name of the bank. Don't tell me you didn't know about it. You've always been your father's pampered son!"

Quintín had no idea what Rebecca was talking about. It was the first time he had heard anything about a bank account in

Switzerland. "He *must* have told you the account number before he died," Rebecca said angrily. "There are several million dollars in it!"

Quintín assured her that Buenaventura had never mentioned it, but Rebecca didn't believe him. "If these funds exist, I'd like to know where they came from, Mother," Quintín asked, his voice shaking slightly. "Where did Buenaventura get that money?" Rebecca looked at him, the blood drained from her face. "All I know is that once a month your father received a registered envelope from Europe," she stammered. "At first it came from Germany, later from Spain, and only recently from Switzerland. The envelopes began arriving soon after the Second World War, but I've no idea who sent them."

"You want to know what I think, Mother?" Quintín said. "It was the payoff the German government made to Father for the military secrets he sold them during the war. And if Buenaventura didn't tell any of us about it, it was because he wanted to take the secret to the grave with him."

Rebecca pretended not to hear. She thought Quintín was hedging; trying to get her off on the wrong track. Treason was a dangerous subject to discuss publicly, in any case, and so she kept silent.

A few days later Rebecca asked Quintín to bring her Buenaventura's bank statements, his personal checkbook, and the company's account books. She even pored over Buenaventura's old address book. But the name of the Swiss bank and the secret number of Buenaventura's account didn't turn up. Rebecca went with Quintín to the office and had Buenaventura's safe opened in her presence; she examined all the documents: business shares, bank notes, every single receipt, dusty and yellow with age, of Mendizabal's transactions. But she couldn't find the magic number.

Rebecca went home frustrated. If the account wasn't found, they would never have access to the deposits in the Swiss bank. And if it remained inactive for a long time—if Quintín truly didn't know where it was—who knew what might happen to the money? The bank might keep it in trust for years, waiting for someone to claim it, but eventually the Swiss government might confiscate it. This was what had happened with the Czar's bank account after the Romanoffs' assassination. The situation was serious indeed, but there was nothing anyone could do.

The account was never found. A few weeks later Quintín informed Rebecca and his sisters that the family would have to alter its lifestyle. They wouldn't have to skimp or be uncomfortable; it wasn't anything like that. They simply couldn't keep up their extravagant expenses.

Quintín grew more and more somber as the days went by. He couldn't lie still in bed at night; he paced up and down the apartment for hours. He was terribly upset; after Buenaventura's death, he had thought Rebecca would ask for his help and admit he was the only one who could take Buenaventura's place at the company's helm. But he was wrong. She had gone to the office and given orders that no decision was to be made at Mendizabal's without her approval, and that Quintín was to sign no more checks. She also gave instructions that Quintín's pay was to remain the same —in case he had contemplated giving himself a raise. She had no idea who was going to be the next president of the company, she said, but she certainly knew who was acting president now.

Buenaventura had always believed in the law of primogeniture. "It's the firstborn's right to be president of the family business at the father's death," Quintín and I had heard him say more than once. "It says so in the Bible, and God should have punished Rebecca for deceiving Isaac! In Spain we still abide by that law; the eldest son always inherits the titles."

Rebecca fumed. "Inheritances should be distributed equally among all siblings," she retorted angrily. "That's the only way to prevent the vendetta's knife from turning up buried in one's front door."

Buenaventura and Rebecca often argued like that about Mendizabal & Company in front of the family, as if Quintín and Ignacio were made of stone.

Ignacio was a senior that year at Florida State; he came home to attend his father's funeral. He stayed a few days longer, and tried to calm everybody down when the Swiss account didn't turn up.

When he heard of his mother's meddling at the office, he laughed and took it all as a joke. "Don't worry, Quintín," he said. "You're the only person capable of keeping the family business afloat, and one day I'll let you manage my shares. I think you should be president." But Quintín was deeply worried. That evening he complained bitterly to me about Rebecca's attitude.

A few days after Buenaventura's will was read, Quintín went to the house on the lagoon and asked to see Rebecca in private. They retired into the study. Quintín's hair was tousled and his shirt rumpled. He was at the end of his wits.

"You know I'm the only one who can take charge of the family business, Mother," he said to her with a touch of desperation. "Don't pretend you can be president, because you can't; you'll only ruin us. I promise I'll go on working for you for the same salary I'm drawing now. I'm sure that, with discipline and order, the company will pull through. But I want you to draw up a will leaving me enough shares so that I'll be Mendizabal's next president when you die. That way you'll be doing Father's bidding and at the same time you'll be assuring the company's future. If you refuse, Isabel and I will be on the next plane to Boston tomorrow—I still have some property I inherited from Grandmother Madeleine—and you'll have to fend for yourselves."

It had all been a bluff, but Rebecca believed him. The next day Mr. Domenech was called to the house and Rebecca's will was drawn up in front of Quintín.

Rebecca ignored Quintín's advice, however. She went on spending thousands of dollars on clothes, jewelry, and expensive furniture. Patria and Libertad couldn't care less about what Quintín had said; they simply pretended they hadn't heard. The shopping trips, the presents to their husbands and friends, the train of nannies for the babies—all went on as before. Ignacio went back to school and forgot about the whole thing. Money gushed out of the house on the lagoon as if from an open faucet. Before the year was over, Quintín had to take a large loan from the bank, and soon Mendizabal & Company was seriously in debt.

The one thing Rebecca did economize on was the servants' salaries. One day she called Petra up to the house. Petra had been forbidden to set foot in it since the day Buenaventura had died, and we hardly saw her anymore. Rebecca was in the study, trying to make sense of all the unpaid receipts that were piled up around her on the desk. She told Petra that now, with Buenaventura gone, the family couldn't go on paying the same salaries as before. Her daughters, nieces, and nephews would receive half of what they had been earning. Those who didn't accept would have to go back to Las Minas. Petra didn't say anything; she just bowed her head and went silently back to the cellar.

That same evening she announced the news to the servants from her high-backed chair, surrounded by green Cobras smoking on the floor. It was a hot night. Quintín and I were on our way out for a boat ride on the lagoon, and the strange scene impressed us both. Many of the servants were crying and singing praises to Buenaventura as they knelt around Petra. Listening, we learned that Buenaventura had been very generous with the people from Las Minas. Often he had sent Petra there with money to help out, without telling anyone.

Rebecca wanted Petra to leave, but she didn't dare kick her out because she knew the other servants would leave as well. Since Buenaventura's death, servants had to go directly to Rebecca for their orders and she often bullied and intimidated them. If they got sick and couldn't work, the day's wage was deducted from their pay. When Buenaventura was alive, Petra had always counted the family's Reed and Barton sterling silver at the end of the day, and no pieces had ever been missing. But now Rebecca did it herself, because she didn't trust anyone, and every week she discovered a fork or a spoon missing. She would fly into a rage, a police officer would come to the house and search through the servants' rooms in the cellar, but nothing was ever found.

Rebecca was convinced Quintín was mismanaging the business; in her opinion, he had no commercial abilities at all. The sales he managed to make weren't due to his skills. Mendizabal's products were so good, she thought, that they sold themselves; the Mendizabal wines and gourmet foods were still the best on the island. Rebecca said as much to Quintín in public, which embarrassed him terribly. Quintín was still trying to win his mother over. He worked like a slave all through that year and was paid a pittance. He bore all the responsibility and made all the decisions but took no credit for anything. Every Sunday morning he went to the house with a basketful of goodies from Mendizabal—smoked salmon, pâté, Swiss chocolates—which he left for Rebecca on the dining-room table. But she never thanked him.

Rebecca's preference for Ignacio had been a thorn in Quintín's side since childhood, and the situation grew more painful when Ignacio came back to live at the house. In December of 1959, Ignacio graduated from Florida State University with a degree in art appreciation. The day he unpacked, Rebecca offered to send him on a trip to Europe as a graduation present.

"He can't go on a pleasure trip now, Mother," Quintín said, soberly shaking his head. "There's too much work at the office. With Buenaventura gone, I need all the help I can get." Rebecca was upset; it was as if she believed money grew on trees.

Ignacio loved it when Rebecca pampered him. He had forgiven her for having insulted Doña Ermelinda and for not allowing him to court Esmeralda Márquez; and Rebecca wanted to make it up to him. Now that Petra couldn't make Ignacio her delicious desserts (she was forbidden to go into the kitchen)—the guava meringues, heaven's bacon, and rice-and-coconut milk he loved—Rebecca made them for him herself. Ignacio seemed reconciled to his fate as a bachelor. He had an active social life; he went out with friends and was always joking and making people laugh, but I thought he was sad. He reminded me of someone looking at the world through the wrong end of a telescope; it was as if he saw everything upside down.

He was very good at doing watercolors on paper, but he never thought his sketches were beautiful enough. He liked to go walking in Old San Juan at dusk, to paint the ramparts of the city when they are bathed in purple light and seem to melt into the blue of the sea. But if you praised his work he would laugh and dismiss it as of no importance. If a young woman walked up to him at a party and told him she thought art appreciation was an interesting career because it enabled you to live while studying beautiful things, he said that good art was usually a combination of tragic circumstances and hard work. What I found even sadder was his lack of commitment to anything. When you asked Ignacio if he believed in independence for the island, he asked what you believed, and if you said you were for independence, he said he was, too. But five minutes later a Statehooder asked him if he believed in statehood, and he would say he did. Ignacio was so sensitive to disagreement that if you offered him a lemonade and he didn't want it, he'd drink it anyway; it distressed him to say no. It was as if he were transparent, incapable of having his own opinion about anything or of thinking evil about anyone.

Ignacio had many artist friends and would often invite them to the house to read poetry or play classical music on the piano, which was wheeled out to the gold-mosaic terrace in the evenings. This was something Rebecca thoroughly enjoyed. On these occasions Ignacio always dressed as if he were going to a vernissage: he wore a white linen suit, had a red silk handkerchief in his vest pocket, and his gold-rimmed glasses—always immaculately clean—shone like polished wafers on his nose. When Rebecca sat down to listen to Ignacio play the piano or recite Pablo Neruda's love poems, his blond hair blowing in the gentle breeze that rose from the lagoon, she found him the handsomest young man on earth.

Ignacio wanted to be on good terms with Quintín, though Quintín's disapproval of his romance with Esmeralda Márquez had left a deep scar. His love for Esmeralda had been all-consuming, and he had acted against his family's code. But when he tried not to love her, something tore in his heart. More than four years had gone by since Esmeralda's marriage, however, and he had begun to see things in a different light. One day he confided to Quintín that he, Quintín, had been right to face up to him when he had asked for his help in getting his family to accept Esmeralda. The slap in the face had been a salutary measure; he should never have fallen in love with her; she deprived him of his inner peace.

Quintín asked Ignacio to lend him a hand at Mendizabal & Company, and Ignacio began to go in regularly. He would arrive early and stay until five, helping to supervise the warehouse. But the sawdust from the wine cases made his asthma worse, so he began to work at the office. He had a meticulous approach to everything. If a crate of champagne was to be delivered to a private club for a wedding, for example, he would make sure all the bottles were in good condition and had them inspected one by one. If a can of Aranjuez asparagus was slightly swollen or dented, he would have the whole shipment sent back; he didn't want his customers to get sick. The intricacies of accounting bored him, and giving pep talks to the salesmen exhausted him. But he was interested in designing new labels for Mendizabal's products, and he spent hours making them more colorful and artistic.

Ignacio was convinced of the importance of advertising, and he maintained that half the value of a product was in its marketing. He designed a new package for the smoked hams, for example, which were now sold in gold cellophane with red poinsettias on them; the asparagus cans were adorned with an elegant picture of the Plaza de Armas in Old San Juan; and the *chorizos* and *sobreasadas* bore a reproduction of Luquillo Beach.

What Ignacio enjoyed most was designing new, beautiful bottles for after-dinner liqueurs. Liquor concentrates were shipped to Mendizabal & Company from all over the Caribbean, but it was at the Mendizabal plant that they were processed and finally bottled. Mandarin Napoleon essence from Martinique was bottled in a beautiful, crinkly glass container with a green bow on it; guava-berry liqueur from St. Maarten in a guava-pink glass; chocolate-mint liqueur from Grenada in a frosted glass which resembled an after-dinner mint. And Ignacio proudly labeled each and every one of them "Made in Puerto Rico." Quintín, with his fervent belief in statehood, didn't like this one bit. But he refrained from mentioning it to his brother, for the sake of family harmony.

Ignacio's favorite bottle was the one he designed for Parfait Amour, a delicious liqueur of purplish hue that made one think of poison, and which was concocted at Mendizabal's plant from a French concentrate. Ignacio considered this liqueur well named, since love *was* a poison and purple should be its color, and he designed a spectacular bottle for it—elliptical in shape and with a hollow at its center, which was just how one felt in the throes of unrequited love.

SIX MONTHS AFTER Ignacio began to work at Mendizabal, Quintín and I were having breakfast at the apartment—it must have been around six in the morning—when the doorbell rang. It was Mr. Domenech, and from the expression on his face we both knew what had happened.

"It's your mother," he told Quintín. "She died of a heart attack last night. They didn't want you to know until today, when everything is ready for the wake." Quintín and I got dressed and hurried to the house on the lagoon. Rebecca had promised Quintín that the will she had drawn up with his lawyer would be her last, but he couldn't be sure she had kept her word. He had contacted a number of lawyers in the city, asking to be alerted if his mother made a new will. But the minute he got to the house he knew Rebecca had dodged his net. Patria and Libertad themselves opened the door. Mr. Purcell, the family's new lawyer, stood by their side.

Rebecca's open coffin was in the living room. Quintín and I walked in alone; his sisters and Mr. Purcell went out on the terrace, so we would have some privacy. No one else was there. It was seven in the morning, and people hadn't started arriving to pay their respects. Quintín stood looking at his mother, his chest heaving as if something were stifling him. "She's beautiful, isn't she?" he said, his eyes full of tears. "Her face is as delicate as ever; it looks as if it had been carved on a Grecian urn." And he bent and kissed Rebecca on the forehead with his eyes closed.

I have to admit *I* didn't cry when I saw Rebecca in her coffin. There had been so many Rebeccas, she had played so many roles in her life—the Queen of the Antilles, the would-be poet and dancer, the political rebel, the defender of the Independentista ideal, the feminist stamp collector searching for stamps with the initials RF (for Rebecca Francisca *and* République Française), the religious fanatic, the obedient rebel, the perfect *Hausfrau*, the jealous wife, the spendthrift socialite, the unforgiving mother —that I couldn't help thinking this was just another of her metamorphoses. I couldn't believe she was dead.

The following afternoon, when we all came back from the cemetery, we sat around the living-room table in front of the lawyer, exactly as we had done after Buenaventura's funeral, and Mr. Purcell read Rebecca's will aloud. She had left each of her children an equal number of shares in Mendizabal & Company, and the shareholders were to elect a new president.

"I think it's the fair thing to do, don't you agree?" Libertad asked Quintín when Mr. Purcell finished. "This way, we'll all have a say in the company's future." Quintín stared, pale with anger, and escorted me out of the house.

27

Quintín's Odyssey

᠙

A MONTH AFTER REBECCA'S WILL WAS READ, the family was supposed to convene at Mendizabal & Company for a shareholders' meeting to choose the new president. Patria and Libertad approached Ignacio a few days beforehand and told him they wanted to vote for him, but Ignacio begged them not to. He trusted Quintín's judgment and was content to go on working as he had been, taking care of the promotional side of the business. He wanted peace, he said. Quintín was the older brother and it was right that he should be president.

Patria and Libertad insisted. They were convinced Quintín was a skinflint; the company's situation wasn't as bad as he said. Quintín wanted to save and reinvest every penny in Mendizabal & Company, and they were expected to make great sacrifices. But that just wasn't right.

"I have two children and a baby and they need a lot of attention," Patria said. "I couldn't possibly do without my three nannies. Can you see me washing shit off diapers? You know how our parents brought us up, Ignacio; it's not my fault if I have such a sensitive nose!"

Juan and Calixto's father had passed away in Spain and had left them two important titles: Count of Valderrama and Duke of

Medina del Campo, which his sons had to lay claim to before any of his nephews did. But it would cost them ten thousand dollars each to do so. When Patria and Libertad heard about the titles, they were ecstatic. To be married to a count and a duke was beyond their expectations, and they immediately went ahead and purchased the titles for their husbands.

Libertad was upset with Quintín because he wanted Calixto to sell Serenata, a beautiful black Arab mare he had just purchased from General Trujillo in Santo Domingo for twenty thousand dollars. Of the two Osorio brothers, Calixto had had the most difficulty adapting to life on the island, and he had often told Libertad that he wanted to go back to Spain. In despair, Libertad asked her mother to lend her some money so that Calixto could buy a few *paso fino* horses, because he loved to ride. Rebecca complied and Calixto bought himself a stable with six horses, on the outskirts of San Juan. For the first time since he arrived in Puerto Rico, Calixto was happy and hadn't mentioned going back to Europe again.

"If Quintín is president and Calixto has to sell Serenata, he'll leave the island and it will break my heart," Libertad said to Ignacio. "You must accept the position, so he'll stay."

When Ignacio heard Patria and Libertad's arguments, he felt sorry for them. It was foolish to spend all that money on nannies, titles, and horses, but he thought things could be worked out if each side was willing to give a little. Perhaps two nannies instead of three, and four horses instead of six, would do it. The money that was saved could be reinvested in the company. Sometimes Quintín was too demanding, instead of doing things step-by-step. Even so, Ignacio didn't want to be president; he didn't want to fight with his brother. Patria and Libertad refused to accept his decision, however. They begged Ignacio to think it over.

On the day of the meeting, the whole family—Patria, Libertad, Ignacio, and Quintín—met at La Puntilla, and sat around the heavy oak conference table in Buenaventura's office. Juan, Calixto, and I were also present, but we couldn't participate in the election. The brothers and sisters were to write the name of their chosen candidate on a piece of paper, fold it, and drop it into Buenaventura's *sombrero Cordobés*, the same one he had been wearing when he arrived from Spain. The hat went around the table, and they dropped their votes in it. Then Quintín spilled the papers on the table. He opened them one by one and lay them in front of us: Ignacio had two votes in his favor and Quintín had one. One piece of paper had nothing written on it: Ignacio had abstained from voting.

"You know you can't be president, Ignacio," Quintín said, looking pale. "You studied art appreciation and are used to dealing with beautiful things. I'm the one who has business experience, in addition to the benefit of Buenaventura's coaching. You've admitted you made a mistake in falling in love with Esmeralda Márquez; you almost ruined your good name then. If you accept this absurd nomination, the whole family will be ruined."

Ignacio looked at Quintín over his gold-rimmed glasses. Disagreeing with his brother made him perspire, and his glasses kept misting and sliding down his nose. In his heart, he would have preferred to leave everything in Quintín's hands so he wouldn't have to worry. But he was uncomfortable with his brother bringing up Esmeralda's name; what he had said about her had been in the strictest confidence.

"Don't listen to him, Ignacio!" Libertad intervened. "Quintín is always making everyone think he's the only one who can do things right. You know your advertising campaign has been a success, and thanks to you, our products are now selling better than before. You're just as intelligent as Quintín; I know you can be president!"

"Esmeralda was one thing, and Mendizabal & Company is another," Ignacio said to Quintín, straightening up in his chair. "I'll give the job a try, and see if I'm able to deal with the beautiful *and* the practical."

Quintín was furious with Ignacio, and we left the meeting. I had no idea what he was going to do next; he was so angry he refused to speak to me for two whole days. Then he asked if I could lend him my diamond engagement ring—the one Rebecca had bought us when the first one splintered in two. He needed it for a while, he said, but of course he would return it. Then he pawned it and bought a round-trip ticket to Spain. When I asked him why Spain, he looked at me soberly. "I'm afraid I can't tell you, Isabel. I have my reasons, but I can't talk about it now."

He left for Europe the following week, and for a month I had no idea of his whereabouts. I knew he had flown to Madrid and had stayed at the Puerta del Sol, a small commercial hotel in the center of town, but after that I lost track. I was mad with worry and didn't know whom to get in touch with. Spanish authorities were notorious for their incompetence, so I telephoned the American consulate in Madrid. They pointed out that there were dozens of missing American citizens in Europe; a month wasn't enough to request an official search. My husband might simply have decided to take a long vacation by himself. There was nothing I could do; I simply had to wait.

I still had some income from Mother's inheritance in Ponce, but I had to be careful with expenses. The economy in Ponce had taken a downward turn and the lease on Mother's properties, the two houses downtown and a warehouse on the waterfront, had expired. I was having a hard time renting them again. The Union Carbide plant, as well as Corco's oil refinery, had closed down because of the upsurge in oil prices; electricity was as expensive as liquid gold in those years. I had no access to Quintín's paycheck, which was waiting for him at the office, so I barely had enough money to survive.

It had been weeks since I had been to the house on the lagoon. With Rebecca's death, Patria and Libertad had stopped calling; they hardly missed us and I certainly didn't miss them. Not having to visit the house was a relief. Now I could stay home as much as I wanted to; I didn't have to pretend I enjoyed being a socialite.

The only thing that worried me was Quintín. I suspected he had fled the island because he couldn't face Mendizabal & Company. I also worried that once he realized the seriousness of the situation, he might take some drastic action.

Eventually I received a telegram from Switzerland that put an end to my worries. Quintín was feeling much better and he would be home soon. A letter arrived a few days later, giving me a detailed account of what had happened in the past month. It was quite tender, and after all these years I still have it.

August 20, 1960
Bern, Switzerland

Dear Isabel,

Please forgive me for all the worry I must have caused you after my sudden departure for Spain, and even worse, for my disappearance after I left Madrid. I realize how inconsiderate this was on my part. You must have been distraught with worry, but at the time I felt so miserable there was nothing else I could do. My family's ungratefulness hurt me deeply, and I became terribly depressed. I had slaved for them for years, and they weren't willing to acknowledge what I had done.

When I arrived in Madrid I realized I had brought very lit-tle money, only enough to pay for a week's stay at the Puerta del Sol. I rented a car, put my bag in it, and drove west for eight hours until I reached Valdeverdeja on the road to Cá-ceres. The village was almost deserted. Most of the houses had been abandoned; the town had suffered a severe decline in population. The young people no longer want to raise pigs and pasture cattle on the dry, rocky plains of Extremadura. The ham industry has long since died out and the municipality is very poor. The young people all travel north to Madrid or south to Seville and never come back.

I hadn't brought the address of my two great-aunts, Ange-

lita and Conchita, but I only had to ask one of the local peasants and he pointed out the Mendizabals' house. It was an abandoned ramshackle building, very different from the gay whitewashed house with pots of geraniums on the windowsills and a roof of red terra-cotta tiles that Buenaventura had described to me when I was a child. I knocked on the ancient, weather-beaten door and an old woman answered. She had been my aunt's servant ages ago and now lived in one of the front rooms where the roof didn't leak. She told me my aunts had passed away long ago, and since there were no descendants, the municipality had expropriated the house.

I felt my heart tighten as I listened to her. For some absurd reason I had believed I could stay there, find shelter under the same roof where Father had been born. I thanked the old woman and walked despondently to the square, dropped my bag on the pavement, and sat down on the ground, leaning against a tree. I was at the end of my tether; I had no idea where else to go. Then a bell began to toll in the tower of an austere Romanesque church close by. It was made of the same gray granite Buenaventura had imported when he rebuilt the house on the lagoon. He had used it to build the archways of our house, the stone turrets of our roof, even the granite stairway with its bizarre banister of iron spears. He had even had the family pantheon at San Juan Cemetery made of that stone. I got up from the pavement, walked to the church, and slid my hand tenderly over the façade. All of a sudden I felt comforted, almost as if I could draw strength from its steel-gray surface.

Then I remembered that Buenaventura had talked to me once about a monastery near Valdeverdeja where the Conquistadors had been blessed by the monks before they left for the New World. Buenaventura used to visit it periodically—every three or four years—and would spend several days resting there. I got back in the car and drove over the Sierra de

Guadalupe until I found it. It was the Monastery of the Virgin of Guadalupe, the Virgin of the Conquistadors. I told the monks I was Buenaventura Mendizabal's son, and they welcomed me with open arms; they said I could stay as long as I wanted. They assigned me to one of their cells and invited me to share their meals with them in the refectory. I was there a week, at the end of which my wounds were almost healed. I felt Father nearer than ever before. I kept hearing his voice in my dreams: "Willpower is the only road to power. If Francisco Pizarro, my ancestor, was able to defeat forty thousand Indians with four hundred soldiers, you shouldn't be afraid of your present situation, my son, because it's only three against one."

A few days after my arrival, I talked to the prior; I had made up a story to get him to help me. I had come to the monastery in search of spiritual help, I said. I was distraught after Mother's death, which had come less than two years after Father's. When I left the island, I had brought barely enough money to live on for a week. I needed a loan for the rest of my trip, and I would pay it back scrupulously the moment I got back home. The prior believed me. He was used to seeing Buenaventura and Rebecca arrive from Madrid in a Bentley limousine when they came to visit, and they had been magnanimous donors to the monastery. That kind of fortune didn't just vanish into thin air. The prior lent me a thousand dollars, which was just what I needed, and the next day I drove back to Madrid.

I wired the different wine and food companies that Mendizabal had done business with in Europe over the years, and asked for an interview with their owners. I knew them all by name; I had been corresponding with them for the past four years, since Father had been partially retired, and I had signed all the purchase orders with the title of vice president. I was the administrator of the company, the one who signed the checks, and they recognized my name immediately.

For two weeks I didn't eat, sleep, or drink. Once the interviews were set up, I traveled day and night. First I traveled throughout Spain: I took a train to Rioja, to the great wineries of the south; from there to Aranjuez, where our asparagus came from; then to Segovia, where we purchased our sobreasadas and sausages; then on to Barcelona, where our Codorniu champagne is made. After I finished my business in Spain, I flew to France and visited the Count of St.-Emilion near Bordeaux; then to Italy to see the Marquis of Torcello, who has his Bolla distillery near Venice; and finally to Glasgow, where I met with Charles McCann, who sold us Scotch for more than twenty years. I met confidentially with all of them and explained the family situation. I was Buenaventura Mendizabal's older son. My mother, Buenaventura's widow, had died recently, and my sisters and brother had taken over the company. But they didn't know the first thing about business; in their hands Mendizabal & Company would be ruined in less than a year. I wanted to rescue it and was inviting them to transfer their accounts to me. The new enterprise would be called Gourmet Imports, and in addition to selling their products on the island, as we had always done, we would serve as a link with the United States and would market their products there. With that kind of arrangement, they would maintain the same comfortable incomes they had had—I quoted these easily, as I knew each account by heart—and they wouldn't have to worry about a thing.

My interviews were surprisingly successful. In less than a month I had flown all over Europe and I had contracts from fifty-five percent of Father's old partners in my pocket. I could have added more, but I wanted to leave some to Ignacio, I didn't want to strangle Mendizabal & Company. Buenaventura was right, Isabel, willpower is the only road to power! The world belongs to those hardy souls who, having Fortune against them, win the struggle for survival by dint of their own efforts.

I'll be back home in a week, darling. I'm anxious to see

you, so we can celebrate our good luck. I still have your engagement ring in my pocket and will soon put it back on your finger with a renewed vow of love.

Your loving husband,

Quintín

28

Ignacio's Martyrdom

❧

WHEN I FINISHED READING Quintín's letter, I didn't know what to think. It was obvious that money was being thrown away at the house on the lagoon, and this seemed to justify Quintín's decision to strike out on his own. But I still had my doubts as to whether it was the right thing to do. A voice kept whispering in my ear that if Buenaventura had known about Quintín's leaving Mendizabal & Company, he would have turned over in his grave. Having convinced so many of Buenaventura's old partners to trust him and join Gourmet Imports was no mean accomplishment, however; I had to admire Quintín for having achieved this feat.

What finally changed my mind about Quintín's decision was, ironically, his sisters' selfish behavior. In normal circumstances Patria and Libertad would have had my sympathy from the start. Women usually get the short end of the stick in family inheritances, and I would have rallied to their cause. But Rebecca had always denied them the possibility of being president of the company. In her mind, the position could be held only by one of the two brothers. Patria and Libertad never did anything about that. They never wanted to attend a university; they were to be elegantly "finished" at their finishing school and then they would get married. They were vain and superficial; they wanted only to enjoy themselves and figure prominently in San Juan society. That still didn't make Rebecca's decision right. But Juan and Calixto were as disinclined toward work as ever. It wasn't that they were lazy or shiftless; it was just that, as with most Spanish nobility of the time, they were used to leading "beautiful" lives. The American Puritan work ethic was totally foreign to them.

"One should work to live, not live to work," they insisted genially, drinking their cool dry sherry before lunch at La Mallorquina. Life was full of too many wonderful pleasures like good food, beautiful women, and the siesta at three o'clock to sacrifice it all for a little gold star in Quintín's notebook of good behavior. When I heard them talk like that, there was no doubt in my mind that Quintín was better qualified than either of them to be head of Mendizabal & Company.

Ignacio's case was different. I wasn't at all convinced of his ineptitude. He had done a good job at advertising, was disciplined, and led an orderly life. I knew Quintín liked to manipulate other people, and I didn't believe what he said about his brother. Ignacio meant well; he didn't want to take advantage of the situation his sisters had put him in, and I felt sorry for him. I didn't understand why the brothers couldn't alternate the presidency from year to year and share equal responsibilities, with equal salaries. Then Quintín wouldn't have to sever himself from Mendizabal & Company.

I suggested as much to Quintín when he came back from Europe, but he was adamant in his decision to strike out on his own. The problem wasn't Ignacio, Quintín said. The problem was that he had to support his sisters and their husbands, as well as their six children. I had to admit Quintín was right, and for the next month I tried to forget about Ignacio, and about the rest of the family.

Quintín was busier than ever. He bought a modern building in San Juan with air-conditioning in every room, and an adjacent warehouse with all the latest improvements. There Gourmet Imports opened its offices. At the time it didn't occur to me to wonder

where the money was coming from; it was only later that I began
to question it. Quintín had to work harder than ever to establish
a name for himself and for his new business. He stayed longer
and longer at the office, and we saw each other only at bedtime.
Gourmet Imports was immensely successful from the start. Quintín
had so many orders from his local customers, as well as from new
patrons in the United States, that he could hardly keep up with
them.

Something else happened at that time which also helped me
forget about Ignacio and his sisters: in October 1960 I became
pregnant with Manuel. Quintín and I were both very happy about
the news: we had been married five years and were anxious to
have a family. But it was a difficult pregnancy. For the first three
months I didn't sleep well, and in the mornings I was dizzy and
couldn't keep anything down. The only thing that helped was
walking down to the beach and lying under a palm tree with a
book in my lap. When I was six months pregnant, Quintín told
me he wanted us to go to the house on the lagoon to visit his
sisters. He thought it was important that we patch up family differences. Patria and Libertad had called at the apartment several
times when Quintín was at the office, but I had refused to see
them. They hadn't so much as phoned when Quintín disappeared
and I had been left completely on my own, so I didn't see why I
should be nice to them now. Quintín went off to see them by
himself. A few weeks later he asked me to go with him again, this
time to say goodbye to his sisters.

"You mean Patria and Libertad are leaving the island?" I asked.

"Patria, Libertad, their husbands, the whole tribe," Quintín
said exultantly. "They've practically chartered the *Antilles*, the
French passenger ship that sails from here to Vigo, all for themselves. Last week they came to the office and asked for a loan;
they had to purchase ten tickets and they didn't have enough cash.
I lent them six thousand dollars, which of course I'll never see
again. But who cares! 'When the enemy retreats, offer him a silver

bridge,' as Buenaventura used to say. Those six thousand dollars will probably be the best investment of my life."

That afternoon we went together to the house on the lagoon. I hadn't been there in over a year, and I was impressed by how different everything seemed. All of Rebecca's gilded Louis XVI furniture had disappeared; Patria and Libertad were taking it with them to Spain. The piano, the Spanish Conquistador's dining-room set Buenaventura had been so proud of, the wall tapestries, even the lamp in the entrance hall, which Buenaventura joked was an iron wheel that had been used to torture the Moors during the Spanish Conquest, were gone; Patria and Libertad had sold them.

The rooms were dirty and unkempt. Petra was still there; I could hear her in the pantry talking to Carmelina, her great-granddaughter; and Brambon was watering the plants in the garden. But the rest of the servants were nowhere to be seen. Later I discovered that when Ignacio had run out of money to pay them he had made them each a generous present—a goat, a cow, a hen—and told them they could leave. He gave away all of Buenaventura's farm animals except his two dogs, Fausto and Mefistófeles, who were still in their pens, under Brambon's care.

When we rang the bell, Patria herself opened the door. She was dressed for the trip, in a beige linen suit. She looked thinner but seemed in good spirits. She had one of her babies in her arms, and one of her little girls was following her around. She let Libertad know we had arrived, and the four of us were soon sitting out on the terrace, talking animatedly about a thousand things, as if nothing disagreeable had ever happened. Quintín was extremely solicitous of his sisters and asked them about their trip. He even offered to send on what they couldn't take with them on the ship to their new address in Spain.

Patria explained that they were going to live in Madrid, where Juan and Calixto had many friends among the nobility. It wouldn't be difficult for a count and a duke to find something to do there.

"They'll be able to hunt and ride on their friends' haciendas all they want, and we'll be much better off ourselves. Servants get paid very little in Spain, and one can have as many as one needs," she said. "And, of course, rents are much lower than over here. By the way, we're grateful you bought our part of the house from us—the money will be useful to help us get settled."

I was startled by her comments. It was the first time I had heard about Quintín's purchase of the house on the lagoon; he hadn't mentioned it to me. But I pretended to know all about it.

Quintín offered suggestions as to what his sisters should do when they arrived in Spain—visit the American ambassador, make sure they didn't forfeit their passports, remember to reenter the United States every six years so they wouldn't lose their American citizenship. I kept looking to see if Ignacio was around, but I couldn't find him. Finally I got up the courage to ask about him. What was he going to do? Was he going to stay here alone? Had he sold his part of the house, too?

"Ignacio?" Libertad burst out angrily. "I couldn't care less what he does. We wouldn't have to leave the island and go live in Spain if Mendizabal & Company hadn't gone bankrupt. It's all his fault!"

Libertad took out her handkerchief and began to cry, and Quintín tried to calm her down. She mustn't take things so hard, he said. He was sure their move to Madrid was only temporary and that someday they'd be able to return home. The sisters still owned some real estate on the island—two apartment buildings that had belonged to Rebecca, which Quintín had managed to save from the catastrophe. Ignacio had mortgaged them to keep Mendizabal & Company afloat a few months longer, and Quintín paid back the loan. He would manage the buildings and send on to Spain the rent he collected.

Juan and Calixto soon walked out onto the terrace, leading the older children by the hand. Brambon came behind them, loaded down with suitcases, and Eulodia and Petra brought the rest of the luggage. Juan and Calixto shook Quintín's hand and kissed me affectionately on both cheeks. But they didn't sit down to talk with us. The taxicabs had just arrived and were waiting on the avenue to take them to the wharf.

We walked down the hall to the front of the house and milled around the cars, kissing and embracing and shaking hands once again. Patria and Libertad were about to get into the taxis when Ignacio suddenly appeared at the top of the stairs, under the granite arch of the entrance. When I saw him, I was amazed; he had lost at least twenty pounds, and his hair was gray. He looked twenty years older than Quintín. He kissed his sisters goodbye and gave each a going-away present: two beautiful watercolors of the house on the lagoon. Patria looked anxious. "Are you going to be all right?" she asked him. "I'll be all right," Ignacio said. "You mustn't worry about me." Patria hugged Ignacio, but Libertad took the watercolor without thanking him. Then they all got into the taxis and drove away. Ignacio stood there smiling and waving goodbye as if nothing extraordinary had happened. It was the last time I saw him alive, and every time I think of him, I remember him that way.

When we returned to our apartment, I felt so bad I had to go to our room and lie down. Quintín followed me and sat next to me on the bed. I begged him to explain what had happened. Why was Mendizabal & Company bankrupt? Why did Ignacio look ill? If I remembered rightly, Quintín had said he had left enough commercial lines open in Europe for his brother and sisters to live on. He hadn't taken over all of Mendizabal's accounts during his lightning trip through Europe. Or had he?

I could tell Quintín was angry; he didn't think I should have brought up the subject at all. It was very simple and he'd try to explain it to me again, he said slowly, although I couldn't remember when he had explained it the first time. Ignacio didn't know anything about business. He thought that merely by sitting at the office doodling he was going to get things sold, and when they didn't sell, his European partners began to cancel their contracts; in a year the business had gone down the drain. Quintín had a clear conscience; he had tried to help Patria and Libertad as much as he could—they were empty-headed but they were his sisters. But Ignacio was another matter. He was a man; he had to learn to be responsible for himself.

I looked at Quintín skeptically and kept silent; I didn't want to provoke him any further. But I couldn't believe what he had said.

What I had seen and heard that day made such a deep impression on me that I began to have severe contractions. I was seven months pregnant and the thought of a miscarriage terrified me. It had taken me five years to get pregnant and I wanted very badly to have the baby. Quintín was worried and he took me to the hospital, where I was given a sedative that knocked me out. When I woke up, the contractions had stopped, but the doctor ordered me to stay in bed for the duration of the pregnancy. I was supposed to sleep as much as I could, and the doctor prescribed small doses of Librium that would calm me down.

Quintín was in a very good mood and catered to my every whim. I had a nurse at my side twenty-four hours a day, and Quintín always came home early from the office. The Mendizabal clan had finally disappeared and he only had to answer for me and his future child. Our two worlds, the Mendizabal and the Monfort, would finally merge into one.

For two months I lived in a mist. Ignacio began to recede from my mind; it was almost as if he had never existed. I suppose I wanted to forget about him, and it was easy. He had always been so sweet and obliging; I wanted him to go away and he had done so like a polite ghost. I had lost count of how many days had gone by when I finally gave birth to Manuel on July 14, 1961. When I came out of the hospital and Quintín took me home, he told me Ignacio was dead. He had shot himself two weeks before.

The news shocked me. I wanted to know more, but Quintín refused to discuss it. It wasn't wise to talk about unhappy things now, he said sternly. I had to think about our baby and about the kind of life we would lead from now on. We had to be grateful the family nightmare was finally over. I had no alternative but to be silent.

A week later I told the nurse there was an errand I had to run in the afternoon, and I left the baby with her. I wanted to talk to Petra; I was certain she'd be able to tell me the real story. I drove to the house on the lagoon and found the door open. The house was in an even worse state than when I had visited it some months before, the day Patria and Libertad left for Spain. The windows had been left open; the rain had warped the parquet in the living room, and there were crabs scuttling about on the damp floor. I went down to the cellar and found Petra there, sitting in her old wicker chair. She was as massive and enigmatic as ever, with her beaded necklaces wound around her neck. She was peeling a manioc root, and it was difficult to distinguish her dark, gnarled hands from the tuber's knobby surface. I pulled up a stool next to her and she set the manioc root down with the knife on a table. For the first few minutes I didn't say anything but just sat there in silence. Finally I sighed and put my head on her lap. Petra didn't say anything, either. She stroked my hair softly.

I was tired, confused. Finally I said, "I want to know why Ignacio killed himself and why Mendizabal & Company went bankrupt. Quintín wouldn't talk about it, but it's important. Quintín and I just had a son. If I can understand why Ignacio killed himself, perhaps I can prevent the Mendizabals' violent nature from taking root in my child."

"Buenaventura has a grandson? That's wonderful news!" Petra said softly, as if she hadn't heard my question. "You should be happy and follow Quintín's advice."

I sat up and looked her straight in the eye. "Don't try to protect Quintín, Petra. Living with a secret like that would be like living with a time bomb. I want to know the truth."

Petra closed her eyes and lowered her head. "All I can tell you," she said, "is that one day Quintín came to the house and they locked themselves up in Ignacio's room to talk. I could hear what they were saying. An empty house is like a seashell; even whispers can be heard through its walls."

"Why don't you sell me your part of the house, like Patria and Libertad did?" Quintín asked Ignacio. "The money could tide you over for a while. You could rent an apartment in Old San Juan until you figure out what to do." But Ignacio didn't want to sell. He didn't want to move out of the house. He was born here and had never lived anywhere else, he said. Instead, he asked Quintín for a loan—five hundred dollars, I think it was—until he could find a job. But Quintín wouldn't give him the money. He was convinced Ignacio wasn't really looking for work; he wanted to go on doing nothing and living comfortably at the house on the lagoon.

"When Quintín left," Petra continued softly, "Ignacio locked the door to his room and refused to come out. I could imagine how he felt, but there was nothing I could do. Ignacio was so sensitive about everything, he was terrified that his father's friends might recognize him and ask about Mendizabal's bankruptcy. He didn't even dare cross the street to buy cigarettes; he sent me, instead. Eventually, the electricity in the house was cut off for lack of payment, and we had to use candles at night. Then the water was shut off. But we still had Buenaventura's spring, and Ignacio could take a bath in it. I went there every day with large kettles to bring drinking water up to the house. Ignacio had no money to buy food, but my relatives came to visit me periodically in their rowboats, and I would prepare Ignacio soups and stews with the vegetables and tubers they brought over from Las Minas, and every once in a while a large crab.

"Finally, one day Ignacio simply couldn't stand the shame anymore. He asked me to wash and iron his white linen suit; he went to Brambon and begged him to cut his hair and shave him; and he took a long bath in Buenaventura's spring. Then he got dressed and lay down on the bed. The last thing he did before pulling the trigger of the gun on the left side of his chest was to take out his handkerchief and carefully clean his gold-rimmed glasses, so that they would shine like polished wafers on his nose."

Petra finished her story, which she had told in a perfectly controlled voice. There were no tears, no sobs, no recriminations of any sort. I hadn't realized how loyal she was to Quintín until then.

"I think Quintín was heartless," I said. "Ignacio must have been in hell. But you still haven't answered my question, Petra. Was Ignacio's suicide Quintín's fault? Did Quintín go to Europe just to open new commercial lines for Gourmet Imports, as he told me, or did he go to Switzerland, where there were three million dollars in cash in Buenaventura's bank account? Maybe he *did* know the secret number of the account, after all!"

Petra sat there silent as the Sphinx. She didn't admit anything, but she didn't deny my accusations. "There are secrets in the Mendizabal family you know nothing about, my child," she said softly, shaking her head. "But I'm not the one to tell you about them."

I wiped my tears and shuddered. If what I suspected was true, Quintín was a scoundrel and I should leave him. But what was I to do without money and with a newborn child? The only thing I could do was to wait. In time, Quintín's innocence or guilt would be revealed to me.

QUINTÍN

Quintín told Isabel in no uncertain terms that they had to get rid of Petra. She was over ninety, too old to do any work around the house. She could have an accident at any moment and they would be responsible for her. It was best if her relatives took care of her in Las Minas. He'd be willing to pay her a generous pension; she wouldn't want for anything.

Isabel hedged. First she told him Willie loved Petra and would miss her terribly. Then she pointed out that Petra was the only one who knew of Manuel's whereabouts. Manuel had gone to live in Las Minas with one of her relatives, and if they got rid of her now, they would lose track of him completely.

Quintín knew that wasn't true. He could have a detective on Manuel's case any minute. But he didn't want to contradict Isabel. He felt sorry for her, she was so completely under Petra's spell. There was no alternative but to keep Petra around awhile longer. But he knew she would never relent. Petra was going to keep on driving Isabel until she finished the novel.

The three new chapters in the manuscript were all the result of Petra's sorcery. He laughed to himself when he remembered thinking—a few weeks earlier—that the novel could become a work of art. And he had been naïve enough to believe that he could help Isabel write it!

The focus was now on him. History—national or familial—had become much less important. He felt as if he were before a camera with a telephoto lens; every time Isabel took a shot at him, she brought him nearer and nearer. And behind Isabel's lens he felt Petra's malevolent eye following his every step, listening to his every word.

As he read on, Quintín began to worry that he was in some kind of danger. But it was all so absurd! What could Petra do to him? Isabel could rant and rave, paint him as a monster and accuse him of all sorts of crimes, but it was only on paper. As long as the novel wasn't published, she couldn't hurt his reputation and she certainly couldn't hurt him physically. Or could she?

Quintín looked up from the manuscript. His heart was racing like a hunted animal's. In the half-light of the reading lamp, he could see the study was in perfect order. Everything was as it always had been. The books were aligned on their shelves. The celadon vase on the antique coffee table was full of fresh flowers. Rebecca's magnificent Empire desk with its bronze caryatids gleamed in the half-darkness. The Mendizabal family photographs in their brightly polished silver frames stood atop the side table. But none of it reassured Quintín.

29

The Art Collector

※

FOR YEARS I HELD Petra's story buried deep in my heart. I never told Quintín what she'd said, and I tried not to think about it. Abby used to say adaptability was the secret of survival—one's soul should bend and then it wouldn't break. I had decided to heed her advice. Quintín and I had been married six years. It had been a turbulent period of our lives—we had both lost our parents and had been on the verge of bankruptcy. Ignacio had killed himself, and I grieved for him as if he had been my own brother. We had weathered those storms together and now we had a child. I wanted desperately to believe Quintín was innocent.

Two months after Manuel was born, Quintín decided we should move to the house on the lagoon. We sold our apartment and with the money from the sale we made some improvements on the house. I felt better when I saw white paint covering the walls like an emulsion; it was as if we were spreading a coat of forgetfulness over them, erasing everything that had happened inside. Quintín sold *La Esmeralda*, Ignacio's sailboat, as well as Buenaventura's silver Rolls-Royce—which was now an antique. Juan had taken his red Porsche with him to Spain, and Calixto had sold his *paso fino* horses before he left. Quintín and I bought modern furniture, new kitchenware, new sheets and towels.

Petra, Brambon, and Eulodia stayed on as our servants, although Quintín explained that we wouldn't be able to pay them very much at the start. Brambon was understanding and agreed to his terms. "The house on the lagoon is our house also," he said to Quintín quietly. Petra returned to the kitchen, Eulodia dusted and ironed, and order was once again established in our daily routine. There was never any silverware missing, food was well prepared and served on time, the house was immaculately clean. Carmelina was fifteen, and we put a small bed for her next to Manuel's room, so she could help take care of him. Quintín had a soft spot for her and treated her almost like a member of the family.

Petra had cared for both brothers when they were children, but her love for Quintín had always been special; she had helped him find his way out of Rebecca's womb with her prayers and magic unguents and he had been born into her arms. She saw him as the warrior-hero who would be fighting for the well-being of all of us as head of the household and of Gourmet Imports. Quintín, moreover, had been very generous with Carmelina. He was paying for her tuition in a very good high school near Alamares, and for her books and clothes. And he had promised Petra that he would send Carmelina to the university.

Quintín began to look for ways to invest our income from Gourmet Imports, and instead of buying bonds or securities in both our names, which is what I would have wanted him to do, he began to purchase works of art. Mauricio Boleslaus, a Bohemian count who was one of Quintín's acquaintances, served as his purchasing agent and informed him of everything that was going on at the European auction houses. Mauricio was later to become a good friend of mine, but at the time I found him too eccentric for my tastes. He had a perfumed goatee, wore a silk shantung jacket with a plaid handkerchief in his pocket, and sported a bow tie. He also wore gray suede gloves, which I found ridiculous considering the heat of the island but which he insisted were necessary because in his trade things had to be delicately handled.

Mauricio himself told me the story of his life. He was born to a noble family in Bohemia. His family had a small castle with a moat, and his parents sent him to study in Paris. He lived there as an art student for three years, until 1939, when the Germans invaded his country and his family was no longer able to send him money. At the end of the Second World War, he chose not to return to his homeland but remained in Paris. He made his living copying Picasso and Modigliani sketches and selling them as authentic works of art to the local galleries. One day the Paris police got on to Mauricio and he landed in jail. When he was released ten years later, he boarded a plane for New York and from there flew to Puerto Rico, which he had picked at random on the map because it looked faraway enough so he could live incognito. A short time after his arrival, he opened a small but very chic art gallery, the Golden Goblet, in Old San Juan.

Once on the island, he mended his ways and never forged anything again. His expertise was so great that he could survive easily by buying and selling paintings and sculptures, since the local bourgeoisie was starting to develop a taste for art. In the sixties he still had relatives in Czechoslovakia and friends in Paris who ransacked the run-down palaces of the European countryside for works of art, which he would purchase at very low prices. They were sound investments. After all, there was a limited supply of Old Masters, and as they diminished in number, they rapidly increased in value. Mauricio's local clients were enchanted; several were powerful people, and soon he became a legal resident of the island. Thanks to Mauricio, by 1970 Quintín had amassed a serious art collection and had invested more than a million dollars in paintings and sculptures. Mauricio had sold him a magnificent Madonna by Carlo Crivelli; a dramatic St. Andrew nailed to an X-shaped cross, by Giuseppe Ribera; a blind St. Lucia, who stood holding her own eyes in a little transparent saucer, by Lucca Giordano; and an impressive painting by Filippo D'Angeli, *The Fall of the Rebel Angels*, in which a dozen handsome angels were tumbling into the abyss of hell.

Mauricio had another side to his business dealings, however, which I thought was the real reason he wore suede gloves. He was very sociable and had numerous acquaintances on the island. Ever since he opened the Golden Goblet, he made a point of being scrupulously honest, and people with money trusted him. When things went well with a collector and his business affairs prospered, Mauricio would offer him the best buys in the art world. If things went badly for his client, however, Mauricio could be an even greater help. As soon as he found out one of his buyers had gone bankrupt and government authorities were about to go into his home and put a lien on everything he owned, Mauricio would don his silk shantung jacket and his gray gloves and he would pay a visit of condolence.

"Life is difficult these days," he would say to his client in commiserating tones as he sat politely in the living room, drinking tea. "What with the worldwide rise in oil prices and the way our island's government is always veering the ship of state in opposite directions—now to the right toward statehood, now to the left toward commonwealth or independence—consumers and creditors are exceedingly jittery. It's no one's fault if a business suddenly takes a nosedive and one wakes up one day with no credit at the bank. But you mustn't worry, my friend. You have a treasure around you, which you have acquired thanks to me. All you need to do is let me dispose of it as diligently and as discreetly as possible." And his client, who was usually at his wit's end, would run to his safe at the house, take out his wife's jewelry, and give it to Mauricio, together with the paintings, sculptures, and other art pieces he had acquired, so Mauricio could sell them away from the island.

Mauricio was the one who let Quintín know he was squandering one of his greatest artistic resources: the house on the lagoon itself. "Milan Pavel, my fellow countryman, was one of the geniuses of our century. You're living in his masterpiece, and you're not doing anything about it," he said one day. "All it would take to restore this house to its original glory would be a little archaeological research. I'm sure the original arrangement of the rooms can be traced with some digging here and there, because the foundations are all in place."

Quintín didn't need much convincing. He had always had an enormous admiration for Pavel and in his youth he had wanted to write a book about him. If he could restore the house to its original state, he would feel closer to Rebecca; the house had been very much a part of her. He immediately set himself to the task. He visited the archives of the School of Architecture at the University of Puerto Rico, and sure enough, he found Pavel's copy of the Wasmuth Portfolio, which the Czech architect had taken from Wright's studio when he fled Chicago with the original plans for many of his houses. One of them was the plan of the house on the lagoon.

A month after his conversation with Mauricio, Quintín had us move to the nearby Alamares Hotel. A demolition crew was brought to the house and in a matter of days it leveled Buenaventura's Gothic arches and granite turrets. Slowly a fairy-tale palace began to rise from the rubble. Artisans were brought from Italy, and they restored the glittering mosaic rainbow over the front door. The Tiffany-glass windows, the alabaster skylights, and the burlwood floors were all reproduced, so they looked exactly as they had in Rebecca's time. When the house was almost finished, the scaffolding and wooden partitions were removed, and it was joined once more to its original Art Nouveau terrace. In September of 1964, a year after construction had begun, we moved back into the house.

The house *was* spectacular, but I couldn't help feeling uncomfortable about spending so much money on it. How could we afford such luxuries? Was it true, as Quintín had told me, that the sales of Gourmet Imports had skyrocketed in the past two years? The difficult economic situation on the island—gasoline was twice as expensive as on the mainland, and unemployment was up twenty-five percent—had been exacerbated by the recent political violence. There were strikes and student demonstrations every day; one couldn't go out into the streets without encountering a rock-throwing mob around the corner.

In spite of everything, Gourmet Imports was making money, and Quintín began expanding into the food-processing business. He opened tomato-, mango-, and pineapple-canning plants on the outskirts of the city. My life was blessed in many ways. I had a beautiful son and a magnificent house. I could read and write as much as I wanted, once I finished supervising the household chores. And yet I never felt truly happy. When I least expected it, I would feel a tiny doubt begin to sprout like an alfalfa root deep in my heart. Where had the money for the restoration of the house come from? Where did Quintín get the income for his expensive works of art? It was true Quintín worked from sunup to sundown, and he was very knowledgeable in business. But after my conversation with Petra, I could never be sure of anything.

MANUEL DEVELOPED INTO A STRONG BOY. He had inherited his great-grandfather Arístides's imposing physique and grew to six feet two inches in height. He was always good-natured. As a baby he drank milk from a bottle which he held by himself, and went to sleep the instant you put him in his crib. He was very obedient. When Quintín asked him to give Fausto and Mefistófeles a bath before going out to play baseball, for instance, he never argued, but would bow his head and do as he was told.

Manuel took after me in only one respect: his eyes. They were large and flint-black, like all the Monforts'. When he was brought to my hospital room the day after his birth, I remember thinking his eyes were so dark his tears would probably look like ink. I took him in my arms and stared at him enraptured, and he stared right back as if examining me in turn. I couldn't believe he was so perfect—his flesh a part of my flesh, his blood my own blood.

Manuel was remarkably self-assured. I never saw in him the least hint of violence; no tantrums, no fits of temper, no useless tears. The few times Quintín ordered Manuel to do something he shouldn't have—he once asked him to do his homework over again when it was already perfect—Manuel gave his father one of his silent Monfort looks and Quintín didn't dare say anything more.

One day about a month before Manuel's third birthday, Quintín came home early from the office and sat down next to me on the study's green leather couch. He looked tired and had deep shadows around his eyes. "Today Mother has been dead four years," he said, sighing, "and I've finally made up my mind to ask you to do something I've been thinking about for a while. I don't think we should have any more children, and I'd like you to take steps to prevent it."

I looked at him in dismay. "Why?" I asked. "You know I want a large family. Besides, kids are healthier when they grow up together."

Quintín got up from the couch and began to pace morosely in front of me. "That's precisely what worries me, Isabel," he said softly. "I don't want a big family. I'm tired of siblings flying at each other's throats. I simply couldn't take it if it happened to us."

"And what if our second child were to be a girl? I never had any sisters and I would love to have a daughter; she'd keep me company." But Quintín wouldn't even consider it. "You know how much I love you, Isabel; you're the most important person in my life. But if you get pregnant a second time, I'll have to ask you to get an abortion; I'm simply not going to go through the same anguish I went through with Ignacio all over again."

I know I should have been angry with Quintín when he said that, but instead, I was terribly sad. All of a sudden I saw myself when I was three years old, playing with my dolls under the terebinth tree behind the house at Trastalleres. I could hear Mother's cry again as she fell on the bathroom floor. I swore I would never have an abortion.

30

The Magic Birthmark

ꙮ

IT WASN'T UNTIL THREE YEARS AFTER Ignacio's death that
Quintín began to feel guilty. I couldn't understand why he had
such a delayed reaction; maybe it had to do with loneliness. Quintín
had always been a loner. He'd go fishing in his Bertram yacht
early in the morning, with Brambon accompanying him once in a
while, or he'd play tennis at the Sports Club with casual acquaintances, but he'd never get together with them off the court.
He had no social life; the family had always been his whole world.
The Mendizabals were a clan; they hated and loved each other,
but for them the rest of the world didn't exist. And all of a sudden
the clan had vanished into thin air. Strange as it may seem, Quintín
began to miss them. He would go whole nights without sleep and
spend hours wandering about the house without turning on the
lights. One Sunday when we were at church, I overheard him
talking to the priest, asking him to say a Mass for Ignacio's soul.

The only thing that eased Quintín's melancholy was his art
collection. He stopped going to the office and would spend hours
sitting in front of his Carlo Crivelli Madonna, which hung in our
living room, over our blue damask sofa. It was a traditional composition: the Virgin in profile, hands piously folded in prayer,
surrounded by a colorful garland of fruits and flowers. The Ma-

donna had a serene beauty: her face, especially her high forehead and her temples, seemed almost translucent, as if chiseled in alabaster. In the months that followed, Quintín went through a second religious conversion. He bought many paintings with spiritual themes, which he found consoling and inspiring. He would stand before these paintings for hours, meditating on the suffering allotted us in this world. "We are all born on Christmas Day," he would say to me, "and in the end we are all crucified."

Margarita Antonsanti arrived from Río Negro at the house on the lagoon on May 15, 1965. I'll never forget the date. Quintín was working in the garage, fastening the last glass globule to our new crystal chandelier, which was to be hung in the living room. When Quintín saw Margarita get out of the car, he was amazed. She had delicate Renaissance features and wore her hair in golden tresses fastened around her head, exactly like the Madonna in his painting. Quintín opened the door of the car and greeted her cordially. But he had only seen her in profile. When Margarita stepped out and he saw her face, he was so horrified he dropped the globule he was holding on the floor, and it broke in two. On the right side of Margarita's alabaster forehead, half an inch above the perfect arch of her eyebrow, she had an oval-shaped birthmark out of which grew a glossy black lock of hair. Margarita was conscious of the strong impression she made on strangers. She didn't dare return Quintín's greeting; she simply turned around and carried her old suitcase up the stairs.

Margarita was my second cousin and she was nineteen. Her father, Uncle Eustaquio, and my mother had been first cousins, and her parents had come to visit us in Ponce when I was a child. When Grandfather Vicenzo Antonsanti sold his coffee farm in Río Negro, Uncle Eustaquio's father—my great-uncle—continued to live there. At first Uncle Eustaquio—a widower—had been lucky not to have sold his part of the farm. Three years before he came to see me at the house on the lagoon, Uncle was visited by a group of scientists from the mainland who said they were interested in buying the farm to build a giant ionospheric observatory on it. The topography was just right, they said; the mountains rose all around, forming the rim of a perfect hollow. A mesh radar could be built at its center, aimed at the stars. The radio observatory would be the largest in the world, and its mission would be to discover whether or not there was intelligent life somewhere in the universe other than on Earth.

Uncle Eustaquio was a hardworking farmer and his coffee farm provided him with a reasonable income. But he found the idea of listening to the stars fascinating. He refused to sell his land to the scientists, but he was willing to lease it to them for five years. He was thrilled that such an important experiment could be performed on his own farm, and he could go on growing his coffee shrubs under the observatory's radar; it would shield his crop from the sun, but wouldn't prevent the rain from getting to it.

The ionospheric observatory was built, and Uncle Eustaquio couldn't believe his eyes when he saw how large it was. It was as if the astronomers had hung a huge mosquito net over the entire forest. But he soon realized he had made a mistake; his coffee shrubs produced fewer and fewer beans. Nobody could explain why the radar was affecting the crops, but Uncle Eustaquio was losing money and had to take out a loan from the bank. The following year he couldn't pay it back, and had to request a second loan. When he realized he was going to lose the farm, he came to San Juan to ask Quintín if he could tide him over for the third year of his contract. He had no money to pay us interest, but he could send us Margarita, his youngest daughter, who could work for us, and we wouldn't have to pay her anything.

"This could be your chance to atone for what happened to Ignacio," I told Quintín after hearing Uncle Eustaquio's story. "If you can save an old man and his family from bankruptcy, maybe God will forgive you and you'll be able to sleep again. A good deed will make amends for your sin."

Quintín lent Uncle Eustaquio the money, and Margarita came

to work for us. She was a high-school senior at the time and had to leave school, but it was only temporary. She would go back to school as soon as her father had repossessed the farm. I wasn't going to let her work for us gratis, in any case; I opened a savings account under her name, so she could use the money to go to the university. If Quintín was doing as much for Carmelina, I saw no reason why he shouldn't help out Margarita, who was from my side of the family.

Margarita became like a daughter to me; having her around the house was a pleasure. Her smiling face brought me fond memories of mountain outings and family picnics. But the real reason she made me happy was that I finally had someone to talk to. I was from Ponce and didn't have many friends in San Juan. Quintín and I had gradually grown apart. It was as if we stood on opposite shores of the lagoon, and no matter how we shouted, neither could hear what the other one was saying. I felt very lonely sometimes.

Margarita changed all that. She brought me news of my cousins who were still living in Río Negro, and of relatives in Ponce. We talked about books and music, gossiped to our heart's content. I could tell Margarita about my fears and hopes almost as if she were an adult. Her dreadful birthmark made her aware of other people's needs, made her more compassionate and sympathetic than anyone I had ever known. After so many years living in the midst of people who were loyal to the Mendizabals, I felt I now had someone I could trust.

Margarita was educated and had been brought up to be a lady. I thought she would do an excellent job of caring for Manuel, and soon after she arrived I suggested to Quintín that we put her in the small bedroom next to our son's, where Carmelina had been sleeping. Carmelina could go back to the servants' quarters.

From the moment Margarita arrived at the house, Petra declared war on her. She was polishing silverware in the pantry when Margarita walked up the stairs with her suitcase in her hand. "That must be the new girl, just arrived from the country," Petra said to Eulodia. "With that hairy cockroach sitting on her forehead, nothing good can come of this." She was furious when she found out that Margarita was to sleep in Carmelina's room and that she would be taking care of Manuel. Now Carmelina could go to school in the morning and clean house in the afternoon.

"Margarita isn't a servant," I explained to Petra a few days later, when I couldn't bear her long face anymore. "She's my second cousin. She's only spending a few months with us and has generously offered to teach Manuel to read and write, as well as help take care of him."

Margarita was able to smooth things over between herself and the servants. She was modest and good-natured; when Petra railed against her, she humbly accepted the scolding and asked to be forgiven. She took excellent care of Manuel; she was patient, and didn't miss an opportunity to teach him manners. She washed and ironed his clothes, cleaned his room, and kept his toys in place. Two months after she came to us, Manuel had learned to read.

I soon discovered there was something special about Margarita. Her presence in a room had a calming effect. If Quintín had a marketing problem at the office, Margarita would walk in and he would think of a solution. If Petra was making a soufflé and Margarita came into the kitchen, the soufflé would be perfect; if she came into the study when I was trying to write, the sentences would fly from my typewriter as if by magic.

Carmelina was nineteen, the same age as Margarita, but they were very different. Margarita was ethereal-looking—tall and willowy; Carmelina had a sensuous body, "with rounded hips that moved like caldrons on the stove," as Quintín would say. Margarita's skin wasn't white. It was more the color of sandalwood, as is often the case with people from the mountains.

Margarita wore her hair carefully braided; Carmelina's stood like an unruly halo around her head. Margarita washed her face every day with soap and water; Carmelina loved perfume, creams, and powders, and she was always filching them from my bathroom.

Margarita wore modest cotton frocks and Carmelina liked brightly colored T-shirts and Levi's. "You're a timid turtledove, and I'm a black swan," I heard her say to Margarita once. "We were brought to this duck pond by mistake, and one day we'll both fly off and be free."

Carmelina was quick-tempered and high-strung; she often talked back to Quintín and to me. Petra said we shouldn't mind; she blamed it all on the bolt of lightning that had fallen near her crib when she was a baby. Petra was immensely proud of her great-granddaughter and she admired her independent spirit, the way she spoke "of the ways of whites," as opposed to "the ways of blacks." When I heard her talk like that, I wondered if somehow she remembered Patria and Libertad's silly prank, when they had painted her all white and she almost died.

Carmelina hated what she called "white man's food," like T-bone steaks or coq au vin; she enjoyed pork chops and *mofongo*, green plantain mashed with pork rind. She loved crabs, and one of her favorite pastimes was setting traps for them. She built the traps herself—a small wooden box with a sliding lid in front, held by a wire which came in at the back, with a piece of ham dipped in honey attached to the end of the wire. She knew crabs loved honey and were carnivorous—something unusual in crustaceans. She liked to watch them seize the sliver of ham with a claw, as the lid in front of the trap suddenly fell.

Carmelina and Margarita became good friends in spite of their differences. Carmelina was carefree; she was always singing romantic songs as she dusted the furniture and mopped the floors. She was never put off by Margarita's deformity. She was used to seeing worse in Las Minas, she said, which was full of maimed veterans of the Vietnam War. On Sundays the girls went to the amusement park or would board the ferry that crossed from San Juan to the town of Cataño every fifteen minutes. For ten cents they could ride the waves for half an hour and dream of sailing one day to distant shores. Margarita would then reminisce about the coffee farm where she was born, and Carmelina would relate how her lame mother had been raped by a black sailor and how she had been brought to the house on the lagoon after being fished out of the mud in Las Minas. She wasn't going to be like her mother, though. *She* was never going to have children. When she graduated from high school, she was going to move to New York, where she would become a black fashion model for *Ebony* or *Jet*, one of the black magazines she had seen at the drugstore.

Margarita listened and agreed. She was never going to get married or have children, either; besides, no one would ever want her, because of her ugly mole. Her father had said she'd better get used to being single, because she was going to stay at home in Río Negro and take care of him when he got old. But she wasn't sure she wanted to do that. With Carmelina by her side, she wouldn't be afraid to live in New York. Leaning on the boat's railing at dusk, the girls looked at the receding lights of the city and dreamed of the day they would leave for New York together, have their own apartment, and live their own lives. I worried about this close friendship, but there was nothing I could do to prevent it.

One day Quintín came into my room and pronounced it "unwise" for Manuel to go on looking at Margarita's deformity. "The beautiful and the good should always go together," he said, "and with her around, Manuel will take ugliness for granted. Don't you think it would be a good idea to have her operated on? Of course, she's your relative. I'll leave it up to you."

I smiled at Quintín's puerile reasoning, but I thought the operation wasn't such a bad idea. I was concerned about Margarita's future. Her dreams of going to live in the States, which she had confided to me one night during one of our tête-à-têtes, seemed not only impractical but risky. Margarita had led a sheltered life —as Uncle Eustaquio's favorite daughter—and she wouldn't know how to fend for herself in the urban jungle, as Carmelina undoubtedly would. Carmelina was streetwise and resourceful; no one could put anything over on her. But Margarita was not cut out for a life of adventure and danger. She would be much happier in her own home, with a husband and children.

The more I thought about it, the more I became convinced I had to help Margarita find a good husband. And without her mole she would have a much better opportunity. A few weeks later I mentioned the operation to her. At first she was adamant and wouldn't even consider it. "The mole has always brought me good luck," she said. "I'm never conscious of it, and if someone really wants to be my friend, it doesn't bother them."

"But what would you do in New York?" I asked. "Carmelina can work as a model, waitress, hotel maid, whatever she wants; but I don't see you doing any of those things." On the other hand, if she made a good match in San Juan, she could have her own family. "Once you have your operation," I said, "we'll introduce you to some of our friends—there are many nice young men in San Juan, and eventually you'll find your other half." Margarita laughed. "Mother was like you," she said. "She also thought the operation would help me to find a husband, but we never had enough money for it." And then she whispered, "Are you sure it's possible? Do you think I can be like other girls and find someone who can love me?" I didn't reply; I simply took her in my arms.

When Petra found out that Margarita was to have her birthmark removed, she was very upset. She was first and foremost a medicine woman and was genuinely concerned about Margarita's well-being. She went to her room, knelt on the floor in front of Elegguá. "Olorún, ka kó koi ké bé! Holy of Holies," she prayed. "Please have pity on the poor girl. The mole sitting on her forehead protects her from the evil eye. The day they take it out, the same thing will happen to Margarita that happened to the warrior who slew the dragon in the mountains and took a bath in its blood. A mango leaf clung to his back and the blood didn't get to it, and that's where the enemy struck."

When I heard Petra's prayer, I began to worry, but all the

arrangements had been made. Quintín and I took Margarita to the hospital; she went into the operating room and was given anesthesia. No sooner was the mole removed than she went into convulsions, and a few hours later, bizarrely, she was dead. The doctor's official report was that she had died of advanced bilharzia—a parasite common in mountain rivers which enters the body through the soles of one's feet. It lodges in the liver, the doctor said, and isn't noticeable until many years later, when the person is already near death. But we knew better at the house.

Uncle Eustaquio came down from the hills and insisted on taking Margarita's body with him to Río Negro; Quintín and I paid for the burial expenses. I was overcome with grief. Uncle Eustaquio had entrusted Margarita to me, and I hadn't known how to care for her.

QUINTÍN

The last few days, Isabel had been almost cordial toward Quintín. She was affable at dinnertime and one night she began to discuss with him Choderlos de Laclos's Les Liaisons dangereuses, *which she had been reading. She found it fascinating. The literary convention of the letters exchanged between Monsieur de Valmont and Madame de Merteuil was particularly effective. The characters communicated indirectly, through a delayed echo. "Between the writing and the reading of a text, things change, the world goes round, marriages and love affairs are made and unmade. Wasn't all storytelling, in a sense, like that?" Isabel asked, as she took a sip of wine from her glass. "Each chapter is like a letter to the reader; its meaning isn't completed until it is read by someone."*

So she knew he knew about her manuscript and was deliberately teasing him, taunting him! His only recourse was to play along with her, try to get the upper hand at her own game.

"Literature is fluid," Quintín admitted, "like life itself. History, on the other hand, is something very different. It is also an art, but it deals with the truth. As a record of human endeavors, history is unalterable. A novelist may write lies, but a historian never can. Literature never changes anything, but history can alter the course of events. Alexander the Great identified himself with Achilles, for

example; he became invincible and almost conquered the world. Therefore, history is much more important than literature."

Isabel looked at him with her flint-black eyes. "I don't agree with you at all, Quintín," she said. "History doesn't deal with the truth any more than literature does. From the moment a historian selects one theme over another in order to write about it, he is manipulating the facts. The historian, like the novelist, observes the world through his own tinted glass, and describes it as if it were the truth. But it's only one side of the truth, because imagination—what you call lies—is also a part of the truth. Like the dark side of the moon, it's no less real because it can't be seen. Our veiled passions, our ambivalent emotions, our unaccountable hates and preferences can best be understood through novels, and heard across the centuries. But I know you'll never agree with me, so we may as well drop the subject."

But Quintín wouldn't give in. He wanted to bring the conversation back to Isabel's manuscript, make her admit she was writing it, but he didn't know exactly how. "A novel can also be a form of escape—a way out of a desperate situation," he went on. "It's like a bottle with a message in it, thrown into the sea to be picked up by a tourist on a faraway beach."

"And it can also be a Molotov cocktail," Isabel retorted, evidently annoyed. Quintín laughed nervously at her joke, and an uneasy silence hung between them.

In spite of their disagreement, that evening Isabel approached Quintín tenderly, apparently bent on reconciliation. He gave in and that night they made love, after almost two months. Petra had gone for a week to her granddaughter Alwilda's house in Las Minas, and took her two great-nieces, Georgina and Victoria, with her. Willie was in Florida, spending a week with one of his friends from Pratt Institute. Only Brambon was in the house, and he never came up from the cellar.

It was a moonless night, and the sky was a dome of fiery pinpoints above their heads. It reminded them of their nights in the garden *of the house on Aurora Street in Ponce. They undressed in the dark and walked hand in hand out onto the terrace. A cool breeze rose from the lagoon as Isabel mounted him, wrapping her legs around his thighs, her skin like warm marble. She clasped her hands behind his neck and began to sway back and forth slowly, pulling him toward oblivion.*

31

The Forbidden Banquet

❧

QUINTÍN BLAMED ME for Margarita's death, in spite of the fact that he was the one who had suggested the operation in the first place. If I hadn't asked him to help Uncle Eustaquio, he said, we would never have brought Margarita to the house and she wouldn't have died. Not only had I lost a cousin who was almost like a daughter, I had to renounce my own world all over again. Now I would have no one to talk to about my childhood home and about the memories we shared.

We all cried for her. Manuel kept asking for Margarita and missed her at night; Petra and Eulodia kept mentioning all the things she had done to help out at the house. Carmelina, on the other hand, was angry and dry-eyed; she kept whispering half-crazed things under her breath, reproaching Margarita for having gone off by herself, leaving her behind. I felt crushed by the loss, and by the emotional turmoil around me.

The consequences of Margarita's death went beyond anything I could ever have imagined. After my return from the funeral at Río Negro, Quintín began accepting invitations to all kinds of parties, which I didn't have the least desire to attend. "I'm tired of so much praying and crying!" he said. "I don't want to see any more long faces in this house because of Margarita Antonsanti's death.

Good sailors prove themselves in bad weather, like Buenaventura used to say, and we have no alternative but to outlast the storm!"

A month after Margarita's burial, Quintín suggested we go on a picnic to Lucumí Beach, and asked Petra to make the arrangements. Petra was seventy-six and hardly did any work at the house. But when Quintín asked her to do something, she threw herself into it, heart and soul.

Quintín ordered the best wines and delicacies from Gourmet Imports. Petra cooked up a caldron of *arroz con gandules*, pickled a pig that would be roasted in plantain leaves at the beach over an open fire, and tied a dozen live crabs to a long pole that Brambon carried across his shoulders on a boat all the way to Lucumí Beach. Six crabs hung on each side, so he'd be able to keep his balance; they were to be stewed on the beach. Crab had always been Quintín's favorite food—he had acquired the taste as a child, when Rebecca had exiled him to the cellar—and he hadn't had any for a long while; all of a sudden he had a craving for them.

We set out for Lucumí at eight in the morning in Quintín's forty-foot Bertram yacht, the *Buena Ventura*, which he kept moored at the pier under the house. There were seven of us—Petra, Brambon, Eulodia, Carmelina, Manuel, Quintín, and myself. We motored through the maze of mangroves, skimming over Morass Lagoon and holding our breath to avoid the stench, and arrived at the beach after an hour-long trip. Manuel and I sat on a dune under an open parasol, almost wilted by the heat. It felt strange to visit that beach again after so many years. The last time I had been there with Buenaventura, I had discovered the Mendizabal Elementary School full of blue-eyed black children.

The place was just as beautiful as ever: the same green light filtering through the nearby mangroves, the same aquamarine waves licking the sugar-white sand, the same surf rolling in the distance like snow. And sure enough, several black women soon ambled up through the bushes, their heads wrapped in gaily colored turbans, and began to give Petra and Eulodia a hand with the food. But it was strange: every time they crossed in front of Petra, they would do a little step, almost like an obeisance, as if performing a dance in her honor.

The women went immediately to work: they put the wine bottles in buckets of ice, spread several tablecloths on the sand, and set out the food. They brought some tin cans from the bushes, made a fire with dry palm fronds, and started dropping the crabs one by one into the boiling water. I sat on the sand and watched them dejectedly. I felt so melancholy I could hardly look at the food. But Quintín was in a good mood. He joked with Petra and Eulodia, and asked the women of Lucumí to tell him stories about Buenaventura's youth. When lunch was finally served, he ate almost half a dozen crabs and drank a whole bottle of wine.

I lay down under a palm tree next to Manuel to take a nap, and Quintín went off by himself. Petra, Brambon, and Eulodia went with the Lucumí women into the bushes, and I assumed they would visit the nearby village. Carmelina stayed behind on the beach, sunning herself in a two-piece bathing suit made of a rough brown cloth. She had a beautiful body, and the coconut oil she had rubbed on herself made her skin gleam like dark mahogany. I could see why Quintín was always comparing her to a Nubian fertility goddess. She looked sad, though. All through lunch, she had been silent; she hadn't taken part in the servants' animated conversation. I knew she was thinking about Margarita, and I felt sorry for her.

After a while Carmelina got up and went into the water; then she vanished into a thicket of mangroves. I closed my eyes and dozed off; I didn't see or hear anything for more than an hour. When I saw Carmelina again, she looked her usual self. And it wasn't until afterwards that I found out Quintín had followed her into the mangroves.

We got back on the boat a little later and made the trip to Alamares Lagoon without mishap. But that night Carmelina disappeared from the house. She waited until everybody was asleep and slipped out in an old rowboat that was kept moored to the cellar pier. She took all her clothes with her, as well as our sterling-silver Gorham water pitcher. She didn't say anything to anyone or leave any message. When Petra discovered that she had left, she sank to her knees on the floor, letting out a wail that shook the walls of the house. It was like watching a mountain crumble.

32

The Love Child

❧

ROUGHLY NINE MONTHS after the picnic at Lucumí Beach, we were having guests for dinner and I went down to the cellar to see about our stock of wine. Petra was in the servants' common room with a beautiful mulatto baby on her lap. She was sitting in her old straw peacock throne, and as she rocked the baby, she said softly, "You got your skin from the Avilés side of the family and your eyes from the Mendizabals. But you have nothing to lose, because you won't be long for this world. Everything's ready for your last bath," she went on. "I've boiled the bay leaves with rue and rosemary and poured them in the grotto's blue basin. In a few minutes I'll take you to Buenaventura's spring, and your soul will follow the water's route back to its origin, just like your grandfather's did when his time came." I couldn't believe what I was hearing. "What are you talking about, Petra?" I asked. But she was distraught and didn't seem to notice me.

I called Eulodia and Brambon. "What's Petra saying?" I asked. "I can't understand what she's mumbling under her breath. And I'd very much like to know who brought this baby into the house." Eulodia bent her head, not daring to look me in the eyes.

"Carmelina arrived the night before last, Isabel," she said sadly. "She was in labor. The baby was practically peeking out from between her legs when she was carried from the boat and brought to the cellar. A few minutes later she silently gave birth. Petra herself delivered the baby in her room, and we helped her as much as we could. It all had to be done so fast—she cut the umbilical cord with a heated kitchen knife and tied a knot in it with a plain wrapping cord. We had no time to come upstairs and tell you. And now Petra wants to drown the baby in the underground spring, so no one will know about it."

"And where is Carmelina?" I asked.

"She left this morning," Eulodia said. "She was so weak she could hardly walk, but she said she couldn't stay here. She asked the boatman to take her to Las Minas, where she'll stay with a cousin for a few days. She's flying back to New York next week and wanted to leave the baby in Petra's care. She said she didn't want it—its skin is too light. She's been living with some of Petra's relatives in Spanish Harlem for the last nine months and returned to the island only a couple of weeks ago."

I took the baby from Petra's arms and looked at it more closely. He was tiny and as delicate as a bird, with gray-green eyes that were barely open. His skin wasn't light, but it wasn't black, either; it was closer to buckwheat honey. Obviously he wasn't more than twenty-four hours old. "If it's Carmelina's baby, we should send word to Alwilda to come and get him. We can't keep him at the house, and Alwilda is his grandmother. Or maybe one of Petra's relatives from Las Minas can take care of him," I said.

Petra got up from her chair and demanded I give the baby back to her. She had been ailing the past few months and at times her mind didn't seem quite sound. I didn't want to upset her. But I didn't give her back the baby, he snuggled so peacefully in my arms.

Petra called me to a corner of the room. "Carmelina told me a secret before she left," she whispered. "She was raped the day of the picnic at Lucumí Beach, and that's why she disappeared so mysteriously."

She was so flustered I could hardly make sense of what she was saying. Lately, Petra had been making up fantastic stories—once she swore she had seen a two-headed chick break out of an egg, the heads furiously pecking at each other; another time, she had hung half a dozen red handkerchiefs from the mangrove bushes, calling to Elegguá to ward off the evil spirit that had been moaning there all night. No one paid attention to her stories. But this baby was different. It was real, and I couldn't get over my amazement that it was in the house. "Such a beautiful baby," I said, caressing his velvety-brown cheeks. "He looks a lot like Carmelina, except for his eyes. But they'll change from hazel-green to brown later, of course—that's what usually happens with mulatto babies."

Petra began to weep bitterly. "Carmelina was too proud for her own good!" she said. "Otherwise, she wouldn't have been so bold as to have this baby, but would have boiled rue leaves to get rid of it." Seeing her so upset, I began to worry. Something must have happened at the picnic—maybe Carmelina had been raped, after all. "I'm going to find out what this is all about right now. You and I are going to have a talk with Quintín," I said to Petra.

I went up the stairs with the baby in my arms, and Petra followed behind. Quintín was in the study, reading the evening paper. We went in and closed the door behind us. He was sitting on the green leather couch, drinking a glass of red wine. "Meet Carmelina's baby," I said, laughing, as I showed him the child. "Do you know what Petra is saying? That you're the baby's father, because his eyes are the same color as yours!" I had meant it as a joke, but Quintín turned pale and dropped his glass.

The wine spilled on the beige carpet and an ominous red stain spread at his feet. "I can't believe you're Buenaventura's son!" Petra told Quintín angrily. "It was your duty to care for my great-granddaughter Carmelina, but you took advantage and raped her the day of the picnic on Lucumí Beach." Quintín cringed, without admitting or denying anything. "Is what Petra says true?" I demanded.

"Yes, Isabel," he said softly. "The devil put Carmelina before me. She asked me to swim out to the mangroves and I couldn't resist the temptation. It started out as a game, and it was over before I realized what I'd done. I know I have no right to ask you to forgive me, but I'll do what I can to bring the child up as my son." Appeased by what Quintín had said, Petra went silently back to the cellar with the child in her arms. I followed, slamming the study door behind me.

"Carmelina will leave the island," Petra assured me. "You have nothing to worry about. But I want you to know it wasn't her fault. Carmelina has the god of fire smoldering in her cunt."

For days afterwards, I felt as if someone had died. My only consolation was that Abby would never know what had happened; she probably would have put a gun to Quintín's head. Whenever I saw Quintín now, I felt myself stiffen and walked by as if there was nobody there. He was contrite to the point of being sheepish. At dinnertime he kept swearing he loved me and promised he would never be unfaithful again. After all, Abuelo Vicenzo had had his flings too, he said. And Abuela Gabriela hadn't stopped loving him or left the house in Río Negro because of it. She had pardoned him. Couldn't I do the same?

Strangely enough, it wasn't Quintín's betrayal which hurt me the most, but what I had done to myself. Soon after Quintín said he didn't want any more children, I went to my gynecologist and asked to be sterilized. Quintín signed the necessary documents and the following week I went into the hospital. The operation was simple; my tubes were tied and I was out in a day.

Once I got home, I realized what I'd done and felt miserable. I was now barren *because* of Quintín. Rebecca was able to conceive Jacob when she was beyond all hope, but I wouldn't have such luck. Yet God was now giving me a second chance—Carmelina's baby, whom I could raise as my own son. That's when I began to see things in a different light.

That very afternoon I gave Quintín back the Mendizabals' heavy gold signet ring, as well as my wedding band, and moved to the guest room. " 'Love is the only antidote to violence,' you once said to me on the veranda at Aurora Street. And now, instead of love, there's treachery. Three weeks have gone by and the baby's eyes are still hazel green. I think that's proof enough he's your son." And I added bitterly: "If I sue for divorce on the grounds of adultery, and it's proven, the court will rule in my favor and I'll take Manuel away from you. But if you adopt Carmelina's child legally and give him your last name, I'm willing to stay on at the house." Quintín agreed to my conditions; he knew I would make good my threat.

We let out the rumor in Alamares that we wanted a second child, and since I hadn't been able to get pregnant again, we'd decided to adopt a baby in the United States. Two weeks after Carmelina left the house, we made a trip to New York, taking the baby with us to have him examined at Children's Hospital and make sure he was in good health. When we came back, we told everyone we had adopted him, even in front of Petra—and she went along with the story.

Quintín was wary of Petra. Now that we had adopted her great-great-grandchild, he thought, anything was possible: she might demand that we buy her a home or expect us to help out Willie's relatives in Las Minas, who kept coming to the house by the dozen every afternoon, asking to see "the beautiful new baby." They brought him all sorts of extraordinary gifts: an ebony calabash full of whispering seeds, an ivory ring with rare feathers which whirled noiselessly from the top of his crib, a tortoiseshell comb which was supposed to prevent him from ever growing bald. I, for my part, preferred to face reality and made Petra swear she would never tell anyone the truth, especially Willie. Petra was dignity itself and promised she would say nothing.

We had a christening party for our son at the house on the lagoon. He was baptized William Alexander Mendizabal Monfort by the bishop himself at San Juan's Cathedral, and after the ceremony we invited all our friends to come and see him. Whatever Quintín intended, we ended up doing the right thing. It was a wonderful feeling.

Petra was beside herself with pride. She took the baby out of his crib whenever she had the chance and paraded him up and down Ponce de León Avenue, pushing the baby carriage herself. She wouldn't let anyone else wash and iron Willie's clothes, and she hung a tiny *azabache* fist from the gold chain on his neck with the tiny gold cross we had put on it. "It's only a good-luck charm," she reassured Quintín when he asked her about it. "Elegguá's *Figa* will protect him from the evil eye, and death will be powerless against him." Quintín went to Mass and Holy Communion daily, so he took the charm off and gave it back to her. "The only eye Willie has to fear is God the Father's, Petra," he said solemnly. "He sees all our actions and that's why, when we do something wrong, we must face the consequences." But Petra fastened the *azabache* with a safety pin to the underside of Willie's shirt, so Quintín didn't see it.

Manuel was Buenaventura's grandchild and Petra cared for him very much; but in Willie she saw her own ancestors. There were no African descendants living in the neighborhood of Alamares; blacks were never seen in church, at the Roxy or the Metro, much less in the drawing rooms of the well-to-do. And this was a terrible thing for Petra to accept; she had always been proud of being an Avilés. So when she saw Willie in the Mendizabals' bronze crib, and saw that Quintín and I didn't mind it when her Avilés relatives came and brought the child magnificent presents, a sense of optimism began to well up in her.

We put Willie's crib in the room next to his brother's, and at Quintín's suggestion we bought him exactly the same furniture—an English dresser, an Italian lamp that looked like a red mushroom, navy-blue wall-to-wall carpeting, curtains with tiny sailboats on them—the best that was available. When the boys were old enough, Quintín bought them Schwinn bicycles for Christmas—

one red and one blue—skates, electric trains. We dressed them both in seersucker suits from Best and Co. We sent them to the same private school in Alamares. Later they were both accepted at Boston University, but Willie chose instead to attend Pratt Institute in New York. Everything Manuel had, Willie had to have, too. That way, the possibility that one would feel favored over the other when they grew up would be avoided.

None of our friends in San Juan would have dared do what we did, to adopt a mulatto child as our own and give him our last name. Whenever we walked into one of San Juan's elegant restaurants with Willie, or if we spent the day with him at the Berwind Country Club, even when we went to the Casals Festival or to the opera at Bellas Artes, people would turn around and stare. We gave San Juan society more to talk about than all the love scandals of the past decade put together. But I didn't care. Was it Abby's defiant spirit that had come to haunt me in middle age? Was it a whim to bring out into the open a thorn which had been buried deep in my heart since Esmeralda Márquez, my best friend, was spurned by the Mendizabals because she was part black? Was it seeing Willie so frail and vulnerable, with his green eyes shining in his beautiful nut-brown face? Whatever it was, I felt better than I had in years.

When I saw that Quintín was going out of his way to be fair with his two sons, my heart went out to him. A year after Willie arrived at the house on the lagoon, we were reconciled. I moved back to our room, and we shared the same bed again.

QUINTÍN

It was late August; summer was coming to an end. Quintín hadn't been feeling well for some time. He complained of pains in his chest, and he went to a specialist for a thorough examination. The cardiologist did an electrocardiogram and told him his blood pressure was sky-high. He was suffering from angina pectoris; he had to take better care of himself. Drugs were prescribed which Quintín would have to take for the rest of his life. He had to exercise every day, couldn't have salt, and had to avoid undue stress if he wanted to live. He knew he would have to give up reading Isabel's manuscript, and he was crestfallen.

He'd never thought he would die early. He was only in his fifties; he still hadn't attained all his goals. He went to church more often, though he did not go to confession or Holy Communion. He believed it was important to be part of a spiritual congregation, even if he was a freethinker at heart. All religions were good, he felt, if they helped you overcome the trials you faced in this world. But he didn't think Catholicism was better than any other religion. Religions were important because they helped you live in harmony with yourself, not because they might reinforce a belief in immortality. Quintín didn't believe in the immortality of the soul, anyway, only in the positive energy of the universe. And this positive energy was what permitted scientists, historians, artists, to create their great works. But he had never been able to create anything, and he feared that when he died his memory would be erased from the face of the earth. This made him feel sad and dejected.

Isabel went to Mass with him once in a while, but he knew her religion was only skin-deep. She prayed with her lips, she didn't pray with her heart. She knelt next to him on the cathedral's mahogany bench and played with her rosary's crystal beads, as her eyes roamed lazily under the dusty archways of the cathedral, looking for an open window to gaze out of. Who was she praying to, Quintín wondered, Jesus or Elegguá? Since she had fallen under Petra's influence, he couldn't be sure what his wife believed in.

Pain changed everything; it made you look at the world in a different light. Gourmet Imports didn't seem so important to Quintín any longer. He had begun to think more about his art collection. If he could never be an artist, at least he had managed to put together a magnificent collection of works of art. Maybe he still had time to turn the house on the lagoon into a museum, into a shrine of art. That way, he would always be remembered, and so would his family, as the founders and donors of the Mendizabal Museum. The house on the lagoon, Pavel's masterpiece, was a landmark on the island. To turn it into a museum would be relatively easy. All he had to do was start proceedings to create the Quintín Mendizabal Foundation, which would make it all possible after his death.

Once he hit on this solution, Quintín immediately felt better. But he didn't want to lose the attention Isabel had begun to lavish on him after the doctor's diagnosis, so he masked his newfound feeling of well-being. Isabel had ordered Georgina and Victoria to cook Quintín salt-free meals, and she now did the shopping at the supermarket herself. She insisted on getting up at six every morning to walk briskly with him around the lagoon. Quintín was very grateful—but he didn't completely trust her.

One night he could hold out no longer, and went into the study to look for Isabel's manuscript. There were four new chapters since he had last searched for it. He sat with them on his lap for a long time, trying to decide what to do. He felt miserable. Not knowing what Isabel had written made him feel as if he were sinking into the mangrove swamp, as if he were losing his grip on reality. But he didn't dare read the new chapters. He put them back unread in the secret compartment.

33

Willie and Manuel

⚜

LIFE CHANGED AFTER WILLIE'S ADOPTION. Quintín pulled out of his depression and began to go to the office regularly, shoring up business with his European partners and those in the United States. He became quite devout, and we frequently went to church together to pray for Ignacio's and Margarita's souls. In time, I was able to put what had happened with Carmelina out of my mind, and Quintín kept his promise and never looked at another woman again.

We were both in good health and our lives were reasonably pleasant. Sometimes we read books and discussed them; we traveled to Europe every two or three years, and had a relatively active social life. We enjoyed seeing our children grow up and shared in their upbringing. Manuel had begun to work with his father at Gourmet Imports and Willie was painting, happy to be enrolled at Pratt. They were both on a steady course.

I had made up my mind not to worry anymore about Ignacio's reason for committing suicide or Buenaventura's secret account. If I wanted to be happy, it was wise to lay the family ghosts to rest. "Time is like water," I told myself. "It wears even the sharpest knives down, and oblivion will eventually overcome us all. Why should I keep painful memories alive, when the rest of the world has forgotten?"

The island was going through a tranquil period also. The political instability of the sixties had disappeared as if by magic; in the seventies, people seemed more interested in making money than in finding out whether they were Puerto Ricans or Americans. The national obsession—should we remain a commonwealth or become a state in the Union or an independent nation—seemed to be in temporary remission, and politics ceased to be the seed of angry arguments at every bar and corner drugstore on the island. And the same thing happened in my heart, which had calmed down considerably. If in my youth I had discussed politics heatedly with Abby and later with Quintín, I now experienced only a faint stirring of embers and was more interested in keeping the peace than in whipping up controversies.

I was content to be Quintín Mendizabal's wife and willingly took over the role of mistress of the house on the lagoon. I kept myself looking as young as possible, was concerned that our children perform well at school, saw that the cooking and the laundering were impeccably done, took care that Brambon fed the dogs and kept the mangroves properly pruned so that they wouldn't encroach on the house. I even joined several charity associations, like the Carnegie Library Ladies Club, the Red Cross Charity Ball Committee, and the Cancer Committee, and would often give tea parties for its members. Once in a while I also invited Quintín's friends to the house, San Juan's most successful businessmen and their elegant wives.

Quintín and I didn't talk to each other very often, but fortunately we had common interests. I had begun to enjoy our beautiful house more and more, and, like Quintín, found comfort in being surrounded by paintings, sculptures, and antiques. I had fallen in love with Pavel's mosaic terrace, which gleamed like a pool of gold in the late-afternoon light. I took pride in the Tiffany-glass windows, the alabaster skylights, the sculptures and paintings, and supervised their upkeep. Every minute of my day was full, and I wrote very little, if at all. At night I lay awake for hours, thinking of everything I would write the next day, and when I got up the next morning, I would rush from one thing to the next and wouldn't put down a single word. Was my hard-earned marital bliss keeping me from my goal? Did Isabel Monfort, who at her wedding twenty-six years before, had vowed to become a writer, still exist?

It was only three months ago—on June 15, 1982, to be exact —that I began to write *The House on the Lagoon.* I was tired of playing Penelope, forever postponing my own accomplishment.

I had been writing for a long while and had filled pages and pages, but I didn't know if what I was working on was a biographical novel, a diary, or just a handful of notes which would never take a definite form. Then, after Willie was born, I set my manuscript aside and didn't write another word for years. When Quintín and I came back from Manuel's graduation at Boston University, I finally heeded Willie's prompting. He was always telling me how important art was. It was the one thing that helped make the world into a better place, he insisted. I was a writer; I only had to believe in myself. He had been after me for months to stop scribbling aimless pages and write a novel, and I told myself that now was the moment to begin.

WILLIE WAS BORN IN 1966, and he brought a breath of fresh air into our home. Manuel was my own flesh and blood, but when I looked at Willie, something curious happened. He didn't have a drop of my blood in him and yet in many ways he was a lot more like me than Manuel was. Willie wore his heart on his sleeve and was sensitive to everything, as if his nerves were made of silk. He was intuitive by nature. If I was worried or sad about the slightest thing, he perceived it immediately and would kiss me on the cheek.

Petra was seventy-seven when Willie was born, but she didn't look it. It was as if she had gained a new lease on life. She followed him everywhere, flapping her arms like a mother hen. Her feet were deformed by age and arthritis, but she cured them herself very effectively, slicing aloe from a large plant in the garden and making compresses with it. Petra was very proud that Willie was Buenaventura's grandson as well as her great-great-grandson. But she kept her promise and was silent as a tomb about his secret. It annoyed me that both boys went to her for permission for just about everything, coming to me only later to tell me what they had already done: gone to a baseball game, for example, or for a swim with friends. The boys worshipped her, and I finally gave up trying to compete.

Petra went out of her way to make sure the boys got along with each other. There was always space enough in her lap for both— she had wide, strong thighs, and when she sat down, her starched apron crumbled into deep folds, so both boys could burrow into them and fall asleep. At other times she'd let them climb on her back and jangled her metal bracelets gaily before them, and they laughed and shrieked as if they were riding a humpback whale. She sang them the same songs, told them the same stories, and always tried to be affectionate to Manuel, so he wouldn't feel that Willie had displaced him.

One day when Willie was no more than three years old, I was out on the terrace reading while he was playing with his toy train. Suddenly he collapsed. His eyes rolled upward, and he had a speck of foam at the corner of his mouth. I raced with him to Alamares Hospital, and the doctors diagnosed a mild epileptic fit. I was terrified: there was no epilepsy in the Mendizabal family; I didn't know about the Avilés side. That night I visited Petra in the cellar. "Can you do something to cure him? Is there any medicine he can take?" I asked her in anguish. She quietly reassured me. "There's nothing to worry about, Isabel," she said. "In Africa, what Willie has is not a sickness. It means there are great things in store for him."

Manuel loved sports, and sometimes Quintín played basketball with him on Sundays. Or they would sail out of San Juan Bay in the Bertram yacht and go fishing in the choppy waters of the

Atlantic, coming home on the verge of sunstroke, but happy. Quintín had taken Manuel to statehood political rallies since he was five, and when he asked the child what he believed in, Manuel would cry out, "U.S.A.!" which amused Quintín no end. Manuel did everything effortlessly. He learned to swim practically the first time he went into the water; he was a star player on his school basketball team, and he was a clever fisherman. But it would take him twice as long as Willie to do his homework. Quintín had mellowed and he taught Manuel the lessons he had learned from his father, but without the rough edges. There was no need to bring Manuel up the spartan way Buenaventura had raised him.

Willie was more artistic than athletic; he had inherited all of Rebecca's and Ignacio's creative talent. He was truly inspired and lived for his art. Petra and I both believed him to be a child prodigy. At ten, he could play one of Mozart's early sonatas on the piano; at eleven, he was a star in the drama club at school; and by twelve he already knew he wanted to be a painter. Petra used to call him her "little lightning rod," because "he turned everything into a flash of inspiration."

Willie had a sixth sense which told him when it was better to be silent and toe the line, to keep his father from losing his temper. Quintín scoffed good-naturedly at his avant-garde paintings, but he let him do as he pleased. He never took him to political rallies or to basketball games. He was obviously relieved that Willie had no interest in business and wanted to strike out on his own as an artist. That way, Manuel would be by himself at Gourmet Imports, and there would never be any strife between the brothers.

34

Fire Coral

※※

THE WEEK MANUEL GRADUATED from Boston University, his
father had him start working full-time at Gourmet Imports. Manuel
was pleased; he had studied business administration and had
planned to go into business with Quintín when he got out of college.
Manuel's office was small but nicely furnished; his basketball
trophies shone on his desk, his framed diploma hung on the wall,
along with an old tapestry of Valdeverdeja which Buenaventura's
aunts had embroidered for him long before.

"This is where you'll be working," Quintín told him, "right next
to me. From now on, you're going to be my right hand. You'll
have to learn everything from the bottom up, and I want you to
learn it quickly because I'd like to retire." And he gave Manuel
Buenaventura's gold signet ring, the one I had given back to him
when Willie was born. "This ring belonged to your grandfather,
Buenaventura Mendizabal," he said. "And before Buenaventura,
to our ancestor, Francisco Pizarro, Conquistador of Peru. Take it
and wear it as a sign of authority. That way, when I'm no longer
around, everyone at Gourmet Imports will obey you." Quintín was
proud to have Manuel working by his side. He was carrying on a
tradition and was glad to be able to treat his son better than
Buenaventura had treated him.

A little later Quintín came back into Manuel's office, carrying four large leather-bound books. "Buenaventura was an accountant, and he believed the secret of every successful business was keeping the company books in order," he said, putting them down on Manuel's desk. "Father kept the account books himself. He said a good businessman should never trust them to anyone, because they were as precious as his wife. Eventually Buenaventura made me his chief accountant, and I kept track of every penny that was spent and earned at Mendizabal & Company. I want you to do the same at Gourmet Imports, from your first day." Manuel looked at him with grateful eyes. He trusted his father and was happy that Quintín had confidence in him.

That summer Willie was also home. He had done well his freshman year at Pratt and wanted to devote his vacation to painting in Old San Juan. He loved to get up when it was still dark, ride his red Vespa to the Old City, and set up his easel near the walls of El Morro Castle, to paint the sunrise.

One Sunday, the day Willie and Manuel discovered the Ustariz sisters had come back to the island, Manuel decided he would go with him to San Juan. It was a date to remember, and later Willie told me all about it in detail.

Manuel planned to jog for an hour in El Morro's open field while Willie painted. Manuel could do five laps on the fort's rolling grounds easily, and afterwards they would breakfast together at La Bombonera—coffee and toasted *mallorcas*, the sweet, turban-like muffins they had loved since childhood. They arrived at La Rogativa late; unlike Willie, Manuel wasn't an early riser. Willie had waited for him until nine and finally knocked on his door. Manuel still didn't wake up, so he poured a glass of water on him. Manuel wasn't fazed. He simply sat up and blinked, like a heifer after a shower. "What's up, kid? Practicing to become a fireman?" he said, tackling him at the knees. And they both fell laughing to the floor.

They parked their Vespas—Manuel had a blue one exactly like Willie's red one—next to one of the old bastions of La Rogativa's square, near the bronze sculpture of the Bishop's Procession. The statue was one of Manuel's favorite landmarks in San Juan. "It's a perfect example of how propaganda can have a positive effect on one's life," he said to Willie. "San Juan was besieged by the English during the eighteenth century, and there weren't enough soldiers to defend it. The Bishop roused the women of the city and they had a procession around the walls with lighted torches; the English believed there was a huge army stationed inside. They fled, and the siege was lifted."

Willie set up his easel in the square, put a canvas on it, took out his tray of oils, and began to paint. He enjoyed the cool breeze that rose from the bay forty feet below. Manuel began to warm up before jogging, doing stretching exercises, then pushups. Several pigeons scattered around him as he flexed his arms. Willie looked up when he heard a noise, and stared at the pink house behind them, a red bougainvillea vine clinging to the balcony. Suddenly his brush stopped in midair. "Just look at that!" he cried. "I think I picked out the wrong subject; there are two much more interesting sculptures than La Rogativa on the balcony above us!" Two girls in bikinis were sunning themselves, lying on colorfully striped deck chairs. One was a redhead and the other one had raven-black hair.

"I think I know who they are," Manuel said. "Didn't we visit that house with Mother when we were children? I remember the steep marble stairs and the prickly bougainvillea. We both got scratched when we ran up the steps."

"That's Esmeralda Márquez's house, Mother's best friend from Ponce," said Willie. "Don't you remember Perla and Coral Ustariz, who moved to the States? I remember them clearly."

Manuel was always amazed at his brother's memory. Willie couldn't have been more than four years old when Isabel visited Esmeralda, and yet Willie remembered the episode better than he did. Manuel got up and they stood side by side, staring open-mouthed at the two pigtailed brats turned into Venuses, whose bikinis seemed no larger than postage stamps. "They must have glued them on," Manuel said in wonder.

"Perla and Coral Ustariz, hear us! God bless your beautiful tits, as well as your gorgeous bottoms, the best foundations possible for an old friendship!" Manuel shouted, climbing on the Bishop's billowing cassock and waving exuberantly at the girls from La Rogativa's pedestal. He let out a whistle which landed on Coral's ear like a pesky mosquito. Willie climbed up on the medieval walls and began to wave his arms at the girls, too.

Coral nudged Perla with her foot. She was barefoot and her toenails were painted a bright red. Perla had fallen asleep on her chair, cooled by the breeze that wafted through the mahogany balusters. "Get up and get the pitcher of lemonade from the refrigerator," Coral told her, "so we can get rid of those monkeys pounding their chests down there." Perla opened her eyes and looked down. "What a pair! The short one looks like a hairy caveman and the tall one looks like a Viking. What do they think we are—birds in a cage for them to ogle?"

Manuel replied promptly, "We don't think you're birds at all, just two beautiful chicks! Come down and say hello to your old friends."

Perla laughed and stared back. The short one had dark skin and a curly—almost kinky—cushion of hair on his head. But his features were finely chiseled, and she found him very good-looking. He was wearing orange shorts and a Save the Earth T-shirt, the same as the tall, brawny one. Coral, annoyed, nudged her sister again, and Perla went inside and came back with a ceramic pitcher full of iced lemonade, which she promptly emptied over the balcony's rim.

The sticky downpour didn't discourage the pair at all. They went on making such a racket that soon the neighbors opened their windows to find out what was happening. But by that time Perla and Coral, amazed that the "crazy monkeys" should know their names, had run inside the house and shut the balcony's doors.

CORAL WAS BORN six years after Esmeralda's marriage; Perla was born six years later. Quintín would have been very upset if he had known, but I had visited them at Doña Ermelinda's pink house in San Juan many times. On one of these visits I took Manuel and Willie with me, and later we all went to the beach together.

In 1969, Ernesto's father passed away. Ernesto sold the farm, Esmeralda packed everything they owned into two trunks, and they moved to New York with the girls. They took an apartment in Washington Heights, and Ernesto finally enrolled at New York University Law School.

Ernesto was a brilliant student and he had specialized in immigration law. He didn't need the money; the fortune he had inherited from his father was enough for him to live on without working for the rest of his life. But Ernesto wasn't like that. After he graduated, he found a job in the city at an office which dealt with illegal immigrants. He was a liberal and a socialist sympathizer, and soon made a reputation for himself among radical politicians.

Ignacio Mendizabal's suicide, five years after Ernesto's wedding to Esmeralda, had made a strong impression on him.

Ignacio had been seventeen when Ernesto met him at the Bougainvillea Ball, and he remembered him clearly. Ignacio had a crush on Esmeralda, and he was two years younger than she was. Esmeralda felt sorry for him and tried not to hurt his feelings. The Mendizabals, however, had hit the ceiling when they saw how taken Ignacio was with her. Esmeralda and Doña Ermelinda had gone to the party at the house on the lagoon because she wanted to see me. Since Quintín and I had gotten married at the beginning of the summer, I hadn't been back to Ponce.

When Rebecca knocked off Doña Ermelinda's turban at the party, Doña Ermelinda was furious, because she was sure it had been intentional. When they walked out the door of the Mendizabals' house, people had laughed at them; they felt humiliated. That night, before they went to bed, Doña Ermelinda told Esmeralda: "The Mendizabals think they're better than everyone else just because that ham peddler got off a cargo ship from Spain thirty-eight years ago! But neither of their daughters is as beautiful as you are. Ignacio Mendizabal will never be able to get you out from under his skin. Let that be a lesson to Rebecca, so that she'll never dare insult us again!"

Ernesto, when he heard the details of the story, at first laughed them off as absurd. But on his wedding night, when Ignacio turned up at the house, firing right and left like some cowboy out of a spaghetti Western, he had had second thoughts. He never mentioned it to Esmeralda, but the memory of what happened that night had a lot to do with his decision to return to the island. He took the job that a legal firm affiliated with the federal government offered him in San Juan to investigate racial discrimination. San Juan's bourgeoisie were among the most prejudiced in the world; they concealed their racism with polished good manners, but there were very few blacks on the corporate ladders in San Juan or in high posts in the local government. Now he wouldn't have to feel guilty about being away from his country for so long. He could contribute hands-on to making things better.

Esmeralda hadn't been able to study at New York's Fashion Institute as she had hoped, because of the injury she had suffered on her wedding night. The little finger of her right hand had to be amputated after Ignacio's attack, and writing had become awkward for her; drawing fashion models even more so. She had managed to cope with it, however, and had been happy with Ernesto all those years. Her daughters were a joy to her. Coral took after her father—she was a live wire and very political. She had just graduated cum laude from Columbia University with a degree in journalism and the minute she arrived on the island landed a job at *The Clarion*, the English-language newspaper. Perla was more relaxed than Coral and wanted to be a nurse. They both spoke Spanish as well as English; Ernesto and Esmeralda had insisted they speak Spanish at home. "For every language you speak, you're worth another person," Ernesto would say. "Each language gives you a new set of tools with which to solve life's problems."

THE FOLLOWING SUNDAY, Manuel and Willie rode their motorcycles to La Rogativa again. They had both gone to Zabós Unisex Salon the day before and had had their manes shorn off. They were wearing linen pants and elegant navy sports jackets with red silk ties. The girls were lying in their deck chairs again, sunning themselves. This time, Manuel and Willie didn't whistle but knocked politely on the door of the house. Esmeralda herself answered, and the boys introduced themselves as Isabel Mendizabal's sons. Their mother had told them the Ustarizes were back, and she wanted them to say hello on her behalf to Esmeralda and her family.

Esmeralda embraced them warmly and a few minutes later Perla and Coral came downstairs, wearing T-shirts over their bikinis. Esmeralda introduced her daughters and asked the young men if they remembered them. Coral was the redhead and her skin was light gold; Perla was dark-haired, with a pearl-white complexion, which was why Esmeralda had named them as she had. Willie said he did; Manuel said he didn't.

"Of course you do," Coral said to Manuel. "The last time I saw you, we were down at the beach with our nannies. A jellyfish stung my leg and you took out your little dick and peed on it to cure the burn." Then she kissed him on both cheeks. Perla stared at Willie, an impish look in her eyes. "That was a quick change! From hairy caveman to silk-tie Romeo," she teased. But she was glad to see him and kissed him on both cheeks also.

From that Sunday on, they were a foursome. The girls came often to visit us at the house. Manuel and Coral spent Saturday afternoons water-skiing in the lagoon, while Willie taught Perla to paint. Everyone on the San Juan social scene took it for granted that Ernesto Ustariz's daughters and Quintín Mendizabal's sons were going steady. They never went out on their own. If Manuel and Coral wanted to go on a picnic to El Yunque, for example, Willie and Perla would go with them; if Willie and Perla were going to Luquillo Beach, Coral and Manuel went along. The blue and red Vespas, with the couples astride, roared up and down the island like two noisy, lovesick drones.

One day Coral invited Manuel to go to a political rally with her; she had to cover a story for *The Clarion*. "It's an Independentista rally, of course," she said to him. "I wouldn't cover rallies for any other political party, it would go against my principles." They were riding the Vespa down the road, and the wind kept sweeping away Coral's words. "There's going to be a referendum on the island in November," she went on, "and the only honorable thing we can do is ask for self-determination." Manuel was surprised to hear her say that; he wouldn't have guessed she sympathized with independence. "But you've spent more of your life in New York than on the island; don't you feel you're an American?" Manuel asked. Coral looked at him reproachfully. "Don't tell me you're for statehood. Because if you are, I never want to see you again." Manuel was amazed. He knew how passionately his father supported statehood and had always believed in what Quintín believed. So he was silent when Coral spoke.

Coral was unquestionably beautiful, and Manuel was taken with her from the start. She was lively and impetuous—she wanted to do everything on the spot. She had a volatile temper; when she argued, she jumped from one idea to the next, her words like sparks fanned by gusts of wind. Manuel, with his peaceful, somewhat slow disposition, felt irresistibly drawn to her. It was as if he could live more intensely when she was near. When they were together, he rarely spoke; he let her do most of the talking and would simply hold her hand. I liked Coral, too—much better than Perla, who had a quiet, almost humdrum personality. But Coral was interesting; she always had controversial things to say and she knew her own mind.

Coral explained to Manuel that political ideals were very important. Believing in something made you think; it kept your spirit alive. Independence for the island was the purest ideal anyone could strive for, but statehood was anathema. It meant English would be our official language and we would have to *talk* and *feel* in English, would have to pay federal taxes, couldn't participate in the Olympic Games under our own flag, wouldn't be able to take part in the Miss Universe Contest—all blows to our pride and to our sense of identity. "Just think, we're a country that in its five hundred years of existence has never been its own self. Don't you think that's tragic?" But Manuel wouldn't say a word. He didn't want to be disloyal to his father, so he just lowered his head and looked at her with lovesick eyes.

35

Manuel's Rebellion

❧

THE FOLLOWING SUNDAY, Manuel and Willie, with Perla and
Coral hanging on behind, rode their Vespas noisily up the mountain
road to Lares, the site of the Independentista rally. "Do you know
what Lares means?" Coral asked Manuel as they roared up the
winding road. "It's the Latin name for the gods that protect the
home. 'Lares' is the hearthstone, the place that's always kept warm.
As long as Lares is kept alive, there will always be hope for our
island."

At Lares they heard speeches and sang patriotic songs; someone
gave Manuel a Puerto Rican flag—a lone star on a blue field with
red stripes—and he waved it over his head to please Coral. When
he got home, he tacked the flag to the wall behind the bed in his
room, because it made him think of her.

That evening, when Quintín went to say good night to Manuel,
he saw the flag on the wall. "And what is that flag doing there?"
he asked, his eyebrows arched in surprise. "A prank for All Saints'
Day?" "It was a present from a friend, Father," Manuel said
nonchalantly. "After all, it's our flag, even if one day we become
a state."

"I don't like the kinds of friends you've been going out with
lately, Manuel," Quintín cautioned him. "Remember, you're from

a well-to-do family, and the island is full of people who would take advantage of us. Think it over, but by tomorrow I'd like you to take that flag down."

The next evening, however, when Quintín looked in Manuel's room, the flag was still there. This time Quintín was more direct in his comments, but he still managed to keep his temper in check. "Nationalism has always been a curse in our family, Manuel," he explained patiently. "It was because your grandfather Arístides Arrigoitia was forced to take part in a Nationalist shootout that he fell ill and left. It was your Uncle Ignacio's preference for Puerto Rican products that first made me worry about his abilities as a businessman. Independentistas are not to be trusted. That's the reason why, when we interview someone for a job at Gourmet Imports, the first thing we do is ask his political affiliation. If he says he's for independence, we have no work for him. I think you'd better take that flag down."

Manuel didn't have any preference for independence; he had no political ideals whatsoever. In spite of Coral's insistence, he hadn't given the matter much thought. But he was stubborn, and he didn't like to be told what to do. The next morning, when Quintín opened the door to the room, the flag was still there, tacked firmly to the wall over Manuel's bed. Quintín didn't say a word. But when Manuel went to Gourmet Imports, he learned that his father had ordered his desk removed to the back of the warehouse, where the liquor plant was located. He was no longer chief accountant, he was told, but would be in charge of checking the liquor bottles for imperfections. He was to stand in front of a conveyor belt, looking into the empty bottles before they were filled with rum, to make sure there were no cockroaches in them, or that they weren't wobbly or marred by air bubbles. Several times a day, he had to drive a pickup truck to the garbage dump and dispose of the flawed ones. Manuel wasn't upset at all. "It's only understandable that I should prove to you that I'm trustworthy, Father," he said to Quintín that evening. "I don't mind it if you

343

want to try me out, before you put Mendizabal's account books in my care."

A few weeks later, Manuel and Willie invited Perla and Coral to a picnic at Lucumí Beach in the Boston Whaler Quintín had bought for them. At the last minute, Perla came down with the flu, so Coral went alone with Manuel and Willie. It was a beautiful day, and Lucumí was deserted. The three of them sat on the dunes and had salami sandwiches with white wine. Willie had a bit too much wine, lay down, and went to sleep under a palm tree. Coral and Manuel dove into the water together. They didn't plan it; neither would have guessed what the other was going to do. But as they floated under the green shade of the mangroves they began to feel so good, so relaxed, it was as if they were in another world where neither gravity nor heat could affect them, and they slowly took off their bathing suits. There was an undertow and the cool water caressed their bodies and tickled their groins. Gently they drifted toward each other, Manuel floating on his back, with his arms and legs spread apart, and suddenly his penis rose up like a sail. Coral, for her part, was the bay where Manuel's ship would come to berth. "Death must be like this, my darling," Coral whispered. "You're wrong, my love," Manuel replied. "This is what our life will be like from now on."

The following morning Manuel told Quintín there was something important he wanted to talk to him about, but Quintín told him to wait until after dinner, when they would have time to themselves. Manuel had been acting strange for some time. I had heard about his trouble at the office, but instead of being downcast, he was walking around with a smile on his face as bright as the moon. When I tried talking to him, he would stare off into space, hug me, and tell me what a wonderful mother I was.

That evening he came down to dinner in a coat and tie instead of a T-shirt. His hair was carefully combed and he was wearing the Mendizabals' gold signet ring, so I knew something was up. Willie finally arrived, dressed in Levi's and a madras shirt. His

hands, as usual, smelled of turpentine because he had been painting up to the last minute. Quintín was wearing one of his elegant
Ralph Lauren suits, and we all sat around our Majorell dinner table, the one with legs carved like lilies which we had bought on a
trip to Barcelona the year before. I searched for the bell beneath the
kilim rug with the tip of my shoe, so María would begin serving us.

During the meal Quintín went out of his way to be civil to
Manuel; he wanted him to know he didn't hold anything against
him, in spite of his headstrong nature. When dinner was over,
Quintín took Manuel into the study. "I'm only waiting for you to
take that flag down to give you back your job," he told him,
laughing, as they went into the study. "Have you done it yet?"
Manuel sat up very straight in one of the study's red leather chairs.
"No, Father, I haven't," he said. "But you mustn't worry about it,
because I'm not an Independentista; I'm not interested in politics
at all. I want to talk to you about something much more serious."

Quintín looked at him, mystified. He couldn't understand his
son's attitude. One day Gourmet Imports would be his, and all of
Buenaventura's valuable commercial lines. He had simply wanted
to put Manuel to the test with the silly affair of the flag. And he
liked the way he had reacted. Manuel hadn't lost his temper; he
had stood by his guns and proven his mettle. Quintín was going
to move him back to the front office the following day, so he could
teach him his business secrets. What Manuel said took him completely by surprise.

"I'm in love with Coral Ustariz, Father, and she loves me,"
Manuel said in a quiet but steady voice. "We'd like to get married,
but we're going to need your help at first." It hadn't even occurred
to Manuel that Quintín might not like the idea. "We're both twenty-
one, old enough to decide for ourselves," he added. "But I didn't
want to go ahead with our plans without letting you and Mother
know about them."

Quintín was sitting behind his desk and for several seconds he
stared incredulously at Manuel. Then he picked up a pencil that

was lying in front of him and, taking out his pocketknife, began to sharpen the point. It was so quiet you could almost hear the yellow slivers of wood falling on the green leather surface of the desk.

"Has anybody told you who Coral Ustariz's mother is?" Quintín asked Manuel slowly.

"She's Esmeralda Márquez, Mother's best friend from Ponce," Manuel replied innocently. "When Willie and I were children, we visited the Ustarizes' home, and we've known her ever since." Quintín stared hard at his son: "Isabel took you there?" he said. "Of course she did, Father. Why shouldn't she?"

"I'll show you why," said Quintín. And, taking his pocketknife, he made a small incision on the tip of his finger, so that a spurt of blood appeared on it. "You see this blood, Manuel?" Quintín said. "It doesn't have a drop of Arab, Jewish, or black blood in it. Thousands of people have died for it to stay that way. We fought the Moors, and in 1492 we expelled them from Spain, together with the Jews. When our ancestors came to this island, special books were set up to keep track of white marriages. They were called the Bloodline Books and were jealously guarded by the Church. Esmeralda's marriage to Ernesto Ustariz doesn't appear in any of them, because she's part black. *That's* why Isabel shouldn't have taken you to Esmeralda's house when you were a child. And *that's* why you can't marry Coral."

I was listening in near-panic on the other side of the door. Then there was deathly silence. I knocked timidly, but there was no answer. When I pushed open the door, Quintín and Manuel were standing by the desk. At first I thought they were embracing, but in fact they were trying to wrestle each other down. The scuffle lasted only a few seconds. Before I could reach them, Quintín pushed Manuel away. "Get out of here, you ungrateful bastard. I never want to see you again." Manuel went to his room, packed up, and left the house without another word.

36

Quintín's Folly

I TRIED TO BRING QUINTÍN to his senses. "You're a bully and a despot, just like your father before you," I said as we got ready for bed. "You think Manuel is like you, that he'd do anything to inherit Gourmet Imports. But he doesn't care about money the way you do, and he's proud. Esmeralda's daughter is wonderfully accomplished, and she's also very nice. You must apologize to Manuel and let him marry Coral."

But Quintín wouldn't listen. "Buenaventura and Rebecca would never forgive me," he insisted. "I'd rather be dead than have mulatto grandchildren and be related to Esmeralda Márquez."

"What about Willie?" I asked. "Where does that leave *him*?" But Quintín wouldn't answer.

The walls of the house on the lagoon had ears, and by evening everybody knew Quintín and Manuel had had a serious argument. Eulodia told me Petra was terribly upset; she had been praying to Elegguá for hours. That evening, she sent Eulodia with a message that she had something important to tell me. At ninety-three, Petra hardly ever came up to the first floor of the house. Her arthritis kept her from going up the stairs, and she was visibly strained from the effort as she entered my room.

"Manuel came to the cellar to see me before he left," Petra said gravely. "He said his father had told him to get out, but he didn't know where to go. He didn't have any money for a hotel, so I told him he could stay with Alwilda in Las Minas. She has a relatively comfortable place; she gets a disability check from the federal government every month. I also told him not to pay attention to Quintín, to go to work tomorrow morning as if nothing had happened. 'Quintín will eventually get over his tantrum,' I said to calm him. 'Your father is upset because he thinks you're too young to get married. But he's a good man. He'll come to his senses.' Manuel promised he'd follow my advice."

I could see Petra was very concerned, and I was grateful. But I didn't add any comment to what she had said. "Quintín is always letting me down, Isabel," she said somberly, shaking her head. "He's going to make Elegguá very angry if he doesn't let Manuel marry Esmeralda Márquez's daughter." And then she added: "I'm not sure if I want to go on working in this house if Quintín goes on like this."

Petra's words shocked me—she had always been so loyal to Quintín. "It's Rebecca's blood coming out in him," I said to appease her. "You know how much stock Rebecca put in public opinion, and sometimes Quintín can't help being like her. It's one thing to adopt Willie and be liberal-minded, another for everyone in San Juan to know the Mendizabals are marrying mixed blood. You must be patient, Petra. This is not easy for Quintín; but I'm sure in the end he'll come through. Right now, Quintín needs you more than ever. You mustn't leave."

THE NEXT DAY I WENT to see Esmeralda in San Juan to inform her what had happened. She knew already; Coral had heard from Manuel, who had told her everything. Alwilda had moved out and left her cottage at Manuel's disposal. The upsetting thing was that Coral had also left her parents' house. "She didn't even ask permission from Ernesto and me," Esmeralda told me agitatedly. "She simply told us she was leaving. We're glad she's with Manuel—

we think he's a wonderful boy and we hope they'll get married. But we're worried something may happen to her in that awful slum of Las Minas if she goes there alone."

I explained to Esmeralda that half the population of Las Minas was related to Petra, and both Coral and Manuel would be perfectly safe there. "Petra is like a sovereign in the slum," I told her. "People worship her. Once they know Manuel and Coral are under her protection, they'll do everything to help them." I thought of trying to get in touch with Manuel myself, but it was difficult to do. The only way to reach Alwilda's house was by boat, and I didn't want to phone him at the warehouse. Quintín had made it clear he didn't want me to try to patch things up. He expected Manuel to come to him and ask forgiveness on his own.

In the next few weeks I tried to convince Quintín to take the first step and make peace with Manuel, but it was no use. I could tell he was unhappy. He had begun to grow heavy, not fat, but solid—as if the flesh had hardened on his bones. At night, when he went to sleep next to me, he reminded me of a medieval warrior laid out in full armor. He refused to speak to Manuel when he ran into him at the warehouse, paid him three dollars an hour—the minimum wage—canceled his medical insurance, and expected him to work from six in the morning until six in the evening. Manuel wasn't one to complain; he was punctual and didn't miss a day of work.

One Sunday morning, Manuel came to the house in one of the company delivery vans to get the rest of his things. When I saw him load up his personal possessions—his clothes, his basketball, his camera, his fishing tackle, even his blue Vespa—my heart broke. I went to the study and begged Quintín to relent and ask Manuel to stay, but he sat stone-faced in the red leather chair reading the newspaper; he didn't even lift his eyes from the page. "Tell him to return the van to Gourmet Imports as soon as possible. I didn't give him permission to use it, but I won't dock his salary this time," he said.

Willie was with his brother, helping him move. I went upstairs and sat on the terrace overlooking the lagoon, sure that Manuel would come looking for me after he had finished packing. But he never did. He went to the cellar to say goodbye to Petra, and after a while I heard the van's motor start, and then I heard it leave. I felt as if someone had died.

WILLIE COULDN'T UNDERSTAND why his father was being so headstrong, but he didn't want to judge him. Quintín had always been good to him; he had gotten along well with both his sons. He used to talk to Willie about the Spanish Conquistadors and about the pride he should take in their tradition of excellence. Willie thought that, because he was adopted, he didn't have the Conquistadors' blood in him, but nonetheless he shared in the family mystique. As to his recent disagreement with Manuel, getting married was a very serious thing, Quintín told him. One didn't take such a significant step unless one was completely independent. Buenaventura wouldn't give Quintín permission to get married until he had worked for more than a year and had his own income. Willie should remind Manuel of this when he next saw him. Willie didn't entirely believe his father, but he was willing to go along. He looked at him with his sad gray-green eyes and hoped that time would wear down Quintín's objections.

Willie didn't have his brother's problem. He was sixteen going on seventeen, too young to even think of marriage. But he was one of those people who are born old. He had innate wisdom. When he went out with Perla, they touched and kissed, but it never went beyond that. They went to the movies and held hands in the dark. They dreamed of getting married one day but wanted everything to be as it should.

Willie was worried about Manuel and spent hours trying to figure out how to help him. When Manuel first moved to the slum, Willie wanted to move there, too; he felt bad about staying in a comfortable house when his brother was living in such dire conditions. So he brought him food, clothes, records, the LP player and portable television set they had shared. But Manuel didn't appreciate Willie's efforts to keep in touch. Sometimes Willie felt Manuel wanted to shoo him away like a pesky bird.

Willie would arrive at Alwilda's house in the Boston Whaler at ten or eleven in the evening, when he knew his brother would be there. He could hear him breathing through the weather-beaten planks of the walls. There was no electricity in Las Minas and it was terribly dark; there were so many mosquitoes Manuel had to keep all the windows and doors shut. Willie would get out of the boat, climb up on the rickety balcony, and knock repeatedly on the door, listening to the breathing inside and growing more and more concerned. Was Manuel sick, or was there something wrong? He pleaded with him to tell him if he was all right.

One day Manuel got tired of his brother's naïveté and decided to give Willie the message. He turned on the battery-powered lantern on the floor next to his bed, and through the tiniest chink in the wooden planks Willie saw a wreath of arms, legs, and thighs, and Coral's red hair flowing over Manuel's shoulders like a fiery shawl. That was the last time Willie went to Alwilda's house looking for his brother. Now he knew why Manuel didn't have any time for him.

I began to suspect Coral had something to do with Manuel's painful rejection of me also and asked Esmeralda to tell her that I wanted to see her. "I'll try to arrange it, Isabel," Esmeralda said to me anxiously, "but we haven't been able to talk to her in days. She left her job at *The Clarion* and is working with the Independentista Party full-time. She hardly ever comes here anymore." But a few days later Coral came to see me at the house on the lagoon. She was wearing a tight pair of jeans, no makeup, and no bra. Her breasts were drawn against her puckered-cotton voile blouse like alabaster moons, and all of a sudden she reminded me of Estefanía and how much we had enjoyed shocking the people of Ponce when we were young. But Coral was different; she had a cold beauty, as if she had been sculpted in marble. She was no frolicking temptress like Estefanía, but more like a determined Amazon.

I was in the study, and when Coral came in I made a place for her next to me on the couch. I liked Coral. She reminded me of myself when I was her age; I had the same intensity, the same need to empty life's cup to the dregs. She chose to sit on one of the red leather chairs opposite me, however, took a cigarette from her purse, and lit it without smiling. "I hear Manuel and you are planning to get married, and I think that's wonderful," I said to her. "You mustn't worry about what Quintín says; he's terribly old-fashioned, but eventually he'll come around. You can count on me for anything. Why don't we go together to look for a nice apartment for you two? Las Minas isn't the place to live." Coral said she'd think about it, and I didn't insist.

She got up from her chair and went to look at the family photographs, which stood in silver frames on the desk: Buenaventura as a young man recently arrived from Spain, with his *sombrero Cordobés* jauntily perched on his head; Rebecca as Queen of the Spanish Antilles, wearing her crown of pearls; Arístides Arrigoitia as chief of police, standing next to Governor Winship at a reception in the Governor's Palace; Arístides in his gala uniform, with Quintín sitting on his knees as a child. Coral picked up a photograph of Willie and Manuel when they were children and looked at it closely. They stood smiling under a palm tree at the entrance to Alamares High School, Manuel's arm affectionately draped around Willie's shoulders.

I broke down and opened my heart to her. "It's sad, isn't it? For the first time in their lives, Manuel and Willie have stopped talking to each other. We haven't heard from Manuel since the day he left the house; he hasn't come to see us once. Is he all right? Is he living in Las Minas with you because of his Independentista friends?"

"Manuel and I are living in Las Minas because we *want* to, not because we have to," she told me sternly. "The slum is part of our way of life now. We believe that, if one wants to change the world for the better, one must become part of the proletariat. Manuel hasn't come to see you because he hasn't had the time; when he gets out of Gourmet Imports he works until late at night at the Party's headquarters. But he's happy; now he has something to live for."

I had heard from Esmeralda about Coral's radical political ideas, so it didn't surprise me to hear her talk like that. To appease her and try to win her over, I told her that in my youth—before I met Quintín—I had worked with Abby in the slums of Ponce, teaching poor children skills like sewing and photography to help them survive in the world. "I've never reproached Manuel for being an Independentista," I said. "I think Quintín made a terrible mistake."

Coral burst out laughing. "I know all about you, Isabel, and your 'liberal' ideas. Manuel talks about them all the time. But this house, the life you lead, is a complete contradiction of them. All private property is the result of theft! You're nothing but a sellout and a sham."

QUINTÍN

Quintín was worried. The private detective he had hired told him that Manuel was in serious trouble. He had left the house and was living with Coral in Las Minas; they had joined an Independentista terrorist group called the AK 47. Statehood was ahead in the plebiscite polls and the Independentistas were sure to carry out violent reprisals before the voting took place.

But Quintín was even more concerned about Isabel. Isabel had become very depressed and hardly went out at all; she sat in the study for hours gazing out toward the lagoon.

Quintín felt guilty because once he had discovered the manuscript, instead of being understanding and patient with Isabel, instead of talking to her about how she was being poisoned by Petra's gossip, he had gotten angry and thrown in some disparaging remarks about Isabel's family. It had been a stupid mistake not to try to approach her once he had found the novel. They should have brought things out into the open and confessed their worries to each other.

Since Quintín had gone into the study the last time, there were four new chapters in Isabel's manuscript. This made eight chapters in all he hadn't read. In spite of the doctor's recommendation, Quintín tore through them. "The Forbidden Banquet," Quintín had to admit, was surprisingly faithful to reality. The affair with Car-

melina Avilés had happened; there was no way to deny it. For seventeen years Quintín had paid the price; Isabel had never let him forget it. She had had the moral upper hand in their marriage for years, and he had been smothered in guilt. What did one do in a situation like that? The spirit was strong but the flesh was weak, and Quintín was neither the devil Isabel portrayed in her novel nor the angel she wanted him to be. He was simply a man, and temptation was always present in a man's life.

Quintín's heart was pounding. After the trouble with Carmelina, he had tried to be a loving husband, a good father, a good provider. He had even adopted Willie without being sure he was his child, just because Isabel had asked him to. After all, Carmelina had left the house immediately after their encounter and had lived in New York for almost a year. She was nineteen years old then and could have had any number of lovers. But Quintín knew that Petra would have testified against him in court and he couldn't stand the thought of a public scandal. What hurt him the most, though, was that Isabel wouldn't forgive him. So he gave in, and they took in Willie, as they had taken in Carmelina herself many years ago.

Isabel had always been partial toward the child. Her love for Willie was almost an obsession; she grew incensed if she thought Willie was being slighted in any way. She was capable of insulting strangers in the street and even her own friends if she thought they were being prejudiced. Quintín had to be on his guard and try to be as fair as Solomon to escape Isabel's ire. He had come to terms with the situation easily enough when the boys were young; he was sincerely fond of Willie. But he couldn't deny he loved Manuel more, because he was his own flesh and blood.

Quintín tried to go on reading, but he began to feel ill. His head was reeling and he couldn't breathe. He loved Isabel above all else; the thought of losing her was unbearable. She had to believe him rather than Petra.

He put the manuscript down and made up his mind to give Isabel an answer. He would write down his version of what had happened with Carmelina. The trouble was, he knew he couldn't write as well as Isabel could. His efforts at correcting her were puny and sketchy by comparison. He could write with ease about Doña Valentina Monfort, about Margot Rinser, adorning the facts here and there, because those people weren't important to him. But how did one put one's personal tragedies down on paper for all to read? How did one say one's heart was breaking without sounding melodramatic? If only he was able to write about himself, to confess what he really felt at that moment, his shameful passion for a woman who had betrayed him—but he couldn't do it. He felt beaten. All he could manage was a dry summary of what had taken place.

Quintín took out his pencil and began to write on the back of one of Isabel's pages:

"The day of the picnic at Lucumí Beach, I was making a great effort to appear gay and lighthearted, but that was far from the way I really felt. Margarita's tragedy had affected all of us. Manuel needed cheering up, and so did I. Isabel didn't make the least effort to lift the family's spirits. For days, she was resentful and distant. If I tried to comfort her, she would push me away with a hand as cold as ice. I got only despondent looks, gloomy unresponsiveness, irritable answers to my questions.

"Crab is an aphrodisiac—anyone who has had it knows that— and that day at the beach I had washed down half a dozen with a bottle of cold Riesling. All of a sudden, the combination of the crab's strong taste and the wine's delicate bouquet made me inexplicably happy. For the first time since Margarita's death, I managed to dispel the ominous cloud I had been living under. I got up from the sand dune where I was sitting and looked over at Carmelina, who was swimming at that moment toward the mangroves. What took place between us was something no one, not even God Almighty, could have prevented."

37

AK 47

❧

AT FIRST MANUEL JOINED the Independentista Party just to please Coral, but his resentment toward his father radicalized him. Every evening I imagined them lying on Alwilda's old mattress in the little wooden house built on stilts, listening to the waters of Morass Lagoon drifting by under them. Knowing Coral, I suspect they probably didn't talk about love or about their plans for the future, as lovers usually do, but mostly about politics.

"The plebiscite will cause a crisis on the island. We must stop being Hamlets and make up our minds to *do* something," Coral proclaimed to Manuel one day. "Only radical action can change the dangerous course our island is on right now."

The political struggle *was* escalating, and we were all surprised when the polls showed statehood ahead by a slim majority—it had forty-nine percent of the vote. Commonwealth had forty-seven percent, and independence four percent. But polls were not to be trusted; voters were fickle, and the situation could change from one day to the next. Commonwealth and independence sympathizers warned against losing our culture and our language if we became a state in the Union. Statehooders wielded economic arguments; their advertising campaign was like a barrage from a machine gun that fired coins at you. The island at present received eight and a half billion dollars in federal funds and with statehood it would receive three billion more; the benefits of social security and of national health programs would be double what they were. Even after paying federal taxes, which the islanders didn't do under their commonwealth status, they stood to gain enormous economic benefits, four to five billion additional dollars, under statehood. "There's no stopping statehood now," the radio and television blared. Coral and Manuel thought it was a losing battle—independence didn't stand a chance, and even commonwealth, which had been the island's status since Luis Muñoz Marín's time, was threatened.

As more and more voters lined up behind statehood, the atmosphere in San Juan grew volatile; disputes took place everywhere. Our current governor, Rodrigo Escalante, was a white-maned politician who spoke in favor of statehood with the hysterical fervor of an Evangelical minister. Governor Escalante was nicknamed the Silver Cock by his enemies, and he had taken the insult as his trademark. He spoke English with a thick Spanish accent and had a white American rooster brought to all his political rallies. He announced that if statehood should win by 51 percent *The Star-Spangled Banner* would be our national anthem and the American flag our flag.

Governor Escalante was famous for his strict measures against dissenters. He thought it was his duty to impose discipline on the land, so voting would take place in an atmosphere of law and order. When a strike broke out at the University of Puerto Rico, he sent in paratroopers, and several students were killed. *El Machete*, the Independentista newspaper, went up in flames one night, but no one was caught or punished for it. The police made a list of all citizens with Independentista leanings, identifying them as subversives despite the fact that the Independence Party was recognized legally and would take part in the referendum. Having an Independentista come to one's house for a visit was dangerous; it put one on the list as a sympathizer. Homes, telephones, and cars of Independentistas were bugged. Every once in a while, a band of brigands would surround one of their houses at night and beat whoever tried to leave or go inside. In August, three months before the plebiscite was to take place, Coral convinced Manuel to join the AK 47. We found out about it later from the reports of the private detective Quintín had hired to keep track of Manuel's activities.

The AK 47 held study sessions in the slum, in a shack near Alwilda's. Manuel and Coral began to go to them regularly in the evening. Most of the members were young and very serious about their studies. They had to learn Chairman Mao's *Red Book* by heart, read and discuss Karl Marx's *Das Kapital*, as well as Albizu Campos's incendiary speeches. Manuel was a slow reader and had a hard time sitting still for so many hours, trying to understand those boring texts, but with Coral by his side helping him, he eventually made progress.

They also studied civil and economic reports which detailed the island's soaring rate of drug abuse, twenty percent unemployment rate, thriving black market, illicit minimum wage, and the shameful condition of public schools and municipal hospitals. In the AK 47's opinion, these ills were the result of the island's colonial status, which led to a confused sense of identity and a lack of self-respect.

The impending plebiscite was the moment for the AK 47 to show that the spirit of independence wasn't dead on the island, that there were still people who shared in its dream. Puerto Rico should be a socialist republic, loosely structured on the Cuban model. For the past twelve years, the country had been politically split almost down the middle. Fear kept it balanced on the edge of a knife. Voting by halves, after all, was a way of not making up one's mind. Fear of what, Manuel asked the AK 47. Fear of choosing a definite path, they said, of leaving the collective schizophrenia behind. The confusion as to whether we were Puerto Rican or American, whether we should speak Spanish or English, had gotten the better of us and turned our will to mush. That was why, when election time came around, half the country voted for statehood and half for commonwealth or independence—the country could not make up its mind what it wanted to be. Now that there was finally going to be a plebiscite, it was the duty of the AK 47 to give the country a definitive push, so it would find the courage to vote for independence.

When Manuel and Coral heard these arguments, they were convinced the AK 47 was right. They threw themselves feverishly into their work: they raised money, helped organize strikes, sold *El Machete* on street corners, waving it above their heads like a flag as they forged their way on foot through traffic.

They wanted an island where everyone could be free—from drugs, from ignorance, from poverty—where no one would sleep in beds with embroidered linen sheets and pillows of swan feathers like those in the house on the lagoon, while others had no sheets at all. And even more important, they wanted a country where waving one's flag and singing one's national anthem was not a crime, where one could confidently fall asleep with the windows open and no one would batter down one's door. And as everything was fair in love and war, the members of the AK 47 told them, and they professed a true love for their country and for the proletariat to which they now belonged, all methods were valid to reach their goal. Manuel and Coral thoroughly approved.

When the AK 47 found out that Manuel was the great-grandson of Chief of Police Arístides Arrigoitia and the son of Quintín Mendizabal, the millionaire owner of Gourmet Imports, they asked him to contribute to their cause. After all, the Mendizabal family had benefited more than most from the unequal distribution of wealth on the island. The house on the lagoon was a virtual myth in Las Minas. Everyone had heard about its terrace of .22-karat gold mosaics where people danced and laughed until the wee hours of the morning, and about the dark cellar where the servants lived. It was his duty to donate generously. Manuel told them he didn't have any money, that he had quarreled with his father and had been kicked out of the house, but they wouldn't believe him. Manuel felt guilty and tried to raise as much money as possible. He sold his fishing tackle, his camera, his stamp collection, even his blue Vespa, and gave them the proceeds, but they only laughed at him and said it wasn't enough.

The AK 47 then asked him to invite Willie to their study sessions. If Manuel couldn't contribute money, he could at least bring a collaborator to the cause. His brother was smart; they would soon find a way to get him to help them. Manuel sent Willie a message through Perla to come to Alwilda's house; he needed to talk to him. Willie was happy to go, being eager to see his brother. Together they went to several meetings.

Manuel and Willie sat next to each other at the study sessions and read from the red book of Mao Tse-tung's thoughts. Manuel took it all very seriously—too seriously, Willie thought. The group never played music or made small talk. What was worse, they never smiled—they seemed to be always frowning. Willie noticed that when Manuel read aloud from Mao his voice trembled and he lowered his head in reverence; it was as if Manuel were praying. But Willie didn't say anything. He was glad to share in what Manuel was doing, so he could see him more often. And basically he agreed that there were many social and economic evils on the island. The oligarchy, his family included, had too much money; they lived in palaces and all of them had second homes—in Vail, Colorado; in Stowe, Vermont—while the poor lived in slums.

Willie was a fast learner. He soon had all the information he needed at the tips of his fingers and he began to write short notices for *El Machete*, book reviews and articles pointing out social ills. One day, the group's leader said he wanted to talk to him in private. He asked if Willie would work for the AK 47 full-time, writing ads for the Independentista Party's campaign. "With the plebiscite only three months away, we need all the help we can get to further our cause," the leader said. "We can't pay you for your work, but you'll be earning points toward the future. Maybe someday we'll be able to return the favor, when we get rid of all the traitors in power." Willie declined the offer. If he worked full-time for them, he would have to stop painting, and he couldn't do that. He was working on some important canvases right now which he hoped to take back with him to Pratt after the summer vacation was over.

The leader of the AK 47 didn't take Willie's refusal kindly. At the next meeting he publicly denounced him. His paintings were self-indulgent; all Willie wanted was to convey hedonist pleasure. When the country was in such dire need of artists to denounce the political morass, it was shameful to refuse.

Willie expected Manuel to speak up, but Manuel just sat there, staring stolidly at him. He didn't say a word. Willie got angry and left the room, slamming the door behind him, and motored back to the house alone in the Boston Whaler. That was the last time he went to an AK 47 meeting or tried to contact Manuel.

38

The Strike
at Gourmet Imports

※

AFTER HIS FIGHT WITH MANUEL, Quintín began to have trouble sleeping again. He was often up all night wandering around the house in the dark. But if I got up and went looking for him or tried to get him to come back to bed, he got very angry. He would stand for hours before Giuseppe Ribera's painting of St. Andrew nailed to the cross, praying to him aloud. "I know every man is crucified at the end of his life, but I didn't know it would happen to me so soon. I've worked like a slave for Manuel, and now he's betrayed me."

Manuel had left his job at Gourmet Imports and news reached us through Petra that he was still living in Alwilda's house. Quintín's private detective followed him everywhere and found out he did all sorts of chores for the AK 47, even cooking, and cleaning Party headquarters. It was as if Manuel had become their ward. But what bothered Quintín most was the rumor in Alamares, the Casa de España, and other social circles of San Juan, that our son had become a radical Independentista.

Manuel was twenty-one; he had the right to be what he wanted and live as he wished. But his silence was like a knife in my heart. Not a word, not a call in more than three months; we could have died and he wouldn't have known. "If you love someone, you must learn to give him up," I heard Petra say once after Carmelina left for New York. Now I had to give up Manuel. "But that doesn't mean we've lost him," Petra added. "He'll turn up when we least expect it."

"The AK 47 is a very dangerous organization," the private detective told us. "They're terrorists, and the police have been after them for some time. They're simply waiting for the right opportunity to force Manuel to do something risky, and then he's going to have to face the consequences." Soon after that, we received an anonymous letter, warning us to leave Manuel alone if we cared at all for our safety.

Quintín was incensed and ordered the surveillance of Manuel intensified. Several agents from the local police force, in addition to the private detective, followed him everywhere. Thanks to his Grandfather Arístides, Quintín still had many friends at headquarters. Quintín was also worried about Gourmet Imports. He was afraid that if something happened to him, Gourmet Imports, as well as our house and the valuable collection of paintings, would fall into the hands of the terrorist organization that had gotten hold of our son.

The day after we received the threatening letter, just before he left for the office Quintín told me he was thinking of making a new will. He wanted to leave his money to a foundation, which would manage his holdings until Manuel came to his senses. If Manuel never did, the foundation would keep everything. "And what about Willie?" I asked. "He doesn't have anything to do with any of this. It's not right for him to be left out of our inheritance, and have to pay for Manuel's folly." But Quintín insisted. "I can't leave a fortune to Willie if Manuel isn't going to inherit anything," he said. "Especially since I can't be sure Willie is my son." I couldn't believe Quintín would go ahead with such an unfair plan.

That same day, after Quintín left for Gourmet Imports, Eulodia came to my room and told me Petra wanted to see me. She was waiting for me in the servants' parlor—Brambon and her three nieces standing next to her. "I want you to take a message to Quintín, Isabel," Petra said quietly. "You've already lost Manuel because of your husband's foolishness, and now Quintín is forgetting that, when he 'adopted' Willie, he did so because the Avilés family *let* him adopt him. But Willie belongs to us. If Quintín disinherits him, we'll tell him who his father is, and you'll lose both your sons, because Willie will think you're ashamed of him." I went upstairs overcome with anxiety, and waited for Quintín to come home, to tell him of Petra's words.

Quintín returned early, but I never had a chance to talk to him. He was very upset about an unexpected development at Gourmet Imports. "We've never had a labor union before, and all of a sudden Anaconda has gotten hold of Gourmet Imports," he said angrily as he sat down to dinner. Buenaventura had taught Quintín to screen workers who might become members of the Anaconda or the Black Bear, the two most powerful labor unions on the island. Quintín would interview applicants personally and always had a private detective do a little footwork before he hired anyone. "I've told the workers in no ambiguous terms: 'I won't have it.' Now they're threatening to strike." He was so angry he kept wielding his dinner knife at an imaginary foe. I didn't dare tell him about Petra.

The next day Quintín fired fifty of his employees, half the workforce of Gourmet Imports. He had spies among them, and easily found out who the troublemakers were. But it was too late. Early the next morning—it couldn't have been later than six o'clock, because we were still in bed—Quintín got a telephone call from one of the guards at the warehouse, telling him a mob was gathering in front of the building. He drove immediately to Old San Juan and found the workers demonstrating in front of the heavy wooden gates, with placards aloft and an elaborate speaker system blaring their propaganda from a pickup truck. The pavement was littered with broken wine and liquor bottles that had been thrown against the building, as well as sausages, smoked hams, and overturned codfish crates. An army of stray dogs was already digging into them. Several of the windows had been broken; stones and debris were everywhere. Quintín telephoned the police, and a squadron of armed men arrived on the scene. They went after the demonstrators with billy clubs and water hoses, scattering them in every direction.

In four hours the situation was under control, and by five in the afternoon Quintín had returned to the house. He was furious. A stone had grazed his right temple when he had come out of the warehouse earlier in the day. Moreover, an entire sales season would be lost because of the strike. It was only September, but Gourmet Imports had been gearing up for Thanksgiving, which had become almost as important as Christmas on the island. Orders for all kinds of wines, stuffings, chestnuts, and other imported foods were already coming in. But he wouldn't be able to deliver, because he didn't have enough workers. He was going to have to put ads in the papers and set up interviews for a whole new workforce. He swore he was going to find out who was responsible for the strike if he had to rake Gourmet Imports with a steel comb.

That evening—it must have been around ten o'clock—as Quintín lay asleep on the bed with an ice pack on his head—I happened to look out the window and saw to my amazement strikers gathering on Ponce de León Avenue, in front of the house. They had brought their placards and streamers with them and were angrily haranguing a crowd of onlookers with a small portable microphone. Our neighbors—the Berensons, who lived in a porticoed Victorian mansion with elaborate trellises; the Colbergs, who owned the home next to ours, designed by Pavel with a prairie-style veranda in front—came out into the street to see what was going on. I worried what they might think of us. A strike in Alamares was unheard of; whoever had organized this one evidently wasn't intimidated by the surroundings. People from the working quarters of San Juan—from Barrio Obrero or Las Minas, for example—rarely dared set foot in Alamares, where a police officer was usually very efficient in getting non-residents to move out of the neighborhood. But this time it was different. There must have been at least fifty workers marching up and down the palm-lined avenue as confidently as if they owned it.

First the Berensons' maid, then the Colbergs' nanny and their chauffeur, and finally the neighbors themselves began to congregate on the sidewalk, listening to the gross insults being hurled at Quintín. "Quintín, you pig, you rip off the worker and reap benefits!" "Quintín, you pig, you starve the poor and feed the rich!" My face was stinging with shame; I couldn't believe what was happening. The strikers circled the street right before our front door, in front of Pavel's Art Nouveau rainbow, waving Puerto Rican flags and shaking their fists at us. Quintín was sound asleep. The air-conditioning drowned out the commotion outside. A shout from one of the strikers finally roused Quintín, and we ran out into the street together. Willie stood on the sidewalk next to Petra, Eulodia, and Brambon, his face drawn with worry. I called out to him and he joined us. "Go inside and call the police!" Quintín shouted at him, picking up some rocks and throwing them at the demonstrators. But Willie didn't budge. He stood next to me on the sidewalk as if he had grown roots. The leader, a tall, dark-haired man who was marching in front of the picket line, was chanting: "Quintín, you pig, selling truffles, and mincing your workers to bits." The strikers had thrown stones at the streetlamps and the street was dark. But we recognized him instantly. It was Manuel.

"I know how to take care of these scoundrels!" Quintín shouted and disappeared into the house. I thought he was going to get his gun, and I cried out to Willie to stop him. But he had thought of something else. Two black forms streaked out from the back of the house and sprang at the demonstrators. Quintín had let Fausto and Mefistófeles loose.

The dogs were ferocious. They were let loose only late at night, and they patrolled the grounds with such diligence that no one had ever dared break into the house. I stood petrified as they flew at the strikers, snarling and frothing at the mouth. Neighbors, workers, servants, everyone ran for cover—except Manuel and a few reckless workers, who defiantly stood their ground.

Then the police arrived, responding to a neighbor's phone call. Manuel bounded off and I looked for Willie. I couldn't see him, but then I spotted him running alongside Manuel, trying to ward off the billy-club blows the officers were showering on him. They had mistaken him for a demonstrator and there was blood on his face. Manuel had long legs, but Willie was an easy catch. In a minute he was handcuffed. Manuel and the workers, on the other hand, ran toward a construction truck that was waiting for them at the curb. Several of them were hurt and bleeding, but they all managed to clamber onto the truck as it began to move.

Then Manuel jumped back onto the pavement and faced the dogs. One of his companions threw him an iron rod from the truck, and he wielded it like a spear. Mefistófeles recognized Manuel and stopped in his tracks; he began to wag his tail. But Fausto was enticed by the smell of blood and lunged straight at him. Manuel threw the rod and it pierced his abdomen. Then he ran after the truck again, climbed on, and disappeared. Quintín ran to Fausto and took him in his arms, but the dog was dead.

I ran to where the police wagon was stationed at the other end of the avenue, looking desperately for Willie. I wanted to tell the officers it was a mistake, Willie wasn't one of the strikers. But I was too late. They were beating him mercilessly. I screamed at them to stop, but they didn't hear. They were lined up like a blue wall of muscle, oblivious to anyone or anything else. Willie collapsed to the ground, foaming at the mouth, his eyes rolling back in an epileptic fit.

I pushed and kicked at the men in front of me and managed to get to Willie's side, but Petra had gotten there before me. She looked like a giant gone mad. Her huge arms flew like the blades of a windmill as she distributed blows right and left, her metal bracelets clanging like spearheads. The officers were so taken aback they didn't dare block her way. Between the two of us, we picked Willie up and carried him back to the house.

Willie was unconscious for hours. The doctor came and said it was better not to move him from the house. He prescribed medication to prevent blood clots, in case of internal hemorrhaging. Petra and I tended Willie all night, putting compresses on his wounds and feeding him medicinal teas. "The only reason he's alive is because of Elegguás' *Figa*, the tiny black fist I hung around his neck when he was born," Petra said. The next day Willie came to, but he was very weak, and his right eye was swollen shut. "Why didn't Quintín help me when he saw what the police were doing to me?" he asked. I tried to explain that in the melee, Quintín hadn't realized what was happening—and I could see Willie wanted desperately to believe me.

Manuel had disappeared. He had left Alwilda's house, and now no one—not even Petra—knew where to find him. Coral may have known where he was, but she said nothing. She had stopped seeing him and went back to her parents', so as not to give him away. Quintín was sure Manuel had gone underground.

"I want the police to find him," he demanded. "I'm not going to let him get away with this! He's not only made me the laughingstock of Alamares—he murdered Fausto, who was sired by Buenaventura's favorite Doberman." Willie was convinced Manuel had been kidnapped by the AK 47 and had been forced to take part in the strike, and he told his father so. But Quintín only scolded him for trying to make excuses for his brother. I was terrified. The anger I had seen on Manuel's face had made my blood run cold. I hardly recognized him; he looked like one of the tortured souls in Quintín's painting *The Fall of the Rebel Angels*.

The doctor came to the house again and examined Willie's right eye. The beating had left him partially blind, and he might never recover his sight completely. I was furious with Quintín for not coming to Willie's aid, but was so emotionally drained I didn't have the energy to reproach him for it. Adrenaline fueled strange reactions in men; it made them blind to everything except the source of their anger. Maybe he hadn't seen what was happening to Willie.

In a few days my hostility toward Quintín abated. He was suffering—he had lost his son also. We should comfort each other, share our tragedy. But soon I realized Quintín wasn't sad; he was smoldering in anger.

Manuel's presence at the head of the Independentista strike prompted him to draw up a new will. "Manuel is a leader of the Anaconda union, and a member of the AK 47. Do you think it's fair he should inherit Gourmet Imports?" he asked, a steel edge to his voice. "He'll donate our fortune to the Independentista cause, and Willie will go along with him, because he adores his brother and does what Manuel tells him. Neither of them cares a damn about Buenaventura's reputation or about mine. Gourmet Imports and even our art collection will go to subsidize the Independentistas and the Nationalists, those fanatics who have been our family's proverbial enemies for over half a century. I can think of much better things to do with my money." That same day our attorney, Mr. Domenech, came to the house to draw up the will, and Quintín made me sign it with him.

I didn't try to defend Manuel; I had given up hope in his case. But Willie was different. He was not part of the strike; he was beaten, and he was innocent. It was unfair to disinherit him. But I wanted to believe Quintín would change his mind later, once he cooled down.

39

Petra's Threat

※

THE FOLLOWING DAY AT BREAKFAST, Petra walked with surprising energy into the dining room. She was wearing the coconut-
white apron tied to her waist, as she used to, and her gay bead
necklaces. I was amazed at her transformation; just a few days
before, she had hardly been able to climb up the stairs to take
care of Willie, so painful was her arthritis. Georgina was the one
who usually served us breakfast, and I asked Petra what had
transformed her. The servants had gone to Las Minas for the
christening of one of her great-grandnieces, Petra said, and
wouldn't be back until that afternoon. She poured us some freshly
brewed coffee and brought a platter of home-baked *mallorcas* from
the kitchen.

"I'm serving you breakfast because today is Buenaventura's
birthday," Petra said to Quintín gravely, standing next to him.
Quintín was just opening *La Prensa*. He put on his glasses and
read the small print at the top of the page. "You're right, Petra,"
he replied, after confirming the date, "Buenaventura was born on
September 18, 1894. He would have been eighty-eight years old
today. It's nice of you to remember."

"It was your father who brought me to this house more than fifty
years ago," Petra said, still more solemnly. "I was with him when

he died, and I was with Rebecca when you were born. I've served you faithfully since. Even when temptation got the better of you and you got tangled with Carmelina in the mangroves, I never questioned what you did, because you were Buenaventura's son. I have a question for you now, however. Is it true you disinherited Willie and left all your money to a foundation?" Her face had turned gray.

Quintín looked at her distractedly and went on dipping his *mallorca* into his cup of coffee. "And what if the answer is yes? It's none of your business," he said briskly. Petra stared at him. She stood very near his chair, straight and tall as a tree, holding the steaming silver pot of coffee over his head. All of a sudden I had a terrifying vision of Petra bashing in Quintín's skull, or pouring the scalding coffee down his back, but she didn't do either. "Willie is Buenaventura's grandson, but he's also an Avilés," Petra reminded him. "If you disown Willie, I'll tell him Carmelina's secret, and the whole Avilés family will oppose you." Petra's booming voice echoed through the house.

Quintín pushed his chair back and got up calmly from the table. "I'm sorry, Petra. I've always tried to help Willie as much as possible; no one in San Juan would have been as generous as I have. But if you say Willie is my son, I'll deny it in court. You have no proof."

"Go ahead and disinherit Willie, then," Petra said defiantly. "But I swear to you by Eleggua—he who is more than God—that one day you'll be sorry!" And with that, she turned around and went back to the cellar.

I was stunned. It was the first time I had ever heard Petra openly defy Quintín. She had supported him in his most difficult moments. She had never reproached him for what had happened to Ignacio; in her opinion, Mendizabal's bankrupcy had been a matter of the survival of the fittest. It was sad, she had said, but the stronger warrior always won over the weaker. But with Willie it was different.

I got up from the table and ran after Quintín as he walked down the hall. I put my hand gently on his arm. "You have to excuse Petra," I whispered. "She's very old and doesn't know what she's saying." "Of course I excuse her," Quintín replied brusquely. "But it's time she went to live with her relatives in Las Minas. Tomorrow she'll have to go." I felt totally helpless. I had agreed with Petra in everything but was so afraid of Quintín I didn't dare open my mouth.

QUINTÍN

That night Quintín went over everything Petra had said, and began to see clearly her motives for hating him: Willie had been brought up thinking he had been adopted. He had never been told he was Quintín's son, as Petra believed, or that the Mendizabal name and fortune were his birthright. And then Quintín had made a new will leaving his money to the Mendizabal Foundation. It was his money; he had earned it with the sweat of his brow, and could do with it as he pleased. The Mendizabal Foundation was a noble cause; it would enable the house on the lagoon to become San Juan's first art museum. Moreover, he wasn't going to disinherit Willie or Manuel, as Isabel's manuscript falsely stated. If anything happened to him, both his sons would have generous lifelong incomes, as would Isabel. But none of this made any difference to Petra. She wanted Willie to inherit everything—Gourmet Imports, the art collection, the money in the bank.

The reason for the manuscript's existence suddenly hit Quintín like a thunderbolt. Isabel wasn't under Petra's spell at all, as he had deluded himself into believing because he couldn't stand the thought of losing her. She was Petra's ally, and they were writing the manuscript together in order to destroy him.

They wanted the novel to be such a scandal that the Mendizabal

Foundation would be stillborn, discredited from the start. How could Quintín turn the house on the lagoon into a museum when the Mendizabal family was in disgrace? This time he was going to take the situation in hand. He was going to destroy the manuscript.

Quintín walked into the study. He took out the desk drawer and opened the secret compartment. But Isabel's tan folder was missing. He groped around for it desperately, but it was not there.

He went directly to the bedroom and turned on the lights. Isabel sat up in bed, startled, and asked what was wrong. Quintín shook her violently by the shoulders. "What have you done with the manuscript of The House on the Lagoon?*" he hissed, his face white with anger. "It was in Rebecca's desk the night before the strike."*

"How dare you read my manuscript!" Isabel cried out angrily. "You had no right."

"How dare you write it!" Quintín retorted, beside himself. "I'll turn this house upside down until I find it. And if I don't, and you publish it, I'll kill you."

"You'll never find it!" Isabel said. And then, with a strange calm, almost in a whisper, she said, "I'll kill you first."

PART 8

When the Shades
Draw Near

ISABEL

The day of Quintín's argument with Petra, I decided to go down to the cellar to talk to her. I wanted to assure her that I didn't have anything to do with Quintín's decision to disinherit our sons. I had grown so used to hearing her pray to Elegguá that I had begun to believe a little in him myself, especially after seeing how Elegguá's Figa had protected Willie. All of a sudden the idea came to me that if I put the manuscript in Elegguá's care maybe peace would come once more to our house. Manuel might leave the AK 47 and ask his father to forgive him; Willie might regain his sight; Quintín could change his mind about the will.

I got up from where I was sitting and went into the study. I took the manuscript folder out of the desk and carried it down to Petra. "These papers are very important," I said as I gave her the folder. "I'd like you to keep them for a while. I've made a promise to Elegguá so that he will protect my sons."

It was three years before I wrote again. With the help of Mauricio Boleslaus, our art-dealer friend, Willie and I moved to Florida, where we took refuge in a small hotel on Anastasia, a narrow island on the peninsula's western coast which appealed to us because of its peaceful atmosphere. Every month we get a check from Mauricio and we manage to get along nicely thanks to him.

A year after we arrived, Willie's epileptic fits had almost disappeared, and he had recovered enough so he could begin to paint again. I was enormously relieved. A few years later he would become an accomplished artist, and today his work hangs in important galleries all over the country. Petra had been right after all when she foretold Willie's success.

There was a small pier in front of our hotel where fishermen brought their catch early in the morning, throwing the fish that were too small to sell at the local market back into the sea. Huge white pelicans dived after them, and a flurry of cries and whooshes ruffled the tranquil surface of the water, as the eternal struggle to eat and escape being eaten went on beneath its surface.

After the pelicans' daily banquet, I would sit on the wharf for hours, staring at the pale, cold Atlantic and at the desolate beach, its solitary pine tree undulating in the wind. I missed our warm waters glimmering like a sapphire around San Juan, our graceful palm trees swaying like winged angels, but I had no desire to go back to the island.

I probably would not have recovered without Willie's help. Looking at the Atlantic was comforting. The living and the dead were held fast by its embrace: Abby, Mother, Father, and Manuel on one side; Willie and I on the other. It made me think of what Petra had said before she died; she had insisted that water was love, that it made communication possible, and she was right. It wasn't until a year later, when the peace of Long Boat Key finally healed my wounds, that I returned to The House on the Lagoon. I know publishing it may have dire results, but a tale, like life itself, isn't finished until it is heard by someone with an understanding heart.

Quintín never read these pages. He never had the chance to scribble angry comments on the margins or introduce his thoughts in long, third-person monologues on the back of the manuscript pages, as he did in previous chapters. But he did know how the novel ended; that's the story I'm about to tell.

40

Petra's Voyage

to the Underworld

❧

THE DAY AFTER PETRA'S ARGUMENT with Quintín, Eulodia
knocked on the door of our bedroom early in the morning. It was
still dark—it couldn't have been more than five o'clock. Six women
had arrived on a boat from Las Minas and were waiting downstairs
in the cellar. "They want to see Petra," she whispered through
the half-opened door, "but I went to her room and called her
several times and she didn't answer. I tried to open the door, but
it was locked. I'm afraid something's wrong." I put on my bathrobe
and went down to the cellar with Eulodia, the master key in my
hand. When I opened Petra's door, I found her lying on the bed
with her eyes closed. I suspected she might have had a stroke
during the night, but then I saw her clothes laid carefully around
her: her best red satin skirt, her *mundillo* lace blouse, and her
beaded necklaces. When I drew nearer, I realized Petra was still
breathing.

I was about to leave the room to call for help when I saw the
six black women who had arrived by boat. They entered the room
softly and stood around Petra's bed in a semicircle. I recognized
them instantly. They were the women I had seen years before at
the picnic on Lucumí Beach; only now they were dressed in white,
with white turbans on their heads. "You mustn't worry, Isabel,

we'll take care of everything," they said quietly. "Soon everyone will begin to arrive." I stepped back and stood against the wall to let them do as they wished. I never found out how they knew Petra was dying, but I had given up trying to understand Elegguá's mysteries.

The women began to pray in low voices as they rubbed Petra's body with unguents and herbs. I couldn't make out the words, but they sounded similar to what Petra used to sing to Carmelina when she was a baby, when she tried to make her fall asleep: "Olorún, ka kó koi bé re; dá yo salú orissá; dá yo salú Legbá." When they finished anointing her, they dressed her and carefully combed her hair. A few minutes later Petra's relatives began to arrive by the boatload. As I hurried upstairs to get dressed and tell Quintín and Willie that Petra was sick, I saw Georgina and Victoria helping Eulodia with the food. They passed around trays of freshly brewed coffee, as well as sweet cakes and jiggers of rum; it looked suspiciously as if everything had been planned in advance.

By the time Quintín, Willie, and I came down to the cellar an hour later, it was crammed full of people; there must have been at least a hundred of Petra's relatives there. They brought her bed out into the common room and lit candles around it. A small altar decorated with flowers and covered by a black cloth had been made for Elegguá at one end of the room. Petra's conchshell, several cigars, and more than half a dozen red rubber balls her relatives had brought were laid out on it as offerings. People were kneeling, chanting and praying, thanking Petra for everything she had done for them. When I came nearer, I could see she was still alive, but was evidently near the end. Her onyx-black skin had turned ashen and her lips were dry.

The rum soon lifted the mourners' spirits. They began to talk animatedly among themselves and seemed to be waiting for something to happen. Quintín and I moved to the back of the room, to keep out of the way as much as possible, but Willie knelt by Petra's bed. He wasn't afraid of death; he had glimpsed its face often enough during his epileptic fits. He took Petra's hand and kissed it and then took a handkerchief out of his pocket and slowly wiped away the beads of perspiration on her forehead.

"Can I do anything to make things easier for you, Grandmother?" he asked in a low voice, not sure if Petra could hear him. I was surprised that Willie should call her that, but he said it quite naturally, and I supposed it was a term of affection. Petra's huge eyes opened and she looked straight at Willie. "Yes, you can," she whispered, quite distinctly. "My relatives are all waiting for me to give Elegguá a new home. It's the custom, before one dies, for the saint's stone to be passed on to the worthiest of the Avilés family. But I want you to have him."

Petra had the women bring Elegguá's effigy to the bed, as well as a square cardboard box, which she said held Elegguá's toys— the rubber balls, the cigars, and the conchshell that had been on the altar a minute ago. Willie took them both reverently and held them against his chest. The six black women then lifted Petra up from the bed and carried her to the underground spring. It surprised me that they seemed to know exactly where to go, almost as if they had been there before. They walked into the cement trough together, without bothering to take off their skirts, and slowly dipped Petra's body in the water. When she felt the cool liquid run over her, Petra seemed to find new strength, as if a great weight had been lifted from her breast. A half-smile appeared on her face. Willie came near and stood next to her, water up to his waist. "Buenaventura was right," I heard Petra whisper to him. "Everything begins and ends in water. That's why one must learn to forgive." Then she heaved a great sigh and closed her eyes.

That evening, Petra's relatives placed her body on an open bier, carried it to a barge covered with flowers, and headed for Lucumí Beach. She had asked to be cremated there, so the mistral would blow her ashes toward Africa. The caravan of boats that followed was so long it reached all the way from Alamares to Morass Lagoon, cutting across the mangrove swamp. For one brief moment the procession linked our elegant suburb to the slum of Las Minas. Quintín stayed home and didn't go to the funeral; he said he wasn't feeling well. But Willie and I went in the Boston Whaler. And as we wound our way, singing and praying, across the maze of mangroves, candles flickering among the branches full of sleeping herons and creatures that scuttled away in the dark, I thanked Petra for everything she had done for us. Her name had suited her well: Petra means rock, and for the many years I had known her, she had been the rock on which the house on the lagoon had stood.

41

Quintín Offers

to Make a Deal

⋈

THE DAY AFTER PETRA'S FUNERAL, at breakfast, Quintín affectionately took my hand. "I think it's time we discussed your manuscript in the open, Isabel," he said in a conciliatory tone. "I've been reading it for weeks, and I know you know I know. I'm willing to make a deal. If you promise not to publish it, I promise I'll tear up the will and won't set up the Mendizabal Foundation. I'll forgive you if you forgive me."

I stared at him in astonishment; I couldn't believe he had finally had the courage to speak out.

"One can't be the warden of one's fortune after death," Quintín added appeasingly. "In any case, I'm still young; I hope to live awhile longer. Who knows what may happen in the future? Two years from now, Manuel may not be an Independentista any longer, and he'll want to work with me at Gourmet Imports. The police informed me that Willie had nothing to do with the strike, just as you said, so it was wrong of me to want to punish him. I've called Mr. Domenech and he's bringing the new will over so we can tear it up together. Then we can get rid of your manuscript once and for all, too."

I bowed my head and felt resentment well up in me like a tide. "What did you think of it?" I asked, my voice tightening. "Is it any good? If we destroy it, you'll be my first and only reader, Quintín."

He was heartless. "Your novel has some good passages in it, Isabel," he replied. "But it's not a work of art. It's a feminist treatise, an Independentista manifesto; worst of all, it distorts history. Even if we weren't going to make a deal, I would advise you not to publish it."

"My novel is about personal freedom, Quintín, not about political freedom," I said calmly. "Its about my independence from you. I have a right to write what I think, and that's what you haven't been able to accept from the start."

And then I added: "I'm sorry, but I can't make a deal with you. I've lost track of the manuscript; I have no idea where it is. I gave it to Petra for safekeeping after the strike, and Petra died that very night. I never had the chance to ask her where she put it. It could be anywhere in the house, or she might have taken it with her to the other world. You'll have to go there to ask her where to find it, Quintín."

Quintín didn't believe me. He looked everywhere: he emptied closets and drawers; he had all the books in the study removed from their shelves, and turned the cellar practically upside down, but he couldn't find the manuscript.

I searched on my own without Quintín's knowledge, but I had no luck. At first I was distraught; I couldn't believe that something which was so much a part of me was gone. Then I gradually became reconciled to my fate. Maybe it was just as well the novel was lost. It was my secret offering to Elegguá, so that he would protect my sons.

42

Willie's Clairvoyance

❧

WILLIE HAD SUFFERED a detached retina from his beating at the hands of the police. When our friend Mauricio Boleslaus heard the news he came to visit us at the house. He had exhibited some of Willie's paintings in the gallery at Old San Juan, and they had had very good reviews; he had even sold some of them. I hadn't seen Mauricio for months, and just having him walk into the house, with his gray suede gloves, his perfumed goatee, and his colorful plaid handkerchief in his pocket, cheered me.

We talked all afternoon. I told him about the strike and about Willie's brutal beating. Manuel's adherence to the Independentista cause had been a shock to all of us, I said. But his parading up and down Ponce de León Avenue with the strikers had created a scandal out of all proportion, and my neighbors were all gossiping about it. I was sick of them and was sorry I had ever invited them to my house. Mauricio patted my arm affectionately. "You should take a long trip, visit Paris, London, Rome. There's so much beauty in the world, and life is still worth living. I'd love to be your escort; it would be an honor to accompany you," he said, winking mischievously. I laughed and thanked him, but told him that would be impossible.

Willie came and sat with us on the terrace. He was feeling

better, he said to Mauricio. He told him about Petra's death—which I was loath to mention—and about her strange wake. He had buried Elegguá's effigy in Petra's room, not because he believed in the rites of *santería*, but out of respect for her. Since Petra had spent most of her life in the cellar, he thought it was appropriate that Elegguá should be put to rest in the same place. He had taken the cardboard box full of Elegguá's sacred toys to his room and put it away under his bed.

Mauricio had always found Petra fascinating, and whenever he came to visit he asked Willie about her. His interest in Picasso, Modigliani, and other modern artists who had been influenced by African cultures made him curious about the rites of magic. Once he had asked Petra to show him Elegguá's effigy, but Petra was offended at the suggestion. Mauricio had had to humor her, and bring her a box of chocolates so she would get over her annoyance. "Now that Petra's gone, I'd love to see what the idol looks like," Mauricio hinted. "We could all go down to the cellar and dig it up." But I refused to humor him. "Petra prayed to Elegguá every day for many years," I said. "Sometimes I have more faith in him than in my own God."

WILLIE WAS STILL feeling weak and he decided not to go back to Pratt that fall, but to do his sophomore year at the University of Puerto Rico, where classes had already begun. He also asked Quintín for a part-time job at Gourmet Imports. He was very good with a computer—I had given him one as a birthday present when he turned sixteen—and he could write advertisements, put together jingles and ditties, and design ads for Gourmet's products. Quintín agreed. He even gave him a secondhand 1975 Toyota which had belonged to one of his salesmen, so he could commute from the university to Gourmet Imports.

Willie hadn't said anything about Petra's secret, and I thought it best not to bring up the subject. I wasn't sure if he knew, and I was afraid he might resent his father for keeping him from inheriting what was legally his. I prayed he would take it all in stride, that his kind nature would keep him from any rash action, and I thought it a good idea that he work for Quintín. Perhaps some fences would be mended that way.

We talked about Petra often. "I've been thinking a lot about Petra's words before she passed away—'Everything begins and ends in water,' " Willie said one evening when we were having dinner by ourselves on the terrace. Quintín was away on a trip and I had put a small table outside; we were enjoying the cool breeze that came up from the lagoon at sunset. "Maybe I had to become partially blind to understand what she meant. When I realized I might never be able to paint again, I cried so much I couldn't believe the body could hold so much water. Tears, saliva, semen, blood—our bodies are mostly water.

"Petra knew that water is love," Willie went on. "Every time we wet our feet or wade into the sea, we touch other people, we share in their sadness and their joys. Because we live on an island there is no mass of mountains, no solid dike of matter to keep us from flowing out to others. Communication is possible, Mother. Through water, we can reach out and love our neighbors, try to understand them." I wondered about all this philosophizing, unsure of what Willie was driving at.

He was silent for a moment, and then he added softly: "Water permitted the Avilés family to travel from Morass to Alamares Lagoon in the first place," he said. "After all, I was conceived in the swamp, isn't that right, Mother? And it was in the mangroves that Carmelina Avilés fell into Father's arms."

Willie's question hung in the air. Now I knew why he had wanted to talk to me about water. It was his way of coming to Petra's secret, of letting me know he knew.

43

Perla's Gift

❧

THE DATE FOR THE PLEBISCITE was drawing near, and the whole island was preparing for it. The three parties—the New Progressive Party, the Popular Party, and the Independence Party—had intensified their campaigns. Television as well as the newspapers were full of political commentary, as the parties strove to explain their different positions in detail. Statehood and independence sympathizers both maintained that Puerto Rico was a colony of the United States—that only statehood or independence would put us at the helm of the island's destiny. Commonwealthers declared that Puerto Rico's status had been legally established and was even recognized by the United Nations.

When the polls began to show that Statehood had only a slight edge, Quintín was visibly concerned. He would have liked the advantage to be larger. "If we win only by a slim margin, there's bound to be a violent reaction," he said. "The plebiscite is really a struggle between Statehood and Independence. If Independence wins, we'll end up eating bananas and shooting each other down like pigeons, like our Caribbean neighbors." The situation was volatile; anyone could see that trouble was brewing. With the difficulty Congress was having retaining English as the official language in the United States, I thought, letting a Spanish-speaking territory become a state would be like letting a fox into the chicken coop. But I didn't dare say anything to Quintín.

We still hadn't heard from Manuel and the police had no clues as to his whereabouts. Every time I looked at his photograph, I cried. There was nothing I could do but mourn. By chance, Willie ran into his brother in Old San Juan one afternoon, and he told me about it. Manuel didn't want Quintín to know; he made Willie promise he wouldn't tell us. Willie was afraid of the police, and with good reason.

"Are you all right?" Willie said, embracing his brother. "Where have you been? We've been worried sick." Manuel's greeting was warm. He had lost weight and his coal-black eyes stood out even more in his gaunt face. Thankfully, there were crowds of people in the street, so it was easy to escape notice. Willie asked Manuel to have a beer at a small bar nearby. They took a table at the back, an electric fan whirling slowly above their heads, and ordered hamburgers and Budweisers.

"I don't have an address," Manuel said. "Every night I sleep at a different house. That's the best way to keep the police from finding me. But things are going well for our cause; independence may stand a chance, after all."

Manuel sat in the shadows, looking attentively at his brother. "Are you sure this is what you want to do? Why don't you leave the AK 47 now, before it's too late?" Willie asked. "They had no right to make you take part in the strike and insult Father." Manuel laughed at his brother's naïveté. "No one made me join the strike, kid; I organized the whole thing myself. We're not children anymore. I'm a Puerto Rican and Father thinks he's an American. He'd have us speaking English and forget we ever spoke Spanish. He thinks that way he could peddle his hams more efficiently on the mainland."

"You mustn't talk like that about Father," Willie reproached him. "We all have our faults—Father, too—but he loves you."

"I'm not being disrespectful toward Father!" Manuel replied, nettled by Willie's words. "I'm doing exactly what he taught us when we were children. Remember how he used to say we had to be like the Conquistadors and not let anything stand in our way if we wanted to achieve something? That's what I'm doing now. Only he wants statehood and I want independence."

When he saw Willie's anguished expression, Manuel let up. He examined his brother's swollen eye, the face that was still black and blue around the temple. "It's just like them to do that. They never pick on the strong ones, only on the weak."

Willie took a swallow of beer and shifted around in his chair. He didn't like his brother to think of him as weak. "Another thing," Willie said. "I'm not going back to Pratt for now. I'm studying at the University of Puerto Rico and working with Father part-time. He's given me your old office, the one with the moth-eaten tapestry of Valdeverdeja hanging on the wall."

Manuel put down his beer. "Has Father brainwashed you about carrying on the Mendizabal family tradition and all that crap? No one should inherit Gourmet Imports. All private property belongs to the state."

"Petra told me Father made a new will, and that he's going to leave all his money to a foundation," Willie said. "In any case, I don't care. I'm not thinking of the business but of helping Father." Manuel didn't believe what Willie told him. He got up angrily, overturning his chair, and walked out of the bar. A few days later Willie found a note stuck to the windshield of his beat-up Toyota. "Gourmet Imports is a Fascist institution!" it read. "If you go on working there, you'll be sorry."

Perla was Willie's great consolation in these troubled times. Unlike Coral, she didn't go in for ideologies; she hated it when Coral talked about politics. She came to see Willie every day at the house and told him about her nursing work, which she was more enthusiastic about than ever. She was visiting the slums, where there were many abandoned children and where drugs were a problem. "Boats from Colombia come at night and drop packages wrapped in plastic in the water when the current from Morass Lagoon is coming in," Perla told him. "They float right up to the wooden huts lining the shore. The people there have lookouts who . pick them up—there are waterproof flashlights in the plastic— and deliver them to the drug moguls. But some of it always trickles down. There are hundreds of drug addicts in Las Minas; getting high is almost a rite," she added, shuddering. "They share the same spoon to mix the heroin with water, the same candle to heat it up, the same rubber band tied around the upper arm, the same needle to inject themselves."

There was a medical dispensary in the slum, and Perla was going there daily. She had a delicate constitution but a strong will. Like Doña Ermelinda, she wasn't afraid of anything. She twisted her long black hair into a braid, put on a pair of beat-up Levi's and a T-shirt, and walked fearlessly through the labyrinth of shacks. She helped out in any way she could, counseling patients on how to deal with addiction, on how to find moral support in meeting with other people who were also addicted. The saddest were the children. Sometimes a skeleton of a woman would walk into the dispensary carrying a baby in her arms, place the child on the floor, and walk out. "They leave them at the dispensary and never come back," Perla told Willie with tears in her eyes.

Willie began to visit Las Minas with Perla in search of abandoned children. "If I were old enough, I'd take this one home with me," she said to Willie one day, holding up a black baby who was so thin he looked as if he had the bones of a sparrow. They found him in an abandoned shack, asleep under old newspapers. Willie's heart went out to Perla. She was the only one who understood Petra's message.

Four days before the plebiscite, tragedy struck. Terrorism had been escalating on the island: a navy bus was blown up in Sábana Seca, killing two sailors and injuring nine others. Soon after, an ROTC vehicle was gunned down at the UPR campus. Governor Rodrigo Escalante swore he would find the culprits, and ordered the National Guard to comb the housing projects for Independen-tista suspects. Armed with machine guns and rifles, they were stationed at the entrance to the city's slums, and would frisk anyone coming in or out. One day, Perla's car broke down and she had to take the bus from San Juan to Las Minas. As she was getting out at the stop in Barrio Obrero, a shootout between a National Guard patrol and a crowd of slum dwellers erupted. Perla was hit in the head and was killed instantly.

44

Perla's Funeral

❈

ESMERALDA AND ERNESTO fell to pieces; they seemed to age
drastically in a matter of weeks. There had been so much pain in
our family: Abuelo Lorenzo, Ignacio, Father—all had suffered
violent deaths. But this was different. Perla was only sixteen,
she'd hardly lived at all. I went to the hospital and saw her before
they took her to the morgue. Esmeralda had brushed her long dark
hair and arranged it around her pearl-white face. There was no
justification, no pardon for people who committed crimes like that.

The ballistics experts couldn't say for certain if the stray bullet
had come from the slum crowd or from the National Guard. Esmeralda and Ernesto were so distraught they couldn't care less
who was at fault. But Quintín was sure Perla had been killed by
a terrorist bullet, perhaps from the AK 47 itself. "You have no
evidence," I said quietly. "It could have been one of the gangs of
drug traffickers that run wild in the slum." But Quintín refused
to listen.

All the way to the cemetery, Quintín kept repeating that the
Independentista terrorists had killed Perla. We were standing
around the coffin as the priest read the *responso*, when Coral
arrived. She wore a black leather miniskirt, with patent-leather
boots hugging her thighs, her red hair worn Afro-style. She began

to cry as they lowered her sister's coffin into the earth, but she managed to get hold of herself to read a poem she had brought with her: "*El llamado*," by Luis Palés Matos—the poet Rebecca's artist friends had admired long ago. It was beautiful, about death being a call we must all obey in the end. But Quintín found it disrespectful, because Palés Matos was a well-known Independentista writer. "You shouldn't be here," he told Coral. "The AK 47 killed your sister, and you're one of them. That makes you an accomplice in her murder." Coral looked at him in horror and fled.

But no one else thought Coral had anything to do with what had happened to her sister. Not all Independentistas were terrorists; there were plenty who were law-abiding and wanted to attain independence through peaceful means. Esmeralda and Ernesto, for example, both sympathized with political self-determination though they never admitted it publicly.

The day after Perla's funeral, Coral moved from her parents' house without telling anyone where she was going. I was sure Coral had gone back to Manuel—wherever he was—and that he would take good care of her. He could comfort her better than anyone.

The plebiscite took place on November 7, two days after Perla's funeral, and as the results began to come in, Quintín grew more and more belligerent. The polls had shown that statehood had a small advantage over the other options, but at the last minute the voters had changed their minds. Commonwealth got forty-eight percent, Statehood forty-six percent, and Independence four percent. The combined votes of Commonwealthers and Independentistas made it impossible for Puerto Rico to ask for statehood.

Quintín was stunned; he felt sure the island was on its way to independence. "Statehood lost because of fear," he insisted. "The Independentistas' terrorist campaign reaped excellent results—people were afraid to vote for statehood." The island was poised on the brink of disaster, he said. If we persisted in "our collective madness," one day Congress would tire of the whole thing and take away our American citizenship. When I heard him talk like that, I simply got up and walked out of the room.

The night of the plebiscite, Governor Rodrigo Escalante went on television, his white mane ruffled like a fighting cock's, blue shirt soaked in perspiration. He was standing on a platform at the New Progressive Party's headquarters and below him a crowd of ten thousand people frantically waved American flags. He looked more than ever like a Latin American *cacique* as he thundered against his enemies and accused them of stealing the elections. "The result of the plebiscite is a declaration of war," he said. "From now on, Statehooders will have to be more careful than ever." They had been threatened and bullied by the Independentistas and their Commonwealth sympathizers, he said, but even so, Statehooders had respected the law. It would be different now. Statehooders were going to take measures they should have taken long ago. The party members gathered beneath the platform cheered wildly. Outside, you could hear automobiles ceaselesssly honking their horns as they cruised up and down San Juan's avenues with the Puerto Rican flag waving from their windows. They were the victors that night, Commonwealthers and Independentistas.

A few days after the plebiscite, several caricatures were published in the nation's newspapers. *The Washington Post* ran a drawing of a little mustachioed Latin lover in bed with a huge Statue of Liberty, and underneath them the caption: "Why get married when we can continue to live together?" Quintín took the caricature as an insult to the Puerto Rican people. We were living in adultery with the United States, and Commonwealthers were abetting our illicit status. He was furious.

Governor Escalante told his followers there would be a confrontation and they should prepare for a full-fledged conflict on the island. Quintín took his words literally. He set aside a room in the house and turned it into an arsenal of firearms. He went to Gourmet Imports at night and patrolled the warehouse aisles himself to make sure there hadn't been any sabotage. At home he stood guard at the study's Art Nouveau windows, staring out toward the lagoon with a gun in his hand. He'd be delighted if Manuel came to visit, he said: he'd get what was coming to him.

Little by little, I became a different person. I had lost my old spunk and could stand up to Quintín less and less. He blamed me for everything. What had happened in our family was all my fault, he said, because I had taken Manuel and Willie to Esmeralda's when they were children. If Manuel hadn't met Coral, he wouldn't have become an Independentista terrorist, the strike wouldn't have taken place, and Willie wouldn't have been hurt. I listened with bowed head. All my Corsican fighting spirit went up in smoke.

After Petra died, Brambon, Eulodia, Georgina, and Victoria left us, and I could only get part-time help. The new women who came to work during the day were not dependable; I had to do half the work at the house myself, because Quintín was afraid they might damage his art. I wasn't writing anymore and that also depressed me. Quintín, of course, didn't notice. He wanted everything to be as perfect as when Petra was alive. I was so afraid of him I went around on tiptoe and never dared mention our sons.

45

A Whirlpool of Shadows

❧

WILLIE'S HEALTH TOOK A TURN for the worse after Perla's death, and he was having epileptic fits again. I spent as much time as I could with him. He was on heavy doses of medication and had stopped going to the university or to work. It was dangerous for him to drive a car or even cross the street, and though I drove him to class, the university didn't want to take responsibility for him.

Our doctor said there was a good possibility that Willie would get worse. To a large extent, his illness was emotional; the best thing would be to send him away so he could forget Perla. If he stayed home, he had little chance of recovering. But Quintín was unmoved. He refused to let us travel anywhere. He saw Willie as an invalid—the best thing would be to institutionalize him, and there was an excellent hospital for epileptics in Boston.

It was then that I resolved to leave Quintín. It had taken me twenty-seven years to find out that Abby had been right from the start: our marriage was a terrible mistake. He would put Willie in an institution over my dead body.

I gathered up my courage and went to see Mauricio Boleslaus at his gallery in Old San Juan. I told him there was something urgent I needed to discuss with him. He ushered me into his private office, which opened onto a small inner patio with a stone fountain in the middle and a large *yuca* plant in the corner. Dark rings circled my eyes, but Mauricio didn't ask any questions. He sat down in front of me, folded his hands in his lap, and smiled.

It was as if a dam had burst. "You're the only one who can help me," I said, sobbing. "I've got to take Willie abroad with me. The doctors have said that's the only way he's going to get well, but Quintín refuses to give us any money for the trip. You sold us our art collection, so you know how much it's worth today."

Mauricio told me not to worry, he would be only too glad to help. He promised he would be very discreet. He asked me if by any chance Quintín would be taking a trip soon. Fortunately, Quintín was planning to be away the following week. On Wednesday, he had to attend a wine convention in New York; he was interested in acquiring a new line of California wines for Gourmet Imports. He wouldn't be back until Friday.

Mauricio set the date for the following Thursday. All I had to do was leave the door to the cellar open that evening, and around three in the morning his helpers would come into the house and quietly remove those paintings I would indicate to him in advance. They would stow them in Quintín's forty-foot Bertram. They would borrow the yacht just for one night, Mauricio promised, and have it back the next day, moored at one of San Juan's public wharves. Quintín would have no trouble finding it there.

The Bertram would navigate across Alamares Lagoon and Morass Lagoon, and somewhere near Lucumí Beach Mauricio's yacht would be waiting, with Mauricio on board. He would supervise the unloading of the paintings and sail with them to Miami, where he would sell them at an excellent price. "You'll soon have enough to take Willie around the world if you wish, my dear," Mauricio told me reassuringly.

I went back to the house saddened but relieved, and during the next two days I made my preparations. I didn't tell Willie anything at first; his health was so frail I didn't want to distress him in any way. I hoped that when the moment came he would understand my reasons and would come with me.

Quintín left early Wednesday morning. On Thursday afternoon I went down to the cellar with our suitcases to make sure everything was ready for the trip. I hadn't been there since Petra's death and was surprised to see what a mess it had become. Petra's wicker chair lay upside down in a corner, and the mangroves were pushing their roots through the mud-packed floor of the common room. A stench of wet earth came from the dark rooms at the back, and there were crabs everywhere. They had begun to creep up the Art Nouveau iron beams supporting Pavel's terrace. I wondered why there were so many, but then realized what had happened. The servants who used to trap them for food were now gone, and Mefistófeles was dead; there was no one to keep them in check. The crabs had multiplied, and their claws could be heard tapping on the ground, a spiny horde slowly on the move.

The Boston Whaler was moored at one end of the pier under the beams of the terrace. I walked over to it with my bags, one of which held my clothes, the other one Willie's, and hid them under a plastic tarpaulin at the prow of the boat. I checked the gasoline tank to see that it was full; I'd asked the new gardener to fill it up the day before, and gave him a big tip not to mention it to Quintín. I left the keys in the ignition switch of the Boston Whaler, and in Quintín's Bertram.

Mauricio had told me I could probably get half a million dollars for three of the paintings: the blind St. Lucia, the Carlo Crivelli Madonna, and *The Fall of the Rebel Angels*. I didn't feel the least bit guilty about taking them with me; after all, I had paid for them in part. For years, when my properties in Ponce were still bringing in a good income, I had given Quintín the proceeds, and he bought many works of art with them.

It was six when I went to Willie's room; I wanted to bring him an early dinner. I found him sitting in bed, propped up with pillows, listening to music. I smiled and gave him a kiss on the forehead as I set the tray on his lap. "There's something important I have to talk to you about," I said, sitting down by his side. Willie turned down the volume of his record player—he was listening to Charlie Parker's *Cool Blues*.

"I've decided to go away for a while. I can't stand not having any news from Manuel. I want to know how he is, but he won't come near this place because of his father. Manuel is sure to get in touch with us when we're living somewhere else. And I'd like you to leave with me, Willie."

Willie understood. He wanted to leave also, he said. There was nothing for him on the island anymore. He couldn't paint, he couldn't work with his father. But at least he could take care of me. It was just like Willie to think something like that. He could hardly take care of himself, but he wanted to take care of me. I hugged him and gave him a kiss on the forehead.

"When would we go, Mother?" Willie asked.

"Tonight, darling. Mauricio Boleslaus has offered to help us; he says he can sell some of our paintings for a very good price in the United States." And I explained that Mauricio was coming that evening to remove the paintings.

Willie looked at me in amazement. "Sell Father's paintings? You can't be serious. He'd be furious if you did that!"

I spoke gently to him. "Those paintings belong to me as much as to him," I said. "He bought them in part with my money, many years ago. I have a perfect right to sell them if I want to. And we need the money to get away."

I went out on the terrace and sat on one of the wrought-iron chairs, waiting for time to pass. I was downcast but at peace; I knew I was doing the right thing. I wasn't angry with Quintín, only deeply disappointed.

The only thing that made me nervous about the trip was Willie. He was already so frail, I was afraid the excitement might make him worse. As the sun went down, its last rays caught the Tiffany-glass panes, turning them red and gold. I got up from my chair and walked to the curve of the terrace, where it jutted out over the water. I could see the whole house behind me. It glimmered in the half-light and I looked at it with a curious detachment. Perhaps Buenaventura had been right all along, and there was a curse on Pavel's houses. I was glad to be going.

Later that evening, when I had turned on the lights in the hallway before going to bed, I heard a key rattling in our front door. I stood at the head of the stairs, holding my breath. All of a sudden the door opened and there was Quintín. "The wine convention was over early," he said, removing his key. "I went to the airport to see if I could get a flight today, and there was an empty seat on American's five o'clock flight." He picked up his carryon and walked slowly up the stairs.

I pretended nothing was the matter. We walked together to our room at the end of the hallway and I asked him if he wanted anything from the kitchen—a glass of milk or some poundcake. But he said he'd had dinner on the plane and was tired; he just wanted to go to bed. I helped him hang his clothes in the closet and went into the bathroom. I had to pretend I was going to bed, too, so I put on a nightgown. When I came out of the bathroom, Quintín was under the covers; he had turned off the lights and was asleep.

I lay there in the dark for what seemed like an eternity, scarcely daring to breathe. Quintín's snores soon began to reverberate over the air-conditioner's even hum. I knew Mauricio's people would be able to enter the house undetected, and I hoped they'd remove the paintings without a sound. I looked at my Rolex and saw it was only twelve o'clock. In a little while I would get up quietly from the bed to see if they had arrived.

I must have dozed off. The next thing I knew Willie was standing by the side of the bed, dressed. He put his finger to his lips in warning, and signaled for me to follow him. I looked at my watch and saw that it was half past three. I got up very slowly and walked barefoot after him to the door. Fortunately, the room had thick carpeting, and our footsteps went unnoticed. Once outside the door, I stopped to put on my shoes and bathrobe. "There's a strange orange glow in the sky," Willie whispered, and when I went to the window at the end of the hall, I saw that a brushfire had started near the walls of the house, on the side looking out toward Ponce de León Avenue.

We ran toward the back of the building, to where the dining and living rooms faced the lagoon. Quintín's paintings had been removed—but not just the three I had indicated to Mauricio; all of them. Quintín's sculptures and his valuable collection of Art Nouveau vases had also disappeared. Open containers littered the floor; wrapping paper and packing material were strewn all about. There was a noise in the kitchen and Willie was about to investigate when all of a sudden the fire alarm went off. Quintín came running toward us, his .42 caliber gun in hand. He was struggling to put on his pants and he was barefoot. "Fire! Call the Fire Department!" he shouted, his face white with fear.

Suddenly a long line of men came noiselessly up the stairs. There must have been at least a dozen, carrying automatic weapons. They were dressed in black pants and sweatshirts, with black hoods masking their faces. I stared in amazement. Only their eyelids moved, and I remember thinking how funny they looked, like clams caught in a sock. Quintín held the gun in his hand, but one of the men, a tall, brawny one, grabbed it from him and pushed us toward the study. Once we were inside, he locked the door.

We tried to force the door, but it was no use. We banged and screamed and nobody answered. Quintín kept asking, "Who are they? Who gave them the key to my armory?" as if we knew who the intruders were. I ran to the telephone and tried to make a call, but the line had been cut. Willie raced to the window and looked out toward the lagoon. There was no fire on that side yet, but we couldn't jump out; it was too high. We could smell the smoke coming from the far end of the hall, seeping under the door.

I have only a blurred recollection of what happened next. It could have been five minutes, it could have been an age. We were certain we'd be burned alive, when the door of the study was flung open and the same man reappeared, the butt of his automatic rifle resting on his hip. Two other men came in behind him, and pointed their guns at us. "You and you," the man said stiffly, signaling to Willie and me. "Come this way. You can escape through the cellar." I started to walk toward him but Willie ran in the opposite direction, to the hall that led to the bedrooms. He came back a few seconds later, a square cardboard box under his arm. "It's Elegguá's sacred toys," he said, holding on to it as he went toward the stairs. But Quintín got in front of him. "Why are you in such a hurry to take Elegguá's toys with you?" he asked. "They've taken everything else; you might as well let them have Elegguá's toys also. They should make good kindling!" And he grabbed the box with both hands. But Willie wouldn't let go. Suddenly he erupted at Quintín, and pushed him hard against the chest. Quintín slapped him in the face with the back of his hand, and Willie's glasses fell to his feet and shattered. Father and son rolled on the floor, and just then the pages of my novel spilled out from the box.

The tall man fired his rifle and Quintín came to his senses. He let go of Willie and got up from the floor. But Willie lay there motionless. The tall man knelt beside me. "He'll come around," he said in an even voice. "Here, let me help you." And he picked Willie up and told one of his men to gather up the papers. The man put the manuscript back in the box and handed it to me. Then they ushered us rapidly toward the door.

We ran down the stairs. The tall man carried Willie, unconscious. But Quintín wasn't with us. "Where's Quintín?" I asked, stopping. "He's not going with you. He's staying behind," the man said. I felt a void in my stomach. The tall man stopped in front of me. We were alone on the stairs, the smoke rising around us. "Then I'm not going, either," I said. And I sat down defiantly on the landing. "Either you let the three of us go or we all die."

The other men were in the pantry, stuffing silverware into plastic bags as fast as they could, just two steps ahead of the fire. I began to shake so hard I couldn't stop. I had seen the heavy gold ring on his finger. It was Manuel.

"He's your father," I said. "You'll live with the guilt for the rest of your life." He turned around and faced me silently, still holding Willie. But seconds later, when one of his men came in, he ordered him to release Quintín.

The men pushed Quintín brutally down the stairs. Then we headed for the cellar. Quintín hardly looked at Manuel, as if he hadn't recognized him. When we got to the pier we bent down to avoid the terrace's iron beams, and got on the boat. I went first, and Quintín came after me. Manuel handed Willie to him, and we laid him down on the deck, up by the bow. I pulled the blue tarpaulin from under the prow, where the suitcases were hidden, and put it under Willie's head as a cushion. Then I put the box with the manuscript next to him and stood at the controls, Quintín sitting in front of me. A second later I turned the key in the ignition, and we moved slowly out from under the terrace.

We couldn't have been more than fifteen yards from shore, headed toward Alamares Lagoon, when Quintín noticed our two suitcases under the prow's wooden seat. "So you didn't know where your manuscript was?" he asked softly, contempt in his voice. I looked up from the controls to face him in the light emanating from the house. "And you didn't know who those people were. Where were you going with these? Could it be you were running away, once the AK 47 had finished their job?"

"It's true. I'm leaving you, Quintín," I said. "But I wasn't in league with anyone. I didn't know Willie had the novel. And I have no idea who those people are."

Quintín was on his feet. "You're lying," he said softly. "You're part of the conspiracy. Don't tell me you didn't recognize Manuel!"

I didn't have time to react before Quintín began slapping me back and forth, striking me on the head. I crouched helpless at the bottom of the boat, trying to protect myself with my bare arms. Then I saw my life unreel before me like a film: Quintín rising from our rattan sofa at Aurora Street, taking off his belt and whipping the sixteen-year-old boy for singing me a love song; Ignacio shooting himself and Petra standing all alone by his grave; Margarita coming out of the operating room, pale as an alabaster statue; Carmelina and Quintín making love among the mangroves; Quintín unleashing his dogs so they would attack his own sons and making me sign a will to disinherit them; Perla in her coffin, her dark hair flowing around her like a shroud. And I told myself nothing, nothing in the world could justify such violence.

Slowly I got up from where I had fallen on my knees. Somehow I managed to hold on to the steering wheel with one hand and the gearshift with the other. I swung the boat around and pushed down full-throttle. The boat lurched forward as we raced back under the terrace. Quintín was facing me, about to strike me again. He never saw the iron beam approaching. It hit the back of his head, and he fell forward into the mangroves. I cut the engine, slowed the boat, and looked on with an almost surreal awareness. Quintín lay motionless off the starboard side, floating facedown in the water, half lying on the mangrove roots. Then I saw the crabs moving slowly toward him.

I left him there and quietly pushed out toward the lagoon. When I looked back at the shore, I could see the flames shooting out of the Art Nouveau windows. And there was Manuel standing guard on the golden terrace, machine gun at his hip, watching the house on the lagoon burn to the ground.